A DEADLY TRADE

By Michael Stanley and available from Headline

A Carrion Death
A Deadly Trade

A DEADLY TRADE

MICHAEL STANLEY

A DETECTIVE KUBU CRIME NOVEL

headline

Published by arrangement with HarperCollins Publishers

Published in the USA under the title *The Second Death of GoodluckTinubu*
by HarperCollins Publishers.

First published in Great Britain in 2009 by
HEADLINE PUBLISHING GROUP

Cataloguing in Publication Data is available from the British Library

ISBN 978 0 7553 4407 9 (Hardback)
ISBN 978 0 7553 4408 6 (Trade paperback)

Typeset in Garamond by Avon DataSet Ltd, Bidford on Avon, Warwickshire

Printed in the UK by CPI Mackays, Chatham, ME5 8TD

Headline's policy is to use papers that are natural, renewable and recyclable products and
made from wood grown in sustainable forests. The logging and manufacturing processes are
expected to conform to the environmental regulations of the country of origin.

HEADLINE PUBLISHING GROUP
An Hachette UK Company
338 Euston Road
London NW1 3BH

www.headline.co.uk
www.hachette.co.uk

For Bill and Jean Trollip
and
Teda, Douglas and Brunhilde Sears

CAST OF CHARACTERS

Words in square brackets are approximate phonetic pronunciations. Foreign and unfamiliar words are in a glossary at the back of the book.

Banda, Edison	Detective sergeant in the Botswana Criminal Investigation Department (CID) [Edison BUN-dah]
Beardy	See Khumalo, John
Bengu, Amantle	Kubu's mother [Ah-MUN-tlé BEN-goo]
Bengu, David 'Kubu'	Assistant superintendent in the Botswana Criminal Investigation Department [David 'KOO-boo' BEN-goo]
Bengu, Joy	Kubu's wife [Joy BEN-goo]
Bengu, Wilmon	Kubu's father [WILL-mon BEN-goo]
Boardman, Amanda	South African curio collector and dealer, wife of William
Boardman, William	South African curio collector and dealer, husband of Amanda
Chikosi, Joseph	Retired general in the Zimbabwean army [Joseph chi-KOH-zee]
Du Pisanie, Morné 'Dupie'	Ex-Zimbabwean. Helps to run Jackalberry Camp [MOR-nay 'DOO-pee' doo-piss-AH-nee]
Gomwe, Boy	South African music salesman [Boy GOM-wé]
Jabulani, Peter	Zimbabwean guest at Jackalberry Camp. Calls himself Ishmael Zondo [Peter juh-boo-LAH-nee]

Khumalo, John	Zimbabwean criminal, referred to as Beardy [John koo-MAH-loh]
Kokorwe, Enoch	Ex-Zimbabwean. Helps to run Jackalberry Camp [E-nock kok-OR-wé]
Langa, Sipho	Goodluck Tinubu's travelling companion to Jackalberry Camp [SEE-poh LANG-uh]
Mabaku, Jacob	Director of the Botswana Criminal Investigation Department [Jacob mah-BAH-koo]
MacGregor, Ian	Forensic pathologist for the Botswana police
Madrid	Foreigner in Zimbabwe with ulterior motives
Mankoni, Johannes	Zimbabwean tough man [Johannes man-KOH-nee]
McGlashan, Salome	Ex-Zimbabwean. Owner of Jackalberry Camp concession
Mooka, Joseph 'Tatwa'	Detective sergeant in Botswana Criminal Investigation Department [Joseph 'TUT-wuh' MOO-kuh]
Moremi, Suthani	Cook at Jackalberry Camp [Soot-AH-nee mo-RÉ-mee]
Munro, Judith	English freelance journalist, sister of Trish
Munro, Trish	English freelance journalist, sister of Judith
Serome, Pleasant	Joy Bengu's sister [Pleasant sé-ROE-mé]
Tinubu, Goodluck	Ex-Zimbabwean now living in Botswana, guest at Jackalberry Camp [Goodluck ti-NOO-boo]
Zondo, Ishmael	See Jabulani, Peter

JACKALBERRY CAMP

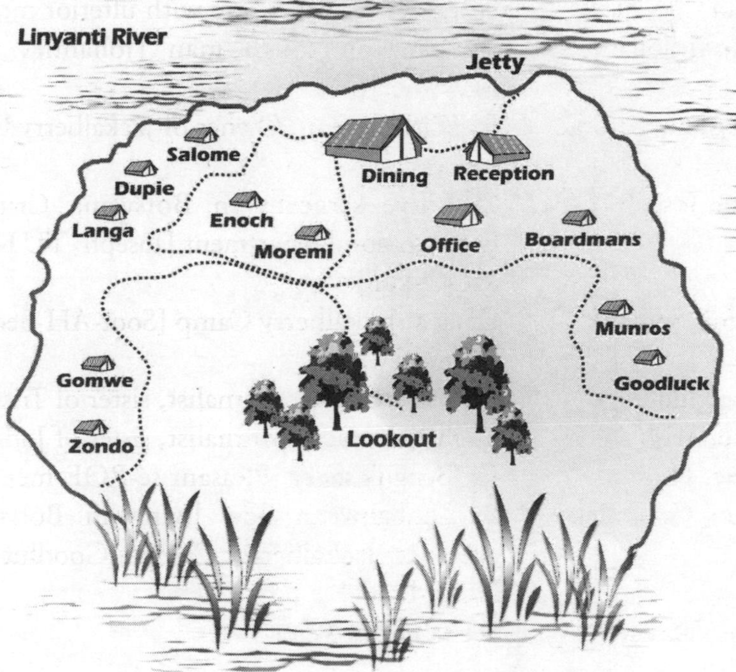

Design by Jacky Smith

BOTSWANA & SURROUNDING COUNTRIES

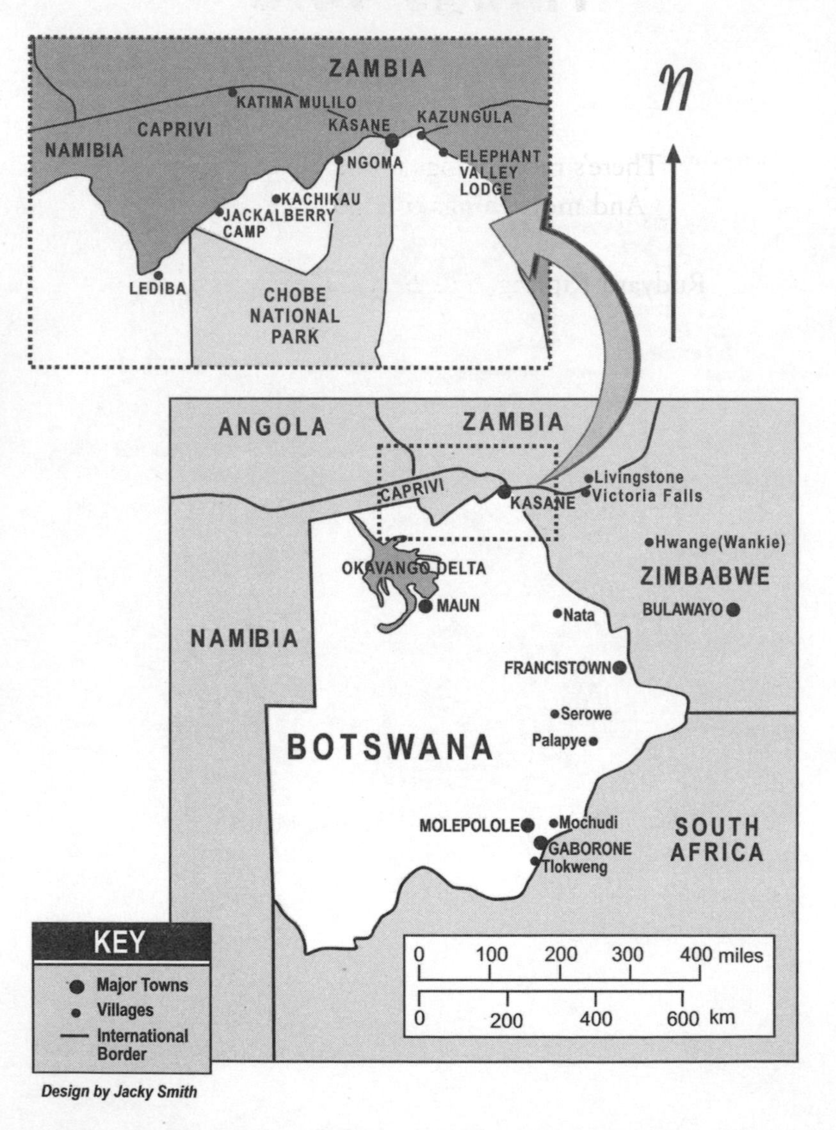

PART ONE
Things Told

There's more things told than are true,
And more things true than are told.

Rudyard Kipling, *The Ballad of Minepit Shaw*

CHAPTER 1

The farewells had been said many years ago, so Goodluck hugged his old comrade and left without a word. He zipped the tent door closed and started along the path to his own bush tent. The waning half-moon had risen; he was glad he did not need his flashlight. Goodluck came to a fork. Straight ahead the path led past the centre of Jackalberry Camp to the guest tents on the other side. The right branch turned up a small hill to a view of the lagoon. It was a spectacular spot at sunrise, popular with early risers. Now it would be deserted, and on a whim he climbed the short distance. The moon silvered the lagoon, making him think of the great river that downstream defined his homeland. One day he hoped to end his self-imposed exile and return with dignity.

He heard a noise – rustling leaves? But there was no wind. Despite the many years since the war, his bushcraft took over, and he faded into the thick brush with no hint of shadow or silhouette. A moment later a man appeared, walking along the main path almost silently. He seemed to be looking for something. Or for someone. He glanced up the path to the lookout, hesitated, but then continued straight. From Goodluck's position in the thicket he couldn't see the man well, but his face was black, and he was heavily built. As he moved, the moonlight caught white sneakers. Goodluck sucked in his breath, let the man pass, and then followed soundlessly. Shortly afterwards the man turned off towards the main area of the camp. Goodluck was puzzled. Was it coincidence, or had he been followed? If so, for what reason?

Arriving at his tent, he saw flickering light within. He had left the storm lantern on the bedside table. Suspicious now, he peered around the edge of the fly-screen window so that anyone inside would be unable to see him. But the tent was empty. Everything seemed exactly as he had left it. Satisfied, he entered, zipped the flap door closed, and got ready for bed. He was tired and still tense, but long ago he had learned to sleep quickly and deeply, even under threat.

About two hours later he was wakened by the sound of the door zipper. In his war days he would have been instantly alert, but he awoke momentarily confused and blinded by the beam of a strong flashlight, and it took him a few seconds to react.

That was much too long.

The next morning the camp staff went about their business as usual. The cook lit the wood stove, clattered about with his pans, and chatted to his pet bird. The cleaner, Beauty, helped her husband Solomon set up for breakfast. The wooden tables, clustered under two ancient jackalberry trees, needed to be wiped down, spread with tablecloths, and laid. Then Beauty would clean the central camp area, and after that would get to the tents of the guests who were up and about. By habit she would start with the one furthest to the east and work back towards the main camp area.

The outdoor dining area overlooked Botswana's Linyanti river to a hazy Namibia on the far side. It was a mesmerising expanse of water, lilies, papyrus and reeds. Hundreds of birds hugged the water's edge, sometimes rising in flocks, other times lunging to catch unwary fish or multicoloured tree frogs. Across the water, six majestic fish eagles perched in a tree, occasionally shrieking their haunting cry. Black egrets in abundance, darters and cormorants, jacanas, black crakes, and pied kingfishers hovering above the water. In the trees nearby, cheeky drongos imitated other birds, weaverbirds flew to and fro selecting grass to thread into their intricate nests, and clouds of red-billed quelea occasionally obscured the sun. Across one of the channels, four large crocodiles lazed on the white sand, pretending to be asleep, but cannily watching for prey through nearly closed eyes. Further downstream, in a deeper pool, the ears of several hippos twitched, their noses barely breaking the water for air. Terrapin swam across the calm water and climbed on to hippo backs to sunbathe.

A DEADLY TRADE

A few hundred metres to the right of the dining area, three *mokoros*, coarsely hewn from the trunks of sausage trees, were pulled up on the grassy bank between acacia bushes. Another glided silently across the shallows towards the bank. A white man with a sunburned face sheltering under a floppy hat, binoculars slung around his neck, perched on a pile of dry reeds in the front of the boat and scribbled notes in a spiral-bound notebook protected by a waterproof cover. At the back, a man past middle age but wiry, with a sweat-stained shirt, stood propelling the *mokoro* with a long pole. When the *mokoro* reached the water's edge, William Boardman wobbled to the front and jumped ashore. After thanking Enoch, the poler, he walked over to the outdoor dining area and joined his wife Amanda, who had already started breakfast.

'Good morning, dear,' he said brightly, putting his hand affectionately on her shoulder. He was rewarded with a warm smile. 'I saw a finfoot and a malachite kingfisher this morning. Enoch saw the finfoot a hundred metres away. He's a great spotter! We must get him to take us out this afternoon.' He leaned forward and whispered, 'I also chatted to him about curios. Dupie's been a bit slack on getting decent stock recently. Maybe Enoch can help us out.'

A few moments later the cook, Suthani Moremi, wandered from the kitchen tent to ask William for his order. As always, on his shoulder Moremi sported a large grey crested bird with a long tail – a common go-away-bird. Each visit, the Boardmans enjoyed a private joke involving the bird. William always insisted that since it was indigenous and not caged, they could add it to their bird list. Amanda pointed out that it was obviously tame – and so ineligible. Fortunately fate inevitably intervened, as wild go-away-birds would descend on nearby fig trees to enjoy the fruit. Over the years, the Boardmans had developed a soft spot for Kweh, who made frequent sorties on to their table at mealtimes, waiting patiently for a treat. His inquisitive eyes and cocked crested head made him irresistible.

Kweh was Moremi's best friend. The cook spoke to him constantly, sharing observations and asking advice: 'Do you think we should serve mango with the fish or just lemons?' Or, 'I think that everyone has had enough dessert. Or should I make some more pancakes?' For his part, Kweh appeared to listen intently, sometimes squawking an answer, sometimes nibbling Moremi's ear. Occasionally, if disturbed, he would let out a raucous shriek that sounded like a shrill 'go away'. The call also sounded like 'kweh', so that had become the bird's name.

At the table next to the Boardmans, a black man sat alone, working his way through three fried eggs, bacon, sausage and chips. He wore sunglasses, jeans and a Hawaiian shirt complete with palm trees at sunset. Sun spots danced across his tablecloth, reflections from a heavy gold chain hanging around his neck. With a nod he acknowledged William as he sat down. William wondered why this man had chosen Jackalberry Camp for his holiday. He did not seem interested in birds, declining yesterday afternoon's motorboat trip up the river. But after a few drinks he became the life and soul of the party, even outdoing Dupie. William had discreetly asked Dupie about the man. His name was Boy Gomwe, his South African passport well used throughout southern Africa. He had given his profession as salesman.

Vaguely William wondered whether the other three black guests had already finished breakfast. But the expectant tables suggested otherwise. Had they gone for a walk together? Up to now they had not seemed particularly friendly.

Trying to be affable, William asked Gomwe if he had enjoyed the morning so far. The man shrugged. 'Slept late.'

'There were wonderful birdcalls at sunrise,' offered Amanda.

'I'm really only interested in birds I can eat,' said Gomwe.

'Let me tell you a story about eating birds.' The voice came from a heavily tanned man with a straggly grey beard and hair to match. He wore an old khaki shirt, patched in several places. His shorts, made from canvas, sagged down to his knees. Brown knee-length socks disappeared into worn leather boots. Everyone knew him as Dupie. Few people even knew his real name was Morné du Pisanie. He was solid and strong and had a stomach that protruded dramatically. It was a sight to behold – the result of thousands of litres of beer. The best view was from the side, which allowed for the proportions of his belly to be properly appreciated.

He walked from the kitchen tent, glass of mango juice in hand, and sat heavily on a chair at Gomwe's table. One leg of the chair sank several centimetres into the ground, causing the onlookers to wonder hopefully if it might tip over, as had happened the previous evening after dinner.

'When I was in the Scouts,' Dupie began, wriggling to find a comfortable position in his chair. 'When I was in the Scouts,' he repeated, looking around at Amanda and William. 'That's the Selous Scouts, not the bunch of cute boys who wear uniforms, collect badges and sleep together.' He winked at Gomwe. 'Well, anyway—'

But Dupie was never to finish his story. He was interrupted by a piercing scream that catapulted dozens of birds skywards. The scream came from behind the kitchen. The three guests leaped up, looking around anxiously. A second scream. Dupie lumbered into the kitchen, returning with a heavy stick. Before he could head towards the sleeping area, Beauty appeared, running, stumbling, hands to her mouth.

'He dead,' she whimpered. 'Someone kill him. Blood all over his throat. Ears gone! He dead!' She threw herself into Dupie's arms and burst into tears.

'Who's dead, Beauty?' Dupie asked, patting her on the back. 'What did you see?'

'In Kingfisher tent. Dead man. Murdered!' Her body shook.

'Get her some water,' Dupie said, passing Beauty to Moremi, who had emerged from the kitchen. 'No, hot tea would be better. I'll be right back.' He ran surprisingly quickly into the reception tent, emerging seconds later with a rifle in hand, an old bolt-action Lee-Enfield .303, probably World War I surplus. He headed towards the last in the line of well-separated tents, perhaps three hundred metres from the reception area, rifle at the ready. When he reached Kingfisher tent, panting, he brushed one flap aside with the rifle barrel and glanced in. Immediately he shouted, 'Enoch! Quickly! Come here!' As he closed the tent flaps, zipping them from top to bottom, the Munro sisters ran up from their tent.

'What on earth's going on, Dupie?' asked Trish.

'We heard somebody screaming,' said Judith, clutching her sister's arm.

Dupie ushered them down the path to the silent group in the dining area.

'He's dead. Looks as though someone slit his throat,' he told them.

'Who's dead?' William demanded.

'It's Goodluck. Goodluck Tinubu.'

'Maybe he's not dead. I've had first-aid training,' William said. 'Let me take a look.'

'He's dead all right,' Dupie responded. 'No one goes into that tent but the police. I'll call them now. Enoch, you stay outside and guard the body.' He handed the rifle to Enoch, who nodded and set off towards Goodluck's tent.

'Are you sure it's Goodluck?' Gomwe asked.

Dupie nodded. 'Seems his name wasn't very appropriate.'

Gomwe shook his head. 'Seems not. I think I'll go to my tent.'

William stopped him. 'We'd better stick together till the police come. We don't know if the killer is still around.' Gomwe began to protest, but then shrugged, collapsed back into his chair, and retreated behind his sunglasses.

'Oh God, was he murdered?' Amanda asked, then blushed as everyone looked at her incredulously. 'Difficult to cut your own throat,' said William. Beauty started to cry again, clinging to her husband Solomon. She calmed down when she got her tea, dutifully delivered by Moremi. Now he stood, Kweh on his shoulder, clutching a carving knife in his right hand and muttering to himself.

'Where's Langa? And Zondo?' asked William.

'Dupie took Rra Zondo to airstrip early this morning,' Solomon said. 'He said Rra Zondo had emergency at home.'

William looked surprised. 'But—' he began, but Gomwe interrupted. 'What about Langa? Has anyone seen him this morning? Was he at breakfast?'

'He didn't come to breakfast,' Solomon said.

'He didn't come to breakfast!' Moremi stabbed with his knife towards the neatly set table. Amanda gave a small scream, and Solomon remonstrated with the cook in Setswana, banishing him to his kitchen domain. Moremi left muttering under his breath. Kweh, however, objected and flapped noisily around Moremi's head.

'Langa,' Gomwe reminded. 'We should check his tent.'

'*We* won't. *I* will!' Dupie said, returning from the reception tent.

At that moment, a woman, anxious and flustered, ran up to the group. 'Oh God, what's happened?' She was tall, with hair sun-yellowed rather than blond, done up in a bun; her arms bare and brown. She wore a khaki top and slacks to below the knee. Tanned and scratched legs ended in worn, flat sandals. Her face, safe from the Botswana sun thanks to a straw hat, looked younger than her forty-three years. Worry now lined it. 'What's happened?' she repeated. For a moment no one said anything, then Dupie told her.

'One of our guests is dead, Salome. Goodluck Tinubu. Someone cut his throat. And we're not sure where Sipho Langa is.'

Salome shook her head. 'Murdered? What are we going to do?'

'I've already contacted the police. They should be here in a couple of hours if they can get a plane. Otherwise it'll take all day.' Dupie put his hand on Salome's arm. 'Take the guests to the bar. Drinks are on the house. I'll be there in a few minutes. I'm going to check Langa's tent.'

William watched Dupie walk off, thoughtful. Then he put his arm around Amanda's shoulders. 'Are you all right, darling? I guess I could handle a stiff brandy at that.'

CHAPTER 2

'There isn't enough blood,' said Detective Sergeant Mooka, known as Tatwa to his friends. His slender body, just shy of two metres, was too tall for the bush tent, forcing him to stoop to look down at the corpse. He held a handkerchief over his mouth; the smell of body waste pervaded the tent.

Dupie, not short himself, looked sharply up at him. 'There seems more than enough to me.'

'I suppose so,' the detective replied, regretting his involuntary remark. He squatted to get a closer look at the body and to relieve the pressure on his neck and shoulders. The victim was a black man, probably in his fifties. He was dressed in a T-shirt and underpants and lay on the floor on his back. There was a bruise on the side of his head with the skin broken. An awful purple slash of congealed blood disfigured his throat, and on his forehead were carved two slashes in the form of a cross. Both ears had been hacked from his head, then rammed into his mouth to stick out like nasty fungi growing from rotten wood.

'It's that stinking mob in Zimbabwe,' Dupie said suddenly. 'I've seen this done before. In the bush war.'

'To a black man?'

'Black, white, the terrorists weren't particular. They'd kill and mutilate anyone who stood up to them. Still do. And they run the place now,' he concluded with disgust.

'You think this could be politically motivated?'

'Hell knows what motivates those people. Tell you what, when you've finished measuring the amount of blood, come up to the bar and I'll tell you who did this. Then you can find out why.' He pushed his way through the tent flaps, leaving the detective with the body.

Tatwa had seen a man with his throat cut before. Then it had seemed as though every drop of blood had been pumped out through the wound. Now, there just wasn't enough blood for that. He sighed. He had better wait for the pathologist before he disturbed the body. He should be here soon, flying by light plane from Gaborone.

Tatwa looked around the tent. Army-style, it was comfortable in a bushy way. Two single beds with cane pedestals on which stood a storm lantern, a candle, two glasses with a little liquid still in them (why two?) and a half-empty bottle of mineral water. To one side there was a hanging area for clothes and a folding stool holding a brown suitcase, on top of which was a black briefcase. They'd need to go through those in due course. There was an adjoining toilet and a shower with a floor mosaic of a kingfisher.

He decided he had better take Du Pisanie up on his offer. He seemed to be in charge of the camp, and probably knew most of what happened in and around it. Perhaps he did have an idea who had murdered this man. He got to his feet – instinctively ducking, as he did even in his friends' houses – and backed out of the tent. The zipper must have been left open when the cleaning woman found the corpse. The fat bush flies had already found their way in.

As he walked towards the bar, he motioned to his two colleagues from Forensics. They would scour the tent and surrounding area for clues.

Tatwa found the entire complement of the camp gathered in the bar. Obviously lunch had been delayed until after his meeting. Dupie introduced him to Salome McGlashan, the owner of the camp concession. Then the guests: Amanda and William Boardman from South Africa, Boy Gomwe also from South Africa, and Trish and Judith Munro, sisters from England. Finally Dupie got to the staff: Enoch Kokorwe, the camp manager; Suthani Moremi, the cook; Beauty, who did the cleaning; and her husband Solomon, the waiter. Tatwa greeted them all with respect and thanked them for their patience.

'Regrettably I have to confirm what Mr Du Pisanie has already told you. One of the guests, Mr Goodluck Tinubu, has been murdered. We have a pathologist on the way from Gaborone, but my guess is that Mr Tinubu was murdered sometime late last night.' He paused, looking around the group.

'I know you must be shocked by what has happened. But there's no need to worry. I've two armed men with me who are searching the area. If the killer is nearby we'll find him. If he's left, which I'm sure he did many hours ago, there's no danger. I'll need to interview all of you later, so I'm afraid I have to ask you not to leave the camp until I give permission. Also, we'll need to take fingerprints from all of you.'

'Are we being treated as suspects then?' Gomwe asked. 'Why do you need fingerprints?'

'None of you are suspects at this point, Mr Gomwe. We need your prints so we can distinguish them from any others we might find.'

'I may be able to help,' William exclaimed. 'I always have a small digital camera with me for pictures of artwork and friends. Happy snaps. I took pictures of everyone at the camp last night. We were all having such a good time after Dupie's chair . . .' He let the sentence drift off after seeing the look Dupie gave him. Tatwa thanked him and said the pictures might be very helpful.

As there were no further contributions, Tatwa added with unintended irony: 'I suggest all of you enjoy a good lunch while I get some background information from Mr Du Pisanie.'

Dupie took Tatwa to the tent off the side of the main reception area, which he described as his office. It contained a table, three plastic chairs, and a metal filing cabinet whose top drawer had slipped off its rollers and was jammed half open. The table was host to a selection of fish hooks and reels, a coffee-stained map of the Linyanti, and a cup, half full of cold coffee, that might have participated in the staining. Piles of documents, old newspapers from both Botswana and Zimbabwe, batches of handwritten envelopes held together with elastic bands, calendars several years old, and stacks of receipts and cancelled cheques covered the table. Pens and pencils lay scattered amongst paper clips and crumpled Post-it notes. On top of the filing cabinet were two old black-and-white photographs, apparently family scenes from a time long past.

Dupie seated himself behind the desk, well back to allow room for his stomach, and waited for the detective to help himself to a chair.

Taking off his ever-present charcoal cap, which honoured St Louis (more likely the American city than the Botswana beer), Tatwa pulled a notebook from his shirt pocket. 'You said you had some useful information, Mr Du Pisanie?'

'It's the dog that didn't bark that is the answer,' said Dupie. 'You know your Sherlock Holmes?' Tatwa shook his head. 'Well, it's who isn't there, you see. The men who aren't with the group outside. One called himself Langa, and the other Zondo.'

'Where are they?'

'Ah, that is the question! That's Hamlet, by the way. Langa has disappeared. Perhaps he took one of the *mokoros*. I don't see how else he could have escaped.'

'Are you missing a *mokoro*?' Tatwa asked.

Dupie shrugged. 'Who knows? Most of them belong to the village on the mainland. Anyone who wants one borrows it and brings it back later.'

'What about Zondo?'

'He left this morning. He was supposed to be here three nights, not two, but he told me last night after dinner that he had to leave first thing this morning. Some sort of family emergency.'

'How did he hear about it?'

'We actually have mobile phone reception here – as unlikely as it may seem. There's a tower in Linyanti town across the river in Namibia. If you have roaming, you'll pick it up.'

'When did he leave?'

'I took him to the airstrip early – before breakfast.'

'When did you last see Langa?'

'At dinner last night. He went to bed shortly after Zondo and Tinubu. Tired, they all said, although they hadn't done much during the day.'

'Do you have an address for Mr Zondo?'

'Oh yes. In Zimbabwe. One of the fat cats. No doubt about that. I know the type. Fat from the gravy train while everyone else starves.'

'Please give me the details. We'll get the Zimbabwe police to help us trace him.'

'Best of luck to you.' Dupie sneered and tossed him Zondo's registration form. Tatwa glanced at it and was disappointed not to see a telephone contact number.

'Does Mr Langa also come from Zimbabwe?'

'No,' Dupie replied. 'He has a South African passport. Lives in Johannesburg, I think.'

'And Mr Tinubu?'

'Well, he's more interesting. He showed me a local identity document so I thought he was a Motswana. But when I checked it, it said he was born in Zimbabwe. Bulawayo, I think. So there could be a connection. In fact, I'd bet on it.'

'I'd like the forms for all the other guests too, please.'

'Sure. I'll get them. Then I'd say it's time for lunch.'

Tatwa nodded. After lunch he'd have to interview the others, but first he had to trace Zondo and start the search for Langa. He needed to report back in any case, and he wondered what had happened to the pathologist.

'Please make sure no one leaves the camp until I say so. I'll need to get more information from all of you later.'

Dupie nodded, then followed his impressive stomach out through the flap of the tent, nearly colliding with a policeman. The constable, ignoring Dupie, addressed Tatwa in Setswana.

'Sergeant, you must come at once. We've found another man.'

Tatwa could tell from the uniformed policeman's demeanour that he had another corpse on his hands. 'You'd better come with us, Mr Du Pisanie,' he said. 'I'm sorry to further delay your lunch.'

They had found the body at the western end of the camp. One of the policemen had walked to the top of a small cliff at the edge of the water and looked down. A man lay crumpled at the bottom of the slope.

It took Dupie and Tatwa several minutes to clamber down to the body and join the other uniformed policeman. There was no mystery about this death, no arcane cross on the forehead, no slit throat, no severed ears. The man had been hit hard enough to dent his skull. He must have been on the path above, because his progress down the scree had marked the rocks with blood. The body was that of a large, well-built black man, wearing shorts, T-shirt and a light jacket, all in khaki. He wore dirty white sneakers without socks, and a pair of binoculars hung around his neck. The face stared sightlessly at the sky.

'My God,' said Dupie. 'That's Sipho Langa! He's been murdered too.'

Tatwa clenched his teeth. Suddenly he had two victims and one suspect instead of one victim and two suspects. The forensics people would have their work cut out to cover two murder sites before dark. Just then a light plane flew low overhead, probably the pathologist. He was glad of that. He needed help. This was his first big case, and he was beginning to feel out of his depth. If Zondo were the culprit, he'd be out of the country already. And if he had the right connections, as Dupie suspected, he would be impossible to shift from Zimbabwe. Since his boss in Kasane was ill, Tatwa decided to call the director of the Criminal Investigation Department in Gaborone directly. He and Dupie walked back to the main camp in silence.

'May I use your office? I need to contact the CID in Gaborone.'

'Why in Gaborone?'

'It's procedure.'

'Go ahead. Call me if you need anything.'

As they walked through the dining area, everyone became silent. Glancing at the river, Tatwa noticed the large crocodiles sunning themselves on convenient sand banks. One was huge – a five-metre monster. Tatwa shuddered. He hated crocodiles; one had cost him a younger brother. Pulling himself together, he walked to the office and made his call to Director Mabaku.

CHAPTER 3

Assistant Superintendent 'Kubu' Bengu had just returned from a day-long investigation of a robbery at a garage in Lethlakeng when he was summoned to see the director. A meeting with Mabaku was an unwelcome intrusion because he hoped to finish his report before going home to his wife and dinner. With a sigh he heaved himself out of his chair and headed for the director's office.

Mabaku growled, 'Why are you always away when I need you?'

Kubu opened his mouth to respond but was cut short.

'It's too late now! Sit down.' Mabaku pointed towards a chair. 'I have an urgent matter to discuss. It concerns a double murder reported this morning.' Kubu had heard nothing of a new murder case. His eyebrows rose.

'This morning a Motswana male was found with his throat cut at a lodge in the Linyanti. Probably happened last night. Then his face was mutilated. Later, another guest – a South African – was found bludgeoned to death and dumped in a gully. There are a number of, shall we say, sensitive aspects to the case, and we have a camp full of tourists stuck there. Detective Sergeant Mooka is investigating. But he's new, and he needs help.'

'Oh, Tatwa!' Kubu chuckled. 'Good chap, even if he is a bit tall!' Kubu had met Mooka as a trainee in Gaborone. They could hardly avoid hitting it off. Mooka had acquired his nickname of Tatwa, a play on the word *thutlwa*, Setswana for giraffe, from his very tall, slim build and occasional slightly surprised look. Because he was gentle and quiet unless threatened, the name suited him remarkably well and had stuck. And David Bengu was nicknamed Kubu, Setswana for hippopotamus, for his impressive girth, his appetite, and, until roused, his deceptively ponderous approach. Even the usually humourless Mabaku had commented that the CID was becoming a menagerie instead of a police department. Then Tatwa had been posted to Kasane, and they had lost contact.

'Why doesn't Assistant Superintendent Dingalo take charge? He's based in Kasane,' Kubu asked.

'He's got another bout of malaria. Kasane is becoming as bad as Victoria Falls. Several CID people are down with some nasty, drug-resistant strain. You'll have to go up and take over.'

'Isn't it time Tatwa went solo on a case? Won't he be demoralised if I take over?'

'Kubu, you're not listening. I said there were sensitive aspects. You know how much the country relies on tourism. The first victim's name is Tinubu. He lived in Botswana. But he's ex-Zimbabwe according to his identity document, and he gets himself killed not far from Zimbabwe. The obvious suspect is registered under the name of Ishmael Zondo, but the Zimbabwe police tell me that the Zimbabwean passport he used is a fake. I think we can take it that his name is also false. At the moment, there's no trace of him. A second man, Sipho Langa, who's South African and apparently unrelated to the first victim, is also dead. All this happens in front of a group of international tourists who want to get on with their holidays. MacGregor is already up there taking care of the bodies. We need this tidied up quickly. And there's the African Union meeting coming up in Gaborone in about four weeks, remember? We don't want to be embarrassed. The manager up at the camp is a chap called Du Pisanie, another Zimbabwean turned Motswana, believe it or not.' He grimaced. 'Catch the Air Botswana flight to Maun in the morning, and have Miriam contact the Defense Force about getting from Maun to the camp. That'll be the third flight we've asked the BDF for today. I hope they don't refuse, otherwise you'll have to hitchhike.' He turned back to his paperwork. 'Give my regards to Joy.'

Kubu sighed as he left. He wondered if the food at the camp was any good.

CHAPTER 4

Kubu looked down at the patchwork landscape of the Linyanti. As they flew over the web of waterways, the pilot pointed out various geographic features and several groups of elephant. It was hard to tell where the water stopped and the land began. Fingers of water moved into channels and then overflowed, silently, with no waves; the flood came like a thief in the night, gently stealing the land.

What snake has slithered into this Eden? Kubu wondered.

In an unusual change of perspective, they looked down on two huge lappet-faced vultures gliding in an updraught a thousand feet above the ground. The pilot pointed out a pod of hippo basking on the bank of one of the channels. Kubu nodded, enjoying the aerial view of his namesakes, and was struck by the dramatic contrast of this water world with the arid dryness of the country's heart. Then the Islander banked, following one of the larger channels to the airstrip near Jackalberry Camp.

The pilot did a low pass over the airstrip. A family of warthogs rushed off with flagpole tails. Satisfied that the runway was free of game, the pilot turned, aligned the Islander with the dirt strip, and brought it down in a cloud of dust and a succession of bumps.

Kubu unloaded his luggage, and after a brief check, the pilot was ready to return to Maun. Kubu moved his bags off the runway and turned his back as the plane taxied for its departure. For a minute it was a dot heading south, then it was gone.

The camp had been informed that Kubu was coming, but he expected a wait. Very little happened quickly in this part of the world. Fortunately, someone had erected a shelter for a small plane – wooden poles topped by a corrugated iron roof. He found a log, dragged it into the shade, and sat, a pole supporting his back. Sandwiches and a cold drink would have helped pass the time, he thought, while inhaling deeply through his nose. This part of Botswana smelled different from Gaborone, with its large population and developing pollution. He could smell vegetation – the lush forests along the Linyanti river. A dust devil swirled close, forcing Kubu to shut his eyes and hold his nose. A few seconds later it had passed, and he was covered in sand. Suddenly he heard a distant trumpet. Elephant! He looked around anxiously, knowing that the six-tonne animals could move silently and quickly through the bush. As luck would have it, not one was to be seen.

To Kubu's relief and surprise, it was a short wait. A Toyota Double Cab pickup truck arrived in a cloud of dust, showing signs of multiple altercations with trees and bushes. The driver was solidly built, wearing the khaki uniform affected by guides at the tourist camps. Sweat darkened his back and armpits. He introduced himself as Enoch Kokorwe, the camp manager. Kubu said he thought the manager was Morné du Pisanie. Enoch shrugged, tossing Kubu's bag on to the vehicle. He was polite but not friendly, and Kubu gave up hope of getting a preview of what to expect at the camp.

Twenty minutes later they came to the channel. Several *mokoros* lay on the bank. For a horrible moment, Kubu feared he'd have to fit his bulk into one of them. If it tipped, the crocodiles would have a field day! But a little further upstream bobbed a rowing boat with an outboard motor. He breathed a sigh of relief.

A short way downstream clustered a small group of rudimentary dwellings, a fishing village typical of the area. An older Land Rover and a newish-model Nissan Pathfinder 4x4 with a Venter trailer were parked under a shady mangosteen tree. Another trailer stood by itself under a nearby wild fig tree. These certainly weren't vehicles the villagers would own. Kubu supposed they belonged to the camp. To the right was a shed, not big enough to garage a vehicle, but perhaps used for storage.

Enoch took the luggage to the boat, which he had pulled up to a rough jetty made from three tree trunks lashed together. He held the boat while Kubu boarded and settled himself, but it was early in the flood season, and the boat grounded with the weight. As hard as he tried, Enoch couldn't shift it, so Kubu had to clamber out, take off his shoes and socks, roll up his khaki pants, and repeat the process with the boat further out into the water.

'Sit right at the front,' Enoch said. 'That may get the prop out of the sand.'

Kubu moved cautiously to the front, causing it to dip precariously close to the water. Again Enoch tried to push the boat into the river, to no avail. He sighed, took off his own shoes and socks, and waded into the water. After several moments of Enoch's lifting and pushing, the boat slid off the sand. Enoch climbed in, maintaining balance, and started the motor. A few minutes later, Kubu made his way back to the middle of the boat, and soon they were heading noisily across the channel, scattering cormorants and darter birds.

The camp boasted a better jetty, and Kubu climbed on to dry land with relative aplomb. He was met by a hefty white man and a white woman, tanned despite her fair colouring. Kubu noted that the man's belly rivalled his own. On the other hand, I have the better overall cover, he thought smugly.

The woman held out her hand. 'Inspector Bengu? I'm Salome McGlashan. I have the concession for this camp. This is my associate, Morné du Pisanie. I hope you can clear this up quickly. Everyone is very upset, and we've other guests waiting to come to the camp. It's all very disturbing.'

Kubu shook her hand and commented that murder often had that effect. Then his large hand disappeared into Du Pisanie's.

'Call me Dupie.' Checking his watch, the man continued, 'We can talk after lunch.' Kubu liked Dupie's down-to-earth approach.

Dupie tactfully seated Kubu and Tatwa at the edge of the dining area, where they could talk in private if they spoke softly. Still, they felt like the floor show, with all the other diners watching them for any hint of developments. Speaking Setswana, they greeted each other warmly and spent a few minutes reminiscing about Tatwa's spell in Gaborone.

Kubu said that he thought Tatwa had grown even taller. Tatwa denied this, but claimed that Kubu had increased his girth. Kubu laughed.

Kubu asked for a steelworks, but was disappointed to have to explain how to make his favourite drink. It came with ginger ale instead of ginger beer, too much bitters, and too little ice. So he was not optimistic about the food, but was pleasantly surprised. The cook produced a dish of lightly devilled eggs garnished with anchovies and capers. Kubu ordered a second helping. He promised himself that he would cut back on the main course of cold meats to compensate. There was always dessert if he was still hungry.

The conversation turned to the case. 'What do you make of this, Tatwa? Tell me what you've found.'

'Well, now that an assistant superintendent is running the show, we should have it all sorted out in no time.' Tatwa sounded slightly peeved. Kubu leaned forward and gave him a friendly shove that nearly knocked him out of his chair. 'Team effort, Tatwa. No one's trying to steal your thunder. First big case. We'll make it your first big success.'

'Of course, Kubu. Sorry. Du Pisanie thinks it's cut and dried. Tinubu was here for a few days. Zondo was a hit man from Zimbabwe. Came in with a fake passport, bumped Tinubu off neatly and then disappeared. Zondo's our culprit. End of story.'

'Motive?'

Tatwa shrugged. 'Perhaps some grudge from the past. Tinubu was from Zimbabwe too.'

'And Langa? Why kill him?'

'Perhaps he came across Zondo after the murder.'

'But you don't believe it,' Kubu observed shrewdly.

Tatwa shrugged. 'For one thing, Langa was found at the opposite end of the camp from Tinubu. According to Salome McGlashan, Zondo made his reservation *before* Tinubu. And Langa didn't have a reservation at all. He just pitched up. And then when I spoke to Enoch, he said—'

Kubu held up his hand. 'Let's interview them all again from scratch. Then you can watch for any discrepancies. In the meanwhile, don't tell me what they said so I won't be biased.' He was eyeing the cold meat platter.

'Won't going over it all again upset them?'

'Exactly! Would you pass that meat? I think there's some cold tongue. Are you sure you won't have some?' Tatwa shook his head firmly. The eggs were fine, but he ate little meat, and certainly not something that had once been in a cow's mouth. Assured that he was not depriving his colleague, Kubu took all the tongue and asked the waiter for mustard. Tatwa could see that the case was on hold until Kubu had satisfied the inner man.

CHAPTER 5

Giving thanks for gas fridges, Kubu had a double helping of ice cream, flavoured with the fruit of a local tree. He was intrigued by the combination of the marula with frozen goat's-milk cream and found it rather good. Even the unadventurous Tatwa liked it. But their enjoyment was interrupted by a tinny version of the Grand March from *Aida* emanating from Kubu's trouser pocket. With obvious reluctance, he hoisted himself out of his chair.

'What's going on, Kubu? What've you discovered so far?' The director's lunch did not seem to be sitting well.

'I've only been here about an hour, Director. I've been catching up with Tatwa.'

'Over lunch, I expect! Kubu, I told you this is urgent. Not at all the moment to be sampling bush cuisine. Phone me back as soon as you have something. I'll be here late. I'll be waiting. You should also phone MacGregor. He told me he'd have a preliminary report on the autopsies this afternoon.' Then he hung up.

Kubu noted with approval that Tatwa had ordered coffee. But the mood was spoiled. Kubu sighed. 'What have we done about finding Zondo?'

'Well, the Zimbabwe police confirmed that all the details he gave here were false, including his name and passport.'

'The director told me,' Kubu said.

'But we have a good description,' Tatwa continued, 'and, even better, some photographs taken by one of the guests – I've got them here. Had them printed in Kasane last night.' He brandished an envelope. 'We've circulated Zondo's photo to all the police stations and border posts, and the surrounding countries, as well as what we think are his fingerprints. Then we've tried to track the plane he left in.'

'And?'

'We've drawn a blank on all counts. No one has seen him. He hasn't crossed the border – at least not using the name Zondo – and there's no recorded flight plan with a stopover here. Probably the pilot flew under the radar and went wherever he wanted to go.'

'Let's take a look at the pictures.'

Tatwa spread them on the table. Kubu glanced at a close-up of the two Munro sisters, looking at each other, laughing, glasses of wine in hand. Then he looked at the ones of the black guests. The first was a striking picture of a handsome middle-aged man with his arms folded against the world. Broad cheeks, closely shaven, pensive. The man seemed to be looking beyond the camp fire into the darkness.

'That's Goodluck Tinubu,' said Tatwa quietly.

Kubu put it down, sorry that he would never meet this man. He picked up the next print. The man's face seemed a bit blurred; perhaps he had moved as the picture was taken. He was older, harder-looking. Kubu could imagine him as a soldier. The man was clutching a tumbler in his right hand as though he might have to fight to keep it. He wore glasses that had reflected the flash, rather spoiling the picture. And he was wearing a felt hat with a spray of feathers. Unusual and incongruous.

'That's our prime suspect, Ishmael Zondo,' said Tatwa. 'However, that isn't his real name, according to the Zimbabwe police. Looks tough. Except for the hat with the guineafowl feathers. Odd.'

The next picture was of Boy Gomwe. A falsely happy face, thought Kubu. He glanced across the dining area. Gomwe was chatting to the Munros, animated, using his hands in the conversation. Good with people, but Kubu found something he disliked about him. The last picture was of a man concentrating on something not in the picture. This must be the second victim, Sipho Langa, Kubu thought. He pushed the pictures back towards Tatwa.

'Okay. Fill me in on Jackalberry Island.'

'Well, in the first place it isn't really an island. It's a peninsula jutting into the river, but it's marshy and has small waterways between here and the solid land.'

'Is it possible that someone came across from the mainland that way? Without using a boat?'

'No, impossible in the dark. It would be a miserable trip, and you'd be wading among crocs and hippos. It's about a fifteen-minute trip by *mokoro*. That would be the way to do it. Silent and low on the water. But even that would be dangerous at night because of the hippos.'

'And the layout of the camp?'

'We're about in the middle of it. The kitchen and staff quarters are behind us. There are three tents behind those two trees.' He pointed to two massive wild figs whose trunks broke into fingers probing the water. Suckers hung from the branches, and clusters of fruit were providing a banquet for a troop of vervet monkeys.

'The two larger ones are where Du Pisanie and McGlashan live; the small one is for their visitors. Since the camp was full when Sipho Langa came, they put him up there. The odd thing is that Tinubu and Langa arrived together.' Tatwa paused, obviously feeling this was significant. 'Dupie told me that Tinubu's car had broken down on the road to Kasane. Langa apparently stopped to help and waited until Tinubu's car had been towed to a garage. Langa was looking for a place to stay, so he decided to join Tinubu here. They drove together to Ngoma, where they were met by Enoch. It takes over three hours to get here from Ngoma. The roads are terrible.'

'They met by chance on a road in the middle of nowhere, and now they are both dead? Hard to believe! What's happened to Langa's car?'

'We drove it to Kasane,' Tatwa replied. 'Forensics will be going over it today.'

'Good. And Tinubu's?'

'We're trying to get its registration. Should have that today, too. Then we'll search for it in Kasane.'

Satisfied about the vehicles, Kubu changed his focus. 'Where are the guest tents?'

'There are three on the east side of this area and two on the west. They're far enough apart to be private and have their own view of a quiet waterway. Nice, if you like water full of crocodiles. On the east side, Tinubu had the furthest tent. Two sisters, Trish and Judith Munro from England, were next to him, then Amanda and William Boardman from Cape Town. On the west side, Boy Gomwe is closest to us, and Zondo was at the end. I'm in Zondo's tent. You can use Langa's. Tinubu's is still closed off.'

'Have the forensics people been through everything in Zondo's tent and Langa's?'

Tatwa nodded.

'I'll use Langa's tent then. How do guests access the tents?'

'There's a path that runs at the back of this communal area, and each tent is approached from behind.'

'So it would be possible to get to a tent without being seen by the occupant, or indeed by the occupants of *any* of the tents?'

Tatwa nodded again.

Kubu pushed away his cup and rose. 'Let's meet the inhabitants. I have to have something to tell Mabaku before close of business tonight.'

CHAPTER 6

Kubu decided to first get the lie of the land. He asked Salome and Dupie to show him around, and Tatwa accompanied them.

'Well, this is the reception tent,' Dupie started, unsure of what the detective wanted. 'We keep all our business records here – in those files at the back. When guests arrive we bring them here to fill out the registration forms, and we take an impression of their credit cards. We do all of that manually because we don't have phone lines.' He stopped and looked enquiringly at Kubu.

'Do you close the tent at night?' Kubu asked.

'Well, we zip it up to keep the dust out, but it's not secure.'

'Have you noticed anything missing since the murder? Any credit-card receipts? Registration forms?'

Both Dupie and Salome shook their heads. 'We checked,' Salome said. 'As far as we can see, everything is here. Dupie gave everyone's registrations to Detective Mooka. We've got the slips they signed at the bar. Dupie doesn't think any are missing. I don't know . . .'

'Anything signed by Zondo?'

Salome shook her head. 'He paid cash in US dollars. We don't take Zimbabwe dollars.'

'Okay,' Kubu said. 'Let's move on.' The group walked the few metres to the tent left of reception.

'This is my office,' Dupie said. Kubu and Tatwa nodded.

'We'll come back to it. I'll use it for my interviews, if you don't mind,' Kubu remarked, not caring if Dupie minded or not.

Next was the entertainment area, comprising the bar and lounge, opening on to an outdoor area where meals were served. The bar area held a bookcase with light reading, reference books on birds and trees, and various games. The walls displayed a variety of bushman artefacts: a full hunting set with a well-worn leather bag, a spear, a bow, arrows and poison containers; a variety of necklaces made from ostrich-egg shell yellowing with age; bangles of seed pods; and several carefully hollowed-out gourds for carrying water in the desert. An impressive collection, Kubu thought. It must be nearly impossible to find sets these days that were actually used for hunting. He glanced at the gas and storm lanterns.

'No electricity?'

'No,' Dupie replied. 'We've got a diesel generator to recharge the batteries for the radio and cell phones whenever necessary, but it's noisy and expensive to run. We use gas for cooking and mainly storm lanterns for lighting. We think it gives the camp a more authentic feel. More like the way Africa used to be.'

Kubu grunted. 'How do you get to the sleeping tents from here?'

'Follow me,' Dupie replied.

The group headed to the line of tents to the right. As they walked the hundred metres or so, Kubu asked Salome, 'How did you get to be the owner of Jackalberry Camp, Ms McGlashan?'

'I'm not really the owner,' Salome replied. 'I inherited the remainder of a twenty-year concession. There is only about a year left. I worked for the previous owner – Andre Cloete was his name – and he left it to me. I was completely surprised. I thought he would leave it to someone in his family. Perhaps they didn't want it.'

'I didn't think concessions could be inherited,' Kubu commented.

'The concession is in the name of a company,' Salome said. 'Andre left me the company. Also, it's not a government lease, but a sublease from the hunters who own the concessions in this area.'

'And before that?' Kubu enquired. 'Were you born in Botswana?'

'I was born in what was called Southern Rhodesia. Now Zimbabwe. On a farm near Bulawayo. I loved it there, but when the war came it was bad. Horrible, actually. Anyway, after the war I didn't want to live there any more and went to South Africa. I worked at hotels in Johannesburg for a number of years. But I hated the noise and the traffic and the crowding. When I met Andre and he offered me a job here, I couldn't wait. I've been here ever since.'

'When was that?'

'March '94.'

Kubu wondered whether it was coincidence that this was just before South Africa was to have its first black majority government.

'Have you ever been married?'

'No. What's that got to do with anything?' she asked sharply.

Dupie interrupted. 'This is the tent that Tinubu stayed in. And was murdered in.'

The tent had police tape tied around the lower section, making it look weirdly gift-wrapped. Kubu pushed the tape aside, unzipped the flap and went in. There was still a bad smell and a few flies, although Forensics had cleaned the place up. This is a typical tourist bush set-up, Kubu thought. Comfortable, but nothing fancy. He looked around at the unpretentious interior, noting its layout, then walked out, closing the fly screen and flaps. He didn't bother with the tape. He doubted if anyone would want to go inside that tent at the moment.

He looked back the way they had come. A sandy path ran from the tent back towards the others. He retraced his steps, checking if someone could be seen. By the time he reached the second tent, he was sure that someone could walk unnoticed along this path from one end of the line of tents to the other. Especially at night.

'This is where the Munro sisters are staying. They're writers from England, here by themselves.' Dupie once again provided the information. 'The next tent is the Boardmans'. They're from Cape Town. They're curio dealers. African art, they call it. And crazy about birds. And the two tents on the other side of the communal area are the same as these. The first is Boy Gomwe's. The other is where Zondo stayed.'

Kubu pointed to a path that forked off the one they were on.

'Where does that path go?'

'To a lookout over the lagoon.'

'Let's take a look,' Kubu said, striding off. After a few steps he slowed to Dupie's pace. 'Where are you from, Mr Du Pisanie? What's your role here at Jackalberry Camp?'

'I've already told Detective Mooka all that stuff,' Dupie said impatiently.

'I know, Mr Du Pisanie,' Kubu said quietly. 'But I need to get the full story for myself. I realise this whole affair is an imposition, but I ask you to be patient.'

Actually, though, Dupie seemed happy to talk about himself. 'I've known Salome for years,' he said. 'We grew up on neighbouring farms near Bulawayo in Southern Rhodesia. After independence, she went to South Africa. I stayed on for a few years, but I didn't like the way things were going, so I left and came to Botswana. I know the bush well, and I'm an experienced hunter, so I hooked up with a safari outfit in Maun. They hired me to lead trips, mainly into the Central Kalahari. Most of our clients were Germans or Americans wanting to bag some big game. They thought they were in the wilds of Africa, but it was pretty tame, really. We set it up so they couldn't miss. Made them feel good, and they paid a lot of money for the privilege. They tipped well, too. Good thing, because the company certainly didn't pay well.' He paused for a moment, then continued.

'Salome and I had kept in touch after she left Rhodesia. When she inherited this place, she contacted me and asked if I wanted to help run it. I was sick and tired of what I was doing, and came here about twelve years ago. We've made ends meet, but only just.'

'And what do you do here?'

'Well, I don't have a specific role.' Dupie shrugged. 'Lots of paperwork, and I fix the mechanical stuff. And I try to keep the guests happy. Man the bar in the evenings and tell stories about Botswana and big-game hunting, and how the area used to be before all the tourists. I know a lot about the history of the area and generally keep people amused. The longer they stay at the bar, the more booze we sell, and that's where we make a bit of money. We've really struggled since the fancy camps have appeared. Camps only in name. Actually they're five-star hotels. We don't want to be like that, just a comfortable and affordable place for people to enjoy Botswana. Trouble is, most of the overseas tourists expect the high-end stuff, which we don't have. And we don't have enough accommodation to attract large groups – our concession only allows ten guests at a time. We stretch that occasionally by using the tent set aside for our personal friends. Nobody knows about that, and nobody really cares.'

At the top of the rise, Kubu stopped to catch his breath. Under a tree stood a picnic table and benches. He looked around. The view was spectacular. Water and islands stretched to the hazy horizon. Wild date palms poked into the sky, hosts to circling palm swifts, moving almost too fast for the eye to track. To the right, the mainland was covered with thick vegetation. Jackalberry, mangosteen and birdplum trees dominated the scene, with an occasional mahogany spreading its heavy branches. And to the left, behind the trees, Kubu knew, were the little jetty and the motorboat.

'This is really beautiful,' he said. 'I can see why people come here.' As though in disagreement, a small flock of Meyer's parrots screeched overhead, flying towards the mainland. Kubu saw immediately why Tatwa had dismissed the possibility of the murderer arriving or leaving on foot. Between the camp and the mainland was a swamp, riddled with pools and covered with papyrus and other reeds. He could see several hippo runs cutting through the area, and a few crocodiles sunning themselves on isolated sandbanks. So the murderer had either arrived and left by boat, or was already on the island the night of the murder.

Reluctantly Kubu headed back to the main path, but just before they reached it, he stopped suddenly. Here there were elegant mangosteen trees, but the brush between them was varied riverine bush, thick, thorny and unwelcoming.

'What's that, Tatwa?' Kubu pointed to some reddish threads caught on a hooked thorn.

'Looks like a snag from a shirt,' Tatwa replied without interest.

'Yes, but why there? In the middle of a bush? Why would anyone be there? It's all thorny and dense.'

Tatwa shrugged. He wanted to get on with the interviews. 'Maybe a child. Could be from anyone.'

'Some branches have been bent here, too. Someone deliberately pushed into the brush between the trees, and then came out again. He didn't force on through or you'd see broken twigs and other signs. I want Forensics to have those threads. If there's a match with one of the victims, it may tell us something.'

'That's a one in a hundred chance!' protested Tatwa.

'Yes,' Kubu agreed. 'Good odds.' He stepped back so that Tatwa could have a clear field to obtain the strands of material. He did so with a poor grace, a pair of tweezers, an envelope, and several scratches as the thorns fought to protect their property.

'Let's go,' Kubu said abruptly. 'I've seen enough.' He turned and headed back to camp.

CHAPTER 7

Ian MacGregor pushed back his desk chair and stretched his legs. He was tired but alert, sucking on an impressive briar that might have appealed to Sherlock Holmes. He could taste the moist richness of the tobacco carefully packed into the bowl. The pipe wasn't alight, of course. He had stopped smoking it after a stand-up argument with his doctor following a brush with pneumonia.

I'm pathetic, he thought contentedly. In my fifties, living in a foreign country far from the lochs of home, no family, more acquaintances and colleagues than real friends. Can't even smoke a real pipe. And I'm as happy as a pig in swill.

There were two great joys in his life, albeit two sides of the same coin. One was the African bush, especially the arid drama of the Kalahari. The other was trying to capture that drama in watercolour paints. He gazed at a desert scene on the wall, a large painting showing the remains of a giraffe carcass with hooded vultures circling. The carcass and the dry grass tufts around it were impressionist, slightly out of focus, with the vultures, sharp and true to a feather, seeming to move against the azure African sky. For once, his hand had captured the vision in his mind. Some people did not feel the painting was entirely appropriate in Ian's office, which adjoined the hospital morgue. But Ian did not care. He thought it the best thing he'd ever done.

There was a perfunctory knock, and Mabaku strode in. At once, the office was too small. 'Director Mabaku,' said Ian, surprised. 'What brings you here?' Mabaku expected people to come to him, not the other way round.

'What do you think I'm doing here, MacGregor? I can't resist seeing you relaxing among your cadavers,' he growled. 'I'm waiting for the reports on Tinubu and Langa, of course. Kubu's waiting too. Probably with a sandwich, a glass of wine, and his feet up. Why am I the only one who thinks this case is urgent?'

Ian chuckled. 'I was just thinking about how to put my report together when you walked in,' he lied, his Scottish brogue stronger than usual. 'Here are the notes.' He indicated a writing pad. The cover had an unpleasant rust-coloured stain. Mabaku grimaced.

'Never mind the formalities. What will the report say?'

Ian decided on a little fun. 'Come on, I'll show you,' he said.

He led Mabaku to his laboratory next door, put on surgical gloves and a face mask, and slid open a cold storage drawer. The smell of formaldehyde pervaded, but Ian did not seem to notice. He lifted the shroud to expose the mutilated body of a black man.

'I finished not long ago,' he said to Mabaku. He pushed some escaping material back into the stomach between his rough stitches. 'Messy lad, aren't you?' he said to the corpse. He lifted up the head and folded the scalp back for Mabaku to see.

'Look here, but don't come too close. Someone hit our friend verra hard. Didn't kill him, though. No fracture. But it would've knocked him cold.' He pointed to a discoloration on the head. 'See the mark where he was hit? The shape and pattern makes me think it was a metal object like a wrench.' Then, as though the idea had just occurred to him, he added, 'Put on gloves and a mask. Then you can feel the indentations for yourself.' But Mabaku declined with a frown. He wasn't enjoying his tour of the late Goodluck Tinubu.

'Now here's the really interesting bit,' Ian continued, indicating the chest cavity, which had been opened with an electric saw. 'I had to take the heart out to check the damage. I have it here somewhere.' He looked around vaguely, pretending it was lost. 'I found a wee hole. Your murderer stuck something long and sharp into the heart. Something like a sharpened bicycle spoke. Very neat. Straight through the right auricle. The heart would have stopped pretty well at once. That's why there wasn't much blood when the throat was cut afterwards.'

'Why cut his throat at all if they stabbed him through the heart? What sense does that make?'

Ian looked at him. 'I tell you what happened. It's your job to make sense of it. The murderer hit him hard across the left temple, knocking him cold. Then he stabbed him through the heart, killing him. After that he cut his throat, probably a few minutes after death, and what blood was around seeped out. Not much. Then, or just before – I can't tell – he used a sharp knife to cut this cross on the forehead.' MacGregor traced it with his finger. 'Then he cut off the ears and stuffed them in the poor man's mouth. From the wounds, I'd say the murderer was right-handed.'

Mabaku had had enough. 'Let's go back to your office.'

MacGregor looked disappointed. 'Don't you want to meet Langa?'

Mabaku shook his head firmly. 'When did all this happen anyway?'

MacGregor returned Goodluck to his penultimate resting place, and started to wash his hands. He shrugged. 'Between two and five that morning is about the best I can do.'

'Anything else?'

'Well, there's this. He was on the bed when he was hit, but I can't tell whether he was stabbed on the bed or on the floor. There was blood on the pillow, which we sent to Forensics; I'm sure it's his and came from the head wound. But the body was on the floor when we found it, and the blood from the throat and ear wounds was on the floor too. Why did the murderer move him? Was he worried about dirtying the sheets?'

Mabaku shook his head. 'Food? General health?'

'Agreed with what the camp people said he had for dinner. No alcohol. He seemed pretty healthy. But there was a time when he wasn't. He had some impressive scars on his lower back. Bullet wounds, I'd say. He was lucky to get out of that lot alive.'

'How long ago was that?'

Ian shrugged. 'A long time. Twenty, thirty years. There's no internal damage any more. Everything healed.'

'What about Langa?'

'Well, that's pretty straightforward. He was hit from behind and then several times from the front. At least one of the blows cracked his skull and killed him. Then the attacker rolled him off the path down the rocky slope. There was blood at several points on the way down.'

'Could he have fallen and hit his head?'

Ian frowned. 'Too many blows. He could have slipped and hit the back of his head, but it's hardly likely that he'd then get up, fall forward, cracking his skull, and roll down the slope.'

Mabaku nodded. 'That's it then?'

Ian fetched his pipe, settled himself, and started to suck it. 'The wounds on Langa's head are similar to Tinubu's. My guess is the same weapon was used on both. I would bet that you only have one murderer, or group of murderers, not two.'

Mabaku just scowled. That was very little consolation.

CHAPTER 8

Kubu and Tatwa commandeered Dupie's office for the interviews. There was barely enough room for three chairs, but it was relatively private. With Dupie's help, Kubu cleared enough of the desk for it to be usable. Kubu shook his head. How could anyone operate in such a pigsty?

When the space was workable, Kubu took Dupie's seat and motioned him to sit down opposite. Tatwa sat near the entrance to the tent, behind Dupie's right shoulder. He was going to observe, not participate. But he was fascinated by an object, perhaps a paperweight, that had emerged from under one of Dupie's piles of documents. It was striking: an opaque glass disc about six centimetres in diameter. The outer ring was deep indigo, then a teardrop of white containing an inner ring of turquoise, and finally a pitch-black centre. It looked like a flattened eye, staring.

'What's that?' Tatwa asked.

'This? It's a souvenir a Turkish hunter gave me when I saved him from a lion. It's called a Watching Eye. Apparently they're all over the place in Turkey. Supposed to bring good luck to businesses and such. Doesn't seem to work in Africa, though, judging by the way things have been going here. But it's useful. I tell the staff it watches them when I'm not here, and they're petrified of it!' Dupie laughed, creating a belly wobble. Then, gauging the reaction from the policemen, he quickly added, 'Just a joke, of course. Just a bit of fun.'

'Mr Du Pisanie,' said Kubu, turning the conversation to business. 'Thank you for showing me around. Now I have to find out what happened here the night before last. I'm going to ask you a number of questions, which you should answer as fully as possible. If anything pops into your mind as we are talking, please tell me. You'd be surprised how often something that seems unimportant can be the key to solving a crime.'

'Look, of course I want to help. But what are you doing about catching Zondo? The longer you sit around here, the further away he's getting!'

'Don't worry. We're looking for him, and the Zimbabwe police are looking for him. We'll find him. I want to be sure we can nail him when that happens. If, of course, he is the murderer.'

'Pretty obvious he's the murderer. Dog that didn't bark!'

Kubu had read Sherlock Holmes, but decided to ignore the remark. 'Where were you when Tinubu was murdered?'

'In my tent. These guests are not much into after-dinner drinking. So I closed the bar about ten.'

'You didn't hear anything during the night, like a scream or a loud thud?'

Dupie shook his head.

'Did you see anybody wandering around the camp later?'

Again Dupie shook his head.

'Did you stay in your tent the whole night?'

Dupie hesitated. 'I went to the bar to get a bottle of soda water at some point. Thirsty. Hot night. Don't actually remember when. Otherwise, yes, I was in my tent until I got up to take Zondo to the airstrip.'

'Can you think of any reason Zondo would murder Tinubu and Langa?' Kubu looked up from his notebook.

'Those terrorists are all the same. Savages. No place for the law. If you think someone has wronged you, kill 'em. That's their attitude. I saw it all too often in the war.'

'That's the civil war in Southern Rhodesia?'

'Call it what you want. It was a bunch of terrorists trying to get rid of the whites. That simple. We gave them hell, but the rest of the world stopped us from finishing them off.' Dupie glared at Kubu, daring him to engage.

'You fought in the war, I take it?'

'Yes. In the Scouts. That's the Selous Scouts, not the—'

'From what I remember,' Kubu interrupted, 'they were the elite troops. Is that right?'

'We were the ones asked to do all the big jobs and all the dirty jobs.'

'Did you by any chance know or recognise Zondo, Langa or Tinubu?' Kubu looked at Dupie, gauging his reaction. Dupie shook his head emphatically.

'Why should I? Never seen any of them before.'

'Other than the fact that Zondo left suddenly, did you see or hear anything that makes you think he could be the murderer? Did he and Tinubu talk to each other? What about Langa?' Again Kubu watched Dupie carefully as he answered.

'I can't say that I noticed anything,' Dupie said. 'Langa and Tinubu sat at the same table at dinner that night. Drank soft drinks.' Dupie managed to add a sneer to the last two words. 'They seemed to get on okay. Didn't talk much. They said they met on the road from Gaborone to Kasane. Tinubu's car had broken down and Langa stopped to help. Langa was looking for a place for a few nights and decided to come here with Tinubu. After dinner, they had coffee. Tinubu left almost immediately, claiming he was tired. Langa stayed a while and offered us all an after-dinner drink. First time he'd been sociable. Zondo declined, but Gomwe had one Amarula, then went to bed. That's a cream liqueur flavoured with marula fruit. Tourists like it.'

'Are you sure they said they'd never met before?' Kubu asked.

Dupie nodded.

Kubu changed tack. 'Was that the last time you saw Tinubu?'

'Yes.'

'And how about Zondo. Had you talked to him at all?'

'Nothing more than small talk. Seemed a little on edge, but didn't say much.'

'You're sure he and Tinubu never spoke?'

'I never saw them, but I don't see everything.'

'Did you see Zondo again before you took him to the mainland?'

'Yes, about half an hour after dinner, I went to the storeroom at the back of the kitchen to get some more Amarula. As I came back, he startled me by walking out of the shadows. He told me he had just received a phone call and had to leave first thing in the morning.'

'Did you ask him why?'

Dupie shook his head. 'No.'

'When was he scheduled to leave?'

'He was going to spend three nights here, so he would have left around lunchtime today.'

'He must've got the call on his cell phone,' Kubu said. 'Do you know if Zimbabwe phones work down here?'

Dupie hesitated. 'There's a Namibian tower across the river in Linyanti. He must have had roaming on his phone.'

'Did he look anxious, angry, perturbed?'

Again Dupie shook his head. 'No. His normal, tense self.'

'So you told him you'd meet him in the morning and take him to the airstrip?'

'That's right. Enoch was taking William Boardman birdwatching, and I said I'd pick up the staff from the mainland. We left at about six thirty, I think. I dropped him off about half an hour later. The plane hadn't arrived yet, so he told me to go. He would wait for the plane. I picked up Beauty and her husband Solomon when I got back to the river. Most days we give them a lift over in the motorboat, if it's convenient. It takes them longer in a *mokoro*. Beauty cleans, and Solomon is our waiter.'

'Did you hear the plane arriving?' Kubu looked at Dupie.

'No. The airstrip is quite a long way away, so it depends on which way the wind is blowing and where they come from and where they're going. I'd say we only hear a few of the planes that use the strip.'

'Is it possible that Zondo wasn't picked up by plane?'

Dupie shrugged. 'The airstrip's in the middle of nowhere. How else was he going to get away?'

'Do any of the other camps use the strip?' Kubu asked.

Dupie nodded. 'Yes, there are about half a dozen places nearby that use it occasionally. It's not busy. A few guests fly into Kasane

International, and we pick 'em up there. But it's a hell of a long trip overland.'

Kubu made a few more notes, then leaned carefully back in the chair. He thought through everything Dupie had said. It seemed to hang together.

'Are you a partner in the concession?' Kubu asked.

'No. It's Salome's.'

'Does she pay you to work here?'

Dupie shook his head. 'No. We use the money from guests to pay the staff and maintain the camp. That includes our food. For the most part guests pay for my drinks. I've some money left over from my hunting days. Occasionally we dip into that if things are not going well here.'

'How are things at the moment?'

'Not great, but not bad. We could really do with a more consistent stream of guests. I wish we could hook up with a tour operator of some sort. That would help a lot.' Dupie nodded, agreeing with himself.

Kubu looked at his notes again. 'Just a couple more questions and we're done. What luggage did Zondo have when he left? Was it the same as when he arrived?'

Dupie frowned. 'I never thought about that. I didn't see him arrive, because Enoch brought him. He left with a carry-on suitcase and a small tote bag. The suitcase seemed quite heavy by the way he lugged it. But you can't imagine how people travel these days. Everything but the kitchen sink.'

Kubu stood up. 'Thank you, Mr Du Pisanie. Please don't leave the island until I say so. I apologise for the inconvenience. Please ask Ms McGlashan to come in.'

When Dupie left the tent, Tatwa took off his St Louis cap, placed it carefully over Dupie's Watching Eye, and left it there. Kubu gave him a sharp look, but did not ask him to remove it. Then Tatwa said, 'Exactly what he told me. I didn't ask about the luggage, though. I wonder what was in those bags?'

'Tatwa, remind me to ask Enoch about the luggage Tinubu and

Zondo brought to the island. See if he noticed anything unusual about any of the bags.'

Tatwa nodded as Salome pushed open the tent flap.

Kubu motioned to the chair. 'Please sit down, Ms McGlashan,' he said, studying her drawn face. 'I'll keep this as short as possible. It must've been a bad shock.'

Salome nodded and looked down at the floor.

'You have a wonderful setting here,' Kubu asked. 'How is the camp doing?'

Salome's shoulders sagged. 'We're struggling. I don't have the money to upgrade the place, and it's not posh enough for most overseas visitors. These murders could be the end of the camp for me. I'm not sure I can go on. And when the concession ends next year, I may not have the money to renew it.'

'Well, I hope it doesn't come to that, Ms McGlashan. Had you ever seen Zondo, Tinubu or Langa before?'

Salome stared at him, and then shook her head.

'Just a couple more questions for now. Did you hear or see anything unusual on the night Mr Tinubu and Mr Langa were killed?'

'No,' she said quietly. 'I heard Dupie zip up his tent around ten thirty or eleven, and I heard him leave the tent early the next morning. Must have been around half past five or so. Otherwise I heard nothing. I didn't leave my tent.'

'When did Mr Du Pisanie tell you he had to take Zondo to the airstrip?'

'Dupie didn't tell me. Enoch told me when I went to the kitchen around seven.'

'A few personal questions to end off.' Kubu paused. 'What is your relationship with Mr Du Pisanie?'

Salome hesitated and twisted a strand of hair around her fingers. 'He and I are friends. We've known each other for a long time.'

'Just friends?' Kubu raised his eyebrows. 'Nothing closer?'

Again Salome hesitated, shifting in her chair. 'Just friends,' she said, her voice tight.

Kubu finished writing his notes, and looked up with a smile.

'Thank you for your time, Ms McGlashan. I may need to talk to you again.'

Salome looked down. 'How long is this going to take? We can't survive a long period of uncertainty and no paying guests.'

Kubu thought for a moment. 'Not too long, I hope. We'll resolve it as quickly as we can.'

CHAPTER 9

Before Boy Gomwe arrived, Kubu's cell phone started playing the Grand March from *Aida* again. He groaned, fearing it was Mabaku checking up on him. To his relief, it was a detective from Kasane.

'Superintendent Bengu, I've got information from Forensics for you. First of all, Immigration has confirmed that nobody by the name of Zondo left the country in the past forty-eight hours. Of course, if he had one fake passport, it's likely he had others.' He paused for Kubu to comment, but the detective did not. 'We've found some interesting things. In Tinubu's tent we found fingerprints from the deceased, the maid, and a partial of Enoch Kokorwe's on the suitcase handle. But this is the interesting part. There were two water glasses in Tinubu's tent – one with Tinubu's prints, and guess whose prints were on the other?'

'Tell me. The director doesn't like to pay for long calls.' Kubu did not like guessing games.

'Well, we're not sure actually, but the prints matched some on Zondo's registration form and several partials we found in his tent. So it looks like Tinubu and Zondo had a chat before Tinubu died.'

Kubu grunted.

'We're trying to get positive IDs on all the prints. Nothing in our computers, but we've sent them to South Africa, Zimbabwe and the UK. Nothing back yet.'

'What was in the glasses?'

'We've sent them for analysis, but it seems to be plain water.'

'What about the luggage?'

'There was a black briefcase. The odd thing is that it was empty. Nothing in it at all.'

'Send it to Forensics in Gaborone for testing. See if they can find out what was in it. What else?'

'Then there was an old brown suitcase. All of Tinubu's clothes were off the shelf, probably bought in Gaborone. His wallet was in his slacks. Hadn't been tampered with, and only his prints were on it. There was his identity document – he lived in Mochudi, just north of Gaborone. Doesn't seem he was married. One hundred and twenty South African rands and two hundred and seventy pula in notes, and a few coins.'

'I know Mochudi well,' Kubu interjected. 'I grew up there, and my parents still live there. I've never heard of him, though.' He wondered why Tinubu was carrying South African currency.

The detective continued. 'Oh yes. He was born in Zimbabwe, according to his identity document. I've sent his information and prints to the Zimbabwe police, and I'm trying to find out when he first came to Botswana.'

'He arrived at the camp by car?' Kubu asked.

'Yes,' the detective replied. 'Rra Du Pisanie told us Tinubu and Langa arrived together. Apparently Tinubu drove from Gaborone, but his car broke down. Langa stopped to help. Langa had been to Botswana only once before, a couple of years ago. What's interesting, though, is that Tinubu was in and out of South Africa the day before. Went through the border at Ramotswa at eleven and returned the same way around three in the afternoon.'

'How often had he been to South Africa in the past few years?' Kubu asked.

'This is the sixth time in fifteen months. Same thing each time. In and out the same day. Then in and out a few days later. Maybe he had a woman over the border.'

'Six times in fifteen months? Can't be a very serious relationship,' Kubu responded. 'Sounds more like he picked something up and then dropped something off. Have you found his car yet?'

'All we've had time to do is get the make and registration number. An old Peugeot 404. We'll send some people out to all the repair shops to see where he left it to get fixed. I'll let you know if we find it.'

'And Langa's car? Have Forensics been through it yet?' Kubu asked.

'Yes. It's a 2003 Focus with a Gauteng registration. We're waiting to hear back from South Africa with the details. They must be overloaded at the moment. Haven't heard back from them about Langa either.'

'Anything of interest in the car?'

'Not really. He got fuel in Zeerust and then again in Gaborone later that night. He also bought some fast food at the garage in Gaborone. The next day he drove up here and refuelled in Francistown and Kasane. We've found all the receipts.' The detective hesitated, then continued. 'One other thing, there were some notes written on the Zeerust petrol receipt. One looks like a Gauteng car licence number – BJW 191 GP. We've sent a query to South Africa. The second is a Botswana licence – B 332 CAX. We're checking on that too. And I've no idea what the rest is all about. First on the list is LC*. Under that WB1. Under that is 1L. And finally under that KGH-A19.'

Kubu wrote it all down and puzzled over it. 'Nothing obvious to me right now. I'll think about it later. What about next of kin for Tinubu and Langa? Have they been notified?'

'We couldn't trace anyone for Tinubu. I've asked the SA police to check on Langa.'

'Let me know if you learn anything useful. Did you find anything interesting in Zondo's tent or in any of the others?'

'Nothing in Zondo's. In Langa's there was his luggage and some clothes strewn around. The only prints we found were his and the maid's. Everyone else's tents were clean too. The Boardmans had an old Bushman hunting kit, with a bow, some arrows, a pair of sandals, a miniature bow and arrows, and a few empty containers that may have been used for poison.'

'And the camp staff?' Kubu asked, not expecting much.

'Same thing. Nothing of interest.'

'Thanks,' Kubu said. 'There's one other thing you could check. Try to track down where the plane could have gone after it picked up Zondo. What airstrips and airports are in range. Let me know immediately if anything turns up. Good work!'

Before the detective could respond, Kubu hung up and said to Tatwa, 'Seems Zondo had a drink with Tinubu – his prints were on a glass in Tinubu's tent. So they did know each other and possibly had something in common. That may lead us to a motive.'

Tatwa shrugged. 'I wonder why they didn't have dinner together. Isn't it odd that they went for a quiet nightcap in the tent without talking beforehand?'

'Water? Hardly my idea of a nightcap.' Kubu shook his head with disapproval. 'It seems they went to some trouble to look as though they didn't know each other. But there seems to be nothing connecting Langa and Zondo.'

'It certainly looks like Zondo is the one we need to find,' said Tatwa.

Kubu wasn't listening. 'There was nothing in Tinubu's black briefcase. I bet it wasn't empty when he arrived.'

Boy Gomwe sat down opposite Kubu and folded his arms. He looked casual, but to Kubu he appeared ill at ease. The detective glanced at Gomwe's registration form.

'Mr Gomwe, I see you're scheduled to leave tomorrow. I'm hoping that will be possible.'

'Yes, well, I'm busy, you know. This was just a short break. Sort of squeezed in.' He hesitated and shrugged. 'Still, doesn't bother me if I stay an extra day. As long as you're paying.'

'Did you know Mr Tinubu or Mr Langa?'

Gomwe shook his head. 'No. The first time I met them was here at the camp.'

'Did either of them seem nervous, then or later?'

'They seemed fine.' Gomwe hesitated. 'There was just the issue of the keys.'

This was news to Kubu. 'What issue was that?'

'Tinubu lost his keys. He was very upset, suggested they'd been stolen. Enoch found them at the salad buffet. Must have dropped out of his pocket. But he was beside himself! It was silly. They couldn't have been far away.'

'What keys? The tents don't lock.'

'I don't know. He had a small bunch of keys with him. Maybe his house keys.'

'Perhaps. What do you do for a living, Mr Gomwe?'

Gomwe played with his neck chain and checked his watch. Does he have another appointment? Kubu wondered.

'I'm a rep for one of the big music companies – EMI. Good at it, too. I've accounts throughout South Africa. And Gaborone. I'm on the road a lot. Last year I got a trip to Cape Town as a bonus for my high sales.'

'Why did you come to Jackalberry Camp?' Kubu looked up from his notebook.

'I needed a break. Someone in Gaborone told me about this place. I decided to give it a spin.'

'It's very quiet here. I would've thought you'd prefer one of the more sociable camps in Kasane.'

Gomwe shrugged. 'I like the quiet. Birds and stuff.' He looked over his shoulder at Tatwa, as if seeking confirmation.

'Any family?'

Gomwe laughed. 'Over my dead body.'

'Did you talk to Zondo?'

'Yes. He was really intense. Seemed to think everyone in the Zimbabwe government was corrupt. And he always wore that silly hat with the feathers.'

'The hat with the three guineafowl feathers?'

'That's the one.'

'Did he tell you what he did for a living?'

Gomwe shook his head. 'I didn't ask.'

'Did you hear or see anything out of the ordinary the night Tinubu was murdered?'

Gomwe shook his head again. 'No, nothing at all. The first time I realised there was a problem was at breakfast when the maid started screaming.'

Kubu heaved himself out of his chair.

'Thank you, Mr Gomwe. We'll let you know when you can leave.'

'Yes. Well, the sooner I can get back to work, the better.' Gomwe got up and left.

'Not much to go on there,' Tatwa commented. 'Everything seems right. Dates and places in his passport match what he said. His ticket shows a return tomorrow. And Salome confirmed that he made a late booking. The bit about the keys is new, though.'

'It's time for a cup of tea and perhaps a biscuit,' Kubu said, stretching. 'Then we can interview the Munros, the Boardmans, and the rest of the staff. Please ask Du Pisanie to make sure Beauty and her husband are available in an hour. We'll speak to Enoch Kokorwe and the cook after that.'

CHAPTER 10

Several hundred kilometres to the south-east, a group of men – four black and one white – were sweltering on a dusty veranda, a lean-to against a corrugated-iron building. The inside of the house, now an oven because of its metal walls, was unbearable in the heat of the late-afternoon Zimbabwe sun. About a hundred metres away was a dirt airstrip. It looked unused; vegetation was starting to encroach. Only the summer drought had kept it serviceable at all. The men had been expecting the plane for some hours. As the wait lengthened, tension increased and tempers frayed. Only the white man sat quietly, looking calmly at the group around him. He called himself Madrid, but one wag had suggested that a colder city would be more appropriate.

Johannes Mankoni, Madrid's man, finally lost patience. 'Where are the bastards?' he yelled. 'They should've been here hours ago. Don't tell me you don't know. Find out! Get the pilot on the radio.'

Others started talking, but the man seated at the head of the table held up his hand, and immediately there was silence. Tall, with greying hair, the man had a military bearing that commanded respect. Even Johannes stopped what he was saying. Only Madrid appeared unimpressed.

'The man we are talking about,' said General Joseph Chikosi, 'is one of my most trusted people. Perhaps there has been a problem, a delay. It's mad to start panicking and talking about stupid courses of action. We wait. If the plane is there, and the pilot is there, there's no need to call. They will get back here as soon as they can. If the pilot is not there, it's the police who will be monitoring the radio.' He pointed to his cell phone lying on the table. 'Why not just phone the police from here and save them the trouble of tracing us?'

Madrid's eyes turned to Chikosi, and he cocked his head. 'It's coming,' he said.

Johannes started to object, but then he heard it too, the distant drone of a light plane engine. Chikosi's face broke into a smile, and the fractious mood lifted. Only Madrid remained impassive. 'But it's three hours late,' he said flatly.

By the time the plane landed hard and bumped to a stop, trailing a cloud of dust, they were all gathered at the end of the strip. But the man who climbed out of the Cessna 172 was alone.

'Where is he?' asked Chikosi. The pilot looked at the faces, now closed, unwelcoming.

'He wasn't there. I waited for three hours. Nothing. Then I took off and did a pass over the area; I thought perhaps their vehicle had broken down. Nothing. From the air I had a cell phone signal so I tried to call him. Nothing. It went through to voice mail at once. After that I got out in a hurry.'

Chikosi's men said nothing while they digested this. It was Madrid's voice that cut through the screaming of cicadas. 'We don't know what's happened, but it's nothing good. We have to take precautions. We don't risk our security. The police might have him. Maybe they were caught, maybe they made a private deal. We move out of here right away. The farm will be safe. For the moment.'

'We may be overreacting,' said Chikosi. 'What about Peter? What do we do about him? We should give this some thought.'

Madrid shrugged as though the matter was of little concern to him. 'If he wants to contact us, and if he can, he will. If I were you, I'd take the plane out right away. Suit yourself. But we're leaving now.' He walked off, followed by Johannes, who gave the group an angry frown over his shoulder as he left.

Madrid did not look back. He knew the others would follow him. People always did.

CHAPTER 11

One of Kubu's delights, rarely enjoyed when on duty, was a leisurely cup of tea, with the milk poured first of course, two teaspoons of sugar, and a plate of mixed biscuits from which to choose. His wife Joy would comment, out of earshot, that it was not a matter of choice but of order, because it was rare that any biscuits were left.

Jackalberry Camp offered Kubu and Tatwa tea and mixed biscuits. Kubu was delighted; Tatwa merely thankful.

Kubu had just delicately removed one side of a lemon cream and was about to nibble around the filling when his phone rang. It was Ian MacGregor. There was no mistaking the Scottish brogue.

Ian told Kubu about Mabaku's visit and his exploration of the corpse. Kubu snorted with delight at the image of Ian handing innards to Mabaku. Serves him right for being so pushy, he thought. Ian gave a quick summary of what he'd found, including his guess that the same weapon, something like a large wrench, had been used to kill Langa and knock out Tinubu. However, he emphasised that Tinubu's death was caused by a stab wound to the heart made by a thin, sharp instrument.

'Could it have been an arrow?' Kubu interupted.

'No, that would have been too thick.'

'What about a miniature arrow? Say one from a Bushman child's toy kit? They're sharpened like the adult ones.'

'I don't think so. The entry wound would have been different, and Bushman arrowheads are designed to come off the shaft. The head would have been left in the body.'

'Oh.' Kubu was disappointed. 'When did the murders take place?'

'By the time I got to Jackalberry, rigor mortis had set in. I estimate Tinubu died between two and five in the morning. It's impossible to be entirely accurate, but I am sure it was after midnight. The same for Langa.'

'Any idea who was the first victim?'

'Can't say, I'm afraid. Does it matter?'

Kubu sighed. Why was it that whenever he asked a question, the response was always to ask his reason for it? As yet, he had no idea what mattered. He changed the subject.

'Do you have any theory about the ears being cut off and stuffed in his mouth or the cross on the forehead?'

'In my experience, sometimes mutilations like this are used as a warning. Sometimes as a statement by the killer.'

Kubu pondered this. He thought Ian might be right.

After a few more questions, Kubu said, 'Thanks for the update, Ian. I should be back in Gaborone tomorrow. I'll give you a call. Perhaps we can have a drink together, but not a bottle of whisky like last time. My head has yet to forgive me.'

After tea, Kubu looked for the Munro sisters. Dupie said they had returned to their tent and offered to call them.

'Don't worry, Mr Du Pisanie. Tatwa and I need some exercise.' The two policemen set off at a leisurely pace.

Trish and Judith Munro were waiting in their tent. They looked to be in their early fifties, and were slim and attractive even in stereotypical khaki bush clothes. They were obviously sisters, but Judith looked reserved while Trish had a ready twinkle. They sat on the beds, and Kubu and Tatwa made themselves as comfortable as possible on the two folding canvas chairs. Kubu's chair bulged disapprovingly, while Tatwa had to sit at a slight angle so that his head did not touch the tent. Trish was having difficulty suppressing a smile. She covered her amusement by offering each of the detectives a glass of water.

'In England it would be tea, of course. Thomas Twining was our medicine man,' she said. 'But all we have in the tent is bottled water.'

Kubu and Tatwa thanked her but declined.

'This shouldn't take long, Miss Munro. I know you've already spoken to Detective Mooka here. I just want to go over a few points. When did you realise something was wrong?'

Kubu looked at Judith, but it was Trish who replied. 'We heard Beauty scream. It sounded dreadful. We thought it might be a hippo or an elephant or even a lion. But we didn't see what we could do, and we were scared. So we just stayed in the tent. Isn't that awful?'

'Probably the sensible thing to do. What happened after that?'

Trish seemed about to speak again, but Judith cut in. 'A few minutes later we heard Dupie at the next tent, so we went to ask what had happened. He said that Goodluck had been murdered – in the tent only metres from us! It was a horrible shock.' Trish nodded agreement.

'Did you hear or see anything during the night? Anything at all unusual or suspicious?'

'We heard his tent zipper about eleven. We were reading. I commented that Goodluck must have found some company at the bar,' Trish said.

'Are you sure it was eleven?'

The sisters nodded.

'I checked my watch. I was surprised how late it was,' said Judith.

'Nothing else?'

They both shook their heads, but then Trish said, 'Something woke me during the night. But I thought it was an animal. There are lots of hippos. We are asked not to wander around after dark.'

'What exactly woke you?' Tatwa asked, but Trish just shrugged.

'It must have been a noise, but I don't recall any particular sound.'

Kubu changed tack. 'Mr Du Pisanie tells me you are writers. Is that correct?'

Judith nodded. 'We write biographical articles for magazines and Sunday supplements. Stories about interesting, but not necessarily famous, people. It's great fun doing the research together. Our pen name is Trudy Munro, by the way.'

'Extremely interesting!' said Tatwa unexpectedly. 'Are you working on something now?'

There was a moment's silence before Judith said, 'No, we're simply on holiday. Even writers stop thinking about writing and go on holiday sometimes, you know.'

Kubu wondered if that could be true. How do writers switch off? 'Do you have any of your work with you?'

Trish dug in a carry-on bag and wordlessly handed him a cutting from the London *Sunday Telegraph* of a few months earlier.

'May I borrow it? I'd like to read it later. I'll return it tomorrow.'

Trish laughed. 'Of course. The only thing writers like as much as being paid is being read! It's about—'

But Judith interrupted firmly. 'Let the superintendent find out for himself, Trish.'

'How did you find this camp?' Again there was an odd pause, and again it was Judith who broke the silence.

'We have a friend who's a travel writer for a London newspaper. She stayed here and wrote a positive piece about it. We were intrigued and thought Botswana would be wonderful to visit.' She smiled.

Kubu nodded. 'Well, I'm sorry your trip has been spoiled by this experience. Perhaps you can write an article about it and recoup your expenses? Or at least make it tax deductible?'

Neither sister knew what to make of these remarks. They started to respond, but Kubu was already on his way enjoying their puzzled looks.

'Thanks very much, ladies. That will be all for the moment. I'm sure we'll see you at dinner.' Tatwa followed him through the flaps, shoulders stooped, head bowed.

After the policemen had left, the two sisters sat in silence for a few moments. Then Judith asked, 'Why did you give him the article?'

'Why not?' Trish replied doubtfully, but then she regrouped. 'Don't you think we should've told him why we came here? And what we thought about Goodluck? It might be important.'

Judith turned away. 'We made a promise. And we were mistaken about Goodluck. We must've been. It would be a crazy coincidence.'

'We'll have to check when we get back to Gaborone.'

'Trish, I have to admit, I was always afraid our research might hurt somebody. Now someone is dead. I think it's time to drop it.'

Trish twisted the ring on her index finger. She did not reply.

CHAPTER 12

Kubu was bored with the interviews, but knew he had to complete them. The Boardmans had wandered up to the lookout searching for birds, so he and Tatwa turned their attention to the staff.

'Four to go,' Kubu remarked to Tatwa as they were waiting for Beauty and Solomon. 'Then we can have a drink.'

Before Beauty and Solomon arrived, Kubu's phone rang again. Mabaku, he thought, answering formally. But he was delighted to hear Joy's voice instead.

'How are things going, darling?' she asked. 'I miss you already. When will you be home?' Kubu smiled. He was so lucky to have a wife like Joy. Best friend, superb cook and lover all in one.

'I'm in the middle of interviewing everyone at the camp,' he replied. 'So far, there seems to be only one person who could have committed the murders, and it seems he's in Zimbabwe already.'

'Will you be able to extradite him?'

'If they find him and want to let him go. They may want to keep him. You know the reputation of the Zimbabwe authorities. What've you been up to?'

'Oh, I've had an exciting afternoon. I won my first karate match! I went to the dojo after work, and we had proper matches. I beat a woman in her twenties!'

'That's wonderful, dear. You're becoming quite a star.' Kubu didn't feel as enthusiastic as he sounded. Joy's obsession with karate had started when he was in hospital after being assaulted while investigating a case. Joy had announced that if he was in danger in his job, she might well be too. So she was going to take self-defence lessons and learn to shoot. Kubu had protested that looking after her was his responsibility. She refused to budge and got Mabaku's support for shooting lessons, under police supervision. Then she joined a karate club.

Kubu had wrestled with feelings he did not really understand. He'd never put any limits on Joy's activities, yet he felt hurt and a little angry that she wouldn't listen to him. But he was wise enough not to interfere. He remembered how he had smugly thought that the phase would last a few weeks and that would be that. How wrong he had been! She completed the shooting lessons, but showed no further interest in firearms. However, she took to the karate and its focus on both body and mind like a gemsbok to the desert. Now here she was a year later winning matches!

Kubu snorted and had to admit, only to himself of course, that he was proud of her accomplishments, particularly since she had never taken part in sport before.

'I've got to get on with my interviews, dear,' he continued. 'I'll phone you this evening, if I can get a signal. With luck I'll be home tomorrow. I love you!'

A few minutes later, Beauty and Solomon pushed back the flap of Dupie's office tent. This posed a problem because there was space only for three chairs, so Tatwa had to stand. They rearranged two of the chairs so that he could stand directly in the middle of the tent and not have to stoop.

'*Dumela*,' Kubu said politely.

'*Dumela*,' they replied.

'Beauty, Solomon,' Kubu said quietly, continuing in Setswana. 'I have to ask you a few questions. I'll try to keep this as short as possible. Beauty, tell me how you found the body.'

Beauty took a deep breath. 'I went to Rra Tinubu's tent to clean. The flap was closed, so I called. No answer, so I thought he was eating breakfast. I opened the tent and went in. He was on the floor. Blood everywhere. Throat cut. He was dead.'

'How did you know he was dead?' Kubu asked.

'A man on the floor with his throat cut is dead,' Beauty replied, looking at Kubu challengingly. Everyone knew that you killed goats and cows by cutting their throats. They always died.

'Don't be rude to Rra Bengu,' Solomon admonished. Beauty shrugged.

'Did you touch anything when you were in there?'

Beauty shook her head. 'I was very scared. I ran to Rra Dupie.'

Kubu turned towards Solomon. 'You don't live at Jackalberry Camp, do you?' he asked. Solomon shook his head.

'No,' he said. 'We live at the village across the water. Enoch picks us up most days.'

'But not yesterday?'

'No, Rra Dupie did. He took Rra Zondo to catch a plane.'

'How do you know he took Rra Zondo to the airstrip?'

'Rra Dupie told us when he picked us up.'

'Did you see him take Rra Zondo? Did you hear a plane?'

Beauty and Solomon shook their heads in unison. 'The airstrip is far away,' Beauty contributed. 'I did hear the motorboat come across early in the morning.'

'What time did he pick you up?'

'About half past seven,' Solomon replied.

Kubu looked down at his notebook. 'Did you notice anything about Rra Zondo? Did he say anything to you?'

Beauty shook her head. 'I didn't see him.'

'I spoke to him,' Solomon said. 'Two times. At lunch and dinner two days ago. He was quiet, but very polite. Thanked me for good service.'

'Did he give you a tip?'

Solomon shook his head regretfully. 'No. Usually only at the end of a visit. And he left too early to see me the next morning.'

'Just a few more questions. When you cleaned Rra Zondo's tent the day before he left, did you notice what luggage he had?'

Beauty hesitated. 'A big suitcase and a bag. Blue, I think.'

'And Rra Tinubu?'

'Brown suitcase and briefcase.'

Kubu made a note in his book, then looked up.

'Thank you both. You may go. You can go back to your village, but don't leave it except to come here.'

Beauty and Solomon nodded, again in unison.

Enoch Kokorwe was next. He sat straight up in the plastic chair, his arms folded across his chest. He just nodded in response to the greetings from Kubu and Tatwa.

'How long have you worked at Jackalberry Camp?' Kubu asked.

'About twelve years.'

'How did you get the job?'

'I know Dupie from hunting trips in the Kalahari. He asked me to come.'

'What do you do here?' Kubu asked, glancing up from his notebook.

'I'm the camp manager. I hire the local staff and keep things running properly. Me, not Dupie. And I know the birds. I guide *mokoro* trips and walks too.'

'Are you from Botswana or Zimbabwe?'

'Zimbabwe. Born near Bulawayo.'

'Had you ever met Rra Tinubu, Rra Langa or Rra Zondo before?'

Enoch shook his head emphatically. 'No.'

'Did you notice anything unusual the night Tinubu and Langa died?'

Enoch shook his head again. 'No. I don't eat supper with the guests. Dupie likes to tell his stories and help the guests drink. I go to sleep. I saw nothing. I heard nothing. I didn't talk to anyone.'

Kubu took a deep breath, banishing an image of three monkeys from his head.

'And how about in the morning? Why did Rra Du Pisanie fetch Beauty and Solomon?'

'Rra Boardman wanted to find the finfoot and the skimmers. We took a *mokoro* just after seven. Dupie doesn't know about birds.'

'Did you see Rra Zondo that morning?'

'Yes. I saw him in the boat crossing to the mainland with Dupie.'

'What time was that?'

'About half past six.'

Kubu scanned his notes before asking the next question.

'When you picked up Rra Zondo . . .' He paused. 'What luggage did he have?'

Enoch frowned. 'Mmm. One suitcase and one tote, I think.'

'Did you notice anything unusual about them?'

'The suitcase was very heavy. He carried the tote himself.'

'And Rra Tinubu's luggage?'

Enoch thought for a moment. 'One suitcase and a briefcase. Nothing special.'

'What about Rra Langa's luggage. What did he have?'

'Just one tote. A small one. Nothing else.' Enoch shook his head.

'Tell us about Rra Tinubu's keys.'

Enoch looked surprised and hesitated. 'He lost a small ring of keys that evening at dinner. He was upset so I helped him look for them. They were under the salad table. He said he hadn't dropped them there. Maybe Moremi's bird stole them.' He shrugged.

Kubu asked a few more questions but learned nothing new. He dismissed Enoch, asking him to call the cook. As Enoch was about to leave, Tatwa casually lifted his cap and placed it jauntily on his head. The Eye glared up at Enoch, who stared and clenched his teeth. Turning, he walked out stiffly.

'Did you see that?' Tatwa asked.

Kubu nodded, and Tatwa closed the Eye again, covering it with his cap.

Suthani Moremi was an enigma. People regarded him as simple, yet he devised and created wonderful meals that were hearty and quite sophisticated, despite facilities that were marginal and supplies that were anything but exotic. Some people thought him a dolt, yet he had a first-class high-school pass, and read books. Some suspected mental problems. He was always talking or singing to himself or chatting to the grey bird that seemed to be attached to his shoulder, yet he was content, reliant only on himself and Kweh for company and entertainment. It was this collection of paradoxes that came into the tent humming a melody that Kubu recognised yet couldn't place. Kweh looked around with brown eyes.

'Please sit down, Rra Moremi. This shouldn't take long. I just have a few questions.'

Moremi did not reply, but continued humming, distracting Kubu as he tried to identify the melody.

'Did you have any conversation with Rra Tinubu, Rra Zondo or Rra Langa while they were here?'

Moremi shook his head in time with his humming. Suddenly he stopped, and said: 'Just the keys. He lost his keys, didn't he, Kweh? Enoch found them for him.' He shook his hand and produced an excellent imitation of keys jingling.

'Whose keys?'

'Tinubu. He lost them. Was very upset. Enoch found them at the buffet. But they weren't there when he lost them.' He started to hum the tune again.

'Does your bird sometimes pick things up?'

Moremi glanced up. 'Did you pick them up, Kweh?' There was no rcsponse, but Moremi seemed satisfied. 'He says he didn't.'

'Did you see any of them together?' Kubu said, trying vainly to keep exasperation out of his voice.

Again Moremi nodded, still humming. But Kubu wanted answers.

'Where were they when you saw them?'

Moremi nodded, causing Kubu to drag himself to his feet.

'Rra Moremi,' he fumed. 'This is a murder investigation. I need answers.'

Moremi's singing stopped. He stared at Kubu. Then, in a strong voice, he said, 'Tinubu and Zondo were friends.'

Kubu blinked and looked over at Tatwa, who shrugged his shoulders and rolled his eyes.

'What do you mean, they were friends?'

'I can see friends when I see people. Or I can see not friends. These men were friends.' He pulled a length of wire from his pocket. Grasping it in the middle and rocking it rapidly, he made its ends hit his left and right thighs alternately. As each end hit, he made a clicking sound with his tongue, first a tick, then a tock. It sounded like a ping-pong game – too fast for a grandfather clock. Kubu shook his head to help him refocus on the interview.

'Zondo wouldn't kill Tinubu,' Moremi added. 'They were friends.'

'What about Tinubu and Langa?'

'Not friends. Not friends. Not friends.'

'Were they enemies?'

'Not enemies, not enemies.'

'Did you hear or see anything unusual on the night of the murder?'

Moremi consulted the bird. 'Did we, Kweh? Anything unusual? I can't remember anything. Can you?'

Kubu took a deep breath and plunged on. 'Tinubu's throat was cut.'

As he finished the sentence, Moremi hissed like a cat.

'Did you notice if any of your knives were missing?'

'No knives missing. No knives missing.' He shook his head vehemently and fell silent. Looking quizzically at Kubu, he waited for the next question. But Kubu had had enough. He stood up.

'Thank you, Rra Moremi. Please stay in the camp until I say you can go.'

Moremi got up, lifted Tatwa's cap, winked at the Eye and covered it again. Then he gave the bird a stroke, causing its crest to rise, nodded to Kubu, and backed out of the tent opening, once more humming the familiar tune Kubu couldn't identify.

Kubu sent Tatwa to the lookout to retrieve the Boardmans. They had their binoculars out, still trying to spot elusive birds, but their hearts were no longer in it. They came down without reluctance. Kubu asked William to wait in the dining area.

'Can't you interview us together?' William asked.

'It will only be a few minutes,' Kubu replied.

After the three of them were seated, Kubu got straight to the point. 'Mrs Boardman, before this trip, did you know either of the two victims, or Mr Zondo?'

She shook her head. 'No, I've never seen them before.'

'Did you speak to them over the past few days?'

Again she shook her head. 'Just the usual pleasantries. We usually sit by ourselves because we always talk about birds. Most people get bored pretty quickly.' Kubu nodded. He could believe that.

'Did you see or hear anything after you went to bed? A scream or shout? A thud? Talking on the path? Anything unusual?'

'No,' she said. 'We went to bed early because William wanted to be up early.'

'Did you leave your tent at all during the night?'

'No. I didn't even go to the loo. I think William did, though. I woke up in the middle of the night and he wasn't there. I thought he'd gone to look for a Pel's fishing owl – we've heard them call almost every night – but his binocs were still on the table. I must have been asleep when he got back.'

'Did you notice what time it was?' Kubu asked hopefully.

She shook her head. 'Ask William. He should know. He wears his watch the whole time.'

Kubu glanced through his notes. 'One other thing. Detective Mooka told me you have a Bushman hunting outfit with you. Are you a collector?'

'Oh, yes!' Amanda brightened. 'The Bushmen are wonderful people. We bought it from Dupie. We've been buying stuff from him for years.'

'So this isn't your first time at the camp?' Kubu asked.

'Oh, no. We've been here several times over the past few years. Five or six, I would think.'

'Have you bought stuff each time?'

'I think so,' Amanda said. 'We're lucky to know someone who has spent time around the Bushmen and can buy their artefacts.'

'Are they genuine?'

'I don't know what you mean by genuine,' Amanda said. 'If you mean were they made by Bushmen, then they are genuine. If you mean are they more than fifty years old, then they are likely not. If you mean were they actually used for hunting, I don't know. All I know is that they are authentic hunting outfits from a group of incredible nomads who are in danger of extinction.'

'Thank you, Mrs Boardman. That'll be all. Tatwa, please ask Mr Boardman to join us.' Kubu did not want any exchange of information between Amanda and her husband.

A few minutes later, William Boardman was seated in front of Kubu.

'Did you talk to either of the deceased or to Mr Zondo?'

'No, other than to say good morning or good evening.'

'Had you met them before this trip?'

'No.'

Kubu glanced at his notebook. 'Did you hear or see anything on the night of the murders? Anything unusual? Any shouts or grunts or thuds?'

'No, I didn't,' William replied. 'We got to bed early.'

'Did you leave the tent at any stage?'

William hesitated momentarily. 'Yes. I heard a Pel's fishing owl calling and went to look for it.'

'And what time was that?'

'I'm not sure. Just after midnight, I think.'

'Did you find the owl?' Kubu asked, looking up. 'Did you see anyone while you were out?'

William shook his head. 'No, I didn't see anyone.' He sighed. 'Nor did I see the owl. So close. It would be the first time I've seen it!'

'How well do binoculars work at night?'

'Oh, they work okay, as long as you can find the bird in your lens. That's the hard part. Finding the bird. They don't stick out as well as they do in daylight.'

'Your wife told me that you left without your binoculars.'

William hesitated, a slight frown on his forehead. 'I must have been so excited hearing the Pel's that I forgot them.'

'You were up early in the morning to go birdwatching. Did you see Zondo before he left?'

William frowned. 'I didn't talk to him, but I saw him with Dupie on the motorboat crossing to the mainland. Zondo was wearing his guineafowl-feather hat. He was never without it. That was around six thirty. Enoch took me out about half an hour later.'

Kubu nodded and made a note. 'Just a few more questions, Mr Boardman, and you can go and have your gin and tonic.' He smiled. 'Tell me about the Bushman artefacts that you have with you. What are they? Where did you get them?'

William raised his eyebrows at this unexpected question. Kubu wondered whether he caught a hint of concern in Boardman's eyes.

'Oh, we like Bushman art. Those are just cheap tourist pieces. Amanda bought them in Kasane, I believe.'

Kubu's mind went back to his youth, and time spent with his Bushman friend Khumanego. It was on their excursions into the scorching desert that Khumanego had taught him how to see not just what was in front of him, but also beyond the obvious. To see clusters of stonelike succulent plants hidden in clusters of real stones. To see the trapdoor of the trapdoor spider's lair hidden in the shifting sands. To see what he wasn't meant to see. It was really Khumanego who was responsible for Kubu's becoming a detective.

'Have you been to Tsodilo?'

'Oh, yes,' said William enthusiastically. 'It's a must. It's brilliant.'

Kubu thought back to the reverence with which Khumanego talked about Tsodilo. He called it the birthplace of mankind, believing that it was where humanity had begun. Hence the thousands of paintings on the four rock masses that rose incongruously from the Kalahari Desert. Kubu remembered Khumanego telling him of a painting of a whale, even though the hills were hundreds of kilometres from the Atlantic Ocean. How had those people traversed such great distances across some of the most inhospitable land in the world? And found their way back?

'Did you know that there are over three thousand paintings there?' William's question brought Kubu out of his reverie.

'And the hunting outfit? Where did you get that?' he asked.

'From Dupie. He's been supplying us for years. He's sourced some wonderful stuff for us. We keep the best pieces for our own collection. The rest we sell in our shop in Cape Town. Did you see the pieces Dupie has in the lounge? Fantastic! They're really old, impossible to get these days.'

Kubu was curious. 'So where did Dupie get them?'

'Must have been gifts from elders. They're priceless. He'd never sell them, of course,' William finished regretfully.

Kubu looked at him for several seconds of silence. 'Are you sure you saw no one? Heard nothing while you were out?'

'Absolutely sure,' William said emphatically. 'Nothing at all.' He held Kubu's gaze. As if he's afraid I'll suspect he's dishonest if he drops his eyes, Kubu thought.

'Very well. Thank you for your time.' With that, he let William go.

Kubu leaned back and wondered. On a quiet night in the bush, no one at the camp had heard anything while two men were violently murdered. Nothing except the sound of a zipper at about eleven.

William and Amanda walked towards the bar.

'I'm sorry I mentioned the binocs,' Amanda said. 'It slipped out. Did you have to explain that to the fat policeman?'

William shrugged and smiled. He seemed in good spirits and pleased with himself. 'No problem. It didn't bother him. Just going through the motions, I think. Silly to go looking for owls with no binocs, though!'

'This business has really spoiled our trip,' Amanda replied. She winced, thinking of how much more it had spoiled the victims' trips.

'Oh, don't worry, my dear. I think we'll be able to afford another trip out here quite soon. And some other things! I'm going to have a double gin and tonic. What would you like?'

CHAPTER 13

Kubu and Tatwa spent the next fifteen minutes comparing notes. The only new information was the story of the lost keys and William Boardman going birdwatching at night without binoculars.

Kubu sighed, turning to Tatwa. 'I have to say that Zondo looks like the only real suspect. I agree with you, though. There's something else going on here. And I felt that Enoch, Moremi and Boardman were all holding back. Not lying necessarily, but not volunteering. We're missing something. There must be a connection between Tinubu and Langa. The two murders can't be a coincidence.'

'Unless, of course, Langa was just in the wrong place at the wrong time.'

'But he was at the opposite end of the camp from Tinubu. It seems very unlikely he'd be killed just because he saw Zondo near his own tent late at night.'

'Why did Langa have binoculars around his neck in the middle of the night?' Tatwa asked. 'Several people said he'd no interest in birds.'

'Hmm. I had forgotten about that,' Kubu said sheepishly. 'Maybe he was spying on someone? But who? And why?' The two men sat in silence, trying to solve this puzzle.

Tatwa eventually spoke. 'Maybe we'll learn something when Kasane gets back to us with the background checks. Maybe one of our charming tourists is a killer.'

'Even so, we'd still have to find a motive.' Kubu paused. 'We don't have one for Zondo either, for that matter.'

'Should we get someone from Kasane to drag the water around here?' Tatwa asked. 'We may be lucky and find whatever was used to knock Tinubu out and kill Langa.'

'Get Enoch to show you their tools. Send the bigger ones to Forensics for testing. It's a long shot, but if we find nothing, we can consider dragging the water around the island. That'll take a lot of manpower, and I'd rather do it as a last resort. Mabaku is always on my case for using too many resources. Speaking of the devil, I'd better phone him and let him know what we've found out. I'll see you at the bar in an hour.'

At that, Kubu stood up, took his notebook, and walked up the path to the lookout point. He needed to gather his thoughts before phoning his boss.

'Mabaku!'

'It's Bengu, Mr Director.'

'Yes?'

Kubu groaned silently. Mabaku had such a way with words!

'Mr Director, Tatwa and I have interviewed everyone here a second time. There is no evidence to suggest involvement in the murders. The only strange thing is that Tinubu and Langa apparently met for the first time on the road from Gaborone to Kasane. Tinubu's car broke down, and Langa stopped to help. I don't believe in coincidences. Two men meet for the first time in the middle of the desert. Then they go to the same bush camp – one of dozens. Then they are both murdered. There's something else going on here.' He waited for a comment from his boss, but none came.

Kubu continued. 'I haven't heard back from Kasane on the background checks. They all seem reasonable people, highly unlikely to be murderers.' He paused again, expecting a reaction from Mabaku. There was none.

'Anything from the Zimbabwe police about tracing Zondo?' Kubu asked, to force a response.

'Nothing more about Zondo. We've sent them the fingerprints we believe to be Zondo's, as well as those of Langa and Tinubu. Who knows if we'll hear from them either way?'

'You mean they may not tell us even if they find him?'

'They have their own agenda. The rule of law isn't exactly alive and well in Zimbabwe.'

Kubu sighed. It was difficult enough trying to keep order in the mish-mash of countries of southern Africa, but when the police themselves could not be counted on to cooperate, it made things impossible.

'Mr Director,' Kubu said. 'Please call me any time if you hear anything about Zondo. It seems he must be the culprit although we don't know why he did it. The way things stand, I don't have any reason to detain the guests here beyond tomorrow morning.'

Mabaku did not respond right away. 'You're right. I don't think we need to detain them,' he said eventually. 'But make sure you get contact information for each of them for the next few days, as well as their home details.'

After wrapping up a few final points, Kubu hung up.

I don't think we're going to find Zondo, or whatever his real name is, he thought. Africa has swallowed him.

Kubu sat for another twenty minutes gazing out at the beautiful waterways and islands, listening to the background of evening birdcalls. Then he pulled out his notebook and looked at the cryptic message that had been written on Langa's Zeerust receipt.

BJW 191 GP
B 332 CAX
LC*
WB1
1L
KGH-A19

The first two were obviously car registration numbers, but the rest made no sense to him. He closed his eyes, hoping to clear his mind and encourage insight. After a few minutes he opened them. He sighed. There had been no inspiration. Maybe my subconscious will take care of it when I'm asleep, he thought.

Remembering his earlier promise, he phoned Joy, and they spoke of private things. Then he sat back, relaxed, with a gentle smile. He tried a Mozart aria softly under his breath, but it seemed out of place, and he stopped. In the distance he could see a lechwe doe edge towards the water to drink, fearful of a crocodile that could pull it to a drowning death, or of a leopard that might appear from nowhere, cling to its throat and suffocate it.

I'll have to bring Joy here, he thought. She would love to be in such a beautiful place. He smiled as he thought of her thoroughly indulging herself. Perhaps Dupie and Salome will offer me a special rate when this is all over. He found himself humming Moremi's tune, but the words still eluded him.

With a sigh, he stood up. 'I declare myself officially off duty,' he said, ambling back to the bar. He ordered a double steelworks from Dupie to settle the dust, with a glass of South African Sauvignon Blanc to follow. Tatwa soon joined him and was pleased to see his colleague with a drink. He ordered one of Botswana's St Louis beers. Kubu thought it had insufficient alcohol, but Tatwa liked it.

'You know, I've been thinking about your problem of attracting guests,' Kubu said to Dupie. 'You need some publicity in the overseas newspapers. Perhaps you could invite a travel writer to stay free for a few days. Have you ever tried something like that?'

Dupie shook his head. 'They only write about the luxury camps. They don't want to stay at a place like this.'

'You've never had any travel writer here?'

Dupie shook his head again. 'Not as far as we know. But a freebie's not a bad idea. I'll chat to Salome.'

Kubu frowned. 'Salome seems pretty depressed. She was talking about giving up altogether.'

Dupie shrugged. 'Well, it's a blow, these murders. But she'll come round. Maybe things will look up. Another glass of wine? On the house? You deserve one for the travel writer idea. Another beer for you?' He looked at Tatwa, realising he had forgotten the sergeant's name.

Just as he was about to pick up his wine, Kubu felt his mobile phone vibrate. Who was calling now? He hoped it was Joy. He walked away from the bar towards the water.

'This is Assistant Superintendent Bengu,' he said.

He listened intently, hardly saying a word. Eventually, returning to the bar, he slumped on a stool and drained the warming glass of wine in a single gulp.

'That was the director,' he said to Tatwa. 'He's heard from the Zimbabwe police. About the fingerprints.'

Tatwa was swatting at mosquitoes with his cap. 'Did they identify Zondo?'

'Indeed. His real name is Peter Jabulani, and he's regarded as a dissident, possibly worse. He shouldn't be travelling anywhere, since they're holding his passport. They're very keen to meet him now. I don't think we'll be seeing him if they get to him first.' He waited for Dupie to refill their glasses.

'And the other fingerprints were definitely those of Goodluck Tinubu. There's no doubt because we gave them a full set taken from the body, and they got a perfect match. There *is* a problem, though.' He savoured a mouthful of wine while Tatwa waited impatiently.

'Goodluck Tinubu died twenty-nine years ago in the Rhodesian war.'

PART TWO
Borrowed Trouble

Borrow trouble for yourself if that's your nature,
but don't lend it to your neighbours.

Rudyard Kipling, *Cold Iron*

CHAPTER 14

As he settled into one of Director Mabaku's uncomfortable chairs, Kubu realised that he had to solve this case quickly. Otherwise he would be living in the director's office – a fate he did not want to contemplate. He had driven directly from the airport north of Gaborone to the CID headquarters in Millennium Park in the vanguard of the western expansion of the city. The still wild Kgale Hill looked down on the intrusion of the new office buildings with disapproval, a tiny psychological barrier to inevitable westward growth. In time, the city would spread around it in an outflanking movement, leaving it isolated and eventually tamed.

'So, what progress have you made?' Mabaku growled.

'No further than where we were last night,' Kubu replied. 'You know what the Zimbabwe police told us about Zondo and Tinubu. Zondo is not Zondo, and Tinubu died years ago. To all intents and purposes, neither exists. Makes solving a murder a little difficult.'

'Don't get me worked up, Kubu,' Mabaku said acidly. 'I'm getting enough pressure from Tourism. They've been on to the commissioner too! Remember those murders in Kenya about ten years ago? No foreigners went there for a year. A disaster!' He walked over to the window. Kgale Hill was sending in guerrillas. A small troop of baboons was scampering down the slope and over the wall into the parking area.

'Tinubu died twenty-nine years ago,' Mabaku continued. 'The Zimbabwe police say there's no doubt about it, although he used the name George then, not Goodluck. His fingerprints match. That obviously doesn't make sense. There's been a screw-up somewhere. They say he fought against Smith's forces in the civil war and was killed in a raid on a farmhouse.' He paused, watching the baboons wander towards the CID building. 'Zondo, whose real name is Peter Jabulani, also fought against Smith, but is now on Zimbabwe's hit list. The security forces there want him badly. Treason, they claim. If they catch him, we'll never get a whiff of him.'

Suddenly he flung open the window. 'Get off my car,' he yelled. 'Fuck off!' The baboons paid no attention and continued to play with the mirrors of Mabaku's old Range Rover. One looked up at him insolently, and with due deliberation defecated in the middle of the metallic silver hood.

'One day I'll have the trainees come over and use them for target practice!' Mabaku fumed.

Kubu said nothing. In fact, Mabaku had a soft spot for the baboons. They did not need to worry.

'Mr Director,' Kubu said. 'We're doing everything possible to find Zondo. Civil Aviation is checking all flights around Kasane and Maun. We've got a photo of Zondo taken by one of the guests, which we've circulated to all northern and central police stations and border posts. We've guys in Kasane, Kazungula and Maun walking the streets on the lookout. There's not much more we can do.'

Mabaku returned to his chair. 'At least there is some connection between Tinubu and Zondo,' he continued. 'They both fought on the same side of a war nearly thirty years ago. We now know Tinubu taught at a school in Mochudi and became the headmaster. He wasn't a salesman, as he put on his papers at the camp. Your friend Edison Banda went to the school yesterday. Everyone was shocked when he told them Tinubu was dead. Very popular, apparently. But this Langa guy is a mystery. The South Africans confirmed his identity, and the car's registered in his name. Never been in trouble. That's all I got from them. There's no obvious connection between him and the other two.'

Kubu wriggled his ample body in the inadequate chair, trying to get comfortable. 'Maybe he just got in the way,' he suggested. 'Maybe his death wasn't premeditated.'

'I don't believe in coincidences,' Mabaku said. 'And the South African police phoned *me* in response to Tatwa's enquiry about Langa. Why did they do that? Why didn't they get back to Tatwa? There's something fishy going on. And I didn't like the tone of the guy who called me from Johannesburg. Seemed reluctant to help with my other questions. I ended up phoning Director Van der Walle in Johannesburg for help. I explained the situation and asked him to let me know what Langa did for a living and who he worked for, and to see if they could find out why he was in Zeerust. But Van der Walle wasn't his usual helpful self either. Listened, but didn't say much. Said he would get back to me, but hasn't yet.' Mabaku pressed a button on his intercom. 'Miriam, two teas, please.'

Kubu blinked. Mabaku did not usually offer tea.

'Mr Director,' he said quietly. 'We can only go as fast as we can go. If Zondo's the culprit, then we need the help of the Zimbabwe police. If he isn't, we'll need a lot of legwork to find out who is. Nobody at the camp is a likely suspect, but we're checking everyone's backgrounds. However, I'd be surprised if we turn up anything interesting. We should have more information this afternoon.'

For Kubu, the arrival of the tea tray was a welcome sight. Miriam poured two cups and offered him a biscuit. He took three and arranged them strategically around his saucer, thus pre-empting the need to reach for more. For a moment, he was lulled into thinking that he and Mabaku were friends. But the moment was brief.

'I want you to go to Mochudi this afternoon,' Mabaku said as soon as his cup was empty. 'See if you can add to what Banda's discovered about Tinubu. Who were his friends? Did he have any enemies? Anything suspicious about his finances? The usual. Report back to me tomorrow at two.' He paused, then continued, 'When you've finished at the school, stop in at your parents. I'm sure they'll want to see you.'

He waved a dismissive hand and pressed the intercom button. 'Miriam, please phone Director Van der Walle in Johannesburg. Tell them it's urgent. I want to speak to him now.'

Walking out, still holding the last biscuit, Kubu wondered what was going on between Mabaku and the South African police.

CHAPTER 15

Kubu was hungry. The summons to see the director immediately after landing nearly four hours after leaving Jackalberry Camp meant he could not stop for food en route to the office.

Now he needed to get to Mochudi for a four p.m. appointment with the deputy headmaster, leaving insufficient time to debrief Edison and also have a decent lunch. The only solution was to eat at the fast-food Wimpy hamburger joint with Edison. Fortunately for Kubu, since he was not fond of their hamburgers, the Wimpy offered its steak-and-eggs breakfast throughout the day. As he ate, he questioned Edison about Mochudi.

'I found very little,' Edison replied between mouthfuls. 'We searched Tinubu's house. Very modest place right next to the school. Bare minimum of creature comforts. Only a few old black-and-white photos on the wall. They looked like school class photos. And one of what must be a young Tinubu and two friends. Not even a television. No personal letters. No sign of a girlfriend. I've asked for all his telephone records for the past year. Should have them tomorrow morning. We can see if there's been anything unusual lately.'

'What about his bank records?'

'I've got them. Nothing unusual. Certainly no large amounts of money ever went in or out. There's a monthly stop order for a hundred pula. I'm waiting for the bank to let me know where that goes. Teachers aren't the best-paid people in the world. There was very little money in his account.'

'What was the reaction at the school when you told them he was dead?'

'I spoke to the deputy headmaster, a man called Madi. He was clearly shocked. No acting there. He said Goodluck Tinubu was the kindest person he had ever met. I also spoke briefly to an assistant and one teacher who happened to be at the school. It's school holidays, you know. They both had the same response. Shock and sadness. They both said the school would never be the same.'

Kubu finished his steak. He had better get going. 'How do I get to the school?'

'On the way into Mochudi, turn left at Rasesa Street. The school is on the left just past the Welcome Bar Part 1. Strange name! Where's Part 2?'

'Oh, that'll be at the high school,' said Kubu, leaving Edison to work out if he was serious.

Most of the way out of Gaborone he needed to steer the vehicle through the apparently random behaviour of traffic, pedestrians and animals, even though the road was a modern highway. The greatest threat came from taxis. Their drivers obviously thought that having the word TAXI hand-painted on their vehicles bestowed unlimited privileges, including exemption from all the rules of the road.

After about fifteen minutes, the traffic thinned and moved more quickly, giving Kubu the chance to phone his parents for the third time since leaving the director's office. Every morning Kubu's father, Wilmon, turned on the cell phone Kubu had given him, convinced it would waste money to leave it on overnight. And every Saturday night he charged it with due ceremony, but he had never used it to make a call. He was proud of the phone and showed it to his friends. 'A present from my son David,' he would say, chest puffed out. 'My son is an important man in the police.'

Kubu was concerned. Wilmon's phone always waited in eager expectation. But Wilmon was nearly seventy. Had he forgotten to turn it on? Had it malfunctioned? Or could the power outages in the Mochudi area the previous weekend be to blame? It would not occur to Wilmon to charge it on a weekday.

The traffic had been unusually light, and having time to spare, Kubu decided to check on his parents on the way to Goodluck's school. He turned off the highway towards Mochudi and drove through the higgledy-piggledy patchwork of houses on small plots along the road. He drove down the main street and turned right into Kgafela Drive, passing the Linchwe II Junior and the Molefe Senior Secondary Schools. Just after the Hungry Tummies Take Away and the Taliban Haircut and Car Wash, he turned right into his parents' street.

Driving towards their small house, Kubu saw his parents sitting on the veranda. Aha, he thought. There's time for a quick cup of tea. As he stopped in front of the house, his mother, Amantle, stood up and waved. Wilmon took longer to get up. He did not wave, but awaited Kubu's arrival at the top of the steps. Kubu extended his right hand, touching his right arm with his left hand in the traditional respectful way.

'Father,' he said. 'You are looking well.'

'David, you are welcome at my house,' Wilmon greeted him in Setswana. It was the same dignified greeting he always used.

Kubu turned to Amantle and kissed her on the cheek. 'Mother,' he said. 'You too look well.' He hesitated, then continued. 'I can only stay a few minutes and would love a cup of tea and, perhaps, a biscuit. I've had a really busy day.'

While his mother bustled off to boil water, Kubu decided to investigate the case of the unanswered cell phone.

'Father,' he said quietly, 'I tried phoning you several times today, but you didn't answer. I was worried. Is the phone okay?'

Wilmon shrugged. 'I decided to leave it off. It uses electricity, which is very expensive. And it is a lot of trouble.'

'But Father, it is useful for keeping in touch.' Kubu did not mention that he paid for the electricity in any case.

'We see you quite often. We do not need it,' Wilmon said stubbornly.

Kubu knew his father, and how he treasured the phone. He thought for a while, then said, 'It's broken, isn't it?'

Wilmon was clearly embarrassed by the question and looked about as if trying to find somewhere to hide on the small veranda. Kubu sat silent, unrelenting. At last Wilmon grimaced and said, 'You know I always charge it on Saturday evenings.'

Kubu nodded.

'Last Saturday we were cleaning the floor, and at six o'clock the sofa was in front of the plug – that is the time I charge the phone. I decided to use the plug in the bathroom instead. I put the phone on the windowsill above the toilet while I plugged the cord into the wall.' He frowned. 'Before I fixed the cord to the phone, your mother asked me to help move a table. When I finished, I had forgotten about the phone.' His embarrassment became acute, but he sat taller in his chair and continued. 'Your mother had need of the bathroom and closed the curtains of the window. The curtains knocked the phone into the toilet!'

Wilmon shook his head. 'It was my fault. I took the phone out of the water and dried it, but I was scared to plug it in again. You cannot use electricity near water, you know.' He was not looking at Kubu.

Kubu managed a straight face. 'Father, you made the right decision. It could've been very dangerous. I'll look at it and advise you.'

He stood up, leaving Wilmon to his discomfort.

A few minutes later he returned and said, 'Father, you did a very good job of drying the phone. I turned it on, and it still works. I also plugged it in – very carefully – and it's charging now. Everything is fine.'

Wilmon broke out in a smile the likes of which Kubu rarely saw from his father.

Twenty minutes later, Kubu had drained two cups of tea and consumed several rusks that he had successfully dunked without losing any into the tea. He briefly told them about the murders in the north

'Father,' he said. 'One of the victims is from Mochudi. A man called Goodluck Tinubu.'

Wilmon's normally impassive face registered shock. 'Goodluck dead? How can this be?'

'You know this man?' Kubu was astonished.

Wilmon snorted. 'Everyone in Mochudi knows Goodluck. I am surprised you do not. He came here many years ago from Rhodesia. He is the headmaster of the Raserura Primary School. A good man, even if he is a foreigner. But then his mother was a Motswana. She married an Ndebele in Bulawayo,' he concluded with a touch of disapproval. 'But we all liked him. He cared about the children.'

'Do you know if he had any enemies?'

Wilmon shook his head. 'Everyone liked him.'

When Kubu took his leave, his father's final words to him were 'Why would anyone kill Goodluck Tinubu?'

'Why indeed?' Kubu muttered as he searched for Raserura Primary School. He missed Rasesa Street and had to ask the way. He turned around, drove a short way, and turned left into a road without a street sign. He wondered whether other countries had street signs that mysteriously disappeared.

Parking, and leaving the car windows slightly open to let the heat escape, he walked through the main entrance. Classrooms were scattered around the property, each colourfully painted with a variety of cartoon characters, as well as letters of the alphabet and numerals. For an instant the buildings towered around him, the perspective of the small boy who had made his way from Mochudi to Maru a Pula school in Gaborone. How lucky he had been. His parents, uneducated and poor, had dreamed of their son being the first in the family to complete secondary school. Their priest, who liked Kubu's soprano hymn-singing and spotted his unusual intelligence, persuaded the headmaster at the recently opened Maru a Pula school to give the young Bengu a scholarship. No doubt Wilmon had something to do with it too.

But the experience was not what Kubu had expected. It soon became apparent that being fat was a hazard. He was teased unmercifully and often bullied by older kids. Despite efforts by the teachers, he could not escape the taunting. Lying in bed at night, he hid his tears, determined to make his parents proud. He would never tell them.

As a consequence of his isolation, Kubu sought activities avoided by the bullies. Although he did not have a great voice, it was good enough for him to be in the school's informal choir. This bestowed respect and the start of friendships. In addition to the African songs he already knew, he also learned songs from all over the world. And then he discovered the soaring choruses from monumental works called operas and oratorios. Some had translations into English, but most were in languages he did not understand but still had to sing. His soul was captured, never to be released.

The other benefit was that there were boys of all ages in the choir, with interests beyond physical prowess. Kubu was soon making friends with boys several years older than himself. He got on better with them than with those of his own age. And they had better things to do than tease him.

Kubu also loved books. By the end of his first year, he was two grades ahead of his classmates in reading. The teachers allowed him to progress rapidly and encouraged him to spend time in the library. He read incessantly.

One day, he picked up a book entitled *Teddy Lester's Schooldays*. He loved it. But more important, he read about cricket, a game he saw the older boys play on Wednesday afternoons but about which he knew nothing. The book's descriptions captured his imagination. And so started a love affair with a game he would never play. From then on, he absorbed everything he could get his hands on and became a walking encyclopedia. He started watching the school teams play and privately kept score. Then one day the cricket coach walked over.

'Hello, Bengu.'

'Good afternoon, sir,' replied Kubu, standing up.

'I see you here every game. What are you doing?'

'I love cricket,' Kubu said sheepishly. 'It's wonderful. I try to keep score, but I keep getting details wrong.'

The coach took Kubu's scraps of paper. 'You're doing a fine job, but you need some help. Let me show you.' They walked to the little pavilion where the players sat waiting for their turn to bat. One boy was keeping score in a large book. The coach showed Kubu how each page was printed to make scoring easier. There was a place to keep track of how many runs each batsman had scored, a place for the total, and even a place where you could record each ball bowled. Kubu was fascinated.

'May I have one of those pages?' he asked eagerly. 'It makes it so much easier.'

'No, I don't think so,' the coach replied. Kubu was crushed. His hopes had been high. 'After the game, take the whole book. Next game I want you to score. You'll be our official scorer.'

For the first time at school, Kubu was happy. Elated was a better way to describe what he felt. The other boys slowly got to know him and to appreciate his skills. He never became 'one of the boys', but he no longer bore the brunt of teasing. For the rest of his time at Maru a Pula, Kubu was a scorer, eventually becoming the scorer for the school's First XI at a younger age than anyone before.

Kubu shook his head, bringing himself back to the present and the buildings to their true size. He found the school administrator, who took him to Joshua Madi, the deputy headmaster. The man who rose to greet Kubu was tall and slim with athletic movements. But there was uncertainty in his step, and his face was troubled.

'Superintendent. Thank you for coming. This news is a great shock to all of us. Rra Tinubu did so much for this school. He was its soul. The school will never be the same without him.' He sounded as though he meant it. 'Forgive my rudeness. May I offer you tea, or *rooibos*?' Despite his recent visit to his parents, Kubu accepted tea, but it came without biscuits.

'When did you last see him, Rra Madi?'

'It was last Friday. He said he was going on a short holiday. A week in the Okavango delta, I think. He'd been working particularly hard on the new curriculum, and we – the staff – encouraged him to go. He said he'd be back for the start of the new term, next Monday.'

'Do you know of anyone who would want to kill him?'

Madi shook his head firmly. 'He came to Mochudi with nothing but the clothes he wore. He was a temporary teacher at a school in town. People were suspicious. They don't like strangers in a small town like this one, let alone foreigners. But he said his mother was a Motswana, and he spoke our language well. When this school opened, he obtained a very junior post and worked without rest to make it the best primary school in the area. These days, parents fight for their children to come here.' Kubu thought of his father's words. Wilmon had known and respected Goodluck.

'Rra Madi, I have to remind you that this wasn't an accident or a mugging. Rra Tinubu was viciously murdered. We believe it was premeditated. Are you sure you've told me everything you know?' Kubu deliberately provoked the deputy headmaster, but the reaction was calm and regretful.

'He was a man much loved and respected. Even though he was originally from Zimbabwe.'

Kubu tried another tack. 'What did Rra Tinubu think about the situation in Zimbabwe? He must've been concerned about the poverty and misery in his homeland.'

Madi thought for a while. Then he said, 'I've often heard him asked that question. Sometimes he just shrugged and praised our government for its policies and kindness to refugees like himself. But if he felt the questioner really cared about the answer, he would respond by telling this story.' He took a sip of tea before continuing.

'When he was young, he had an uncle who lived alone with his dog, near the university in Bulawayo. Sometimes Goodluck would visit him because he told good stories and offered food and drink to his poor student nephew. But the uncle was too fond of brandy mixed with Coca-Cola. Sometimes he ran out of Coke, but he never ran out of brandy. His dog was a huge mongrel, part Rottweiler. It could fit Goodluck's thigh in its mouth. But it was a good dog and loyal, if not fierce enough to suit its owner, who complained of the cost of feeding it. He tried to train it, and would beat it with an old belt if it didn't behave as he thought it should. Once it caught a neighbour's chicken in the road and ate it, so it deserved a hiding. But sometimes Goodluck found his uncle beating the dog for no reason other than too much brandy. Goodluck was sad. He liked the dog, but couldn't take it to his student lodging.' Madi stopped.

'And what happened?' Kubu prompted.

'One day they found the uncle dead. The dog had gone for his throat and torn it out. He was still holding the old belt, and the dog lay next to him, guarding his body.'

Kubu nodded, getting the point. After a moment he said, 'What happened to the dog?'

Madi looked up, surprised. 'I never asked him that.'

'They would've destroyed it,' said Kubu, rising to leave.

Madi, also rising, replied, 'Yes, I suppose they would.' He walked with Kubu to his car.

As they shook hands, Kubu said, 'Rra Madi, I'll need to talk to as many of the teachers as I can. I'll come to the school around nine tomorrow morning. Please try to have as many here as possible. I realise it's the holidays, but do your best. And please try to think of anything that may help us solve this murder of a good man.'

Madi nodded, and watched the large detective drive slowly away.

CHAPTER 16

As Kubu negotiated the traffic back to Gaborone, his thoughts turned to his parents. They were so kind, wanting everything of the best for him. Yet he felt a growing distance, not because he loved them less, but rather because they didn't really understand what he did, or the way he and Joy lived in Gaborone. Other than family matters and local gossip, there was little for them to share. Kubu wondered whether all children found this happening to them. Joy had noticed it too, although she was better at maintaining a domestic conversation. Perhaps if there were grandchildren there would be a different focus for the family, but it seemed that was not to be.

As he turned into Acacia Street, Kubu smiled in anticipation. He had managed to get home without delaying dinner. He and Joy typically enjoyed a leisurely drink after work, catching up on each other's day. It would not be too much of a hardship today to cut that time short. As for wine, his small stock would have to provide for whatever Joy was serving.

As he pulled up at the front gate, he felt a mild twinge of regret. He and Joy were not going to be alone. Her sister Pleasant was there too. Her ancient Toyota Corolla was parked outside. He got on well with Pleasant, but he had been away from home for nearly two days and had a lot to tell Joy. He would be careful not to let his disappointment show.

His thoughts were interrupted by Ilia's frenzied barking, determined to show her pleasure at Kubu's return. She jumped at the gate, yapping furiously. Kubu knew what was to happen next. Before getting out of the car, he opened the passenger door and put his briefcase on the floor. He got out, lifted the latch on the metal gates and opened the left half. The fox terrier flew into his arms, licking his face. Kubu knew he should not allow such uncontrolled behaviour, but did not have the heart to stop it. It gave him too much pleasure. After a few moments he spoke in his sternest voice.

'Car! Car, Ilia!' He put Ilia on the ground. Without hesitation, she jumped on to the passenger seat and sat panting.

Kubu swung the second gate open and drove the few metres up to the house. Ilia waited for him to get out, then sprang out of the car, barking again as he closed the gates. No one would dare to rob my house, Kubu thought. Ilia would tell the whole neighbourhood!

Joy was waiting barefoot for him at the top of the steps to the veranda. He looked at her appreciatively. Of medium height, she had the full figure admired in Batswana culture. Her twinkling eyes were set in a round, happy face, and colourful beaded ornaments dangled from her ears. Lovely legs showed beneath a pair of maroon shorts, and a white tennis shirt strained over ample breasts. Kubu smiled, fully approving of this decidedly non-traditional attire.

'Welcome home, stranger!' She gave him a hug and kissed him. 'It's good to have you home. I've missed you.'

'My dear, you know how I hate to spend a night away from home.' He turned to Pleasant, who was relaxing in a comfortable *riempie* chair, glass of white wine in hand. 'Hello, sister-in-law,' he said. 'Nice to see you. Pleasant surprise!' Pleasant smiled at the perennial jest.

'Well, it *is* a special occasion, dear,' Joy said teasingly.

Kubu ran mentally through his list of important dates. Joy's birthday? Pleasant's birthday? Wedding anniversary? Today was none of those. What could it be? Should he try to brazen it out? Or should he admit ignorance and take his medicine?

'You don't remember, do you?' Joy said. Pleasant giggled from her chair.

'I have to admit, I don't.'

'How could you forget?' Joy said with mock anger. 'A most important day in your life!'

Kubu squirmed. He was sure it wasn't his wedding anniversary. Then it dawned on him. It was nine years ago today that he had first gone out with Joy. He was new to the Gaborone police, having paid his dues at various small towns around the country. She worked as an administrator in the office, dealing with the mountains of paperwork that were inevitable in police work, mountains that had not yet been levelled by the police computer network. He needed some details on a suspect's previous convictions and was told that Joy was the person to help him. He was immediately attracted to her twinkling eyes and her efficiency.

Kubu had little experience of dating. He had always doubted that women would find him attractive, given his size. But Joy was different. She made him feel comfortable, even while teasing him for being so serious. A few days later he found an excuse to visit her again. He was surprised that she remembered his name.

'What can I do for Detective Bengu?' she asked. Before he could answer, she continued, 'What does the notorious Kubu want today?'

He gaped. He hadn't told her his nickname. She had obviously asked around. His heart pounded. Was she attracted to him too? Suddenly his reserve left him.

'This Kubu wants to ask a certain beautiful police administrator out to dinner. Tonight, if possible. At the Mahogany Room at the Sun.'

Joy had feigned shyness.

'Are all detectives this forward?' she asked. 'They must know you well at the Sun.'

Kubu felt his confidence slipping. 'You would be the first person I've ever taken there.' He hesitated, then continued quietly, 'The truth is, I've never eaten there myself. I just wanted to impress you.'

Joy's heart melted. 'I'd love to go out for dinner tonight. But I insist on paying for myself. I can't afford the Mahogany Room, and I'm sure you can't. So let's find a place we *can* both afford.'

Kubu's mind snapped back to the present. 'My dear, I could never forget the first time we went out together. I was so embarrassed! Not being allowed to pay for my guest. I was mortified for weeks!'

Joy and Pleasant laughed.

'Good recovery,' Pleasant said. 'Joy told me she was going to make you suffer if you didn't remember!'

'How could I forget?' Kubu replied smugly.

*

Dinner was leisurely, and afterwards the women retired to the living room while Kubu washed the dishes – something he disliked, but which he did occasionally when they had guests to show his status as a liberated male. He hadn't told Joy that he was setting money aside for a dishwasher. She had a birthday coming up.

Joy and Pleasant chatted about what was happening at their respective workplaces. Pleasant was concerned whether her travel agency would survive.

'It's very difficult now that the airlines are reducing the commissions they pay to agents,' she said. 'Some tour operators are following suit. The Internet is killing us. People can find out so much by themselves, even if they spend much more time doing so. They boast about their good deals, but ignore the time it took to find them. I'm not sure what I'll do if we close. All the agencies are in the same boat, except those that service Debswana and other big companies. Or the government, of course.'

The conversation turned to the day-care centre where Joy worked. She related horrifying statistics about babies born with HIV to parents who would soon die. The number of orphans had skyrocketed as AIDS ravaged the country. Botswana had fewer than two million people and one of the highest HIV infection rates in Africa. It was estimated that about a quarter of the adult population was infected. It was a national crisis that the government was attacking with free antiretrovirals and widespread campaigns advertising responsible sexual behaviour.

'In some ways,' Joy said, 'I'm pleased that Kubu and I can't have kids. It must be a nightmare bringing them up in these times.' Pleasant was surprised at the comment, because it had been so painful for Joy to learn that she and Kubu had little chance of becoming parents. Joy rarely mentioned this situation.

'Of course, *you*'ve nothing to worry about, Pleasant. You have to find a man first. You are so picky, you'll be a spinster all your life.'

'I'm not worried yet,' Pleasant responded, laughing. 'Besides, I do see Kubu's friend Bongani every now and again. I like him, but he is so serious about his work I'm not sure he ever thinks about me. Even when we have dinner, I get the feeling his mind is elsewhere.'

Joy moved closer to Pleasant and whispered, 'Have you been to bed with him yet?'

Pleasant looked at her, wide-eyed. This was not traditional Batswana small talk even between sisters.

'What's wrong with you?' said Joy, eyes twinkling. 'Haven't you heard of sex?'

Pleasant giggled, and the two of them huddled together to devise various not entirely serious plans to get Bongani into Pleasant's bed. Or vice versa.

In the kitchen, Kubu wondered what was causing the low voices punctuated by squeals of laughter. Must be girl talk.

Half an hour later, Kubu was telling Joy and Pleasant about the murders at Jackalberry Camp.

'It's so weird,' Pleasant said. 'He can't have been dead all these years and still be teaching!' She noticed Kubu's quizzical look. 'You know what I mean! There must be some mistake. They must've got the fingerprints mixed up. Not the ones you took the other day. The ones on their records. You should send Joy up to Zimbabwe to sort them out.'

'I agree,' Kubu said. 'It's the only rational explanation. I'm not as surprised about Zondo. If he's a hit man, he'd cover his tracks pretty well. A false passport and name are easy pickings these days.'

'You mean I could get a passport in someone else's name with my photo in it?' Pleasant asked.

'I could have you one in twenty-four hours. Fake passports are as plentiful as quelea these days.'

Pleasant visualised a flock of false documents settling from the sky like the greedy seed-eating birds.

'What I don't understand is why anyone would want to kill Tinubu,' Kubu continued. 'I could understand it if he was killed because he was in the wrong place at the wrong time. But the markings on the body suggest he was the target, while the Langa guy may have been killed because he saw something. He was just bonked on the head and thrown into a gully. The mutilation of Tinubu's body was meant to send a message. To who and about what, I haven't a clue.'

The three sat in silence.

'Do you think you'll find that Zondo man?' Pleasant eventually asked. 'Will the Zimbabwe police catch him?'

'Unfortunately the Zimbabwe police know Zondo under a different name. They tell us he's a dissident. That means he's against the president, and if they catch him, he's in for a hard time. He wasn't supposed to be outside Zimbabwe.'

Kubu paused, ugly images flooding his mind.

'If they get him first, I don't think we'll see him alive.'

CHAPTER 17

The next morning, Kubu set off for Mochudi at about eight. Better to be early than late. He negotiated the traffic chaos and emerged in a better mood than anticipated.

As the traffic thinned, his mind returned to the murders. He knew persistence would pay off, even if the case made little sense at the moment. Somewhere, some time, a clue would emerge or a mistake would be discovered. He had to be alert for that moment.

Mabaku's right, he thought. There has to be a connection between Tinubu and Langa. It's too much of a coincidence that they meet on the road for the first time, and a few hours later they're both dead. Why did Langa write down Tinubu's licence plate number at the top of a scrawled list? And why are the South Africans stalling on the other licence plate that was jotted on Langa's petrol receipt? And what on earth does the jumble of letters mean? Kubu had them memorised:

LC*
WB1
1L
KGH-A19

'1L,' he said out loud. 'That's how I write directions to someone's home. First left. But it could mean almost anything.' A cow lumbered into the road, and he had to take evasive action. Stupid animals, he thought. They're better off as rare steaks with garlic and pepper! Preferably washed down with Shiraz.

'LC*.' Kubu resumed talking to himself. 'LC*?' He frowned. 'L! C! Asterisk!' He broke the group into its parts, pausing between each. It still meant nothing to him. 'Maybe it's LC star? Does that make any more sense?' He did not think so. So he switched to the next group.

'WB1? Way back at the first street?' Kubu sighed. 'I don't think so. But what else could WB stand for? Some place before turning first left? Willie B's? Women of Botswana?' He tried various other combinations, but none made sense.

Kubu tackled KGH-A19 with the same result. He could speculate as much as he liked, but nothing gelled.

He followed the road to the school and prepared to meet the teachers.

Seven teachers had gathered in the staff room that morning, as well as deputy headmaster Madi and a few administrative staff. The reaction was unanimous. It was inconceivable that Goodluck had any bitter enemies. In fact, nobody could believe he had any enemies at all.

When he asked for their opinions of Tinubu, Kubu was overwhelmed by a barrage of comments.

'We loved him,' said a large woman in a colourful dress. 'He would do anything for the children, and he always supported the staff.'

An elderly man chimed in, 'He had been here for many, many years, but he was always working here at the school. I'm not sure he ever slept.'

A younger man stood up. 'I can't believe this has happened,' he said. 'He was quiet and gentle and everyone thought the world of him. What are you doing to catch these men? There is more and more violence these days, and people get away with it! We want some action!'

There was a murmur of agreement and for a moment the group turned hostile. Kubu held up his hand. 'We will catch these men, and they will pay for their crimes. I can tell you the director of the CID has made this our top priority. It is only a matter of time before we solve the case. All we need is your help.'

The young man looked at him for a few moments and then sat down. The mood changed.

'Did Rra Tinubu have any good friends he saw regularly? Someone who knew his plans and could tell us? A girlfriend, perhaps?'

It was a middle-aged woman who responded, with a hint of regret. 'Where would he find the time?'

Kubu was touched by the emotions Tinubu's death had generated. Tinubu must have been a remarkable man. He let the meeting continue for over half an hour, giving everyone a chance to air their anguish. When he decided he would learn nothing more, he thanked the group for their help and promised to keep them informed about the progress of the investigation.

'May I see Rra Tinubu's house now?' he asked Madi. The deputy headmaster led him across the grounds, past the school classrooms, to a small side street.

'That's it. First house. Here are the keys.' Madi seemed reluctant to go into the house. Kubu stepped into a small garden that was ill-tended, with few flowers. Obviously gardening had not been one of Tinubu's hobbies. The house was small and rectangular. Every expense had been spared in its building. As he glanced up at the roof, Kubu caught his breath. He blinked and looked again at the house number. KGH-A19. He looked at the next house. KGH-A20.

KGH-A19 was the last item on the list on Langa's receipt. Could he work backwards and solve the riddle of the other codes? Kubu wanted to jump into his car immediately, but decided to complete his search of Tinubu's house. It did not take long, even though his mind kept wandering back to the puzzle. The house was as Edison had described. Austere to a fault. Few personal items. No signs of a partner. Tinubu had a small alcove with a desk and an office chair, but the desk was clean, no clutter of papers. Well, his school office is just across the road, Kubu thought. Why bring work home? With little expectation, he went through the drawers. Bills and financial stuff. Probably where Edison found the bank statements. The bottom drawer contained some pamphlets on a charity organisation supporting Zimbabweans trying to make a new life in Botswana. There was also a schedule of its meetings in Gaborone. Three had large crosses against them. Kubu pocketed the list and a few of the pamphlets, took a last look around, and locked up. Then he went back to the staff room to thank Madi, who walked him to his car. As he was about to get in, Kubu handed the deputy headmaster his card, asking that he contact him if he thought of anything that had the smallest chance of being significant. Madi looked at the card for a moment.

'There was one thing,' he said. 'Your card reminded me of it. I suppose it means nothing, but it was strange. Two white ladies came all the way from Gaborone in a proper taxi.' Madi shook his head at such extravagance. 'They wanted to see Rra Tinubu, but he'd already left on his holiday. They said they wrote stories for a newspaper and wanted to write about our school. I offered to show them around, but they said they would come back in a few weeks. They were also going on holiday in the bush. Then they drove away in their taxi.'

'Did they tell you their names?'

'They gave me a card. To prove who they were, I suppose. I've got it here somewhere.' He rummaged in his wallet, which seemed to contain everything except money, and produced a dog-eared card.

It introduced Judith and Trish Munro, writers for the London *Sunday Telegraph*.

CHAPTER 18

Kubu sat in his car, pondering what he had just learned. The Munro sisters had told him that they were on holiday in Botswana. However, their story about knowing a journalist who had been to Jackalberry was probably a lie. Now it turned out that they had tried to visit Tinubu a few days before his death, and possibly followed him to the camp where he was murdered. Kubu was fascinated. He would interview them again and crank up the pressure until they explained what they were really doing at Jackalberry Camp.

But of more immediate interest was the puzzle.

'If KGH-A19 is indeed Tinubu's house, it's reasonable to think of the other groups of letters and numbers as a set of directions.' Once again Kubu spoke out loud. 'If I drive down Rasesa Street the way I came, I have to turn left to get to Tinubu's house. If 1L means first left, then it is first left after whatever WB1 is. Let's find out.'

Kubu drove to Tinubu's house at the end of the little street and turned around. At Rasesa Street he turned right, and crept down the road looking to both sides. It was only a few hundred metres before he came to an intersection. He looked around carefully. Then he had it. Across the street was the Welcome Bar Part 1. WB1! Of course. Edison had mentioned it.

He continued down Rasesa Street, wondering about LC*. He reached the main road to Mochudi and stopped. No commercial buildings were nearby.

'LC*. Turn left at C asterisk? Turn left at C star?' Kubu mumbled to himself. Then a small sign across the road caught his eye. It was a sign for a mosque. Next to the words Islamic Centre and Mosque was a quarter-moon and a star. Kubu laughed aloud. 'That's the C*! He had to use another sign because the street sign was missing. That's just the sort of direction I would write down if I was driving alone. Abbreviate easy-to-see buildings or signs. Make it easy to retrace your steps.'

So Langa hadn't chanced on Tinubu for the first time on the road to Kasane. He had followed him to his house – probably from Zeerust – making brief notes of the directions on the only paper he had available – the Zeerust petrol receipt. But why? Perhaps Mabaku would have the information from the South Africans about the owner of the other registration number on the receipt.

Kubu's flesh tingled. At last the chase was on! A few hours ago he had nothing. Now he knew there were connections between Tinubu and Langa, and between Tinubu and the Munro sisters. Next he had to find out what those connections were.

Heading back to CID headquarters, he was actually looking forward to his meeting with Mabaku.

As he encountered the crowded streets of northern Gaborone, Kubu's phone rang its rousing tune. He pulled over and parked on the sandy verge, scattering chickens and receiving dirty looks from scrawny dogs.

'Bengu,' he said.

'Kubu, it's Edison. I've got Tinubu's phone records. He doesn't make too many calls. A few to the deputy headmaster's home, as well as to some of the teachers. He phoned a travel agent a couple of weeks ago. I checked with them, and they confirmed he made a reservation for Jackalberry Camp for three nights. His request, not their suggestion. Paid for it by cheque. And that's it. No other calls.'

'What about calls from his office? Can you get those checked too?'

'I've got the records,' Edison said. 'We're checking them now. That's going to take some time.'

'I asked his assistant if he'd received any calls out of the ordinary,' Kubu said. 'She said that nothing caught her attention. Give her a call and see if she remembers anything last Thursday. Maybe Tinubu said something about going into Gaborone.'

'One last thing. Forensics called to say that Tinubu's briefcase had no traces of drugs.'

'Okay, thanks. I'll check with you when I've finished with the director. I've got to report to him as soon as I get back. He's really revved up about this case.'

When the conversation was over, Kubu took a couple of deep breaths, signalled that he was pulling back on to the road, accelerated, and prayed that it was in no one's interest to run into him.

CHAPTER 19

Had Kubu known what was happening in Director Mabaku's office, he would not have looked forward to his upcoming meeting. Mabaku had a visitor. The two men had known each other for many years and had great respect for each other's skills. There were no titles between them, nor did they use first names. Their relationship was professional and had always been cordial. Until now.

Mabaku shouted as he towered over his visitor. 'You're telling me that Langa was a South African *policeman*? A South African policeman following a Botswana citizen into Botswana! And you didn't let me know! Did you let *anybody* in Botswana know?'

'We didn't expect—' the visitor started to say.

'I don't care what you expected! No policeman – from South Africa, from Namibia, not even from the United Kingdom – no policeman comes into Botswana without notice, unless he's a tourist with his own money and no professional agenda!' Mabaku shook his finger in the visitor's face. 'If it ever happens again, you'll find it impossible to get any cooperation from us!' He crashed his fist on his desk. Everything jumped, including Director Van der Walle of the South African Criminal Investigation Department.

'You have my apologies,' Van der Walle said contritely. 'You know we've been trying to track the hot money on drug routes.'

Mabaku glared at him without a word.

'Mabaku,' Van der Walle continued, 'we didn't expect or authorise Langa to come into Botswana. He was following a money-smuggling suspect. He got to Zeerust and saw a briefcase change hands to your fellow Tinubu. He made a snap decision to follow Tinubu and got the Zeerust police to follow the original courier back to Johannesburg.'

'Snap decision?' snarled Mabaku. 'Since when do plain-clothed police travel with passports and car registration papers? And an overnight suitcase? He expected to come to Gaborone, and you didn't let me know.'

'Sit down, Mabaku,' Van der Walle said, exasperated. 'We've worked together long enough to trust each other. I promise we didn't expect Langa to cross the border. If I thought it a possibility, I would have let you know – in advance.'

'But he would have let the Zeerust police know where he was going. Are you saying you weren't told?'

'The Zeerust police assumed we knew what Langa was up to. They didn't realise it needed urgent authorisation.'

Van der Walle hesitated. 'Look, Mabaku, I take full responsibility. Langa was working for me. He should've known better. That's how it was. I'm sorry.'

Mabaku glared at him, unconvinced.

Van der Walle stood up and extended his hand. 'Shake on it, Mabaku. I'm sorry about what happened. Now let's focus on the case.'

Mabaku sighed and shook his head. 'Okay. Okay. Just don't let it happen again.' The two shook hands and sat down. Mabaku ordered tea and biscuits from an amused Miriam, who had been enjoying the explosions from beyond the closed door.

'What do you know about Tinubu?' Mabaku asked. 'Bring me up to date on what you think is going on.'

'We know nothing about him. The first we heard was a call from Langa in Mochudi, saying he was following a guy who had taken a briefcase from our suspect in Zeerust. He'd spent the night outside his house and was following him north. He reported in at Francistown as well – nothing new, though.'

'You're saying he was reporting back to you while he was in Botswana, and you didn't let us know?' Mabaku's voice had flipped to the other end of the spectrum. Van der Walle could barely hear what he was saying.

The South African rolled his eyes. 'Come on, Mabaku. Cool it. I've apologised. Everyone simply assumed that Langa's activities had been authorised. The detective who took Langa's call didn't raise the issue immediately, but was going to wait until our weekly meeting to report on what he was doing. I don't know what Langa was thinking of. Heat-of-the-moment decision, I suppose. We'll never know for sure now.'

With obvious reluctance, Mabaku let it go. 'And then what happened?'

'The last call we got was that he'd helped Tinubu fix a puncture and was going to join him at a camp somewhere. Then we heard from you guys.' He paused. 'Frankly, it took us a day or two to decide what to do.'

'You mean you were deciding whether to tell me or not!'

'No. It took some time for me to get all the information. When I realised what had happened, I didn't want to make matters worse by giving you wrong information. I decided the best thing was to get down here right away and discuss it face to face. We've a vested interest in this too, you know. One of my men was killed following someone we suspect was involved with drugs.'

'So tell me about this drug thing.' Mabaku's voice returned to its professional volume.

'Okay. As you know, one of the main heroin conduits into South Africa is now through Zambia and Botswana. The other is through Mozambique. It's smuggled from the Far East, first into Tanzania. We've been trying to follow a money trail. We've been watching a number of people who have had unusual financial transactions – large amounts of money changing hands outside the banking system. Usually dollars. We've been unable to pin anything on them. In fact, they all seem squeaky clean. It's very odd. So we decided to do nothing but watch, in the hope we'd give them enough rope.' Van der Walle paused as Miriam came in with the tea. She poured it, offered the biscuits, and left.

'That's what Langa was doing,' Van der Walle continued. 'He didn't know where the Johannesburg guy was going. Ended up in Zeerust. The Johannesburg guy had lunch with someone, who picked up a briefcase and headed back into Botswana – that's Tinubu, of course.'

'Tinubu was a respected headmaster in Mochudi. Left Zimbabwe after the war and settled here. Was a great asset to the community. Never in any trouble. Not even parking tickets. Everyone says he spent all his time working at the school. Nothing significant with his bank account, either. He's a most unlikely candidate for a drug smuggler.'

'What about the murders? Do you have any suspects?'

'The most likely is a man calling himself Zondo – from Zimbabwe. False name, fake passport. We sent fingerprints to Zimbabwe. They tell us that his real name is Peter Jabulani and that he is a dissident. He shouldn't be leaving Zimbabwe because they confiscated his real passport.' Mabaku shook his head. 'We'll have a tough time getting to him if the Zimbabwe authorities find him. Apparently he was quite a hero in the war, but turned against the president when he started making his own rules. I guess he feels that his war efforts have come to nothing.'

Van der Walle nodded.

'The strange thing is that the Zimbabwe police tell us that Tinubu died at the end of the war. They have his fingerprints, death certificate. Everything. There must be a screw-up somewhere. Tinubu was definitely alive before he was killed,' Mabaku said with unintentional irony.

The two sat in silence, finishing their tea.

'Tell me about the guy Langa was following from Johannesburg. The one the Zeerust police followed back.' Mabaku drained his cup.

Van der Walle shifted in his chair, embarrassed. 'Unfortunately they lost him. He must have noticed them and then shaken them off. We don't know who he is or where he is. The car registration – the one Langa wrote on that receipt you found – is false. We blew it! We've got nothing.'

Even Mabaku kept quiet. Van der Walle was suffering enough.

'I'd like to have one of my men work with you on this case. He can stay in Gaborone for a few weeks or until you close the case.' Van der Walle looked at Mabaku.

Mabaku took a deep breath. 'I'm reluctant to allow that after what has happened. I'll let you know each week what's happening here.'

'Come on, Mabaku,' Van der Walle said. 'Don't be pig-headed.

Langa was a South African and a policeman. We have to be involved. Tinubu met someone in South Africa before he was killed. And on top of that, you'll need lots of information from us. My man can act as liaison so that you get what you need right away.'

Mabaku glared at him. 'Getting information at all will be an improvement! But you're right. We need your help *and* you need ours. It's just that I'm still angry that your Langa came into Botswana without my permission.' He paused. 'I'll get over it.'

Mabaku then proceeded to lay out exactly how the detective from South Africa was to operate in Botswana. 'And if he steps one inch out of line, he'll be across the border so quickly his hair will char. Is that clear?'

Van der Walle's smile warmed. This was the Mabaku he knew and loved.

CHAPTER 20

Boy Gomwe sat in the manager's office at the Blast music store in Soweto, a sprawling southern suburb of Johannesburg. He was selling. It was what he did best. At that moment he was sipping instant coffee and making small talk. Part of his sales technique. Chatty.

'You look tired, Joe. You should take a break. Do you good. I was just on holiday. Great!'

Joe Petersen, the manager, nodded, but looked sour. 'Guess that's why you're late. Shit! I was worried. Got commitments, you know. Where'd you go, anyway?'

'Botswana. Nice.'

'What were you doing there?'

Gomwe gave him a look. 'Holiday, like I said. None of your business anyway.'

Petersen shrugged. 'Sure. Just curious.'

'I don't like curious,' said Gomwe. He finished the coffee. 'Let's get to the music. How are the sales?' Petersen started describing what was and what was not selling, and Gomwe pretended to be interested. But he was not listening, and when the manager stopped talking he pulled out an order book. 'Great price on the new Jö Blö CD. Special – fifty rands. How many you want?'

'I don't know. He's not so popular any more. Some people weren't impressed with that Rwanda story, trying to buy that kid and all that.'

'He didn't buy him. It was an adoption. He's loaded. We should be so lucky!' Gomwe gave Petersen a friendly shove. 'I'll put you down for fifty.'

The discussion went on in this way for about half an hour. Petersen heard some snatches from new releases, liking some, disliking others.

Gomwe put him down for all of them. At last he tore off the top sheet of his order book and gave it to the manager. Petersen had learned that he could not reject anything, but he could negotiate on numbers. He pushed up a few and lowered several. Then he gave the order back to Gomwe, who glanced through it sourly. He had his reputation as the company's best travelling salesman to maintain. Hell, he wanted to win the trip to Mauritius. But it looked all right. He nodded.

'You got my other order?' asked Petersen, trying not to sound too eager.

'Of course.' Gomwe opened a case apparently stuffed with music magazines. Actually, there were only a few. The bottom was false. He lifted out a bag of white powder, weighing perhaps a hundred grams. Petersen opened it carefully, smelled it, and tasted a touch on his finger. Gomwe looked on, disgusted. Petersen was pathetic. He probably could not tell the difference between salt and sugar, let alone judge the quality of heroin.

Petersen was satisfied. The packet vanished, and money changed hands. A lot of money. No negotiation here, either.

'I'll get your order processed as soon as I'm back in the office. That new stuff will sell like hot cakes once it hits the airwaves. You'll be glad you put in a good order while we had stock. Five per cent discount if you pay in thirty days. As usual. Okay?'

Petersen said it was fine. He did not see Gomwe out.

Gomwe had one more call to make in Johannesburg. To settle a score.

CHAPTER 21

Dupie maintained his happy-go-lucky appearance despite all the disruptions at Jackalberry Camp. Salome, however, was showing the strain. Police scouring every nook and cranny; the camp being closed to visitors for four days; the endless questions. She was not in the mood to entertain these guests, the first since the camp had reopened. So after dinner she sat quietly next to Dupie, saying very little. Dupie, on the other hand, was in fine form, and the guests were enjoying beers, liqueurs or Dom Pedros.

At least we'll make some money, Dupie thought. He was surprised that the group was hanging together. There were two friends sharing a tent who had arrived at the airstrip in a decrepit Cessna 172. From Maun, they said. The first man was Spanish, short and swarthy. The second, who said he was a Zulu, was big and black, with a barrel chest and heavy muscles. An odd couple. Faggots, most likely, thought Dupie. Then there was an English couple on their first tour of the wilds of Africa; a young South African couple on their honeymoon; and an elderly French couple, whose English was limited. Enoch had met them at Ngoma that morning.

Most of the conversation was carried by the English and French couples, gesticulating energetically to communicate. They were obviously enjoying themselves, and Dupie was happy to keep their glasses filled.

Suddenly one of the women screamed and lifted her feet off the ground.

'A scorpion,' she cried. 'A huge scorpion!'

A large grey creature, about the width of a whisky glass, darted from under her chair into the open near the fire.

'That's not a scorpion,' Dupie said. 'It's a spider. See, it doesn't have pincers or a stinging tail.'

'A spider? It looks more like a scorpion to me,' said her husband.

'No. It's definitely a spider.' Dupie said emphatically. 'Actually, it's a spider endemic to this area. It can be a real pest, especially for people who use rooftop tents. You know, those tents on the top of their Landy or Land Cruiser.'

The group fell silent, sensing Dupie's next story.

'It's called the ladder-climbing spider,' he said earnestly. 'You see those long legs? It jumps from one step of a ladder to the next. People in rooftop tents are safe from lions. But they never think of those spiders!'

The woman drew her knees up to her chest, huddling closer to her husband.

'It is quite scary,' Dupie continued, 'to wake up with one of those spiders sitting on your face.'

Several members of his audience gasped. Salome shook her head and rolled her eyes, like a wife hearing her husband's story for the hundredth time.

'The problem is you can't just run away. A rooftop's a long way from the ground!' He paused for effect. 'But you have to remember they're completely harmless. They feel dangerous when they're on your nose or eyes, but they're not. Just brush them off and ignore them.'

'Will they come into *our* tents?' asked the English lady.

'No, you don't have to worry about them. Your tents don't have ladders, so the spiders aren't interested in you. That's why our tents are on the ground.'

Most of the members of the group sipped their drinks, not knowing whether to believe Dupie. Salome tried to keep a straight face.

Conversation soon picked up again, but Dupie noticed that the women constantly checked whether the spider was near them. When it did reappear, it was running past the Spaniard. With a lightning movement, he stamped it into the ground and kicked the corpse towards the fire.

'Hey, you react fast,' said Dupie, impressed. 'But it wasn't doing any harm.' The man said nothing and continued to sip his beer.

About a quarter of an hour later, the honeymoon couple left for their tent. The English and French couples, now firm friends despite understanding very little of what the other had said, followed soon after. The Englishman was still demonstrating to his French counterpart how the spiders climbed ladders by using one hand to climb his other arm. Salome took advantage of the exodus and said good night as well.

'What can I get for you gentlemen?' Dupie said. The Spaniard, who had the unlikely name of Madrid, and his friend Johannes had nursed an after-dinner drink for all of an hour. 'How about an Amarula on the rocks? Or an Amarula Dom Pedro?'

Both declined with shakes of the head.

'You had problems here this week?' Madrid asked. He spoke good English with a strong Spanish accent.

'We read about it,' said Johannes.

Dupie warmed to the story. He embroidered the gruesome murders and had dozens of police scouring the island for days. 'Of course, I know who the murderer actually was!'

His two guests looked at him impassively and waited.

'He called himself Zondo,' Dupie said, 'and he came from Zimbabwe. Actually, I think he was a drug dealer. He killed his customers and took off with the drugs and the money too.'

'Why do you think it was him?' Madrid asked.

'Zondo?' Dupie paused. 'The murders were on Sunday night. He was going to leave on Tuesday lunchtime. He suddenly changed his mind and left early on Monday. I took him to his plane just after dawn. After I got back, we found the bodies.'

'Who was killed?'

'One called himself Goodluck Tinubu. A salesman from Gaborone, I think. The other was from South Africa, Sipho Langa. Not sure what he did. I think they were buying drugs from Zondo and got bumped off for the money. Zondo leaves with the drugs *and* the money. Nice deal.'

'I didn't know there was much drug stuff in Botswana.'

'Oh, yes,' Dupie responded. 'It's one of the supply routes into South Africa, though the police deny that.'

They watched the crackling logs and grasping flames in silence.

'Were you able to get the registration of the plane?' Madrid asked. He sounded casual, but Dupie looked at him sharply. His skin tingled as it always did when he sensed danger. Who were these two? Why on earth would they want to know about the plane's registration?

'I never saw the plane. When I dropped him off, it hadn't arrived yet. I left right away because I had to pick up some of the staff from the village. Apparently the police haven't been able to trace it either. Flew below the radar, as they say. Mark my words, it's back in Zimbabwe right now, and Zondo is living it up.'

'Nobody heard anything? The camp isn't that big.'

Dupie shook his head. 'Both were hit on the head. No noise. Langa's body was on the far side of the island, down a bank near the water. The blow killed him straight away. We found Tinubu in his tent, throat cut. They were killed in the middle of the night. Nobody heard a thing.'

'Where do the staff sleep? Isn't someone on duty all night?' Johannes' curiosity was insatiable.

Dupie shook his head. 'I sleep at the far end of the tents. Enoch – he picked you up at the airstrip – he and the cook sleep back behind us, out of sight. If I didn't hear anything, they certainly wouldn't have.'

'How did the police get here? It's a long way from Maun.'

'They flew in from Kasane, not Maun. It's closer. The Defense Force brought them up in some sort of twin-engine plane. After that they used a helicopter.' Dupie's skin tingled again. Usually people wanted all the gruesome details of events like these – what the bodies looked like, how much blood, how they had been discovered. These questions were different, more like an interrogation. 'Normally they'd drive, but the camp's miles from anything. Even the landing strip is quite far. A chopper's much easier. By the time they'd finished, I think the chopper had made six or seven trips, what with detectives and pathologists. Must've cost a fortune. The animals around here didn't know what was going on.'

Johannes digested that. 'How'd you call the police anyway?' he asked casually.

'Cell phone.' Dupie was getting increasingly suspicious. He glanced at Madrid, who had said nothing for a while.

'What happens if you lose reception for the phone? How do you contact the outside world?' he asked.

'We have a radio,' Dupie replied. 'We don't use it a lot because it's not private, but it works fine.'

'Did the police agree with your theory about the other guest? Zondo, wasn't it?' Johannes was not about to let up.

'They didn't say anything. Just did their investigation, gathered up the evidence and took off.'

'How was Zondo when you took him to his plane?'

Dupie had had enough. 'He was quiet, that's all. He was quiet when he arrived too. Hardly said a word.' He stood up with some difficulty. He had been sitting in a particularly low chair and had enjoyed several brandy and Cokes. 'Well, I'm off to bed. Have to get up early in the morning. Get either of you a nightcap?'

Johannes said no, and Madrid shook his head. With a wave, Dupie walked towards his tent, leaving them to watch the dying fire. Perhaps I'm wrong, he thought. Perhaps the murders have made me oversensitive. Perhaps they are just curious about a gruesome event.

Salome lay in bed, unable to sleep, her mind racing. She tried lying on her side, on her back, on her front. Nothing worked.

She heard Dupie's tent zipper open and close. That triggered more thoughts. What was he going to do if she shut down the camp? He'd been good to her, helping with everything here, as well as providing humour and support. The camp could not have survived this long without him.

She had known him almost all her life. He'd grown up on the neighbouring farm, and the two families were as one. Doing everything together, they helped each other in times of need, and often holidayed together on South Africa's glorious Natal coast.

Salome rolled over on to her back and thought about the Dupie of today. He was reliable, handy. And they were friends. What other friend did she have? None, she thought. He was the only one.

Salome heard Dupie's tent zip again. Must've had too much liquid! She thought she heard someone speaking, but decided it was her imagination. Suddenly the zip on her own tent opened. Startled, Salome sat up. How should she react if it were Dupie? A bright light momentarily blinded her. A second later, a rough hand clamped over her mouth.

'Don't make a sound! If you do, I'll kill you.' Salome did not recognise the voice. She clawed frantically at the hand, trying to pull it from her face. She felt she was suffocating.

'Stand up!'

The man grabbed her by an arm and jerked her to her feet. She clutched her nightdress at the neck and folded her other arm tightly across her breasts.

'Do what I say and you won't get hurt. I'm going to gag you and tie you up, but no one will touch you. Understand?' Salome stood, frozen. Suddenly the man grasped her throat and started choking her. He took his hand away from her mouth, and as she gasped for air, shoved a rag into it. Then he released his hold on her throat. She started screaming, but the gag dampened the sound almost completely. Finally he wound heavy tape around her head and over her mouth.

Terrified, Salome flailed at the man with her fists. With ease he caught her by the wrist and twisted her arm behind her back. He pushed her on to the bed.

'Put your hand behind you.' Salome did nothing, so gripping the flashlight in his teeth, the invisible intruder jerked her other arm behind her and taped her wrists tightly. Then he pulled her roughly to her feet.

'Move!' He pushed her out of the tent towards Dupie's.

In the adjacent tent, much the same scenario had taken place. Caught completely unawares, Dupie was now trussed, but not gagged. However, unlike Salome, he knew who his assailant was – Madrid, the man of few words. Madrid held a knife to his throat.

'You cause me trouble, I'll cut your throat like a fat pig,' he said.

'What do you want? You think we've got money? You're joking!' Dupie wondered how this was going to end.

Moments later, Salome was pushed into the tent, followed by Johannes, pistol in hand

'Down,' he said to her. She didn't move, so he shoved her down and she landed heavily on the ground. Then he bound her legs with a heavy plastic tie around her ankles, before turning to Dupie.

'Answer the questions. No one gets hurt. You lie, or you try anything clever, I kill her first. You understand?' Johannes jabbed Dupie in the ribs. Dupie nodded. Madrid stepped back so that he could watch Dupie's face.

'Did you take Zondo to the plane? Left him there like you said? Didn't see the plane?'

'Yes! I already told you.'

'Tell me again. Her life depends on it.'

Another jab in the ribs from Johannes. Dupie winced, then nodded.

'Say it!'

'Yes! I took him to the airstrip and left him there.'

'You're lying,' said Madrid. 'He never contacted the pilot.'

'Well that's what he told me.'

'The pilot came to fetch him the next day, but he wasn't there.'

'The pilot works for you?'

'I'll ask the questions!'

Dupie searched desperately for some way out. 'If the pilot works for you, Zondo would've needed a different plane to get away. Stands to reason!'

'Did he take his bags with him?'

Dupie nodded again.

'What bags did he have?' Madrid hissed.

'He had a suitcase and a tote bag,' Dupie said.

'What colour was the tote?' Another jab from Johannes. Harder this time.

'I think it was green. Maybe blue.'

'Where's Tinubu's luggage?'

Dupie grunted as Johannes jabbed his ribs again. 'The police took all his stuff. I think there was a suitcase. A brown suitcase.'

'Why do you think the murders were about drugs?' This time it was Johannes who asked, jamming the pistol barrel into Dupie's solar plexus.

'I'm just guessing.' Dupie gasped. He had been in many life-threatening situations in the war, but this felt different. Johannes was a typical thug, but Madrid's coldness frightened him. He had to find a way of getting out of this alive. 'What else could it be?'

'You'd better tell me what I want to know!' Madrid said. Johannes emphasised the point by pulling Dupie off the bed and kicking him in the belly.

'Where's Tinubu's briefcase?' Madrid asked.

Dupie shrugged. 'I suppose Zondo took it.'

Madrid raised his hand, and Dupie braced himself for the blow, but it was Salome he hit across the face, and the slap left an angry red mark, visible even in the dim light.

'You're lying to me! You said nothing about Zondo taking a briefcase.'

Dupie struggled. 'Leave her alone! It's got nothing to do with her!'

Madrid stuck the point of the knife into Salome's throat.

'I count to five. You don't tell me the truth, I'll cut her throat!' Madrid's voice was harsh. 'One. Two. Three. Four . . .' Salome was whimpering through the gag.

'Wait!' Desperately Dupie grasped for a plan, anything that would keep them alive. 'The police have it! It was in Tinubu's tent. Seemed very heavy.'

Johannes glanced at Madrid.

'Why didn't you tell me this before?' Madrid asked.

'The police told me to say nothing. Said it was top secret. Said I'd be in big trouble if I let on.'

'Did you see who took the briefcase?' Johannes kicked Dupie again.

'The fat detective,' Dupie responded quickly. 'Bengu. He's from Gaborone.'

'If you are lying, I'll cut her into pieces in front of you! Then I'll throw you to the crocodiles.' This time Johannes' kick caught Dupie on the mouth and nose. He felt a tooth break and blood pour down his cheek.'

'It's the truth. I swear!'

Johannes looked as though he was going to kick Dupie again, but Madrid stopped him.

'Maybe it's true. We're not going to get anything more out of them. Shut his mouth.'

Johannes pulled a rag from his pocket. 'Open your mouth!' he ordered.

But Dupie had had enough. '*Fuck* you!' he said, and clamped his mouth shut.

'Open!' Johannes hit Dupie on the side of his face. Dupie kept his mouth closed.

Johannes took the pistol by the barrel and clubbed Dupie on the side of the head. He went limp. Johannes stuffed the rag into Dupie's mouth and taped it tightly.

Madrid glowered. 'Maybe it's true,' he said again. 'Otherwise so-called Zondo is living it up in South America by now. Bastard!'

Johannes looked down at Salome, at the outline of her body, helpless, the terror in her eyes. He liked that. Then he saw the dismal coldness of Madrid, watching him. He shrugged.

'Let's get out of here,' he said.

CHAPTER 22

Dupie regained consciousness and immediately wanted to throw up. A foul-tasting rag was halfway down his throat. He tried to shift it by working his tongue. Eventually he moved it enough to relieve the pressure. He took stock of his situation. The side of his head ached, and some sort of tape was wrapped around his head, across his mouth. The gag was there to stay, and he could free neither his hands nor his legs. And the tent was pitch black. He couldn't see a thing.

Not good, he thought. These guys knew what they were doing. Dupie was thankful to be alive and relatively uninjured. He heard a muffled sound and remembered Salome. She's alive, he thought. Thank heaven. He grunted a response and rolled on to his side and wriggled towards where he thought she was. A few moments later his head touched her, but he could not tell where her head was. He grunted again. She replied in kind.

He wriggled until he thought he was pointing towards the tent door. He used his legs to push himself forward. On the third or fourth push, his head banged into something solid.

'Fuck,' he shouted, muffled through the gag.

He wriggled again, changing direction. Same result. This time his head hit the side of the tent. He turned himself a little to the right and pushed again. More tent. Again he turned to the right. Again, the tent.

I must find the opening, he thought.

But the next advance resulted in another sharp blow to the head.

Fucking hell, he thought. I may never get out.

After what seemed an eternity of turning and pushing, Dupie still had not succeeded. He lay exhausted. He had kicked over the table beside his bed, but it hadn't made enough noise to wake the staff. He lay on the floor, panting, despondent. He might have to wait for morning.

Then, in the distance, he heard the sound of an outboard motor.

The bastards, he thought. They've taken the boat. He ached all over, and the broken tooth throbbed.

Suddenly he heard Enoch's voice.

'Dupie! Dupie! You awake?'

Dupie made as much noise as he could through the gag. He saw a light outside the tent. Moments later the flap zipped open, and the beam of Enoch's flashlight caught Dupie first and then Salome.

'Shit!' Pulling a pocket knife from his trousers, Enoch dropped to his knees and cut Dupie's bonds. Dupie pulled the tape off his mouth and spat the rag out, wincing in agony as the cold air blew across his broken tooth.

'Fucking shit,' he said. 'The bastards!' He grabbed Enoch's knife and freed Salome.

'Are you all right?' he asked. 'Did they . . .'

'I'm fine,' she whispered. 'They didn't touch me.' She felt far away, watching from a distance.

'Thank God!' He helped her to her feet and wrapped her in his arms. She flung her arms around him and started sobbing.

'It's all right,' he murmured. 'We're both alive, and they've gone. I heard the motorboat.'

'Boat woke me,' Enoch said. 'Something was wrong. Something's always wrong!' He cursed in his home language. 'Was it the two men?'

Dupie nodded. 'The bastards. They were after Tinubu's briefcase. I'd better call the police.' He took Salome's hand, leading her to the dining area.

'Sit down,' he said gently. 'Enoch, get Salome a Scotch, then go and boil some water. A cup of coffee will go down well. I'll be back in a minute.' Salome reached for him, but he was already on his way. At the office tent he grabbed the Lee-Enfield rifle and slid a cartridge into the breech. Then he rummaged on his desk for his cell phone. When he found it, he dialled the Kasane police station. While waiting, he dug out his old service revolver, hidden at the back of a filing cabinet drawer.

'Kasane police station? This is Dupie du Pisanie at Jackalberry Camp – that's where the murders took place last week. We've just been attacked by two men connected to the murders. They may still be nearby.' But Dupie was sure they had left with the boat. Why would he be alive if they had wanted to stay? 'When can you get here?'

The policeman explained that they would not be able to get to Jackalberry Camp before morning. It was already nearly midnight, and it would be hours before anyone would be ready to leave. But he promised to contact the station commander.

'You've got to come now!' Dupie yelled. 'They may still be here. They could kill us!'

'I'll call you back,' the policeman said, and hung up.

Dupie cursed. Then he stuffed the phone into his pocket and returned to the dining area, firearms in hand.

He shoved the handgun at Enoch. 'Look after Salome while I check on the boat.'

Dupie walked quietly behind the guests' tents, over the ridge to the jetty. In the dim moonlight, he could see that the boat was gone. Then he went to where the *mokoros* were usually moored. There was nothing there. He shone Enoch's flashlight out to the lagoon, and saw the small boats floating, ghost craft on the glass-still water. He turned back to the dining area.

'All the boats are gone,' he told Enoch and Salome. He called Kasane police station again, telling the constable they had no boats, that they were stranded.

The policeman said he would alert all officers on the Namibian border, but that the police wouldn't get to the camp until the morning.

'They can only get here sometime tomorrow,' Dupie said after hanging up. 'There's nothing we can do but wait. I'm sure those bastards have gone, but we can't take a chance. Enoch, you face that way. Check the revolver's loaded. Salome, you face the kitchen. If you see anything, shout, and I'll shoot them.'

As the three of them settled down to spend the night peering tensely into the darkness, they heard the drone of a small plane in the distance.

Faint streaks in the easterly sky found the three still huddled together. Exhausted from tension and lack of sleep, they had struggled to stay awake, taking turns to walk around and stretch. Fear and mutual cajoling had spurred them on.

Suddenly Dupie's phone rang, causing them all to jump.

'Shit,' cursed Dupie, fumbling for the phone.

'This is Du Pisanie,' he whispered. The other two strained to hear.

Dupie related what had happened the night before. Then he listened carefully to the caller.

After hanging up, he said, 'That was Detective Mooka – the tall one. He'll be here as soon as he can, but he's not sure he can get a plane. He may have to drive. Anyway, it's too late. That plane we heard last night must've been them. No one else would fly a light plane in the middle of the night. It looks as though they've got clean away.'

CHAPTER 23

On Saturday afternoon after lunch, Kubu was sitting on his veranda, cup of tea in hand. Inevitably, his relaxed mood was interrupted by the telephone.

'Kubu,' Joy called from inside the house. 'It's for you. Tatwa.'

Kubu pulled himself from his seat and walked to the phone. Tatwa's found out something about the murders, he thought.

'Kubu, we've got a problem,' said Tatwa, ignoring Kubu's greeting. 'I'm at Jackalberry Camp. It's been attacked again.'

'What do you mean attacked again?' Kubu interjected.

'Well, last night two guests attacked Salome McGlashan and Dupie du Pisanie. They're alive, but Du Pisanie was quite badly assaulted. Happened about midnight, and they were tied and gagged. Then the intruders stole the camp's motorboat for their getaway. That woke Enoch Kokorwe, who found them tied up in Du Pisanie's tent.' He paused for a moment. 'Apparently they wanted to know what had happened to Zondo and where Tinubu's briefcase was.'

'Good heavens! Does Du Pisanie know who they were?'

'He's got their registration papers and so on, but they seem to be false, as you would expect. One was white, said he was from Spain; the other a black from South Africa. Threatened to kill both of them. McGlashan's very scared, as you can imagine. I've arranged to leave a couple of constables here for a few days.'

'What have you learned so far?' Kubu asked.

'Not much. No one on the island heard a thing. The police found *mokoros* from the camp floating on the river. They've all been returned to the camp. They also found the camp's Land Rover at the airstrip. They'd taken the keys from the office. And Dupie and Enoch both say they heard a small plane taking off not long after the attackers left. We've got plenty of fingerprints, to be processed as soon as I get back to Kasane. We've alerted all the border posts and so on, but we'll draw a blank, I'm sure. And, of course, Civil Aviation hasn't any flight plans on file for any plane going to the airstrip.'

'Who picked them up from the airstrip when they arrived?'

'Enoch,' Tatwa replied. 'But unfortunately he didn't note the registration. I would have thought after the murders, that would be an obvious thing to do.'

'Well, this seems to support the Zondo theory for the murders, doesn't it?' Kubu said. 'We'll have to spread our net even further to find him. And now we may have a motive. It sounds like a drug swap, and Zondo got greedy. How're the guests taking it?'

'They're panicked and want to leave immediately. I've spoken to them all and can't see any benefit from keeping them. I've told them they're free to leave. Dupie isn't happy about it because they were booked in for several more nights.'

'And the other staff?'

'The crazy cook says he didn't hear anything at all. Not surprising with that noisy bird in his tent. Beauty and Solomon weren't on the island. McGlashan is sleeping now. Du Pisanie is quite badly beaten up, but he refuses to go to Kasane for treatment. Says he'll take care of his broken tooth when he can. The rest will heal itself.'

After hanging up, Kubu wandered back to the veranda, collapsing into his favourite chair. Joy offered him a fresh cup of tea, and he nodded distractedly. So some other people – not very nice people – had missed Ishmael Zondo. Or perhaps they only missed the contents of Tinubu's briefcase. He wondered what their next move would be.

Madrid barely said a word from the time they had taken the motorboat to the time he landed the old Cessna 172 on the dirt strip on a farm near Hwange in western Zimbabwe. As soon as he touched down, the hurricane lamps marking the runway were extinguished, and everything was again dark. Thank God for portable GPS, he thought. It would be impossible to find this place at night without it.

Madrid was angry, his cold mind sifting through options to recoup his money. He had already invested significant time in this project. Hours spent planning with Joseph Chikosi, the leader of this rag-tag crew, and Peter Jabulani – Ishmael Zondo, as he had called himself at the camp; days on scouting missions; weeks on the farm, training the men.

People, he thought bitterly. They're all the same. Leave them on their own with a lot of money, and they can't resist the temptation.

He walked to the farmhouse. Chikosi was standing at the door waiting for him.

'Well? What did you find out?' Chikosi's voice was tense.

Madrid shrugged. 'Not much.'

'What do you think happened?'

'What do I think? I think your loyal lieutenant double-crossed you. I think your perfect Mr Jabulani took off with my money. Probably the other stuff too. Even the Pope would be tempted! But you sent him alone.'

'Are you sure it's all gone?'

'The manager at the camp said the police found a briefcase – Tinubu's briefcase. Didn't know what was in it, but said it looked heavy. I know who has it. Maybe they'd already switched, maybe not.'

'What are you going to do?' Chikosi asked after a few moments.

'I'm going to find out if the manager was telling the truth,' Madrid replied.

'And the mission?'

'That's your problem! Right now, I couldn't care less. I want to be paid for what I've already done. You better start looking for ways of raising the money. I've spent a lot on this already, and lots of people are waiting to be paid. What're you going to give us instead? More worthless promises? You better pray I find what I'm looking for in Gaborone.'

Chikosi slumped against the door. 'I can't believe it. I'd have trusted Jabulani with my life.'

Madrid sneered. 'Your life's not worth half a million dollars. Know what? I don't think your life's worth even one dollar right now.' With that, he shoved Joseph Chikosi out of his way and stalked into the house.

CHAPTER 24

Sunday was family day in the Bengu household. Kubu and Joy made a point of visiting his parents every Sunday after church. This Sunday they decided to bring the lunch so his mother could have a relaxed day. Of course, his father never cooked. He spent his time tending a small garden of vegetables and medicinal herbs at the back of the house.

Joy had a great love for her in-laws, and they treated her as a daughter. When Joy was fifteen, her mother died of tuberculosis, leaving her thirty-five-year-old husband to care for Joy, her brother, Sampson, and her sister, Pleasant. In typical African fashion, he was supported by his and his wife's families, who absorbed the children into their lives and homes. But five years later, he suffered a massive heart attack and died within a few days. Sampson was then twenty-one, Joy twenty and Pleasant eighteen. The children sold their father's general dealer's shop, and so had a little money for the future.

Joy and Pleasant took a secretarial course and decided to move to the capital, Gaborone, where there was more work and a larger pool of single men. Joy found a job as a clerk with the police department, while Pleasant joined a travel agency, where she soon upgraded her qualifications to become an agent rather than a secretary. Sampson stayed in Francistown and went to work for the government, in the Ministry of Lands and Housing.

Kubu's mother was overjoyed when he and Joy married. She had almost given up hope of her large, hard-working son ever finding a wife. Amantle liked Joy immediately and embraced her as one of the family. Even the reserved Wilmon emerged from his shell, showing her great affection.

Kubu was looking forward to the visit, not only for the socialising, but also for the opportunity to quiz Wilmon more about Goodluck.

On the drive to Mochudi, Kubu was preoccupied with the recent events at Jackalberry, and Joy knew that conversation would be futile. Normally, she and Kubu used this time to catch up, but today Kubu's mind was far away, so she resorted to the Sunday newspaper. Even Ilia had curled up on the back seat. Typically, she spent the entire forty- or fifty-minute trip with her nose out of the slightly open rear window, her stub of a tail wagging nonstop. However, as they turned into the road where Kubu's parents lived, she jumped up, yipping with excitement. She knew from experience that Wilmon and Amantle would spoil her.

After he and Joy had carried the various containers of lunch into the house, Kubu greeted Wilmon.

'Father,' he said. 'You are looking well.' He extended his right hand, touching his right arm with his left hand.

'David, you are welcome at my house.'

Kubu turned to Amantle and kissed her on the cheek. 'Mother, you too look well.'

The duties of the son discharged, Joy greeted both Amantle and Wilmon in the modern way – with warm hugs. Kubu always wished he could photograph Wilmon's face as Joy wrapped her arms around him. The usually impassive face managed to register happiness and reserve simultaneously.

Under normal circumstances, Kubu would not be able to raise the subject of Goodluck until after lunch, when the ladies went inside to wash the dishes and put the leftovers into little packets for freezing or refrigerating. Until that time, Amantle and Joy gossiped, while Wilmon and Kubu listened. However, this time, since much of Amantle's gossip surrounded Goodluck's tragic death, Kubu had an early opening.

'Father,' he said, 'when I was here on Wednesday, you couldn't understand why anyone would kill Goodluck Tinubu. Have you had any more thoughts about that? Or heard any from your friends?'

'When you asked me,' Wilmon said quietly, 'I thought you had made a mistake. I thought you had not identified him properly. I do not understand it.'

Kubu interrupted. 'The police were also worried about that, because when we sent the fingerprints to Zimbabwe, they told us he'd died in the war. So we thought we'd better make sure that it was the same man as the headmaster of the Raserura School. We showed a photo of him taken at the camp to the teachers, and they identified him.'

Wilmon shook his head. 'I know it is important to help the police, so I spoke to the wife of a friend of mine. She works as a cleaner at Raserura School. She says nobody can understand it. He worked the whole time for the children.' He sat quietly for a few seconds.

'Do you know if he had a girlfriend?'

'I thought about that and asked her,' Wilmon replied with a glimmer of pride at anticipating his son's question. 'She told me that no one had ever seen him with a woman.'

'What about Rra Madi?' Kubu asked.

Wilmon did not respond immediately. 'Rra Madi is also well respected in Mochudi. He was the assistant of Goodluck. He too is a good man. He will become headmaster, I think.'

'There's nothing you've heard that might help me? It doesn't make sense – a man with a good heart and no enemies, brutally murdered and disfigured.'

Amantle stood up to clear the table. 'A man like Goodluck, who does not have a wife, must have something to hide. Otherwise he could have been married a hundred times. Every single mother in town wanted to marry him. Maybe he did things or saw things during the war in Rhodesia that were always in his head. Maybe the children were his *muti* – his medicine for the mind.' When Amantle used this tone of voice, no disagreement was possible, because she was certain that what she said was the truth. As she picked up the tray, she continued, 'Maybe he met someone at the camp who was an enemy from the war. I am sure that must be it!'

'But Mother, that was thirty years ago! How would he remember?'

'Your birth caused me much pain,' Amantle said softly. 'And I remember every moment of it.'

*

'That was a strange visit,' Joy remarked as they were driving home. 'Normally it is warm and cosy. This time there was a chill, a sadness, I couldn't understand.'

'I felt it too,' Kubu said. 'It must be something to do with Goodluck's death. It raises difficult questions when someone everyone knows and admires dies violently. Why a man like that? Why did God let it happen? How can God be so callous? I am sure my father prayed about it at church this morning. Perhaps the sermon was about Goodluck. It affects a community like Mochudi deeply.'

They both lapsed into silence, thinking about their own beliefs, their own God.

CHAPTER 25

On Monday morning, Kubu arrived at the office to find his inbox already beckoning with new papers. Reading Tatwa's faxed report of the latest problems at Jackalberry Camp, as well as Dupie's and Salome's statements, his imagination recreated the camp and played out the events of Friday night. It was this introspective mood that was interrupted by the shrill ring of his telephone.

'Hello, this is Assistant Superintendent Bengu.'

'Superintendent Bengu? My name is Smith. John Smith. I was told you're investigating the murder of a very dear friend of mine, Goodluck Tinubu. Is that correct?'

Kubu confirmed this. He did not like the voice on the line. It was cool, falsely pleasant, dangerous. A white-male voice speaking English with an unfamiliar accent.

'Well, you see, I'm interested in recovering something of mine that Mr Tinubu had with him when he died. Do you know what I'm talking about?'

Kubu thought he did, but hesitated while he gestured to Edison to trace the call. 'His briefcase?'

'Yes, exactly. Very clever of you. I spoke to the police in Kasane, but they don't seem to have such an item. Perhaps you felt it would be *safer* with you in Gaborone?'

'Look, Mr Smith, I don't know who you are or what you want. I presume you can prove that you have a legitimate interest in this item? I think it would be best if you came to my office tomorrow, and we can discuss all this properly.'

'I'm nowhere near Gaborone, Mr Bengu.' The trace would later confirm that. 'I don't think it would be healthy for me to appear at the

Criminal Investigation Department anyway. Someone has already been killed for that briefcase, you know. I think we should meet privately. We can make a deal. A good deal for both of us. You do *have* the briefcase, don't you, Superintendent? Much safer with you, I'm sure.'

Kubu hesitated. He was sure that he was close to the core of the case. If he could get information out of Smith, he would understand why Goodluck had died and who was responsible. But how to do that? Smith seemed to think he was a corrupt cop with a valuable item to fence. Perhaps if he played along, he could flush the man out.

'I'm not saying I have it, but I'm not saying I don't. I am saying that we should meet and see what we can arrange. You know the briefcase has interesting contents, so I'm not keen on talking to any of your cronies either, Mr Smith. Only you.' He paused. 'You may find you can push around overweight lodge managers, but I promise you'll be sorry if you try that with me. Very sorry.'

There was a long silence. When Smith replied, it was brief and cold. 'Very well. You'll hear from us, *Kubu*.' Then the line went dead.

Kubu wondered how Smith knew his nickname, and what else he might know. He hoped he hadn't overplayed his hand.

Mabaku was apoplectic. 'Kubu, for one of our smartest detectives, how can you be so unutterably stupid? We don't know who these people are, or where we can find them. On the other hand, they know exactly who you are and where to find you. You've made yourself a target.' He gestured to the electronic inhabitants of his office. 'This is how we work nowadays. Computers, tracing phone calls and e-mails, fingerprint databases, DNA tests. Not standing in the street inviting potshots and trying to guess the direction the bullet came from!'

'Director, they're white foreigners. I'm sure they think I'm the stereotype African policeman. They think they're dealing with a corrupt cop, but actually they are dealing with the might of the whole Botswana Police Force!' Kubu tried to make it sound impressive, but Mabaku was not buying it.

'The might of the Botswana Police Force has other things to do with its time! Other cases to work on! It's pretty clear now what happened.

They were using Tinubu to courier money – drug money, whatever. The other side of the coin – Zondo – decided to keep the money for himself. Open and shut. No attacks on innocent tourists. No international intrigue. And Langa was on their trail and got in the way. Exit Langa. Two and two. Four. Now you've complicated everything! Do you think they'll be happy if you give them an empty briefcase?'

Kubu tried to interrupt the tirade. 'I don't think Tinubu was a drug smuggler. And this was the only thing I could think of to draw them into the open.'

Mabaku glared at him. 'Edison stays in contact with you at all times. You don't arrange any private meetings. I'm informed of everything. Beforehand! We don't know how this Smith is going to react, and I don't want any surprises. No more surprises!' He thumped his fist to emphasise each of the last three words in turn.

Kubu nodded acquiescence and left to find Edison. He was beginning to wonder if he'd been as clever as he had thought. He would be very careful to ensure that the director got no more surprises. He was sure he could manage that.

But he was quite wrong.

PART THREE
Unforgiving Minute

Fill the unforgiving minute with
sixty seconds' worth of distance run.

Rudyard Kipling, *If*

CHAPTER 26

The Munro sisters had made their way through the Okavango delta and were now back at the comfortable Grand Palm Hotel in Gaborone. Trish wanted to rest, and Judith decided to relax by the pool. The visit to Jackalberry Camp had been upsetting and disconcerting, a confluence of events impossible to understand. The unwanted extra days at the camp had added to the stress, particularly as Salome – who had been friendly before – appeared to regret telling them her story and seemed to avoid them.

The Okavango sojourn had been a relief, yet there had been no closure to what had happened at the camp. The answers were here in Gaborone, not in the pristine waterlands of northern Botswana. Judith lay beside the pool feeling sweat form and evaporate, hoping that an hour in the sun would help relieve her tension.

From the other side of the pool, a younger man checked her out and smiled. She smiled back in thanks for the compliment, expecting nothing more. He dived into the pool, swimming strongly while she watched. After a while he pulled himself out and walked over to her.

'Sit here?' he asked, looking down at her. She nodded, smiling again, watching water drip from long black hair on to his tanned shoulders.

'Sorry, English bad. Portuguese. Mozambique. José,' he said and laughed.

She liked his accent and his strong face. 'Judith,' she said, smiling.

'Drink?' he asked, waving to a passing waiter.

She nodded.

'Gin with tonic?'

She nodded again.

José stretched out on the beach chair next to hers. 'Here often?' he asked.

Judith laughed. He laughed too, showing startlingly white teeth in his dark face.

Walking back to her room after an hour of flirting with José, Judith thought about men and love. She and Trish had experienced both – even marriage in her case – but it all seemed transitory. Perhaps she and Trish were too close. Sharing their lives since early childhood, their work, their interests. They were best friends and always had been. Their men never got to play that role. So what was left after the passion faded? Her mind turned to Salome. For her there had been no passion, no romance, perhaps no lovers at all. Just pain and violence that had now resurfaced.

She found Trish sitting on her bed reading the letter from Shlongwane again. Her face was pale and strained. Perhaps she had even been crying. Her eyes looked red. Judith bit her lip. She didn't want to revisit the horror and death. She wanted to tell Trish about José, to have dinner with him, perhaps to play tennis the next morning.

'I'm going to have a shower and get changed,' she said.

But Trish stopped her. 'Shlongwane said he was supposedly killed after an attack on a farm, Judith. An attack on a farm! You don't think . . . ? Surely it's not possible.'

Judith pulled the towel tighter around her shoulders. 'I'm getting cold,' she said.

'I can't bear it. Will you phone the school? Please. I can't face it. I have the number. We have to know.'

Why? Judith wondered. Why do we always need to confirm our fears? Why did we start this? Why must we finish it?

'Give me the number,' she said.

CHAPTER 27

Moremi had been dreaming of far-off lands, of exotic dances, and of colourful markets where women compared saris and talked in strange tongues. When he awoke, he had a hankering for a curry – not one that cauterised the taste buds, but one that seduced with hints of tantalising flavours.

'We'll do a *bobotie*, Kweh. What do you think?' Moremi asked his feathered friend, who was sitting on a kitchen cupboard. Kweh cocked his head and chortled a reply.

'I knew you'd agree. Everyone likes our *bobotie*!' Moremi took three medium onions from the wire vegetable rack, and two large garlic cloves. Then he broke off a couple of centimetres of fresh ginger. At the table, he started peeling them all, sometimes humming, sometimes chatting to Kweh. When he was finished, he used a large knife to coarsely chop them into pieces.

'There you are,' he said. 'Now for the apples.' He took two green apples from a fruit basket and peeled them too. 'This is for the *bobotie*, Kweh! Not for you. You can have the peel.' Moremi threw a long strand of apple peel to Kweh, who let it fall on the top of the cupboard. Then, clutching it in his claw, he nibbled on it, occasionally spitting bits out.

Moremi poured two cups of milk into a bowl and dropped in a couple of slices of bread. Then he wandered over to the oven, struck a match, and lit the gas. 'Two-thirty C means four-fifty F. Two-thirty C means four-fifty F,' he chanted. He took a kilogram package of ground beef from the fridge. 'Better if lamb. Better if lamb,' he muttered, unwrapping it.

Suddenly he stopped what he was doing and turned to Kweh. 'Solomon's *mokoro*, Kweh. It was here. The morning after the murders.

Do you remember? We thought Solomon and Beauty were here to set up for breakfast. But they came later with Dupie. So why was it here? Solomon's *mokoro*?' Kweh looked as if he was concentrating, but didn't offer any insights. Nevertheless the cook nodded. 'Maybe that's it. Maybe it was here the day before too. You could be right. You could be right. We should ask him.'

Getting back to his cooking, he tossed the beef into a frying pan and browned it, spooning it into a large bowl when it was done. Then he threw the onion, garlic and ginger into the pan.

With a little smile on his face, Moremi picked up a piece of onion that had eluded the pan and tossed it to Kweh, who caught it deftly in his beak but immediately spat it out. 'Go away! Go away!' he cried in disgust.

'Sorry! Sorry! Just a joke!'

Moremi rummaged on a shelf in the cupboard, emerging with a container of curry powder. He spooned a couple of tablespoons on to the translucent onions and stirred. 'Too dry, too dry!' He grabbed several lemons, cut them in half, and squeezed the juice into the pan. Now the curry formed a paste. He also added a couple of tablespoons of brown sugar and a sprinkle of salt. 'Stir, stir, stir the pan. Stir it very well.' He spooned the mix on to the beef in the bowl. Then he threw in the grated apple. 'What's left, Kweh?' There was no response. Kweh was finishing off the apple peel.

'Nuts and raisins! You like them!' After another visit to the cupboard, Moremi tossed a cup of raisins and half a cup of slivered almonds into the pot. Then he lifted the bread out of the milk, squeezing all the liquid back into the bowl. Into the pot went the bread, followed by a raw egg. With a gleeful look, he plunged his hands into the pot and mixed all the ingredients, squeezing the mixture between his fingers. When it was done, he licked his fingers. 'Yummy, yummy! Too mild. Too mild.' He washed his hands and added another tablespoon of curry powder. 'Powder too old, Kweh. We'll get some more at the Kachikau market.' Again he plunged his hands in and mixed. This time Kweh flew down on to Moremi's shoulder and peered into the pot. Moremi picked out a raisin and offered it to Kweh, who hesitated before swallowing it. He flapped his wings. Perhaps the raisin was too spicy.

Moremi found a casserole dish and spooned the mixture into it, pushing it down so the top was flat. He cracked two eggs into the milk in the bowl and whipped them with a fork. When the mixture was smooth, he poured it onto the meat, covering it completely. Finally he stuck several bay leaves into the meat.

'Into the oven. Into the oven!'

Fifteen minutes later, when mouthwatering aromas were emanating from the oven, Moremi lowered the temperature, and let the *bobotie* cook for another half an hour. Then, with a flourish, he delivered it to the guests' tables, with a large bowl of steamed rice, coloured with turmeric, and a small bowl of Mrs Ball's original chutney.

'What is it, Moremi? It's delicious! All the different tastes; different textures! It's wonderful.' These guests obviously loved the *bobotie*, because the casserole dish was empty.

Moremi wandered from the kitchen, enjoying their pleasure. Several guests clamoured for the recipe. 'Will I be able to get all the ingredients in the States?' one asked.

'Of course,' Moremi answered with authority, although he'd never left Botswana. The discussion about *bobotie* continued for some time until curiosity had been satiated. Finally the guests retired to their tents to rest through the heat of the day, and Moremi proudly returned to his kitchen. In the glow of his culinary success, the issue of Solomon's *mokoro* was completely forgotten.

Salome had watched a married couple at lunch. She envied their closeness, the shared glances and mutual comfort. After lunch, she spent an hour alone in her tent, thinking. After the attack on the camp, she knew she had to leave as soon as possible. Fear was everywhere. She had to battle to stop herself grabbing the Double Cab keys and driving as far as she could. Anywhere! As long as it was away from the police and away from Madrid and Johannes. All the ghosts of the past had resurfaced. How could they now be exorcised? Options rattled about in her mind as she stared out at the lagoon. When she came to a decision, she went to find Dupie.

He was in his office. The desk had been cleared of papers – and the Watching Eye was nowhere in evidence – but it was now covered with gun parts, squeeze bottles of light oil, and brass ammunition cartridges covered with mouldy verdigris. She hoped they were safe to handle, because Dupie was polishing them with Brasso. His Lee-Enfield rifle was spread in pieces on the desk as was his illegal Rhodesian Army-issue revolver. They were cleaned and polished and shone with gun oil.

Dupie looked up at her. 'They took me by surprise,' he said as though in reply to a challenge. 'That won't happen again. This is an island. Islands are hard to conquer. Ask Winston Churchill.'

Salome shook her head. 'I'm terrified to stay, Dupie. The attack was the last straw. I have to get out.' Dupie touched her gently on the arm. 'Anyway, I've been looking at the accounts. It's not going to work.'

'What's not going to work?'

'The camp was already in trouble before the murders,' Salome continued. 'But now I simply don't have enough to cover our expenses. You sent Enoch to get supplies. Thank God we've got accounts with the shops in Kasane. But when those accounts come in, I'll be hard pressed to cover them. And as for the renewal of the concession next year, we won't come close.'

'Don't worry, Salome. Things will look up. We'll be okay.'

She was touched by the 'we', but didn't want reassurance. She needed to leave. She shook her head without replying.

'We can use the rest of the money in my savings account. That'll keep us going for the moment. Till things turn around.'

'That's finished, Dupie. After paying the accounts and the staff wages this month, there'll be just a few hundred pula left.'

Dupie pouted and pushed his chair away from the desk to allow his stomach more space. 'Well, maybe we need a change.'

She noted the 'we' again.

'There are other opportunities,' he continued. 'Maybe we need to try something else, do something new, go somewhere new. We've got lots of options.' He started assembling the revolver, clicking the chamber into place and loading it with freshly polished ammunition. Then he shoved it into his belt.

Salome looked at the solidity of him, the size of him. It was as though the cramped office with its crude furniture was a theatre set, two-dimensional. Dupie was the only substantial thing. He has always been the only substantial thing, she thought, surprised. Ever since that one particular night in Rhodesia. But as always, her mind shied away from the horror of that night, dragging her attention back to the present, away from the ghosts. For twelve years he's been the anchor here, asking nothing. Hinting, yes, wanting, perhaps, but not asking. And twelve years later it's still 'we'. Suddenly she wanted to tell him how she felt – not suddenly felt, but suddenly understood. But she wasn't sure what to say, or even if he'd want to hear it ten years on. Well, she decided, start and see where you finish.

'Dupie, I—' But she was interrupted by the sudden crackle of the two-way radio coalescing into Enoch's voice. At once Dupie jumped up and adjusted the volume.

'Yes, hello, Enoch. I can hardly hear you. Say again.' There followed a broken discussion of mechanical matters concerning the trailer. Enoch was at the extreme range of the radio, and sometimes his voice was swamped by interference. After frustrating dialogue, Dupie said, 'Okay, just get back to the trailer and hang on there. Wait. With. The. Trailer. Just stay where you are! I'll come out with my tools. Over and out.'

Dupie turned to Salome. 'The trailer's broken down. Sounds like the wheel bearings have seized. Just what we need right now. Enoch wanted to leave it there and pick it up on his way back. That would've been the end of it! Don't worry. I'll get it rolling. I'll need tools.' He was already heading for the office to collect the keys to his vehicle and to the storage shed on the other side of the river. Salome followed him, but she realised that her moment had passed.

'I'll get Solomon to take me over in the motorboat. Tell him to meet me at the jetty. Pack me some drinks, would you?'

She nodded and started for the kitchen, but he stopped her. 'We're not expecting anyone else. Don't let anyone come across until I'm back. No one comes on to the island.' He pulled the revolver out of his belt and offered it to her. 'No one. Okay?'

She nodded and took the gun, liking the feel of it and appreciating the mixture of his concern and his confidence. 'I feel as though I'm in the Scouts,' she said, smiling.

'That's the Selous Scouts,' said Dupie, and laughed.

She leaned over and kissed him on the cheek, avoiding the frontal defence of his stomach.

He looked surprised, pleased.

'I'll be back in a couple of hours. Don't worry.' He gave her a hug and hefted a jerry can of fuel for the motorboat. There was a jauntiness to his step as he headed for the boat, whistling something he'd picked up from Moremi, but out of tune.

Salome hid the gun before organising the drinks and snacks. When she got back to her tent, she listened to the fading sound of the motorboat crossing to the mainland.

When Dupie returned, the sunset was swimming in the lagoon. Salome went to meet him at the jetty. He was sweaty and had taken off his khaki bush shirt to expose a net undershirt, originally white but greyed by repeated washing, and now smeared with grease and dust. He was surprisingly cheerful and complimentary of Enoch. 'Did a good job. Had the trailer up and the wheel off when I got there. But it was nearly two hours up the road.'

'What's wrong with it?'

'Wheel bearing, as I thought. Couldn't fix it properly, so I improvised. Used nylon rope and grease. I was able to tow it back. Enoch will try to get parts in Kasane tomorrow morning. It was too late to go on tonight. Told him to sleep in the vehicle and head in tomorrow. He can cram what we need into the Double Cab. He should be back here by afternoon.'

Salome nodded, accepting all this as in Dupie's domain. 'Moremi is expecting you to do a bush *braai* for the guests. I thought we could all eat together since there're only four of them. He's made a great marinade. Good rump steak too, from that new butcher you found. And salads.'

Dupie nodded and smiled at her, flushed by the sunset. 'I'll take a shower. We'll open a bottle of wine on the house. And some beers. Shit, I could handle a beer. Tell some stories while we cook. Get everyone happy.'

She knew he would. She knew the alcohol would relax her too. She would find her moment after all. Not to tell him her feelings. Just to ask him to come back with her to her tent.

CHAPTER 28

William Boardman left the lounge bar of the Maun Toro Lodge disappointed, and strode angrily outside into the cool air. It was after ten! He had been waiting for over an hour, his voice-mail messages unreturned. He had been looking forward to an interesting and lucrative evening. He had imagined that certain pieces of African art he wanted badly were within his grasp. Either the price would be right, or they could be obtained by less upfront means. But the meeting had not taken place, and the whole trip was largely wasted.

However, tomorrow there would be hell to pay. He would make absolutely sure it was understood that nothing was negotiable. He clenched his teeth and started drafting a letter in his head as he walked. A letter he had no intention of sending, but which he could use to get what he wanted. 'Dear Superintendent Bengu,' it would begin. 'I have spent some time thinking about the events of that awful night and the following morning. Playing it over in my head like a videotape. Trying to ensure that the shock and denial had not caused me to forget something of importance.'

He liked the videotape simile. It sounded serious and genuine. 'I have recalled something that could be significant.' Or perhaps, 'By freezing frames I came across an important item.' That sounded a bit contrived. 'Over the last few days some frozen memory frames have changed my view of what I saw quite dramatically.' Maybe leave out 'quite dramatically'. He was already feeling better, the start of a smile.

He found himself at the door of his bungalow. It was near the end of a row of identical thatched one-bedroom units, efficiently but unattractively arranged. All the surrounding cottages were in darkness, and only an outdoor light at knee level gave a pinkish low-energy illumination. He had to check his key and squint at the number to make sure he was at the correct cottage.

He was still fumbling with the key in the lock when he felt a knife at his throat and a hand over his mouth. He jerked with reflexive fright and felt the knife blade break the skin, warm blood trickling. Then he didn't move.

'Quiet! You don't get hurt. Understand?'

He tried to answer, but the hand was too tight over his mouth. He nodded as hard as he could against the restraining hand. He felt the door open, and he was shoved through. He almost fell, but recovered, and turned to face his attacker. The bedside light he had left on revealed a man – all black. Black tracksuit, black boots, black ski mask revealing only dark pupils. The only contrast was the whites of his eyes in the mask slits.

The man kicked the door closed behind him.

'We talk,' he said. 'Just talk.'

Boardman recognised the assailant's voice. Surprise burst out of him when silence would have been more prudent. 'I know you, damn you! What the hell do you think you're up to?'

The man in black hit him with both fists clenched together. It was supposed to knock Boardman down, to prepare him for what was to follow. But being recognised so easily was a shock, and the blow was not well judged. Boardman collapsed to an unnatural position on the floor, eyes staring at the ceiling.

'Shit!' The attacker hesitated, breathing harder than the exercise justified. 'Wake up, shithead! Or you get hurt!'

When there was no response, he aimed some powerful kicks and felt a rib snap. Then he broke the man's nose with his heel. It was only when his boot smashed into his groin and still there was no response that he accepted that William Boardman was dead. He cursed his bad luck, and did what needed to be done.

Ten minutes later he slipped from the cottage, slunk through the darkness to the road, and disappeared.

CHAPTER 29

Enoch's first stop in Kasane was at a spare-parts shop. He greeted the mechanic in Setswana and explained that he needed a set of wheel bearings for a Venter off-road trailer. The man shook his head. 'We'll have to order them from Johannesburg. We don't keep specialised parts like that. No call for them. Maybe I can patch it up in the meanwhile?'

'Dupie decided to tow it back to Jackalberry Camp,' Enoch told him. 'We got it rolling, and he thinks he can fix it himself. Save a few pula.' He sounded sarcastic.

The mechanic took the details and promised to let them know the price and how long it would take to get the parts from South Africa.

Enoch shrugged. 'I'm starved,' he said. 'I only had a snack for the road and had to spend the night out in the bush. Nothing for supper. I'm off for some breakfast at the Old House. Can I use your bathroom to clean up?' His shirt was streaked with grease and dust, and his hands needed scrubbing. His pants looked as though he'd slept in them.

He emerged looking more respectable, thanked the mechanic, and headed for the casual and friendly restaurant. He explained his grubby, rumpled state to the owner – a Chinese woman whose eclectic menu included the best spring rolls north of Gaborone – and ordered a hearty English breakfast, which would have been a hit in London at three times the price. Enoch worked his way through multiple fried eggs, bacon, sausage, mushrooms, and lashings of toast. It was a special treat. He felt he deserved it.

Satisfied, he toyed with the idea of visiting Lena, his local girlfriend. She lived on the southern outskirts of the town, and would be pleased to see him – unless she had another engagement. He decided against the possible embarrassment. He still had to do the shopping and endure the four-hour drive back to the camp.

His next stop was the liquor store, where he loaded cases of wine, beer and harder stuff. It was around eleven by the time he got to the supermarket, which was not yet busy. He worked through his list, reducing cases to single bottles, skipping bulky items, which would normally go in the trailer. After he had paid, one of the shop assistants helped him to pack the Double Cab. It was a tight fit. Again he had to explain the absence of the trailer.

'Weren't you scared sleeping out alone in the bush?' asked the assistant.

Enoch shook his head. 'Nothing happened.'

His next visit was to Mario's Meat Market on the outskirts of town, where cooler boxes awaited him crammed with frozen vacuum-packed meat. He checked his list to make sure he had everything. Dupie wouldn't be pleased if some item was left off, and Moremi was very particular. With no room in the back, the cooler boxes made a tower on the passenger seat and threatened to collapse on him if he cornered too quickly.

Finally he stopped in at the Mowana Safari Lodge to collect an item left behind there by one of Jackalberry's current guests. As he waited for it, he noticed a man sitting under the thatch overlooking the river. He looked familiar. Enoch walked to a window in the lounge area to get a better view. It was Boy Gomwe. Gomwe glanced up and quickly turned away to face the river. Enoch was puzzled. Gomwe had returned to South Africa as soon as he had left Jackalberry. What was he doing in Kasane a week later? He shrugged. That was Gomwe's business.

Thoughtful, he collected his package, walked back to the Double Cab and headed for the camp, taking the tarred road through Chobe towards Ngoma.

It would be four hours of hard bush driving before he got back to Jackalberry.

Gomwe was shocked. When he had turned to beckon a waiter for another gin and tonic, he had seen Enoch Kokorwe standing in the lounge. Was that coincidence? Or was Enoch checking up on him? If so, why? What did he know? Could the Jackalberry people be on to him? Gomwe turned quickly to face the river. Perhaps Enoch hadn't seen him, but the sooner he tied up his business and got out of Kasane the better.

He had checked into the Mowana Safari Lodge that morning, tired after the drive. He would have liked to relax, but he was waiting for a man whom he knew only as Mandla. He thought back to his meeting in Johannesburg a few days earlier. He had shown that money-man Jarvis who was important. He had been furious that Jarvis didn't want to help after what had happened at the Jackalberry Camp. Jarvis had told him that there was a great opportunity there. That a steady supply of money was headed there. Probably for heroin. That it should be easy to make a killing. Follow the money, he'd said. And Gomwe had.

'Bullshit!' The couple at the next table were startled by the outburst from the man sitting alone. They stood up and moved to the far end of the bar.

Easy to make a killing, he thought. What a load of crap. He wondered whether Jarvis had tried to set him up. He was lucky to have got out of Jackalberry without suspicion. If, indeed, he had. He was worried about being spied on by Enoch.

He took off his dark glasses and polished them on his floral shirt. He looked around for the man he was to meet. Mandla who? he wondered. Still, it was good to be cautious. After all, *he* had been very careful to check that he hadn't been followed.

Jarvis, he thought. Poor Jarvis, who thinks he's a big shit just because his bosses are big money-laundering shits. Thinks he can choose whether to help me. He wanted to back out after Jackalberry. I showed him. Threatened to beat the shit out of him. Fucking coward had snivelled that Mandla was big up here. Speak to him. He'll point you in the right direction. Gomwe put his dark glasses back on. He'd fucking well better!

Gomwe was on his fourth drink when a short, stocky man sat down at his table. 'I'm Mandla,' he said quietly. Gomwe turned at look at him. The man looked around nervously. Another arsehole, Gomwe thought. He'll be just like Jarvis.

'Little late, aren't you?'

'Just being careful. Wanted to be sure you weren't followed.'

'Not a chance,' Gomwe said, louder than necessary. 'After the Jackalberry screw-up, I check my back the whole time. I'm clean.'

'So what can I do to help a friend of Jarvis?' Mandla's lips smiled, but not his eyes.

Gomwe leaned forward. 'I know shit comes through the border around here. I want to expand my business. Into wholesale. I need a contact from the other side, from Zimbabwe or Zambia.'

Mandla didn't respond, but stared impassively at Gomwe.

After a few seconds, Gomwe couldn't bear the silence.

'I've got good contacts all over,' he said, bravado creeping into his voice. 'And my business is growing.'

Mandla continued to gaze at him without saying a word.

'Come on, man,' Gomwe spluttered. 'If you get me the contact, I'll make it worth your while.'

'And what about the people who are already in the business? They won't like it.'

'No, tell them I'm not going to take any of their customers. I have my own. Good, serious customers. I won't touch theirs. I don't need them.'

Mandla stared at Gomwe for a few minutes.

'Very well,' he said quietly. 'There's going to be a trade in two days at a place called Elephant Valley Lodge, just outside Kazangula. I've made a reservation for you there in the name of Boy Biko. The travel agent in the lobby has it. Pay them in cash.'

Gomwe had no problem with that. He was always keen to move the cash he had received from his clients. 'When do I go?'

'Tomorrow. Settle in. Something will happen in the next week.'

'A week! You're mad! You think I have nothing better to do than sit around at a game lodge for a week?'

'Do you good to relax.'

'Why can't I meet these people here? Or if it must be at this other place, why can't you set up a meeting for tomorrow?'

'You think this works on a timetable? The principals aren't here now. They'll be here for a trade in the next few days. Check in at Elephant Valley Lodge. Someone will contact you. Then it's up to you. Everyone will be nervous about you – even with my introduction.' A glimmer of a smile crossed Mandla's lips. He stood up. 'I'd like my money now. The amount Jarvis told you to bring.'

Gomwe pulled an envelope out of his pocket and shoved it towards Mandla.

'I'm paying a lot for fucking little. No names, no arrangement. Just cool my heels and wait for something to happen. This better work out or you'll be hearing from me again.'

'Don't worry. It will work out. Just the way we've planned.' Mandla pocketed the money and left without a further word.

If everyone in the trade is such an idiot, Gomwe thought, I'll make a fortune. They couldn't organise themselves out of a paper bag. He looked around and caught the attention of a waiter. 'Bring me another gin and tonic. A double.'

As Mandla sat down in his car, he pulled out his mobile phone and dialled a South African number. He got voice mail. 'Jarvis, it's Mandla. I met your friend. He drinks too much. He'll be at Elephant Valley Lodge tomorrow. You wanted a favour; you owe me.' Then he cut the connection and drove off. He had other business to handle, important business.

CHAPTER 30

As Kubu walked to Mabaku's office, Edison passed on a message from deputy headmaster Madi. One of the journalists from England had phoned and asked for Mr Tinubu. She had expressed condolences when she heard the news of his murder, but hadn't seemed particularly shocked. Perhaps it was because she hadn't known the late headmaster, Madi had suggested. Or perhaps she already knew he was dead, Kubu thought. He was greatly looking forward to his next meeting with the Munro sisters.

Once again Mabaku was in a foul mood. He glared at Kubu, who to the best of his recollection had done nothing to annoy his boss. Mabaku immediately disabused him.

'Your friend William Boardman got himself killed in Maun.'

Kubu wanted to respond that Boardman was certainly not his friend, but the shock of the news erased that. 'Killed? What happened?'

Mabaku growled. 'Beaten up. Tortured. Murdered.'

Kubu collapsed into a chair without invitation. 'Do we know why? Any suspects?'

Mabaku glared at him. 'Probably the mob that attacked Jackalberry Camp. They want something and aren't particular about how they get it.' He paused, recalling Monday's phone call. 'You haven't heard anything from so-called Smith, have you? No bribes of French champagne delivered to your house?'

Kubu was disturbed by the concern below the sarcasm. 'No, nothing, Director. I suppose he saw through my ploy. I'm not a great actor. But why go after Boardman? He didn't have the brief-case, or anything else as far as we know. Was his wife in Maun with him?'

Mabaku shook his head. 'He was there alone. He was found this morning in a bungalow at the Maun Toro Lodge. Beaten up, with cigarette burns on the face and chest. Room trashed. Eventually they killed him and left, with or without what they wanted.' Worry crept into his voice again. 'That idiot Notu is in charge of the case. He thinks it's a break-in that went wrong. Moron!' He stood up and paced to the window, taking comfort in Kgale Hill.

Kubu pouted. Notu was indeed an idiot, who held his job because he had married the niece of someone very influential. Only his undeniable incompetence had kept him from more senior positions. So far. Now Kubu was up against some very nasty people whose attention was focused on the police, thanks to Kubu himself.

'I'll go up to Maun tomorrow,' he said. 'I'd like Tatwa to come down from Kasane. I think I could use an elevated perspective.'

Mabaku just looked at him and nodded, the joke falling flat. 'Leave early,' he said.

It was a long road, and boring. Just over three hundred kilometres past Mochudi to Serowe, where Kubu allowed himself a quick bacon-and-cheeseburger washed down with a chocolate milkshake and coffee for the caffeine. Then four hundred kilometres on the flat, straight road west to the edge of the Okavango delta. At six p.m., after twelve hours of driving, he arrived at Maun. Once a sleepy gateway to the miracle of the delta, it was now a bustling tourist town shunned by the old-timers who still liked to think of Botswana as the old, wild Africa. Expecting less than enthusiastic cooperation from Notu, he checked into the Toro Lodge in order to have an excuse to do his own snooping. Plus, it was inexpensive; Mabaku would approve. A mediocre supper at the Lodge restaurant completed the exhausting day.

He was too tired to explore. After a hot bath, he crawled into bed with the newspaper, and called Joy. She was bubbling with enthusiasm. Pleasant's boyfriend Bongani had come to dinner with them, and the evening had gone very well. They had emptied one of Kubu's bottles of red wine, perfectly matched with her steak and mushroom sauce, and greatly enjoyed it. Kubu tried to be enthusiastic. He was suffering from heartburn from the doughy chicken pie he'd eaten for supper.

After the call, Kubu fell asleep within minutes, the reading light still on, and the *Daily News* on his chest heaving in time with his snores.

CHAPTER 31

'Well, you've come a long way to take an interest in my case.' Assistant Superintendent Notu's manner indicated that he considered the interest to be interference.

Kubu tried to be diplomatic. 'I think your case may be directly relevant to mine. Ours,' he corrected himself, looking at Tatwa.

'And how is that?' Notu examined his fingers as if expecting a more sensible answer from them.

'Well, the murder victim was one of only ten people on an island in the Linyanti where the double murder we're investigating took place.'

'This man, Broadman I think was his name, was the victim of a violent robbery that went over the top.' Notu shrugged. 'There are such things as coincidences.'

Kubu shook his head. 'I keep hearing that. I don't believe in them. And his name was *Board*man.'

Tatwa interrupted. 'Assistant Superintendent Notu, do you have many opportunistic robberies where the victim is forced into his hotel room, robbed, tortured, beaten to death and his room ransacked? It's certainly never happened in Kasane, as far as I know.'

'*Sergeant* Mooka, perhaps you haven't seen as many robberies as I have. Perhaps *Kasane* is still a bit of a backwater. Here there are too many rich, careless tourists. Easy prey.' He rubbed his chin and then resumed the study of his fingers. 'It's unfortunate,' he finished, without apparent regret.

'Sergeant Mooka is right,' Kubu said firmly. 'It doesn't add up. This wasn't a street mugging. The perpetrators waited for Boardman outside his room. Forced him into it. And beat him to death. For a few hundred pula? In a hotel unit where there was a good chance of him being heard screaming? I don't buy it. Let me tell you what happened on our island in the Linyanti last week.' Kubu described the attack on Jackalberry Camp. 'Do you still think this is a coincidence?'

Notu stroked his jowls again and checked his watch. 'What do you want to know?'

Kubu sighed. 'Please take the time to tell us exactly what happened.'

'I told you what we think. You're the one who thinks differently.' Nevertheless Notu fetched the file. 'The body is still with the pathologist.' He looked up at Kubu. 'Your chap, MacGregor, drove up to examine it at the scene. You should be satisfied with that at least.' He pored over the file again. 'From his examination, he thinks the victim was killed between ten that Monday night and three the next morning. Actually we know he died around half past one.'

He paused, but Kubu was listening intently and didn't comment. Tatwa was taking notes. 'I'll tell you why later,' Notu said, his moment spoilt. 'The man had been assaulted. Punched in the face, kicked, or attacked with a bat. He had cigarette burns on his face and chest. Brutal.' He set aside the preliminary notes from the pathologist and pulled another note towards him. 'His wallet was gone. But his car keys were still in his pocket. They searched the rest of his room too. Threw all the stuff out of his suitcase, ripped up the bed, searched the closet, threw out his toiletries.'

He looked up at Kubu again, pointedly ignoring Tatwa. 'Maybe they thought he had more money hidden in the room? Perhaps they had a tip-off from someone? He'd been going around markets buying items for cash. Plenty of cash. Curio dealer or something.' There was a note of triumph in the last statement. These interlopers ought to appreciate his thoroughness.

'And what have you done about catching the murderers?' Kubu asked, unimpressed.

Notu sighed. 'Well, it's early days yet. We've interviewed the hotel staff and the guests who were around. But no one seems to have heard anything. Except the person who called in.' This was his trump card, and he meant to make them beg for it. This time Tatwa obliged at once.

'Who called in? What did he say?'

'One of the guests. He heard shouting and screams. He phoned reception to complain. He thought it was a domestic row getting out of hand. The reception guy was half asleep but walked around the camp and heard nothing. He checked with the security guard, but he hadn't heard anything either. So he shrugged it off and went back to sleep. He forgot all about it until they found the body in the morning.'

Tatwa was almost out of his seat. 'What did the guest hear, exactly? Did he hear any words? Could he confirm the exact time?'

Again Notu's fingers seemed the better company. 'Actually we couldn't find the guest who phoned. He must have checked out before the body was discovered. But we got a good report from the receptionist.'

'And you haven't tried to trace him?' Kubu was incredulous.

'What more is it going to add? The receptionist noted the time as shortly after one thirty. The caller complained how late it was. Don't you believe Broadman would scream while they tortured him to death? Do you think the caller made it up?' Amazingly, Notu seemed to be vaguely amused by the whole matter.

Kubu swallowed. It was close to lunchtime, and they had achieved almost nothing the whole morning. 'Did the receptionist note the room number of the caller?'

'He couldn't tell. It was an outside call, and the caller didn't give his name or room number. Shouted about being woken in the middle of the night.'

Tatwa was puzzled. 'An outside call? Why was it an outside call?'

Notu gave him a pitying look. 'This lodge isn't the Gaborone Sun, you know. It's free-standing bungalows over several hectares. They don't have phones in the rooms.' He stared over their heads, waiting for the unwelcome visitors to leave.

Kubu had had enough. He was getting hungry. 'Do you mind if we talk to the people at the lodge? Chat to MacGregor when he's through?'

Notu looked offended. 'Help yourself. Director Mabaku said I was to give you every assistance. Now, if you've no more questions, I want to get back to work.'

Kubu and Tatwa left, dismissed. They realised that without Mabaku paving the way, they wouldn't have been granted an audience at all.

Reaching the door, Kubu turned back. Notu was as thick as a plank, and surly with it, but he certainly didn't look undernourished. He likes his food, Kubu thought with grudging approval. Perhaps he could be of *some* help.

'Anywhere good to eat lunch around here? I'm quite keen on Italian.'

Notu didn't look up from his desk. 'The canteen opens at twelve thirty,' he replied.

Kubu had no intention of subjecting himself to a police staff canteen and walked out. But Notu's secretary called after him. 'Excuse me, Assistant Superintendent. There aren't any nice Italian restaurants in town, but the Bon Arrivé is always decent. It's around the corner, opposite the airport. We go there sometimes for a celebration. Bit pricey, but the food is really good. I've been a few times lately.'

Kubu smiled and thanked her. The young lady was attractive, and he imagined she would receive many invitations to dine away from the canteen. Cheerful and bright, she was the complete opposite of her boss.

Outside, Tatwa exploded. 'Idiot! He's done nothing. These bastards are miles away by now, and he sits at his desk looking for ink on his fingers! He hasn't even thought of tracing that call to find out who the caller was.' Kubu just nodded, distracted as he was. He was keen to get to the restaurant.

They found it easily. It had an aviation theme, and model aeroplanes, aviation paraphernalia, and copies of newspapers with aviation headlines adorned the walls and ceilings. The menu was decent, and peppered with aviation jokes. The place was starting to fill up, so Kubu directed Tatwa to a table for four. Tables for two were too cramped for the multiple plates he liked.

When they had ordered, Kubu turned to Tatwa. 'All right, Tatwa. Out with it. You've been dying to tell me something ever since we met at Notu's office.'

Tatwa looked surprised, then blurted out, 'I think I may have a breakthrough in the case. How did you know?'

Kubu laughed. 'I'm a detective. Let's hear your ideas.'

'Well, we finally got something useful out of that guy the South Africans have on the case. I hoped to tie the two murders together, so I checked where all the people who'd been at Jackalberry Camp were when Boardman was murdered.' He paused for effect, and Kubu nodded. 'Good thinking,' he encouraged.

'All the camp staff were running a *braai* for guests at the time of Boardman's murder. Except Enoch, and he was stuck in the bush.'

'Is it possible that he could actually have been driving to Maun when he was supposed to be stuck?'

Tatwa shook his head. 'He was halfway to Kasane towing a trailer when it broke a wheel bearing. Dupie had to drive there, meet him, and tow the trailer back. It would've been impossible to get to Maun in time for the murder after all that. Especially at night. The roads through the Savuti section of Chobe are awful.' Kubu nodded, accepting that.

'The Munro sisters are in Gaborone at the Grand Palm, and they had dinner there that night. I phoned the head waiter to confirm. Mrs Boardman was in Cape Town. That leaves our friend Boy Gomwe.'

'Or a reappearance of Zondo? Perhaps he came back for another victim?'

'I suppose that's possible. But why not bump Boardman off at the camp along with the others? My money's on Gomwe. And I'll tell you why.'

Before Tatwa could explain, a waiter arrived with a plate of pâtés and a basket of bread. Kubu was enjoying his first mouthful when to his amazement he looked up and there stood Ian MacGregor.

'Ian!' Kubu exclaimed. 'What good luck to bump into you here! Just the person we want to talk to.'

'Och, wasn't luck,' Ian said, shaking hands. 'I spoke to Mabaku, and he said you'd be having lunch here.' Kubu was silent. How on earth did Mabaku know these things? Had he phoned Notu and spoken to the secretary who suggested the restaurant? Had he eaten here on a previous visit? Kubu shook his head. Mabaku was always one step ahead. When you stepped out of line, you bumped into him.

Ian settled into a chair and examined the menu. 'Good choice of restaurant. The tripe is delicious.' Even Kubu was glad he'd chosen something a little less exotic. Tatwa looked as though he might pass on lunch altogether.

'Tatwa was just about to explain a theory to me,' Kubu said to Ian. 'You'll be very helpful on the case here. But spare us any grizzly details until after we've eaten.' Tatwa looked grateful for that. 'Go on, Tatwa.'

'I've just explained that none of the group present when Goodluck was murdered – other than Zondo, of course – could've killed Boardman, except Boy Gomwe. We've discovered that he was in Botswana when Boardman was killed, but we haven't been able to trace him yet. So he had opportunity. I think he had a motive as well.' He waited while the other two men digested this. 'It turns out that the South African police have been keeping an eye on Rra Gomwe. They're pretty convinced that he's in the drug business, using his music salesman persona as a front. They don't have much evidence, but he's got an old conviction for possession, and his name comes up in investigations from time to time. Now guess what the major smuggling routes for heroin into South Africa are?'

Kubu suddenly saw where Tatwa was heading. 'You think Gomwe was picking up drugs at the border?'

Tatwa nodded. 'Probably Goodluck too. The South African police were trying to track hot money when they followed him there. Money goes to the border, drugs come over it. Two plus two equals . . . ?'

'But why the murders? Sounds all nice and cosy to me.' Ian was puzzled, but Kubu had jumped ahead.

'What if Zondo decided to keep the money *and* the drugs? Or Goodluck and Gomwe were rivals? So the thugs who attacked Jackalberry would have been after the missing drugs and money. In cahoots with Gomwe? But where does Boardman come in?'

Tatwa frowned. 'I haven't quite worked that part out yet.'

The food arrived, accompanied by soda water for Ian and a Coke for Tatwa. Kubu was pleased to receive an acceptable steelworks. He worked his way through a fine rump steak, while Ian savoured his tripe. Tatwa had chosen a vegetarian dish, which he pronounced very good, but he toyed with it, perhaps put off by the smell of the tripe. Eventually Kubu had to finish it for him in order to avoid waste.

When the empty plates had been pushed back, and Kubu had reluctantly passed on dessert due to his current diet, the three men went back to discussing the case.

'Ian, what can you tell us about Boardman?'

'Well, death occurred at midnight, plus or minus a couple of hours. But, of course, there was the report of screams some time after one and silence thereafter. That's consistent with the medical evidence. The neck was broken. Very hard blow, like a karate chop. There were also a lot of blows – or kicks – to the body. But from the bruising, several of them were post mortem.'

Kubu pricked up his ears. 'Post mortem? You mean he was beaten after he was dead?'

Ian nodded. 'Perhaps the attackers didn't realise they had killed him.'

'And the cigarette burns?'

'Yes, several to the face and chest.'

'Were they before or after he died?'

Ian reflected. 'Hard to say for sure. They might have been after death, but then it could be no more than a few minutes later.' He started to explain why, but Kubu pressed on.

'Ian, this may be really important. Is it possible that the torture was actually just a disguise for the murder? That someone – Gomwe, say – wanted it to look like the thugs attacked Boardman and were looking for something, but actually it was a neatly executed murder? I'm suspicious of a torture angle. How do you torture someone for information in the middle of a resort complex?'

'But there were the screams,' Tatwa pointed out.

'Yes, reported by cell phone by a witness who conveniently disappeared.'

Ian looked worried. 'Really I can't say, Kubu.'

'Is it possible Boardman was killed, then beaten up and burned, and the room trashed?'

Ian thought carefully. 'Yes,' he said at last, firmly. Tatwa looked unhappy. Kubu nodded, satisfied. Deliberately forgetting his diet, he took advantage of the pause to order ice cream, with hot chocolate sauce in a separate jug. 'So that it stays warm,' he explained.

Once the enthusiasm for coffees had been satisfied, Tatwa drove Kubu back to the Toro Lodge, where they learned little new. The maid who had found the body described the scene between sobs. Everything was consistent with what they had been told. The manager showed them the bungalow, but it had been cleaned and freshened on Notu's authorisation. There was nothing to indicate the grisly events of three nights before. And the receptionist confirmed the late-night call.

'It was about half past one. I was asleep. Well, who needs reception at that time of the morning? I'm sure about the time because I looked at the clock when the phone woke me.' He indicated the electric clock on the wall behind him.

'Do you remember what the caller said? What sort of voice was it? Man?' asked Tatwa.

'Definitely a man. Sort of gruff, but really angry about the noise. Told me to get them to shut up.'

'As closely as you can remember, what *exactly* did the man say?' asked Kubu.

'It was something like: there's shouting and screaming coming from the bungalow in front of me. Bastards having a row. No consideration for other people. It's after one in the morning! I've been woken up, and I can't get back to sleep with the noise. You bloody well get him to shut up.'

'Did the man say "him" not "them"?'

The receptionist thought, and then nodded. 'Yes, I think so.'

'And what did you do after that?'

'I asked him where he was, but he hung up. So I went outside and wandered around a bit. Asked Albert – the security guard – if he had heard anything. He hadn't, and everything was quiet. So I went back to the office. No one else called.'

Kubu and Tatwa went back to Kubu's bungalow, where Kubu collapsed into the single comfortable chair, leaving Tatwa to perch, heronlike, against the desk.

'*They're* making a noise but you must get *him* to shut up. I don't think that call came from the hotel at all. I think it was phoned in, perhaps to confuse the time of death. I'd bet that the murder took place earlier. Perhaps the murderer wants to create an alibi. Make sure you trace the call. It'll be really interesting to know what phone it came from. You never can tell.' Kubu pouted. 'Maybe Gomwe was involved. Or Zondo. But why kill Boardman? A curio dealer? How could Boardman have anything the drug smugglers cared about? How could he have known about whatever was in Tinubu's briefcase? I don't get it.'

'Perhaps he saw something, or found something,' Tatwa suggested. Suddenly he jumped up, excited. 'Kubu, remember the lost keys!'

Kubu looked at him, puzzled. Then he said, 'Oh my God, Tatwa. You may be right!'

CHAPTER 32

It was early Friday morning, and Mabaku had skipped breakfast. His stomach complained about the black coffee it had been offered instead, while he tried to concentrate on Kubu's phone report from Maun. What an insufferable idiot that Notu is, he thought with disgust. Kubu and Tatwa had achieved more in a day than Notu had in three despite all his resources.

'Say that again.' Mabaku's annoyance and heartburn had distracted him.

'I said we've contacted about three quarters of all the guests who were staying here at Toro Lodge on the night of the murder. Some of the others are tourists now on bush trips; three were here for their last couple of nights on holiday and have now left Botswana. But the important part is that we have spoken to all the guests who were no further than two rows away from Boardman's unit. None of them remembers any unusual disturbance or noise that night. Obviously no one called reception to complain.'

'And your point is?' Mabaku growled.

'There was no disturbance. The call was made later, probably from a cell phone. I've asked Edison to trace it. I doubt Notu will be interested.'

'Now, Kubu, keep him informed. No need to cause unnecessary trouble.' This produced a grunt from Kubu not dissimilar to what might be expected from his riverine namesake.

'It's consistent with Ian's findings too. He thinks the injuries – other than the fatal blow to the head – were post mortem.'

Mabaku whistled. 'Even the cigarette burns? What's the point of that?'

'Misdirection. Like the phone call. The object of the attack was to kill Boardman. All the rest was to make it seem the attackers were thugs searching for something. A briefcase, for example.'

'Who knows about the attack on Jackalberry Camp last Friday?'

Kubu paused, following Mabaku's line of thought. 'Ah, you mean who knew enough about the attack at Jackalberry to make this look as though it was committed by the same thugs? Good point. All the people at the camp, of course, including the guests who were there when the attack occurred. The attackers themselves would know. But why point suspicion at yourself? And the police in Maun knew. I think Notu could be corrupt, but he's so inept he couldn't organise a paper clip on to a piece of paper. I don't think he's involved.'

'There was a short piece in the *Gaborone Gazette* about it too,' interrupted Mabaku sourly. 'Unavoidable. We couldn't get them to drop it, but they did tone it down. No one would react unless they knew the camp and the recent history.'

'Like Boy Gomwe,' said Kubu thoughtfully.

'And our literary ladies from England. They're waiting to see me now. Apparently they showed up here half an hour ago to see you. I'm taking your place with great pleasure.' Mabaku didn't like to be crossed, and Kubu felt a twinge of sympathy for the Munro sisters.

'I don't believe they killed anybody,' he said. 'And they have an alibi for the night Boardman was killed.' It was Mabaku's turn to grunt. He came to a decision.

'Stay up there for another day, Kubu. Check the forensics – prints, anything. Keep checking the hotel. See if you can get any connections through the curio dealers. You better have a word with Boardman's widow too, if she's up to it. I'll ask Edison to get on to the cell phone issue. And I'll talk to the Munros.' Mabaku's voice rose. 'We have to get this tidied up. We've the African Union meeting coming up, remember? It can't look as though we're less secure and law-abiding than Zimbabwe, for God's sake!'

Kubu sighed. He'd hoped to get back to his home-cooked meals, his own bed and, most important of all, his wife. She would understand, but would be disappointed.

*

Mabaku fixed Trish and Judith Munro with an unforgiving stare. He couldn't judge their ages; the smooth complexion of a certain type of Englishwoman seemed timelessly wrinkle-free. But their body language showed them to be nervous at being ushered into the office of the Director of the CID.

'We wanted to see Superintendent Kubu,' Trish blurted.

'Assistant Superintendent *Bengu* is busy right now, madam. So I'm afraid you'll have to settle for me.'

'Oh, I didn't mean—' Trish started, but Mabaku interrupted.

'He's investigating the murder of William Boardman, who was tortured to death four nights ago at a tourist hotel in Maun.' He watched closely to judge their reactions.

Both sisters were clearly shocked.

'Oh my God,' said Judith, pale.

'He was such a nice man. So keen and knowledgeable about birds. Why would anyone want to kill him?' said Trish, fighting back tears.

But Mabaku was not sympathetic. 'I hope you can help us answer that. If you are willing to tell the truth this time, that is.'

'What do you mean by that?' Judith snapped.

'When Superintendent Bengu asked you how you learned about Jackalberry Camp, you told him that a colleague had written a travel piece about the place. Is that correct?'

Trish nodded. Judith met his eyes, but said nothing.

'Mr Du Pisanie confirmed that no such person had ever visited the camp.'

'Well,' said Judith. 'We must have been mistaken. Someone else may have mentioned it, or perhaps we just found their website.'

'They don't have a website,' Mabaku guessed.

'Well, what difference does it make? We were there on holiday.' This was Trish's contribution. 'There were those awful murders, and now poor William too!'

'And you said you had no knowledge of Goodluck Tinubu, is that correct?' The two women did not reply, uncomfortable. 'Then I wonder why you visited his school in Mochudi? The deputy headmaster showed you around. It's a good operation, but not exactly a tourist attraction, I would've thought.'

The sisters exchanged glances, but Judith tried to stand her ground. 'You must understand, Mr Mabaku, that we are journalists. Our sources are privileged.'

Mabaku was not impressed. 'That doesn't give you the right to lie to the police! You may have your privileged sources, but I have three vicious murders. Now are you going to help us, or do you want to face charges of obstructing justice?'

The two sisters looked at each other. 'We'll tell you everything we can,' said Trish.

Judith began. 'I suppose we'd better tell you the story from the beginning.' Mabaku nodded approval. 'We write pieces for the *Sunday Telegraph* in London, Director Mabaku. We write about people, people with interesting stories but who aren't necessarily famous or even well known. We loaned Kubu one about the vet who looks after the Queen's corgis.' Mabaku nodded. He wanted to see where this was going.

Trish smiled. 'Kubu said he liked it.'

'Well, we wanted to try something different, something that might lead to a series of articles or even a book,' Judith continued. 'So we had an idea – actually I had the idea – and we took it to our usual editor, Chezi Makanya. Perhaps you've heard of him? He left South Africa during the apartheid era and is quite well known as a writer, in addition to being a senior editor of the newspaper.'

'We wanted to try for something deeper,' Trish added. 'We wanted to be taken more seriously. You don't win awards for pieces about handling snappy royal dogs. Sunday readers enjoy that stuff, but it's frothy and doesn't keep you awake long – like a decaffeinated cappuccino, I suppose. We wanted to come up with a double espresso.'

'So you needed a black man for that?' offered Mabaku. He thought it quite witty, but neither woman smiled.

'Chezi is incredibly sharp. Usually he'll decide right away whether a premise has merit or not. But on this occasion he seemed disturbed and said he needed to think about it.' Judith stopped. There was silence for a moment.

'And what was this premise?' Mabaku encouraged.

'We wanted to follow the lives of people who'd been in the Rhodesian war thirty years ago. What had become of the whites and the blacks who'd been sucked into it. Whether there was reconciliation, where they had gone, how their lives had been changed. Some would be in the UK, some in Zimbabwe, some in other African countries.'

Mabaku could see Chezi Makanya's problem. 'Do you think you have the background to try something like that?'

It was Trish who replied. 'We don't know much about corgis either, Director. The question for a writer is how hard you are willing to work, how much time you are willing to invest, and how far you are willing to travel. Well, here we are.' She seemed to think the question was answered.

'Ladies, we have three people violently dead. What has this to do with my murder cases?'

'When we met Chezi the second time, he explained the problems to us. That Zimbabwe would not admit writers from an English newspaper, that many people on both sides had emotional scars and some of the scabs were still raw, and that the people who'd left Africa would be the ones for whom negativity would be a form of self-justification. But he said we could try, and that he'd look at what came out. No promises and no advance. But we decided to give it a go.'

Trish took up the narrative. 'We started in the UK, doing research and interviewing people. But Chezi was right. Lots of people were willing to talk to us. But most were Whenwes. Do you know the term? *Whenwe* were in Rhodesia we did this and we did that, and *whenwe* hunted and *whenwe* farmed and so on. It was all reminiscence. And if the war came up, it was always about how it would've been won if only Britain and South Africa hadn't betrayed the Smith government. Rather pathetic that this perspective has survived thirty years. Nothing with heavy caffeine.'

'Until Chezi put us on to Tito Ndlovu,' said Judith. 'He was different. He had fought for the Patriotic Front and became something of a hero, but he was from the Nkomo faction and had fallen out with the new government.'

'He was an awful man,' said Trish. 'He wanted to tell us about rape and murder as weapons of war. He wanted to tell us the details.' She shuddered. 'The way he looked at us . . . I think he was sorry the war was over. He wanted to shake my hand when we left, but I couldn't. And he just laughed at me.'

Judith was matter-of-fact. 'He didn't want to be interviewed on the record. Didn't want people to be able to trace him, I think. But he did tell us some horrific stories. One was about a terrorist group that attacked a farm outside Bulawayo. Slaughtered the men and raped the women. I asked what had happened, and he said the army claimed they killed all the terrorists that night. But later there were rumours about one man who had escaped. Deserted, sneaked away and fled the country. His name was George Tinubu. 'You should try to find Tinubu,' he told us, and laughed. 'He's more your kind of kaffir.' We would never use a word like that! I asked where this man was, and he told us he thought there was a Tinubu nice and safe across the border in Botswana. Maybe a brother or cousin or something? He thought that was very funny. He didn't know if any of the settlers – as he called them – had survived the attack on the farm, but said we weren't much good as reporters if we couldn't find out.'

Mabaku was starting to see where this was going, and felt a surge of anger. 'You did find out, didn't you? Her name was Salome McGlashan. And you found Tinubu too. A refugee who had made a new life for himself in a small town in Botswana. What right did you think you had to hound these people thirty years after what had happened? And how did you engineer the meeting at Jackalberry Camp? Did Tinubu suddenly get a free offer of a week's holiday?'

But now the sisters came to life, both talking at once and denying anything to do with the meeting.

'It's supposed to be another coincidence?' Mabaku asked incredulously. 'I don't believe in coincidences.'

Judith waved her sister to silence and said firmly, 'We went there to meet Salome, of course, to talk to her about her experiences. When a salesman called Goodluck Tinubu appeared, we were surprised. We had discovered that there was a Tinubu who was the headmaster of a school in Mochudi, and we asked Goodluck if he knew him. He said he did not, that Tinubu was a common name in Botswana these days because many families had fled Zimbabwe during the Rhodesian bush war. We were looking for a George Tinubu. We thought Goodluck Tinubu must be a different person. Why would the headmaster of a primary school go on holiday to a bush camp and pretend to be something else?'

'We only realised he was the same Tinubu when we phoned the school yesterday,' Trish concluded. 'That's when we decided to come and see Superintendent Kubu.'

Mabaku calmed down. 'How did Salome and Du Pisanie react to Goodluck?'

It was a few seconds before Trish replied. 'They seemed fine. Treated him the same as the other guests. But we didn't see much of Salome that day. She said she didn't feel well. Dupie was his usual overbearing self.'

Mabaku stared across his desk at Judith. At last she dropped her eyes.

'This brings a completely different set of possibilities to this case. I have to insist that you stay in Gaborone for the time being. I want you to go over everything again in much more detail with Assistant Superintendent Bengu. He'll be back tomorrow or the next day. I must also ask you to stay in the Grand Palm complex and not wander around the city. We don't know why Boardman was murdered. He seems to have no connection to Tinubu or Langa except that he was present at the camp when they were killed. So were you.' He saw that this statement had had the desired effect.

The sisters left chagrined and depressed, but they looked forward to the session with Kubu. They realised that the Goodluck double espresso was forever lost to them. But a strong black, with lots of sugar, based on the large and boisterous detective, was a real possibility.

PART FOUR
A Woman's Guess

A woman's guess is much more accurate than a man's certainty.

Rudyard Kipling, *Three and an Extra*

CHAPTER 33

It was unusually hot for April, and Joy had walked four blocks from the main road where the minibus taxi had dropped her. Then there had been the boisterous greeting from Ilia – a double greeting, since Kubu was not available to receive his share. The bed had to be made, dishes put away, laundry loaded into the washer. At last she could relax before she thought about supper with Pleasant.

Joy poured herself a glass of chilled orange juice, more refreshing than anything alcoholic. Even a steelworks seemed unattractive with Kubu stuck for another day in Maun. Suddenly Ilia barked. From the window, Joy saw two smartly dressed black men coming up the driveway. Who was visiting at six in the evening? Probably from the Zion Church, she thought with irritation. Why couldn't they leave you alone? After all, she had her own church, and *she* didn't try to convert *them*. She was tempted not to answer the door, and let Ilia see them off. Not very charitable, she thought with a sigh. Kubu would have dealt with them easily. They never thought it worth annoying a policeman.

The doorbell rang, and Ilia barked even more furiously. Strange, she was usually quite friendly. Joy hesitated, but then opened the door halfway. 'Yes?' she said. She made no attempt to call off Ilia.

'Mrs Bengu? I hope we're not disturbing you. We just need a couple of minutes of your time.' The man was smooth, polite, and had an astringent-sweet aftershave. He spoke English, but his accent marked him as foreign, probably Zimbabwean. Joy decided she didn't like him. Ilia had stopped barking, but was still growling.

'I'm sorry, it's not convenient. I'm busy making dinner for my husband and two of his colleagues from the Criminal Investigation Department.' That should do the trick, she thought.

The man leaned forward as if he were going to tell her something confidential. But suddenly he shouldered the door, shoving her into the hallway. The second man followed, and Ilia went ballistic. He tried to kick her, but she kept out of reach. Joy saw that the first man was now holding a pistol.

'Call off the dog. We won't hurt you if your husband cooperates. He knows what we want. He'll give it to us.'

'Ilia!' snapped Joy. The dog was momentarily quiet. 'He's not here. He'll be back shortly. With colleagues from the police, as I told you.'

The man smiled. 'We know where your husband is, Mrs Bengu. We'll meet him later. Now we want you to come with us. Quietly. No one gets hurt.' The second man had taken something from his pocket, a dishtowel wrapped around a small bottle. The sickly-sweet smell Joy had mistaken for aftershave became stronger. She screamed.

At once Ilia rushed for the man and bit his leg through his trousers. He yelled, dropped the bottle, and tried to knock her off with his fist. She let go of his leg long enough to bite his hand before returning her teeth to the fleshy part of his calf. Trying to kick her off, he nearly fell over. The man with the gun was distracted, and Joy saw her chance. Still screaming, she rushed him and kneed him in the crotch as hard as she could. Doubled over in pain, he hardly realised that she had grabbed the gun and backed to the far wall. The other man had freed himself from Ilia, but she circled him, snarling, looking for an opening.

They regrouped and weren't smiling any more.

'If you come any closer, I'll shoot you both!' gasped Joy. They ignored that, but stopped when she competently worked the action to ensure a bullet was in the chamber and released the safely catch.

'Put your hands up and stand against the wall. I'm a good shot. It'll give me pleasure to shoot you both!' She was bluffing, and they could tell, but they did not push their luck. Slowly they raised their hands to shoulder level. Then the one she had kneed started backing towards the door.

'You're not going to shoot me, Mrs Bengu. You don't want to do that. We'll just leave now.' The second man joined him. It was clear that they saw this as a temporary setback, not a defeat. Joy's self-defence lessons had paid off, but her hands were shaking. She let them go.

But Ilia had the last word. She tore down the driveway, barking furiously, and ripped off a piece of trouser leg. She brought it back proudly, and Joy was immensely pleased with her.

'Good girl! Your father will want that for evidence. We showed them, didn't we, Ilia?' Suddenly Joy felt faint and nauseous. She locked the front door, and checked the back door and windows. Then, still tightly gripping the gun, she ran to the toilet and threw up. After a few minutes, she felt better and phoned the CID.

When Edison and Mabaku arrived ten minutes later in a cacophony of sirens, they found Joy surrounded by women trying to comfort her. The neighbours had heard Ilia's frenzied barking and had come to investigate. One had her arm around Joy; another rubbed her back. A third was making tea.

It was only after Edison had shooed the women out of the house that Joy's control finally broke, and she started to sob. Edison put his arms around her, but she desperately wished it was Kubu holding her against his comforting bulk.

Kubu drove through the night and arrived home the next morning just after dawn. All night Edison and Constable Mashu had alternated sleeping on the couch and patrolling the house. Ignoring them, Kubu rushed to Joy, even finessing Ilia's welcome. The little dog would get plenty of attention and rewards for her bravery later. Once he was convinced that Joy was safe and had suffered no obvious ill effects, Kubu settled down and officially relieved the other policemen. Edison headed for home, and Mashu went back to CID headquarters.

Kubu spent the day at home, unable to decide whether Joy was his charge, his wife, or even his patient. In desperation, she fed him a large lunch with a generous glass of red wine, and was relieved when he settled down in the bedroom with her and fell asleep. With a sigh, she left him there and went to clear up. He's feeling guilty about the whole episode, she thought. But whether it was because he hadn't been there, or for some other reason, was unclear.

CHAPTER 34

Built in the Chobe Forest Reserve, Kachikau is a charming helter-skelter of small houses climbing the slope overlooking the Chobe river flood plain. The Kachikau Saturday market is a popular event. People come from as far away as Satau and Kavimba, and everyone has something to buy or something to sell. And it's a good excuse for a chat and to meet for tea and, later, maize beer.

Moremi had grown up in Kachikau and loved the market. He had managed to get a day off and a ride with Enoch, who was driving into Kasane and who dropped him off at the town, roughly halfway. Moremi and Kweh were now browsing the stalls, which were nothing more than camp tables or a patch of ground, tended by a merchant seated on a log. Sometimes Moremi found interesting local herbs that would add a special flavour to his intriguing stews. Local ingredients always appealed to the guests at Jackalberry, although once there had been a problem with a herb used mostly for medicinal purposes. Some of the guests had stayed at the camp the next day, not daring to venture far from the toilets.

Several people stopped to chat to Moremi and to greet Kweh, who had become something of a local mascot. The grey go-away-bird sat on Moremi's right shoulder, balancing himself with his long tail as his owner bent to examine the wares. Moremi had discovered Kweh as a fledgling that had left the nest too soon and found himself on the ground unable to return to the safety of the trees. Moremi had taken him back to the camp and fed him scraps of fruit. Everyone had told him that the big, noisy, clumsy birds couldn't be tamed. In Moremi's experience, when everyone agreed on something with no evidence, it was usually false, and this was no exception.

Kweh had become more than a pet; he was Moremi's friend and confidant.

Moremi tried and rejected the feel of a carved walking stick, and looked around the scatter of stalls in search of the fresh curry powder he wanted. He spotted a fat, overdressed woman trying on a hat. 'Look at that lady, Kweh,' he said, nodding surreptitiously towards her. 'She looks ridiculous!' The hat had a large and rather wilted ostrich feather as its centrepiece. Kweh raised the neat crest on his own head, as if in competition. Moremi wandered on, keeping an eye out for interesting hats to entertain Kweh. Suddenly he stopped, shocked.

'That's Rra Zondo,' he told Kweh. 'That's his hat. You see the felt hat with the guineafowl feathers on the side?' The man was in a crowd around a drinks seller.

'Rra Zondo!' he called out, and would have moved through the crowd towards him, but something more interesting had caught Kweh's attention. He took off with a flapping of wings and landed heavily on a rough wooden table. Its owner, who was selling marula fruit at ten for a pula, according to a handwritten sign, was a stout lady sitting on a wooden stool hardly adequate to support her. She knocked it over in fright and began complaining and flapping at Kweh with a brown paper bag grabbed from a small stack on the table. Kweh was selecting a fruit, but jerked back to avoid the flapping bag, and voiced a loud, alarmed 'Go away! Go away!' Nevertheless, he grabbed the closest fruit and flew to the safety of Moremi's shoulder. Balancing on one claw dug deeply into the shoulder, he held the marula in the other while he ate. Juice dribbled down Moremi's neck.

'You must pay for the marula,' screeched the woman. 'Your bird has stolen one.'

'I will, Mma,' said Moremi. 'I just need to find Rra Zondo, then I'll come right back.'

'No!' said the fruit seller firmly. 'You pay now!'

Moremi was looking around. He could no longer see the felt hat with the feathers. Quickly he fished ten thebe from his pocket, but the woman shook her head. 'Twenty-five thebe,' she said. Moremi wanted to go after Zondo, but felt cheated.

'It's too expensive! I can pick these from the trees by the road for nothing! It's ten for a pula, so each one is ten thebe.' He held out the coin.

The woman shook her head again. 'Special price. You have to buy ten.'

Moremi looked around. He thought he saw Zondo crossing the road some way off, but wasn't sure. The man was wearing a felt hat, but was too far away for Moremi to tell if it had feathers on the side.

'All right. Quickly. Give me ten. But the ripe ones, not the green ones hidden underneath. I'll be back in a minute.'

Again the woman refused, insisting he pay at once. Irritated, Moremi ignored her and started to walk away. 'I'll scream that you are robbing me and stealing my fruit!' cried the woman. Angrily Moremi pulled out a pula and pushed it at her. She accepted it and started filling a bag. Moremi watched to see that he was not cheated. As he took the bag with the nine fruits inside, the bird let out another raucous 'Go away!' startling them both, and flew down to the table to grab another marula. The woman started to scream again and flap with her paper bags. Quickly Moremi pulled a fruit from his bag, dropped it on the table, and moved hastily away. Kweh landed elegantly on his moving shoulder with his new prize in his bill. The woman's loud complaints that the bird had fouled her table followed them, but Moremi was hurrying across the road looking for Zondo.

But the felt hat with three guineafowl feathers was nowhere to be seen.

Moremi and Kweh went to the house of Constable Shoopara. Moremi felt it was his duty to report the matter to the police, and in Kachikau, Constable Shoopara was the police. Because it was market day, he was off duty – although always on call – and he was not feeling particularly friendly.

'You can't bring that bird in here,' he said firmly.

'Kweh does no harm. If I can't bring him in, we must talk outside on the veranda. Or I'll go away if you like.'

Shoopara looked at Moremi. He had known the cook for many

years and, like most of the villagers, regarded Moremi as strange, unusual, but not mad. In fact he thought Moremi smart, but not in ways that made sense in rural Botswana.

'No, it's all right, he can stay,' he relented. 'Now, what's the problem?'

'We saw Rra Zondo – didn't we, Kweh? – the man who was at Jackalberry Camp, the man you're all looking for!' Moremi finished triumphantly.

The goings-on at Jackalberry Camp were well known throughout the area. People here did not rely on newspapers; it was word of mouth. The excitement of the attack on Dupie and Salome had been described variously as another attempted murder and an armed invasion of Botswana from Zimbabwe. But Shoopara knew the true story, and he knew about Zondo.

'Are you sure it was him? Did you see him close? Did you talk to him? Where did this happen?'

'Yes. Not very. No. At the market.'

Shoopara had to replay his questions to decode the answers. 'Let's go and look,' he said. 'How did you know it was Rra Zondo, if he wasn't close?'

Moremi explained while they walked, and Shoopara lost some of his enthusiasm. 'Perhaps there are many such hats,' he said doubtfully. 'Did you see his face?' Moremi admitted that he had not. Nevertheless, they searched the area around the market and questioned the sellers, who were now busy packing up their unsold goods. No one remembered a man wearing a felt hat with guineafowl feathers. Shoopara showed them the picture of Zondo, albeit a poor faxed copy, but no one recognised the man. Worse, no one even remembered a stranger unable to speak good Setswana.

Shoopara gave up on the wild goose. 'I think you were mistaken,' he said firmly. 'You had better hurry or you'll miss your lift. Keep well, Moremi.' And he stalked off to resume his interrupted nap.

As Moremi waited for his ride back to the main road, he hummed and puzzled. 'We did see him, didn't we, Kweh? I'm sure, aren't you?' Kweh had one russet eye fixed on the brown paper bag Moremi was carrying. He chortled, but whether he was agreeing or begging for the food was hard for Moremi to decide. Absent-mindedly he passed the bird another marula fruit.

CHAPTER 35

Tatwa spent Saturday morning following up the remnants of clues and loose ends. He was relieved to know that Joy was fine. He had met her once or twice with Kubu during his time in Gaborone and liked her. More important, Kubu had been good to him and supported him. He was very fond of the big detective.

He had been shocked to see him so haggard the day before, taking off alone on the long journey home. He had offered to help drive, but Kubu had waved this aside. 'I'll be fine. You have to talk to Mrs Boardman tomorrow. I'll call you when I'm home.' Then he was gone.

So in the afternoon Tatwa called on Amanda Boardman at the Maun Safari Lodge. He found her calm, focusing on the details of a death in a foreign land rather than its enormity.

'It's been a nightmare with the plane. You'd think it's the first time they've been asked to transport a body,' she told him. 'The undertaker is an idiot. And the police haven't been helpful either.' She glared at the mild-mannered detective as though the fault were his.

'Mrs Boardman, I'm terribly sorry for your loss. I only met your husband once, but I thought he was a fine man. I wish there was something I could do.'

Amanda seemed surprised and touched by his short speech. 'Thank you, Detective. Well, you can tell me what the police have done to catch his killer.'

'I'm hoping you can help me with that. We – Assistant Superintendent Bengu and myself – don't think this was just a robbery. We believe it was somehow connected with the murders at Jackalberry Camp.'

'Yes, of course. I said as much to Assistant Superintendent Notu, but he couldn't see it. A vicious, brutal murder for a few pula? That would be believable in South Africa, Detective, but not in Maun.'

Tatwa was intrigued. 'So you agree your husband was somehow . . .' He stumbled, not wanting to say 'involved'. 'Somehow *connected* with what happened at Jackalberry?'

'I think there may've been something he knew or guessed about what happened. He seemed almost pleased about it – not about the murders, but in the way you can be pleased when you know a useful secret. He didn't tell me what it was, though. William kept things to himself, business and such, even though we worked together. He'd wait until the deal was closed, then he'd let me know. Almost as though he thought saying it out loud would tempt fate. I know it sounds silly, but he was like that.'

'Why did you think that in this case?'

'There was something about him after the interview with you and the Superintendent. Almost as though something important had been confirmed. Something he'd find valuable in the future. That's the impression I had at the time. But then it was gone, and he was back to normal. I knew better than to quiz him about it.'

Tatwa felt a stir of excitement. Was it possible that Boardman had somehow stumbled on Gomwe's involvement? Perhaps seen him that night when looking for the owl? If that were true, and he'd tried to use it in some way such as blackmail, then Gomwe might have a motive for staging a violent and deliberately fatal attack.

'Mrs Boardman, did your husband say anything about what he was doing here on Monday? Particularly Monday night?'

'Well, of course he was here to buy stock for our shop. He'd done pretty well, judging by his full trailer. But I know he was meeting someone. He usually calls me every day when he's on a trip. He phoned about six, but I was out, so he left a message on the answering machine. He was meeting someone for drinks after dinner that evening. He thought he might be late, so he'd phone the next morning. So you see, he was definitely expecting someone.'

Tatwa hesitated, then asked, 'Could it have been a woman?'

Amanda laughed. 'You're not married, are you, Detective?' Tatwa shook his head. 'Well, if you were having an affair, would you call your wife and tell her you were expecting to have drinks with an unnamed person?'

Tatwa admitted that that seemed unlikely.

'Very unlikely, I'd say. I'm sure William was looking forward to telling me about another of his secret successes in the morning. But the morning never came, did it?' She stared at the ceiling, forced to focus on that gruesome night. Her voice dropped. 'That's all I can tell you, Detective. Perhaps you would leave me now?'

Tatwa nodded, muttered his thanks, and rose to go. 'We'll catch this man, Mrs Boardman, I promise that.'

'Yes, I suppose you will,' she said.

CHAPTER 36

Kubu and Joy came close to one of their infrequent rows that Sunday morning. Kubu was adamant that they should stay at home. Joy was still not feeling well after Friday's frightening experience with the intruders, and he argued that a quiet day with him and Ilia would do her good. Joy, on the other hand, had begun to feel like a prisoner in her own home and desperately wanted to get out and about. It was Sunday, she railed, and on Sundays they visited his parents.

'I'm not going to stay here and be a sitting duck.' Her voice rose angrily. 'They know I'm here. And you want me to stay? Not a chance! We're going to see your parents. I've already invited Pleasant and told your mother we're bringing food for a picnic.' Kubu thought it unwise to challenge Joy in this mood. He decided to live with being told what to do.

Grudgingly he conceded that Joy's choice of a picnic was a sound idea. This way his mother would not have to cook. Although she would complain that Kubu and Joy had brought the food the previous Sunday, she would not press the point too far. 'But,' Kubu said firmly, 'we say nothing about the attack. My parents will worry, and by tomorrow everyone in Mochudi will know. We want to keep this quiet.' Joy understood and agreed, but she knew Kubu very well. She suspected there was something else behind his insistence.

Since there were to be five adults and one dog in his old Land Rover, Kubu decided on a picnic spot close to where his parents lived. With everyone in the car, and Ilia curled up on Wilmon's lap to enjoy her ears being rubbed, he drove up into the semicircle of hills that surround Mochudi. He turned up a paved road near the hospital and followed it as it wound up the *koppie*, through rock fig trees with grasping roots that enveloped huge boulders. At the crest they reached the Phuthadikobo museum – an elegant colonial building, once a school, overlooking southern Mochudi.

After checking that there were no acacia thorns to damage the tyres, Kubu parked off the road near the museum. The entire area was covered with rocky outcrops, and Kubu chose a flat rock in the shade of a wonderboom tree. From there, they could almost see Amantle and Wilmon's house on the east side of town. In the distance, through the haze, Kubu thought he could see Kgale Hill.

Kubu spread a blanket on the rock and unfolded a small table and two chairs, which he offered to his parents. Joy and Pleasant covered the table with a colourful cloth and unpacked the contents of two baskets. Soon a dish of cold meats was surrounded by salads, cold *pap*, and a bowl of chopped tomatoes and onions – Wilmon's favourite. Joy then covered the table with mosquito netting to keep off flies. Finally, Kubu regretfully took only soft drinks out of a cooler – Wilmon would not countenance alcohol on the Sabbath. Kubu had fleetingly considered replacing the contents of a ginger ale bottle with sparkling wine. However, he had rejected the temptation as disrespectful to his father. Wilmon and Amantle ate at the small camping table while the others sat on the blanket with plates on their laps.

After the meal Wilmon said to Joy, 'You look tired, Joy. Are you well?'

She laughed. 'It is Kubu's fault. He is always making me work and giving me a hard time.' They all laughed except Wilmon. Kubu's chuckle was a little forced.

Wilmon looked serious. 'When we go home, I will give you some leaves for making tea. It will make you calm and help you sleep. It is quite harmless. Even Kubu and Ilia can have some.' A glimmer of a smile lit up his wrinkled face.

Wilmon had the reputation in Mochudi of being someone you could trust for *muti* or herbal medicines. He was not a witch doctor, but knew and understood what local plants offered for dealing with a variety of human ailments. Rather than an incantation, Wilmon usually attached a silent prayer to each vial he dispensed – a Christian prayer, of course.

Then Amantle turned the spotlight on Pleasant's unacceptable marital status, as Kubu and Joy had warned Pleasant she would. Amantle's interrogation began slowly and gently with questions about Pleasant's work at the travel agency, how her brother Sampson was faring in Francistown, and whether he was married yet. When Amantle realised that he was in his early thirties and still single, she gave Pleasant a lecture on how distressed her parents would have been had they been alive. Pleasant solemnly agreed that Sampson was shirking his responsibilities and promised to have a word with him. Joy sat back, enjoying the fact that this Sunday she was not being interrogated.

Wilmon, sensing Pleasant's discomfort, voiced his approval of Sampson's government position. 'He will receive a good pension.'

'But who will he share it with?' Amantle demanded, determined not to let the initiative slip. Wilmon lapsed back into silence, unable to respond to this challenge.

Amantle then leaned forward and took Pleasant's hand.

'My dear, you are nearly thirty,' she said in a scandalised tone. 'Soon the only people who will look at you will be dry old men who already have children. Soon you will be too old to bear your own children.'

'Mma Bengu,' Pleasant replied. 'I thank you for your concern, but I'm happy at the moment. I'd like to be married and have children, but I haven't met someone yet who I want as my husband.'

'A man does not like a woman who works,' Amantle said. 'He thinks he will look more important and successful if his wife stays at home. Actually, he is afraid that his wife will earn enough money to do what she wants. Then he cannot tell her what to do. That will make him feel bad. You should give up your job and find a man. When you marry, you can go back to work.'

'Mma Bengu, you are wise,' Pleasant replied. 'But how will I live if no one wants me? I have to work.'

Joy thought it was time to support her sister. 'Pleasant is seeing a very fine man. He is a professor at the university. Very clever and famous. His work is known by people all over the world.'

'Why does he not ask you to marry him?' Amantle asked. 'He must be blind not to want such a beautiful girl as you.'

'I don't think I'm clever enough for him.'

'What nonsense! How can a professor be so stupid? Can he not see you will carry children well? Kubu, you must speak to him!'

'Mother, times have changed,' said Kubu, alarmed by this turn of events. 'Today's young people think differently from you and Father. They do what they want.'

'We know that, Kubu!' Amantle interjected. 'Your father and I nearly gave up on you ever getting married. You were lucky to meet a sensible woman like Joy. I know she had to take charge. You were so blind with your police work.' Amantle turned back to Pleasant. 'Tell me about this professor. I am sure I can help you open his eyes.'

Wilmon had been thinking the matter through. 'Perhaps the problem is the *lobola*. Maybe he does not have enough cattle to pay a proper bride price. And it is hard to negotiate because your father is not alive.' He scratched his head, willing memories to surface. 'I recall that it was necessary to talk to two of your uncles to resolve the matter when Joy and Kubu married. I sorted it out quite easily, though. I wrote them a fine letter – Kubu helped me – and then my brothers and I went to Francistown to visit them. They are fair men, and we discussed all the issues, and when it was all agreed we had a drink on it.' This was such an unusual occurrence for Wilmon that he thought it worth mentioning.

Pleasant had been ready for Amantle's questioning, but Wilmon's suggestion caught her by surprise. 'Rra Bengu, Bongani is a fine man from a good Batswana family. I think he just needs some time. He's very busy with his career. He has studied at the university in Gaborone and in America. He's very clever. He works with computers and satellites.'

'How can he be clever if he does not see your wide hips and happy smile?' Amantle interjected.

'Remember that time when the Botswana Cattle and Mining Company had so many problems?' Pleasant asked, ignoring Amantle's question. 'Bongani helped Kubu solve that case. He used his satellite to find a Land Rover in the desert. Doesn't that prove he's clever?'

'I do not understand these things, so I do not know if he is clever. But I do know he is stupid! Kubu, you must tell him to ask Pleasant to marry him, and your father will help you sort out the *lobola*.'

'Mother,' Kubu said, 'you always know what is best. I'll see him this week and give him your message. I'm sure he'll agree immediately!'

'Thank you, Mma Bengu,' Pleasant said quietly. 'I miss my family every day, so it's wonderful to have a second mother looking after me.' Pleasant seemed genuinely touched by the old couple's concern, but Kubu and Joy were having difficulty keeping their faces straight. It seemed prudent to pack up and drive back to Wilmon and Amantle's small house for tea.

Amantle made tea while Wilmon went to his little garden behind the house to pick the ingredients for Joy's *muti*. Ilia was not sure whether to stay on the veranda and hope for crumbs from the Marie biscuits that Amantle would inevitably serve, or to accompany Wilmon to the garden, where she knew she would have her ears rubbed and her tummy tickled. Having been spoiled at the picnic, she opted for the latter and trotted off to be with the old man.

By the time Wilmon reappeared with a small brown packet, tea was ready. Remembering that his parents had only four chairs, Kubu said that he was tired of sitting and would stand. Everyone else then insisted that they had been sitting for much too long. So the five people stood around the four empty chairs. Ilia was pleased because it meant they had trouble controlling the cups, saucers and Marie biscuits simultaneously. She accepted several dropped biscuit pieces with enthusiasm. After tea, Kubu, Joy and Pleasant said their farewells and started for Gaborone.

As they drove off, they dissolved into laughter. Ilia was puzzled and broke her usual habit of sleeping on the way home to jump around the car, licking faces. Eventually the humans sobered.

'What wonderful parents you have,' Pleasant said to Kubu. 'They've such dignity and concern for other people. You're so lucky to have them. You're their pride and joy.'

'I'm lucky indeed. They've always been good to me.'

The three sat in silence as Kubu threaded his way back into Gaborone through the myriad of taxis, animals and pedestrians.

'Look after my sister,' Pleasant said to Kubu as they dropped her off at her apartment. 'You never know if those thugs may turn up again.'

'She's going to stay at home for a few days with a police guard. They won't dare to try anything. They know I'll rip them apart.'

Pleasant patted Ilia and hugged Joy. As Kubu and Joy drove off, she waved after them. Feeling a little lonely, she started up the stairs to enjoy a quiet evening at home.

CHAPTER 37

On Monday morning, Kubu waited at home until Edison arrived with Constable Mashu, taking advantage of the opportunity to have a proper breakfast and two cups of coffee. Joy was annoyed to be treated as a liability and irritated with Kubu. On the previous night he had insisted on sitting up to guard her in the bedroom with his police pistol. A bottle of Allesverloren vintage port kept him company. The result had been that he snored in the armchair all night, keeping her awake. She appreciated his commitment, but not his macho approach, and certainly not his execution. Having him in bed with her would have been much better.

'Kubu, I'm not staying at home all day. I've things to do. And I'm having lunch with Pleasant. This whole business is ridiculous. I can look after myself. And I have Ilia.' The dog wagged her tail in agreement, perhaps suggesting a reward would not go amiss.

'Joy, my darling, I have work to do and won't be able to do anything if I think you're in any danger. I know you can look after yourself. You proved that very convincingly. But we have to track down these bastards! Please humour me.' He grasped for a straw. 'Edison is very good at Scrabble. Perhaps you can play. Make them some coffee.'

'Scrabble doesn't have enough M or K letters to play properly in Setswana,' Joy replied grumpily.

Edison and Mashu sat quietly waiting for the domestic ripples to subside. They looked at each other and nodded. All men have such problems with their wives.

'I'll phone Pleasant and explain that you're staying at home,' Kubu said. 'Why not make a nice lunch here and introduce her to Mashu?'

'You know she's quite involved with Bongani,' she snapped.

However, she did give Mashu an appraising look. He was well built and had a wide, cheerful face lit by a ready smile. Pleasant might like to meet him. She wondered if she had enough mutton neck to do a curry.

'I'll phone her myself,' she said.

But Pleasant wasn't at work, nor was there any answer at home. When Joy tried her mobile phone, she heard a voice that she recognised at once. The voice with the foreign accent. Suddenly a sweetish, acrid smell seemed to fill the room. She had to throw up. She gave the phone to Kubu and rushed to the sink.

'Hello, this is Assistant Superintendent Bengu. Who am I talking to?'

The others couldn't hear the other side of the conversation, but they could see Kubu's face tighten and his fists clench. Then they could hear the dial tone. Kubu carefully replaced the receiver.

'They have Pleasant,' he said at last. 'They have the nerve to threaten my family and kidnap my sister-in-law! These pigs will rot in jail and then rot in hell. And hell will be a relief for them.' Joy had never seen him so angry.

'Did you speak to her? Is she all right? What will you do?'

'The pig said she's fine. But he is lying vermin! They'll wish they were dead when I get my hands on them.'

'Yes, but what about Pleasant? What about her? Can you give them what they want? You can catch them afterwards.'

'I don't know what the shits want! They talk in riddles. Look, I've got to get to the office. We'll search every house in Gaborone if necessary! Every house! From top to bottom. Who the hell do they think they are?'

Joy spoke very calmly, although her pulse was racing and nausea was building up again.

'Kubu, I need to help you with this. I'll come with you to the CID. I'll be absolutely safe there. You can't leave me here to play Scrabble. Besides, I know how Pleasant thinks. That'll help you.'

Kubu was not listening. 'Darling, I've explained already. I must know you're safe or I'll be distracted. I promise you that Pleasant will be free and with us this evening for supper. I'll phone you every hour, and you can give us any information you can think of. Don't worry. It'll be all right. I promise.' Joy started to reply, but he was already halfway through the door, shouting instructions to Edison.

After Kubu had left, Joy sat involved with her own thoughts. Edison and Mashu kept a low profile, speaking softly to each other. After about ten minutes, Joy got up and seemed more cheerful.

'Did you boys have a proper breakfast? Kubu had bacon and scrambled eggs and *mielie* meal porridge. It's important to start the day with a proper meal.' Mashu was a bachelor and admitted that his breakfast had been bread and jam in the police car. Edison thought he saw a way of distracting Joy and said he was ravenous. A proper cooked breakfast would be wonderful.

Joy started at once. There was still porridge in the pot, which she reheated and gave to them in big plates with milk and salt. She even managed a small joke. 'Kubu will smell this and be home shortly,' she said. 'You'll see!' The two men laughed as they spooned up their porridge. She put on toast and started the coffee percolator. Then she began to whip the carefully cracked eggs, adding milk. 'You have to use milk,' she told them. They were not disposed to argue. Ilia sat waiting, hopeful for some bacon fat.

When the men were faced with a plate heaped with scrambled eggs, well-done bacon, fried tomatoes and toast, she said, 'Now you enjoy that after all my work!'

'Aren't you going to join us?' asked Edison.

Joy shook her head. 'I ate with Kubu,' she lied. 'I'm going to have a hot relaxing bath, and I'll feel much better. There's more coffee on the stove. Oh, and you can play Scrabble if you get bored. It's in the living room.' The men joined her laughter.

'But you shouldn't be alone,' said Mashu. 'Kubu, I mean the Assistant Superintendent, said one of us was to be with you all the time . . .' He trailed off in response to Joy's look.

'Even when I'm in the bath? I'm not sure the Assistant Superintendent had that in mind at all!' She laughed. 'The bathroom is just across the passage. You can watch the door from here. Okay?'

The men gratefully returned to the delicious breakfast. Ilia gave a sharp bark to remind them of her presence. They heard the bath fill.

Edison and Mashu finished breakfast and argued about soccer and which African teams would get to the World Cup in South Africa. Edison was scathing about Bafana Bafana, but Mashu had relatives in South Africa and supported its national team, except when it played against Botswana. They had some more coffee. Then they talked about Mabaku for a while, a perennial topic among members of the CID.

Ilia, who had wrangled a bacon rind or two, got up and went to lie at the bathroom door. Edison realised that it had been three quarters of an hour since Joy had left them. He rose and listened at the bathroom door but heard nothing. He knocked. 'Joy, are you all right? Joy?' There was no response. He tried the door. It was not locked. 'Joy?' He opened the door gingerly. The room was empty, the bath was full of clean water, and the sash window to the garden was open. Edison felt a thrill of fear. Then he saw the lipstick writing on the basin mirror. 'Kubu, I'm fine. I've gone to find my sister. Don't worry, all's well. I have my cell phone. Love you. Joy.'

Edison pouted, but couldn't suppress a smile. Kubu would be furious. But Joy was a very resourceful lady. He wondered who would be the first to find Pleasant.

Mabaku was waiting for Kubu in his office. Kubu wanted to start a house-to-house search for Pleasant at once, but Mabaku was firm. 'Let's get some coffee,' he said. He asked after Joy as they filled their cups from the urn. When they returned to Mabaku's office, Kubu could see that his boss was more than concerned. He was scared.

'Kubu, this case has got completely out of hand. I'll tell you in a minute what I learned from the Munro sisters. They are waiting impatiently to tell you themselves, by the way. But everything has changed now. I don't know what we are up against. International drug cartel? Money-laundering network? Who has the nerve to attack a senior policeman's family? Even if he did invite it,' he finished bitterly.

Kubu was fidgeting; he wanted action, not philosophy. 'We should be going through her flat inch by inch,' he said.

'Under way,' Mabaku responded. 'Now this is how we are going to deal with the situation.' He held up his hand to forestall Kubu's interruption. 'I should take you right off the case, but I'm not going to do that. Frankly, I *can't* do that. You've put yourself in the centre of it, and we're going to exploit that.' Kubu started to thank him, but again Mabaku stopped him. 'From this point on, I'm in charge. Tatwa will handle things in Maun. Edison will do the leg work here. You will be in on everything but you'll never be on your own, and your first priority will be Joy.' Kubu started to protest, but Mabaku was adamant. 'We work this way, Kubu, or you'll spend your time under house guard with Joy until it's over.' Kubu calmed down enough to realise that this was fair.

'Yes, Director, I agree. Now how do we go about finding Pleasant? I've promised Joy she'll be home for supper.' Kubu wondered if he would come close to fulfilling that promise.

Mabaku's cell phone demanded attention. He listened for half a minute. Then he handed it to Kubu. 'Well, it seems your wife has decided to take matters into her own hands. Now we have a double problem.'

CHAPTER 38

Mma Khotso's shop was in African Mall, not a large Western-style shopping centre, but a collection of small establishments clustered around narrow streets and parking places near the middle of Gaborone. Known as Khotso Shop, it sold an eclectic mix of items, anything that appealed to Mma Khotso. But it was definitely a shop for women, and anyone was welcome to come in and browse, gossip and have a cup of *rooibos* ('I've just made some fresh') with as much milk and sugar as they wanted.

Mma Khotso had an unusual sales technique. She always told the truth about her items, even if – in fact, especially if – she used them herself. She sold Bami Beauty Cream. 'It's supposed to keep your skin fresh and a lighter shade and remove wrinkles,' she would tell a customer. 'But it's all nonsense. Every woman has an inner beauty, which shines through at every stage of her life. We don't need these things. Look at me! I use Bami cream all the time, and you can see it makes absolutely no difference.' Although well past youth, Mma Khotso had a particularly smooth and wrinkle-free, silk-like skin. The cream sold like hot cakes.

Then there was the Love Lotion. The label had a rather rude depiction of a nude man, physically well endowed in every area, watched approvingly by a reclining woman. Mma Khotso turned the label away and was particularly scathing if a curious customer picked up a jar to look. 'Love Lotion! When I was with my Jacob we always had a wonderful sex life. He always performed, and I had great orgasms! Of course he liked me to massage the cream into his inner thighs and on his balls and his thing. What man wouldn't? But we never needed it. He was a bull, that man! He could do it two, and once even three times. Do you know, that's when he had his heart attack?' The Love Lotion sold well, too.

When Joy entered the shop, Mma Khotso was showing a customer her new line of handbags, reputedly ostrich skin. 'How could I sell it for a hundred and ninety-nine pula if it was really made from ostrich skin from Oudtshoorn in South Africa? It would be five hundred pula, more likely. And look here, it says "genuine ostrich *lether*". The spelling of leather is wrong! They come from China, my dear. The Chinaman at the takeaway restaurant orders them for me. They probably have people making the holes where the feathers were supposed to go, or maybe they have ostriches in China? I don't know. But I've had one of these bags for years. They're soft and really well made.' She showed the double stitching on the inside. 'I got him to order more, because mine lasted so well. And only smart people like you and me can tell the difference. But ostrich skin for only a hundred and ninety-nine pula?' She shook her head. 'People are so gullible, aren't they?' The shopper bought the bag.

Coming over to Joy, Mma Khotso could see immediately that something was wrong. 'My darling, you look worried. What's the matter? Let's have a cup of tea. I've just made some fresh.' Joy admitted that a cup of tea sounded wonderful. Mma Khotso found a packet of finger biscuits in her cash drawer. 'You look ill, Joy. Better have the tea very sweet for energy. And some of these biscuits. Now tell me what's wrong.'

Joy told her everything that had happened since the two men came up her driveway. Mma Khotso said nothing until the story was complete. 'My goodness, no wonder you're worried! This is terrible! How brave you were, you and Ilia. But your husband has a senior police post. Surely the police will help you?'

Joy shook her head. 'You don't understand, Mma Khotso, our parents are dead. Pleasant is my little sister. She's my responsibility. Our brother is in Francistown, and he works for the government.'

Mma Khotso understood at once. You couldn't expect anyone who worked for the government to do anything constructive.

'What if the police catch these men but Pleasant is hurt, or killed?'

Joy continued. 'Sometimes the police don't succeed in rescuing kidnap victims. Kubu says he doesn't know what these people want, but would he give it to them anyway? The police don't believe in paying off kidnappers.'

Mma Khotso considered this for a moment. Then she said quietly, 'Do you trust your husband, Joy?'

Joy thought about how Kubu had fallen asleep while protecting her because he'd drunk too much port. Then she thought about how much Kubu loved her and Pleasant; how strong and honest he was. Finally she nodded.

'Kubu must be worried sick,' said Mma Khotso.

'No,' Joy said. 'I left him a message on the mirror. And I have my cell phone.' She did not add that the phone was switched off. She felt ashamed. Climbing out of the bathroom window had seemed so clever, but she had no idea what to do next.

'My darling, you don't look at all well. Wouldn't it be better to leave this to the police? It's their business after all. That's why we pay all these outrageous taxes. Let's have another cup of tea.' Without waiting for a response, she poured.

Joy sipped the brew, crestfallen. 'I have to find Pleasant. I can't just run back with my tail between my legs like a little mongrel. Will you help me?'

'Of course, my darling. But what do you want me to do?'

'Mma Khotso, you know everything that goes on in Gaborone. Surely you can help me find these men? Then we'll just get Pleasant to safety. I'll call Kubu, and we'll leave the rest to the police.'

Mma Khotso managed to keep a straight face. 'Ah, well, if you promise to call Kubu as soon as we've found them, that shouldn't be too difficult.'

Joy brightened, completely missing the irony. 'Where will we start?'

'We'll start by asking the women who always know where the men are.' She shouted to the little back room, 'Minnie! Come look after the shop! I'm going out for a while with Joy. And offer the customers some tea. This pot's cold. Make some fresh.'

CHAPTER 39

When he heard what Edison had to say, Kubu was beside himself and directed a few choice comments at Edison about people who cared so much for their stomachs that they neglected their jobs. When he calmed down, he tried to formulate a plan with Mabaku.

'Where on earth would she go?' asked Mabaku. 'Women are impossible to understand!'

Kubu tried to think. 'Well, she's obviously gone to look for Pleasant. It's actually my fault, Director. She offered to come here to help. I just thought she'd be in the way, but she might have helped with suggestions about Pleasant's acquaintances and plans. At least she would have felt useful and involved. And she'd have been safe. Now she's running around looking for the very people who are looking for her!'

Kubu knew he should be able to guess what his wife would do. 'She'll go to a friend,' he said at last. 'She won't do this on her own. Women don't even go to the toilet on their own.' He had a suspicion that this idea was not likely to add to his reputation as a detective, but at least it was something. He started phoning all Joy's friends.

Meanwhile a Constable Tswane was going door to door at the apartment complex where Pleasant lived. Unfortunately, as it was a weekday, most of the tenants were at work, and he was having little success. But four doors down from Pleasant's apartment his luck changed. An old man answered the door and asked what he wanted. He was so elderly that his hair was pure white.

'Rra,' began the policeman politely in Setswana. 'I'm very sorry to disturb you this morning. I'm with the police.' He presented his identification, which the man looked at carefully. After a while he seemed satisfied.

'Very well. My name is Molobeti. Please come in. What can I do to help the police?'

Tswane noted that the small living area had a balcony, with carefully tended potted plants, overlooking the road. 'Rra Molobeti, did you hear or see anything unusual yesterday evening or perhaps this morning?'

The man shook his head. 'What sort of unusual thing?'

'We are looking for a lady called Pleasant Serome. She's missing, and her family is very worried.'

'Pleasant missing? But I saw her last night.'

'You know this lady?'

'Of course. She is my friend. Sometimes she brings me some of her dinner or a piece of cake. She is a kind person. And we talk sometimes. Her parents are dead. She is my friend.'

'When did you see her?'

The old man hesitated. 'She was going out. I saw from my balcony. I like to sit there in the evening with the plants. Sometimes I drink beer if I have some, but last night I had run out.'

Tswane was excited. 'What time was that?'

'About seven o'clock.'

'Was she alone?'

Molobeti shook his head. 'She was with two men.'

'Was she going with them willingly?'

Molobeti hesitated for so long that Tswane began to think he hadn't heard. At last he said, 'I suppose so.'

'Why are you not sure?'

'Constable, Pleasant is my friend. She is a nice young lady and very pretty, so she has lots of boyfriends. Nice young men. Well dressed, like the men last night. She would never drink, you know? Nice girls do not do that.' He nodded for emphasis. 'Now, the other night, she had one young man who was drunk,' he added with disapproval. 'And she brought him here. I am sure she did not want him to go home alone, or she would not have brought him here in that condition. I have a beer myself from time to time. No harm in it. But he had drunk too much.' He nodded firmly. This seemed to be the end of the story, and the policeman was none the wiser.

'But the men last night?' he pressed.

'Oh, they were not drunk. They seemed fine. They were helping Pleasant.'

Suddenly Tswane got the point. 'You mean *she* looked drunk. Was she staggering, unsteady? Were they holding her? One on each side?'

The old man nodded, embarrassed for his young friend.

Tswane felt the urge to defend Pleasant's reputation. 'Rra, she wasn't drunk. She was drugged. She was being kidnapped!'

This revelation cheered Molobeti considerably. A young lady's reputation for sobriety was very important. But then he realised that being kidnapped might be worse. What would they do to her?

'Now this is very important,' Constable Tswane said. 'Do you remember anything about the men? How were they dressed? And did they have a car? Can you remember the colour? Anything will help. Your friend is in great danger!'

Molobeti described the men as best he could, but his apartment was on the second floor, and he had only seen them from behind. But he was interested in cars. He gave a detailed description: green like a wine bottle, small, Hyundai. Tswane wrote all the details down.

'Do you remember anything else that might help?'

Rra Molobeti shook his head. 'Not really. Just the licence number. B 234 JRM. I remember because the numbers are so easy and the letters are my initials.'

The constable thanked heaven for nosy old men with good memories. He shook Rra Molobeti's hand several times and thanked him profusely.

'We will now be able to rescue your friend, and she will be home soon. All because of your help.'

The old man felt very proud. After the policeman had left, he treated himself to a congratulatory cup of coffee.

CHAPTER 40

Happiness House was in a seedier part of the city, in the direction of Tlokweng. Joy and Mma Khotso took a minibus taxi in the direction of the border with South Africa, got out at a café along the way, and then walked a few blocks back from the main road.

The middle of the day was a slack time for the girls, and they were sitting drinking Cokes and eating takeout hamburgers from the Wimpy. Mma Zarte, the madam, was not pleased to see the two women approaching. In her experience, when women came to a brothel they were looking for their husbands or boyfriends, and there would be a scene whether they found them or not. But, like everyone else, she knew Mma Khotso and rose to greet her.

'Good day, Mma Zarte,' said Mma Khotso politely. 'I have brought you two jars of Love Lotion. One of the girls tells me it is useful if a client is a bit bashful when he takes off his pants. And this is my friend, Joy. We are hoping that one of your girls may be able to help us with a small problem.' She carefully did not give Joy's surname.

Mma Zarte looked suspicious, but accepted the lotion. 'Just what is your small problem? We have to be very discreet here, you know.'

'We are looking for a foreign man. Someone new to the neighbourhood. Someone even I don't know. He has an accent.'

'Black man? Why do you want to find him?'

'He has gone off with this lady's sister, and she is trying to track them down.'

Mma Zarte called out, 'Any of you girls had new clients recently? Black man with a foreign accent?'

One of the girls said through a mouthful of hamburger, 'A Zimbabwean? They're hardly foreign any more.' They all tittered.

'Oh, yes,' said Joy. 'He might very well be a Zimbabwean. They cause a lot of trouble these days.' She felt she was on safe ground now. No one would protect a Zimbabwean who was seducing a good Batswana girl.

The prostitute finished her hamburger and wandered over. Obviously she was dressed for work, and Joy was amazed at how little was left to the imagination. It was fortunate that Gaborone was in the grip of a heatwave.

'I'm Rachel,' said the girl. 'So what about this guy?'

Belatedly, Joy realised that men wouldn't leave a forwarding address at a brothel, even if they weren't criminals. 'I want to know where to find him,' she said lamely.

The girl nodded. 'What's it worth?'

Joy would have paid any price, but Mma Khotso interrupted. 'Ten pula.'

'Fifty,' said Mma Zarte firmly. 'Half for me.'

'You got the lotion!' said Rachel.

Mma Zarte gave her a cuff. 'As though it's any use to me! In my day I didn't need cream to get a client to screw me! You girls are all spoiled.'

'It's agreed,' said Mma Khotso, cutting through the domestic tiff. 'Now, what do you know, Rachel?'

'Maybe he's at that house that was for rent on Ganzi Street. Number 15, 17, 19. Something like that.'

'How do you know?' asked Joy, amazed.

The girl looked sullen. 'He didn't tip me enough. Ten pula! He had a good time even if I did make him wear a condom. I went through his wallet while he was using the toilet. He had the address written on a piece of paper between the money. I left it there after I read it.' She did not say how many of the pula notes she had not left.

Joy asked what the man had looked like. Her heart sank when she learned he had a heavy beard. Both the men who had attacked her had been clean-shaven. But it was still her best chance. She was grateful and gave Rachel a hug. Rachel was touched, and volunteered, 'There was a second address on the paper. Not near here, though. It was in Acacia Street. I'm not sure about the number.'

'Was it 26, perhaps?'

'Yeah, that may've been it. How'd you know?'

'Because that's my address,' said Joy quietly. She paid Mma Zarte the fifty pula, thanked her and Rachel, and the two women left.

'We must go there at once,' said Joy. This was not at all Mma Khotso's understanding of the agreement, and she told Joy that the time had come to call Kubu.

Joy shook her head firmly. 'We must get Pleasant out first. Then we'll call the police.'

Mma Khotso took a deep breath. 'Joy, my darling, how are we going to do that? There are at least three men – the two you met and the one with the beard. They're sure to have guns. It's one thing catching them by surprise with a bit of help from Ilia – and that was wonderfully brave of you both – but quite another attacking their fortress. What'll you do? Walk up to the front door, knock politely, and threaten to practise beginner's karate on them if they don't immediately hand over Pleasant?'

'I'm not a beginner,' Joy said sullenly, but she took the point. She had no resources and no plan. It was a job for the experts. 'But suppose we're wrong, and no one's there? Then I'll be back under house arrest and cooking for my jailers. We have to be sure. The house isn't far. Let's go there carefully and see. Then we can call the police.'

Mma Khotso was dead against this idea, which she felt could only lead to trouble. But Joy was adamant. If her friend would not join her, she would go alone. Eventually Mma Khotso capitulated, but on the condition that Joy phoned Kubu the moment they arrived at Ganzi Street. So they set off.

CHAPTER 41

Kubu traced the car to a small local rental agency, which had accepted a fake international driver's licence and a large cash deposit in lieu of a meaningful address. He sent out an all-points bulletin with the description of the car and the licence number. This exercise had temporarily taken his mind off Joy, but once the alert was out he felt lost again. What should he try next? Then his cell phone rang.

'Kubu, it's Joy.'

'Joy, where on earth are you? I've been worried to death.'

'Oh darling, I'm sorry. I couldn't help myself. Do you understand?'

'Yes, sweetheart, I do,' he lied. 'This is all my fault. Just tell me where you are, and I'll come to fetch you.'

'I'm with Mma Khotso. We're in Ganzi Street, near Tlokweng. Kubu, I think they've got Pleasant in one of the houses here. It's a pretty poor area. Not nice at all.'

Kubu felt his throat close and go dry. He did not ask why Joy thought that, nor how she had got there. Instead he asked if there was a green Hyundai parked in the street.

Joy looked around until she spotted it. 'Yes, Kubu, across the road from us. Its number is B 234 JRM.'

'Joy, my darling, listen to me very carefully. That car was used to kidnap Pleasant. Probably the bastards are very close! Stay where you are, but *keep out of sight*. We'll be there in ten minutes, and we'll get Pleasant out and catch these pigs. I'm coming right now.' Kubu was already walking and signalling to Edison. 'Call the director!' he shouted. 'I know where Pleasant is. And Joy's there too!'

*

For Kubu it was a nightmare trip. Every traffic light was red, every lane blocked by the slowest driver in Gaborone. He cursed himself for not bringing a police vehicle with a siren. Soon he emulated the minibus taxis, helping himself to pavements and passing on solid lines. From time to time he checked that Joy was still there, terrified something would happen to her before he arrived. At last he was in Ganzi Street, and there was a small green car parked in front of a run-down house. But there was no sign of the women.

'Joy, where are you?' he yelled into the phone. They emerged from a narrow service alley. He pulled over, and they clambered in.

'You remember my friend Mma Khotso?' said Joy, not forgetting her manners. Kubu nodded, then moved down the street. It was not encouraging. The house was dilapidated, its uncurtained windows watching the street. You could not get close unnoticed.

'We'll go back to the café on the main road and meet Mabaku,' he said. 'We need a plan.' There was no suggestion that Joy would be excluded from the proceedings. Kubu had learned his lesson.

Mabaku drank foul takeout coffee as he listened to the group. This was an extraordinary situation. They were discussing a delicate police operation with two civilians – women at that – and actually deferring to their opinions. But they had solved the puzzle of Pleasant's location swiftly, and the police would have had little success at Happiness House. The problem was what to do next. Kubu is completely out of it, Mabaku thought sourly. No idea what's going on. He wants to call out the army! Mabaku knew that massive assaults on positions with hostages often led to the death of the hostages as well as their captors. That was out of the question. He held up both hands to stop the debate.

'This is what we're going to do,' he said firmly. 'We're going to secure the area and watch the house. Sooner or later they'll contact Kubu. If we can get two of them out of the house, our chances are much better. They'll set up a meeting with Kubu somewhere away from here. My guess is that the one with the beard, who can't keep his pants on, is the hired help and not smart. Brothel down the road, for heaven's sake!' He directed a smile at Mma Khotso.

'Yes, but they won't leave Pleasant unguarded. How do we get to her?' Joy was still desperately concerned for her sister.

'I'm betting they'll leave Beardy for that. And we know what he likes. This is a job for you, Mma Khotso. Do you think you could get one of our younger policewomen looking like one of the ladies up the road?'

Mma Khotso smiled. 'Get me back to African Mall and tell her to meet me there.'

Mma Khotso had a cup of *rooibos* while she caught up at the shop. No sales, again. No one seemed to sell anything when she was not there.

'Must we all end up on the street?' she berated the unfortunate Minnie. 'Did you offer the customers fresh tea? And biscuits? Or did you just try to sell them things they didn't want?' Minnie looked at the large tea leaves floating in her cup. Mma Khotso snorted. 'I can tell your fortune without those!' she said sarcastically. But then she spotted a well-dressed lady examining an elegant Italian rain jacket made in China. She bustled over.

'They're really the height of fashion,' she told the customer. 'But it never rains here, so what's the point? Although it does seem a bit threatening this afternoon. And they are rather pricey. Most people can't afford them, although I do have one myself, of course. Why not have a cup of tea, rather? We've just made a fresh pot.' But the lady was in a hurry, so she bought the jacket and left.

The next woman who entered was conservatively dressed, in a grey suit. She was in her early thirties, short, with curves in the right places, and a face of well-defined features. She looked lost. Mma Khotso realised immediately that Mabaku had sent her.

'I'm Sergeant Amy Seto,' the woman told her.

'Come, my dear, we'll find you some clothes. Then we'll come back and do some make-up. Yours is too sophisticated, I'm afraid.' She shouted back at her assistant, 'Minnie! I'm going out. Try to sell something while I'm away. A jar of Love Lotion at least! Find some man and show him how it works!' Everyone laughed.

Mma Khotso took Amy to a shop that sold clothing for teenage girls and selected the shortest miniskirt she could find. She also bought hip-long black stockings and shoes with suicide heels. Amy had wonderfully shaped legs, and she was quite taken with the effect. She wondered what her boyfriend would think.

Mma Khotso looked at Amy critically. 'That blouse is hopeless. She needs a tank top,' she told the shop assistant.

'Does Madam take a medium or a large?' asked the confused girl.

'A small,' replied Mma Khotso firmly.

The top was so tight that all three were a little shocked by the effect. But Mma Khotso was still dissatisfied. 'Come here, my darling.' She reached her hands into Amy's bosom and carefully slipped her bra cups down so that the breasts were lifted, and the freed nipples stood out clearly. 'Perfect!' she said. The shop girl was speechless, but accepted Amy's money and gave her change. Amy then asked for a cash slip, making the poor girl blush by telling her it was a business expense. Amy did a few turns in front of the mirror, a little smile on her face. It would be fun to dress like this for her man. In private, of course. Mma Khotso smiled too, and decided they would be friends.

'Come, my dear,' she said. 'We need to spoil the excellent way you've applied your make-up.'

The call came at about five p.m. 'Superintendent Bengu? It's time to trade. Now we have something you want.'

Kubu knew he must not be too eager. 'My sister-in-law? Come on! You must do better than that.'

There was a moment of tense silence. 'Look, Bengu, I don't want to play silly games. But I'll add a bonus to the deal. If it all goes smoothly, no hitches, I won't kill your wife. And I was looking forward to that, since she was so uncooperative.'

Kubu folded at once. 'I'll give you the briefcase.'

'The briefcase and the tote.'

'I only have the briefcase.'

'What's in it?'

Kubu bluffed. 'Look, you know perfectly well what I've got. I'll give it to you. You give me Pleasant and leave us alone. That's the end of it.'

There was silence for a long heartbeat, then the voice said, 'Take it to the Gaborone Sun at exactly eight this evening. When you turn into the parking lot, there's a row of carports on your right. Drive to the last one. There's a dumpster there. Put the briefcase in it. Don't stop. Drive straight on. And no stake-outs or other nonsense. It'll be very easy to get to your wife, *Kubu*. At her sister's funeral, for example.'

Kubu wanted to insist on speaking to Pleasant, but the line went dead. It struck him that they would have to catch all the members of this gang if his family was ever to be safe again.

At 7.30 p.m., two men came out of the house, climbed into the bottle-green Hyundai and drove off. It was clear they were heading for the Sun. Fifteen minutes later Amy hammered on the door of number 17 Ganzi Street, the sad house with peeling paint. The man who answered was broad, tall and bearded, matching Rachel's description. His eyes fixed on Amy's protruding breasts and obvious nipples. 'What the hell do you want?'

'Your friends sent me. They're at Happiness House. They said you couldn't leave here. But I do house calls.' She smiled and rubbed her leg against his.

'Bastards! They were supposed to be going to meet someone! Someone at Happiness House, it turns out.' He shook his head. 'Look, darling, you're lovely but I'm busy. Some other time, eh?'

Amy did not have much time. She pulled down one side of the top and let Beardy have a good look. 'Come on, you can't be that busy. A quickie. Whatever you want. It's paid for already.' She gave him an appraising look. 'Not that you'd have to pay anyway, lover-boy.' She considered a wink, but did not want to overplay her hand.

He hesitated. 'All right. Come on then.'

'Anyone else here, darling? I'm shy, you know.'

He laughed. 'No, just us. Let's go to the bedroom.'

Amy followed him to the bedroom, alert for the unexpected. He pulled off his shirt, took a heavy automatic out of his pocket, and put it on top of the wardrobe out of her reach. Then he dropped his pants and pulled off his shoes. He was down to slightly greyed briefs. What was happening inside them made it clear that Love Lotion would not be required.

'Get your dress off,' he said. Obviously foreplay was not his strong suit. Instead he found himself looking at a small-calibre pistol, which had a deflating effect on his ego, as well as the contents of his briefs.

'What the fuck?' He started to raise his hands in pretended surrender, and then with a roar he rushed the diminutive policewoman. With clinical precision, she shot him in the fleshy part of each thigh.

When he heard the gunshots, Kubu was out of the car and moving towards the house faster than his colleagues would have believed possible. But the Special Support Group team in camouflage clothing and flak jackets was already in the building. Following training that they had seldom needed, they searched the house rapidly, securing it. Beardy received no quarter; he was handcuffed before anyone showed interest in his wounds. Then the paramedic checked that he was not bleeding to death from a severed artery. Amy observed his grimaces and heard his bellows of pain with satisfaction. He would not be kidnapping a policeman's family again in a hurry.

With unerring instinct, Kubu headed to the back of the house. 'Pleasant!' he yelled. 'It's Kubu! We're in control. Where are you?' The response came from behind the door of a room to the right. Pleasant, showing her good sense, shouted, 'I'm here! I'm alone! I'm all right!'

'Break it down,' Kubu instructed one of the uniformed men, who tried a powerful kick. The door shuddered but held, the only solid item in the rickety house. The man tried again with similar results.

Kubu pushed the man aside. 'I'll do it myself.'

Giving himself a short run and summoning value from every calorie he had ever enjoyed, he threw his bulk against the door. The lock ripped out, and he landed in a heap. But moments later he was holding Pleasant in his arms and enjoying the warm feeling of rescuing the damsel in distress. The next morning he would be enjoying the warm feeling of a variety of bruises and abrasions, but that was tomorrow.

Kubu found Joy waiting impatiently with Mabaku in the street. She rushed to Pleasant and hugged her. Both started to cry.

'I told her to stay in the car, but she wouldn't listen. For that matter I told you to stay in the car,' the director commented. 'I've radioed Edison at the Sun. He knows we have Pleasant and have secured the house. He'll pick up the Hyundai as soon as it appears. We've got the bastards, Kubu!' His enthusiastic, triumphal punch hit Kubu on his door-bashing shoulder. Mabaku did not notice the wince. A flash of white teeth lit up his face. 'They're about to become guests at the president's pleasure. And for a very long time!'

CHAPTER 42

Shortly after nine p.m., a bottle-green Hyundai slunk into the parking lot of the Gaborone Sun. Well-heeled patrons were leaving, those who had come for dinner or drinks with business colleagues. The night was still young for the blackjack and roulette enthusiasts. This was where Botswana's success was most ostentatiously evident: designer clothes, designer cars, designer gambling losses. The Hyundai made its way through the revellers to the last carport. The driver pulled over, double-parking in front of the dumpster that occupied the last space. He was to wait one minute, phone a cell phone number, walk casually to the dumpster, and describe it. Next he was to light a cigarette, smoke it, and throw the stub into the bin.

It did not take that long. The moment he got out of the car, he found himself surrounded by police holding a variety of intimidating weapons. The driver, scared witless, put up no resistance. The cell phone was knocked out of his hand.

By the time Edison arrived from the car where he had been waiting, the suspect was secured and the area cordoned off. Edison looked at the scrawny youth with surprise rapidly deteriorating to dismay.

'Where are the others?' he asked in Setswana. He grabbed the youth by his T-shirt and yelled, 'Where are the others? Tell me!'

The driver looked at him speechless, bewildered.

'What's this shit? I did nothing!' he said, trying to talk up some courage. Edison snarled at him and let him fall heavily. He turned to the policemen.

'This foul-mouthed punk isn't the right man. Where the hell are the two men who set out from Tlokweng this evening? They're Zimbabweans and probably don't even speak Setswana!'

'He was in the car,' said the uniformed man, indicating the youth with his handgun. 'Must be him!'

Edison gave him a withering look and turned back to the teenager. 'What's your name?'

'Kali Jameng.'

'Tell me everything you know. At once. If you hesitate or leave something out, I will immediately charge you with kidnapping and murder. I'll get a judge tonight, and you will be hanged tomorrow! You better give us the names of your parents.' This piece of complete nonsense was said so matter-of-factly that even the constables wondered if the judge might already be on his way from Lobatse.

'I know nothing,' said Kali. 'I just borrowed the car and—'

Edison interrupted. 'Perhaps I didn't make myself clear. I forget how stupid you are. Let me spell it out for you. People have been murdered. A senior police officer's wife and sister-in-law have been kidnapped and held for ransom.' He paused. 'Perhaps you need some help to refresh your memory.' He turned to one of the uniformed police. 'Constable, get on the radio to headquarters. Tell them to get the interrogation room set up, the electrical stuff, crocodile clips for the testicles. The works. We need answers at once!'

The constable had no idea what Edison was talking about, but caught on quickly, rushed to his car and pretended to be on the radio. 'We need big crocodile clips!' he shouted at the top of his voice.

The youth started gabbling in an unsteady voice. He denied everything. He knew nothing about kidnappings. The problem was no longer to get him to talk, but to get him to stick to the point. He confessed to all sorts of misdemeanours in which Edison had no interest. Soon he lost patience. 'I don't care about any of that. Tell me how you got the car.'

'Rra, I was watching a man at the Nando's takeout. It's a good place to work. Busy and crowded. He seemed very nervous, scared, not concentrating. I had his wallet in a second. He didn't feel a thing!' This was said with a note of pride, which Edison killed with a ferocious snarl.

'Yes, well the problem was that he was with another man, who caught me. They weren't Batswana. Maybe they were Zimbabweans.' Kali shook his head. What was the country coming to with all these foreigners causing trouble? 'I thought they would be angry, beat me up, call the police. But they pulled me aside. Spoke to me nicely.' He gave Edison an accusatory look. 'They were both upset about something. Something bad. They said they'd give us five hundred pula. I just had to wait until half past eight and drive through the parking lot at the Gaborone Sun and phone them. Nothing wrong with that.' His hint of spunk wilted under Edison's glare.

'Who's "us"?'

'My friend Leonard was there. They caught him too.'

'You didn't think it was strange to be paid that much money? Why didn't you just steal the car?'

'It wasn't worth very much,' said the boy sullenly. 'And they kept Leonard.'

'What did you have to do?'

'Drive through the parking lot, stop at the end of the carports, phone them, smoke a cigarette and come back. For five hundred pula!'

'Nothing else? You're absolutely sure.'

'Nothing!'

Edison called to the police car, 'Constable, is the equipment ready?'

'Nothing! I swear!'

Edison sighed. The boy was too gullible to be lying, the story too unbelievable to be invented. He called the constable over. 'The Nando's is our best chance. Pick up this Leonard fellow. Try to find the Zimbabweans. They may still be waiting there.'

They went in convoy, leaving the curious glitterati to their late-night entertainments. As they drove, Edison reported to Mabaku what had happened. The director was furious. It seemed that his celebration had been premature.

'Yes, go ahead,' he said sourly. 'But they'll have left as soon as the cell phone call cut off. You won't find them.'

And they did not. They found Leonard drunk and happy with two hundred pula in his pocket. But the two Zimbabweans were gone. They had left by minibus taxi for the border at Tlokweng. Just minutes before Mabaku alerted the border officials, they slipped across into South Africa. From there they would make their careful way back to Zimbabwe.

PART FIVE
Rung by Rung

We are dropping down the ladder rung by rung.

Rudyard Kipling, *Gentlemen-Rankers*

CHAPTER 43

Mabaku assembled his core team. He had told them to meet by 7.30 a.m., and no one dared be late. Kubu was slouched at one end, brooding over a cup of coffee, with a fatcake for comfort. He had already spoken to his father about the kidnapping because he knew it would be all over the press and TV, and they would hear about it from neighbours. He had assured Wilmon that both Joy and Pleasant were fine. He would tell them all the details at their next visit. They had been upset, but he had calmed them down.

Edison was sitting next to Kubu, morosely sipping black tea. Ian MacGregor was cheerful as always, but wishing he was painting, sleeping, or even examining an interesting cadaver, rather than being at this glum early-morning meeting. Zanele Dlamini was there representing Forensics, although the only thing her group had done was check Tinubu's briefcase for drugs. The rest of the forensic work had been done in Kasane and Maun. But she provided beauty and brains, and the men were glad of both. Joshua Bembo, the South African police liaison, had settled for a glass of water and was fidgeting with his pen. The last to arrive, looking tired, was Tatwa, who had flown from Maun the day before. He was dressed formally in a jacket and tie; his St Louis cap rested on the table.

Mabaku was already on his second cup of strong black coffee. His stomach had hoped for something more substantial for breakfast, and he felt a twinge of heartburn. But the bile was in his voice. He was angry.

'Last night's operation was a disaster! In fact this whole case is a total mess.' No one said anything. 'Kubu was completely out of it yesterday.' He winced from the indigestion, and then added more kindly, 'That was understandable, of course. How are Joy and Pleasant this morning?'

Kubu pulled himself up in his chair. 'They're okay. Treating it as a big adventure and telling all their friends. It'll hit them later. They're both at my house, and Constable Mashu is keeping an eye on them. Both insisted I make the meeting this morning. But I admit I'm worried about them.'

Mabaku nodded. His anger, frustrated by sympathy for Kubu's family worries, turned on Edison. 'Edison, have you never run an undercover operation before? How in God's name did you let the Zimbabweans get away? What tipped them off?'

Edison had slept badly knowing this was coming. 'Director, we don't know what tipped them off, but there was some confusion. We had a lot of men around Ganzi Street and the Gaborone Sun. But we didn't cover the roads in between. That's where they disappeared. We needed some extra police around the hotel. The dispatcher told them it was urgent, but didn't say it was undercover. So they arrived at the Sun with their sirens going.'

'*Some* confusion? *Total* confusion is more like it.' Mabaku pounded the table, rattling the cups on their saucers.

'We think they caught wind of us and decided to wait. Perhaps also they tried to call the bearded character at the Ganzi Street house and couldn't get through. Then they came up with the plan involving the pickpocket. And we fell for it.' Edison shrugged. Early promotion looked out of the question.

'What've you done about catching them?'

Edison shrugged again. 'The usual. We've distributed identikit drawings from Joy and Pleasant throughout the southern African countries. All the border posts are alerted, but the men may be in South Africa already; one of the Tlokweng immigration officials thinks he recognises them from the identikit pictures. But we've got prints, we've got Beardy, we can follow up with the car and the pickpockets. We'll get them.' Edison wished he felt half as confident as he tried to sound.

Joshua came to life. 'Of course, you can count on the full cooperation of the South African police.'

Mabaku gave him a dirty look, muttered that more cooperation earlier would have been helpful, and changed the subject.

'What have we learned from the bearded character?'

'We think he's a hired thug. He hasn't said much yet. But he will.'

Mabaku snorted. 'Okay, I want to review the whole case. Set a few parameters. We've got lots of pieces, let's fit some of them together.' He paused. 'First, I want to make something clear. This is Kubu's case, but now he's too close to it personally. We don't want some sleazy lawyer going after him later. So formally I'm running the show, but it's Kubu's case. That clear?'

Everyone nodded. Kubu thought gratefully how well Mabaku had handled a sticky situation. The previous day the director had said he would take charge. Now he had passed the baton back, albeit under a watchful eye.

'Okay. Let's see what we have. Kubu, lead the way.'

Kubu straightened in his chair, tea and fatcake finished. It was time to get to work.

'Let's start in Zeerust. Joshua, why don't you fill us in?'

Joshua looked bashful. 'Yes, of course. Thank you, Assistant Superintendent. Good morning, everyone. One of our undercover guys – Sergeant Sipho Langa – was following a person with a number of aliases. We believe his real name is Sithole. But it doesn't matter. He's a middle man, launders money, drugs, precious metals, diamonds, you name it. But he's careful, and his principals are always well hidden. It's the principals we want. Sergeant Langa was tailing him. He followed Sithole to Zeerust and observed a meeting with a man completely new to us. Sithole gave the man a briefcase, which we suspect contained a lot of money. We now know that man was Goodluck Tinubu. Langa decided to follow Tinubu and asked for someone else to tail Sithole. Regrettably Langa followed Tinubu into the Republic of Botswana without authorisation.'

He faced the director. 'We greatly regret this. And then we lost Sithole, who's now dropped out of sight. Not our best day.'

Kubu thought this an understatement. As Joshua seemed to be finished, he took up the story.

'We know Langa followed Tinubu across the border to his house. We decoded his cryptic notes giving directions. He watched him overnight, and then followed him towards Kasane. Tinubu's car broke down, and Langa gave him a lift to Kasane and then on to Jackalberry Camp. He reported in once, saying he thought Tinubu was involved in something big. The breakdown seems to have been fortuitous, and Langa was a resourceful chap and took the opportunity offered. Then they met the mysterious Zondo at Jackalberry.'

Much of this was new to Zanele, and she was trying to keep up. 'He was the criminal from Zimbabwe? A hired assassin?'

Mabaku shook his head. 'That idea came from Du Pisanie – the camp manager. The Zimbabwe police said they'd never heard of him. Then they discovered his real name was Peter Jabulani and said he was a dissident. Recently they told us that he's a desperate criminal and murderer. They've started extradition proceedings – as if we had the man in custody! Either they want him very badly, or they have him and want to misdirect us. They've even made a fuss about their president's upcoming visit to the African Union meeting, saying Botswana's not safe if we harbour criminals and assassins. Rich, coming from them!'

Ian piped up. 'Are they being straight with us now?'

'They'd better be!' said Mabaku. 'How can he disappear with half of southern Africa looking for him? And we've got nothing. Not a hint of a trail. We can't even trace the pilot who fetched him from Jackalberry.'

Ian sat back and filled his pipe. He would suck contentedly on the unlit pipe for the rest of the meeting. 'Tinubu was originally from Zimbabwe. Was there anything in his background connecting him with Zondo?'

It was Edison who replied. 'Not as far as we know. In fact he seemed to have had very little contact with Zimbabwe since he came to Botswana years ago. We found out that he volunteered some of his time at a Zimbabwe support group. Kubu found some of its literature in his house.' Edison pouted. He had seen the pamphlets but ignored them. Kubu hadn't been complimentary about that either. 'He usually helped illegal immigrants deal with the system here. I also traced a regular payment from his bank to an individual who lives near

Bulawayo. That was all. No letters at his home, no phone calls, nothing.'

'Regular payments? Could it be blackmail? Have we followed up on this guy?' Mabaku asked.

Edison shook his head. 'It was one hundred pula each month. Far too little for blackmail. I've got the man's name – Paulus Mbedi – and address through the bank, but we haven't followed it up. I'm not sure we want to get the Zimbabwe police on this person's case. He's probably just a friend or relative. Completely unrelated to the case or to Zondo.'

'Let's get to the night of the murders,' Kubu said. 'Over to you, Tatwa.'

Tatwa was nervous in this gathering and felt he should stand. Everyone near him was forced to lean back to look up at his face.

'On the Sunday night, everyone at the camp had dinner together. It was pleasant, everyone was relaxed, but no one was particularly friendly. They all went to bed early. Tinubu was murdered in the early hours of the morning. The most obvious suspect is Zondo. That night he changed his plans and arranged to leave at dawn. We think he cleaned out whatever was in Tinubu's briefcase, because it was empty when we found it. Then he disappeared.'

Zanele chipped in. 'We found nothing of interest in the briefcase. You asked us to check it for drugs, but we found no traces at all. Even sealed bags leave a detectable residue.'

'The clues are confusing,' Tatwa continued. 'We think something like a wrench was used to knock Tinubu out and kill Langa, but it hasn't been found. All the ones we took from the camp tested clean. Also, there were two water glasses in Tinubu's tent, one with his fingerprints and one with Zondo's. So it seems they had a drink together, presumably after dinner. That's interesting, because they apparently didn't know each other.' He sat down abruptly.

Zanele interjected. 'Were there any other Zondo prints in Tinubu's tent? Anything else that linked them?' Tatwa shook his head, and Zanele continued, 'Well, it could be a set-up. Maybe someone planted the glass there, taking it from Zondo's tent.'

Kubu digested that. 'That's an interesting idea. Let's keep it in mind.' He paused. 'Another strange feature was the position of the body. Ian, over to you.'

Ian took his pipe out of his mouth, holding it by the bowl. 'Tinubu was obviously in bed asleep at that time of the night. He was hit on the side of the head, probably hard enough to knock him unconscious. There was blood on his pillow, and he had a head wound. Then he was dragged off the bed, stabbed through the heart with a spike of some sort, and his throat was cut. Overkill, you might say.'

Zanele was frowning. 'Why pull him off the bed? Surely the murderer could stab him there?'

Ian pointed the pipe stem at her. 'Good point. I also wondered about that. And cutting the throat? It must have been obvious that Tinubu was dead. Then the murderer mutilated the body. A message? A warning? Or more misdirection?'

'What about Langa?' asked Mabaku.

Ian replied. 'Sergeant Langa had his head smashed in, probably by the same blunt instrument used to knock out Tinubu. Then he was tossed down a slope into a small gully. No fancy killing methods or mutilations there.'

Kubu took over. 'We think it was the briefcase that linked the two murders. Certainly Sergeant Langa was focused on the briefcase. First the handover in Zeerust, and then a possible exchange at Jackalberry. And when he was killed, he was prepared for a night of watching – jacket, binoculars and so on.

'Let's suppose Zondo was the murderer. He kills Tinubu, takes the contents of the briefcase and goes back to his tent. He doesn't realise that he's being followed by Langa.'

'Surely the sergeant would've raised the alarm when Tinubu was murdered?' Joshua interjected.

'But he probably wouldn't have known,' Kubu replied. 'He couldn't get close enough to see into the tent. And the goings-on there would've been quiet. No shots or screams.'

Joshua nodded doubtfully.

'Now suppose that near Zondo's tent, Langa made a mistake,' Kubu continued, 'and somehow gave himself away. Zondo kills Langa and gets out at first light the next morning as planned.' Kubu rubbed his jowls with both hands, wishing he'd had a longer night's sleep. He clearly had more to say, so the others waited.

'There's another possibility I've thought about. The thread Tatwa and I found up at the lookout niggled at me. It came from Tinubu's jacket and was in thicker bush – as though he'd suddenly needed to hide from a watcher. Who would that have been? Not Zondo, his supposed compatriot. And why hide from anyone else at the camp? He had every right to be there. It could only have been Sipho Langa. Goodluck must've been suspicious. Suppose he went to Zondo's tent – probably to exchange money for drugs or whatever – and realised Langa was on to them. Perhaps Langa even confronted them? They would've had to get rid of him. Exit Sergeant Langa.

'But now Zondo is one step ahead of Tinubu. He realises that once Langa is found, the game will be up. So he decides to make this last trade the most profitable ever. Later that night he kills Tinubu and takes the contents of the briefcase.' Kubu rubbed his jowls again and shook his head slightly.

'You don't buy it?' asked Mabaku.

'Well, if they used a wrench, where did it come from? No one at the camp reported one missing. And the ones we tested were all clean. Whichever way I look at it, it seems premeditated. More important, the whole thing doesn't ring true with Tinubu's character. I can't reconcile his work at the school in Mochudi over all those years with what happened. Tinubu a murderer? Drug smuggler?' Kubu shook his head. 'It was something else. I think Goodluck was a victim.'

Mabaku looked grim. 'Well, I have some information to contribute. The Munro sisters actually came out to Botswana to follow the lives of people involved in the Rhodesian war. One of those people was Salome McGlashan and another was a George Tinubu – the name Goodluck used when he lived in Rhodesia.' He filled the group in on his meeting with the Munro sisters. 'Kubu needs to follow up with them. We haven't had the opportunity with all this other business. The point is that there's now a real chance that Tinubu and Salome knew each other. Maybe they didn't recognise each other, and maybe they did. But it's a connection; before, we had strangers. It raises the possibility of other motives.'

'Revenge is a powerful motivation,' said Ian. 'Could Salome have been the murderer?'

Kubu shook his head. 'Based on my assessment of her, I doubt it. And what about Langa?'

'Maybe he caught her in the act while keeping an eye on Tinubu,' Ian responded.

'Why kill him at the other end of the camp? Hardly likely she'd be able to do that if she'd lost the element of surprise anyway. And how was she going to explain the bodies in the morning?'

'She could blame the murders on Zondo!' said Zanele excitedly. 'Exactly what happened!'

'According to Dupie and Enoch, she didn't know Zondo was leaving early. And how would she know he was going to disappear?'

Zanele was unconvinced. She seemed to like Salome in the role of vengeful fury. 'What if she had help from Du Pisanie? Or one of the other camp staff?'

'Well, Dupie certainly had no love to waste on black Zimbabweans – especially the ones running the country there now. He still refers to them all as terrorists. But to commit murder on the spur of the moment in front of a camp full of people when the truth was sure to come out? He knew where Tinubu lived and could have chosen his moment.' Kubu shook his head again. 'It doesn't add up. But we do need to dig deeper into this issue with the Munros.'

Mabaku looked pensive, but he could not fault Kubu's reasoning.

'Does that mean that it had to be Zondo? Because he was the only one who knew about the briefcase and so had a motive?'

Tatwa broke in excitedly. 'That's what we thought. But it's not right. Tinubu lost his keys at one point and was very upset about it. They turned up, but could easily have been lifted and used to search the stuff in his tent in the meantime. One of them could have been a key to the briefcase. So someone not involved in the smuggling could've known about the contents of the briefcase. Mind you, there wasn't a briefcase key on the ring we found in his tent, but that could be because the murderer needed it to open the case.'

Kubu joined in. 'So anyone who was nosy could've discovered a briefcase full of money, and then would have a motive. The only thing is, he would have to be suspicious to make him look in the first place. Someone who had an inkling of what was going on. And that brings us to Boy Gomwe.'

Kubu looked at Joshua Bembo, inviting him to share what the South African police had discovered. Joshua obliged by filling in the background and their suspicions of Gomwe's drug-running activities, lamenting that Gomwe always seemed to be one step ahead.

'That makes him a suspect. What was he doing at the camp? And he would've guessed or suspected what was in the briefcase. Enough motivation to steal the keys and take a look. And then . . .' Tatwa trailed off, leaving the rest to their imaginations.

Kubu was no longer concentrating. The fatcake was long gone, and he was thinking about breakfast. There was a real danger the meeting would go on all morning. He would have to think of something; he doubted he could hold out until lunch.

Mabaku picked up the story. 'Then on Thursday night two thugs attack Du Pisanie and McGlashan at Jackalberry Camp. They were after the briefcase. That means Tinubu's murder wasn't a hit or a personal vendetta; it was for the money and drugs or whatever. And the thugs knew Zondo. They came to the camp because Zondo wasn't at the airstrip when the plane arrived to pick him up. That looks as though Zondo decided to take off with the lot. To cut his bosses out. Perhaps he thought the Zimbabwe police were on his trail. Perhaps he just got greedy. Then, of course, Kubu stuck his neck out and damned nearly had it chopped off.'

'What we need to do now—' Ian began, but Kubu interrupted.

'What we need to do now is take a break while we order more tea and send out for muffins. Plenty of muffins.' Without waiting for Mabaku's approval, Kubu was on his feet and heading for the door. 'And I need to call home to check on Joy.'

The others were happy enough to stretch their legs. Even Mabaku felt that a muffin might help his indigestion.

Once the food had been assembled, the meeting resumed. Kubu would have liked to eat in peace, but Mabaku was impatient to continue. 'Let's get to the murder of William Boardman,' he said, selecting a banana muffin as his second. Kubu was busy with a chocolate one and waved to Tatwa.

'Boardman was murdered late on Monday night. Assistant Superintendent Notu thought it was an opportunistic robbery, but that makes no sense. Boardman was accosted at his room at the Maun Toro Lodge. Either he was forced into it, or he let the murderer or murderers in. Once again, there was a lot of misdirection. Whoever killed Boardman wants us to think it happened later than it did. Someone pretending to be one of the guests phoned reception at one thirty to report a big noise in one of the bungalows, but Kubu and I established first that no one heard the noise, and second that none of the guests phoned in. In fact, the murderer made the phone call when he was already well on his way. Our trace on the call showed it came from Boardman's own cell phone, no doubt taken from the murder scene. That suggests the murderer wanted to confuse us or establish a false alibi.'

Ian took his pipe out of his mouth. 'Another thing was thrown in to confuse us. I think that Boardman was attacked and killed and *then* tortured. Not much point. Dead men can't talk, as the saying goes. I can't be absolutely sure on the order, but, at the latest, he died very shortly after the torture started.'

'So if it was the thugs who attacked Jackalberry and then Joy and Pleasant, why do that?' Tatwa continued. 'And the search of Boardman's room was exaggerated. Clothes strewn around, toiletries emptied. The thugs were looking for a briefcase, not something small. But they left Boardman's car keys in his pocket and apparently didn't bother to look in his trailer with his African artworks and curios.' He shook his head. 'Also Mrs Boardman told me that her husband was meeting someone that night. Quite excited about it apparently. But that person never turned up – at least not to the meeting. According to the restaurant, Boardman ate on his own – quite late – and then had a couple of drinks, clearly waiting for someone. Finally he gave up and went to his room.'

Zanele had another thought. 'Could Boardman have been involved in the Jackalberry murders? Did he have curios there?'

Kubu turned his attention from the muffins – he was on his third – long enough to reply. 'As a matter of fact, he admitted to wandering around that night, and his wife noticed. And they did have curios. What of it?'

'I was thinking they might've been used to smuggle the contents of the briefcase off the island. Maybe it wasn't bulky at all. Something like diamonds that could be hidden in a mask or drum.'

Kubu didn't like that idea at all. 'If it was that small, anyone could've hidden it anywhere. They'd all have opportunity.'

'Any other prints in the room or other forensic evidence?' asked Zanele.

'Nothing that idiot Notu could find,' Kubu growled.

Tatwa was trying to regain the floor. 'There's another issue. I've looked into it very carefully. If we accept that the Boardman murder and the camp murders are related – and I think we do . . .' He paused, but no one challenged this. 'Then we must look at who had opportunity. Apart from the victims, there were ten people at Jackalberry Camp that Sunday night of the murders – nine excluding William himself.' He counted the potential suspects on his fingers. 'Last Monday night Dupie, Salome and Moremi were all entertaining guests at the camp. Beauty and Solomon were at the village on the mainland as they were on the night of the murders. Enoch wasn't at the camp because he'd broken down on the road to Kasane, and Dupie had to drive out to help him. Enoch slept in the vehicle and went in to Kasane the next morning. That's four of them accounted for. The Munro sisters were having dinner in Gaborone in the dining room at the Grand Palm Hotel. Two more. Boardman's wife was in Cape Town. That's seven in total, leaving only Gomwe and Zondo.' He paused and looked around the group. Now he was enjoying being the centre of attention. No one interrupted.

'So there are only three possibilities. Boardman was murdered by Zondo, who somehow returned to the middle of Botswana with the whole country looking for him and disappeared again presumably the same way. Or the thugs from Zimbabwe did it and maybe hit him too hard, killing him before they could find out what they wanted to know. Or he was killed by Gomwe looking for the valuables.' He looked around. 'And Gomwe's office told me he was expected in Gaborone. He did meet with the owner of a music store here on Saturday morning and stayed at the Oasis Hotel on Saturday and Sunday nights, leaving early on Monday morning. After that he disappeared. No record of his leaving Botswana. No flights under his name. He had plenty of time to drive to Maun.'

Mabaku decided to sum up. 'Okay. Good job, Sergeant Mooka. I think you've put it together very well. Kubu?' Kubu nodded. He had been through it all with Tatwa before and could not fault it. Yet it seemed too pat, too straightforward. Kubu's instinct told him some piece was missing, some assumption not as solid as it seemed. He nodded again but with just a hint of uncertainty, which Mabaku ignored.

'Right,' Mabaku said. 'We pressure Beardy. We try to find the two Zimbabweans and get them into an interrogation room as soon as possible. We smash this drug ring or whatever it is. Big feather in our caps. And we use that as a lever to force them to tell us everything about Zondo. Everything!' He banged his fist on the table again in time with the last word. 'In parallel we go after Gomwe. Get to the bottom of whatever he's up to. And if he's a murderer hiding behind these Zimbabwe thugs, he's going to wish he'd never been born!'

'Right!' said Kubu. 'Let's get to work!'

CHAPTER 44

First things first. Kubu checked if anything new had come up on Zondo and was not surprised to discover there was still no trace of him. Either Zondo had a careful plan to disappear with the fruits of his treachery, or somewhere he had met an unpleasant demise. Kubu was beginning to lean towards the latter explanation as the case developed. Then he checked if there was anything new from the border stations on the Zimbabwean kidnappers. But they too seemed to have disappeared once they crossed into South Africa. Kubu ground his teeth. He wanted to catch them very badly. As long as they were at large, his family was not safe. He tried not to blame Edison for the debacle. Mistakes happened. But he was very concerned. He made another quick call home.

'Kubu,' said Joy. 'This is the third time you've called. The house is swarming with police, Pleasant and I are bored out of our minds, and you spend the day worrying. This can't go on.'

'The house is hardly swarming with police. Just Constable Mashu. How are you feeling now?' The last question was motivated by Joy's persistent nausea. Kubu wanted her to see a police counsellor; Joy thought this was nonsense.

Not in the mood to chat, she repeated, 'This can't go on.'

Kubu sighed. He had thought of a plan but had wanted to get Mabaku aboard before trying it out on Joy. He was not sure how either would react. Well here goes, he thought. He put his proposal to Joy and waited for her to explode. There was silence on the line for long seconds. 'Yes, all right,' she said in a matter-of-fact voice. 'Provided we're left alone there. I'll talk to Pleasant. Now for heaven's sake get to work and catch those horrible men. I'll speak to you later. Bye, darling.'

And the line went dead. Kubu sat holding the receiver for a few moments, listening to the dial tone. I'll never understand women, he thought. Even the great male poets don't understand women. I'm not convinced that even women understand women!

He replaced the receiver, but lifted it again almost immediately. He needed to arrange to see two other women, whom he probably wouldn't understand either. The Munros seemed keen to see him too; they had left two messages with the duty constable during the morning.

It was Trish who answered Kubu's call. 'Oh, Assistant Superintendent. So good to hear from you! Director Mabaku told us to wait here until you contacted us, but we want to leave tomorrow. We've delayed our return twice already, and we really want to get home now. Of course, Judith's in no rush!' She laughed as if this would mean something to Kubu, and then gushed on.

'We're so keen to talk to you, too. Remember that you suggested we write a piece about what happened? Will you help us? Perhaps we could ask you a few things about Botswana and the police and what you do. Just a few. And then you could ask us anything you want to know.' She made it sound like taking turns in a game, and Kubu was not sure how to respond. But then Trish played her trump card. 'Could you join us for lunch? Say in half an hour? The Palm has a very good restaurant, and I'm sure you'll find something to your liking.'

Kubu was tempted, but he wasn't sure socialising was appropriate. On the other hand, the Munros were witnesses in a murder investigation, and there had been a formal interview with Mabaku, so this was really just a follow-up. He had to have lunch, and there was much to do this afternoon if Mabaku accepted his plan. He felt himself weakening.

'The veal with lemon sauce is particularly good,' said Trish. Kubu's mouth was watering as he heard himself accepting their invitation without further ado.

CHAPTER 45

Mabaku decided to join Edison for the interview with Beardy. Kubu had wanted to go, but Mabaku had forbidden it, promising that he would give a full report. On the drive to the Princess Marina Hospital, where Beardy was being held, Mabaku sat silently involved with his thoughts and his after-lunch indigestion. Edison felt it prudent to keep as low a profile as possible and drove carefully at the speed limit.

But once at the hospital, Mabaku cheered up. 'What do we know about this villain?'

'Not much. He's refused to say anything. But we know who he is. The police in Zimbabwe identified him from his prints. His name is John Khumalo.'

'If we do this properly, Detective Banda, we may walk away from here a lot further ahead with this case. I'll lead, but be ready to jump in at the right moment.' Edison wondered how he would know when that would be, but nodded firmly.

'Has he been advised of his rights?' Mabaku asked, and again Edison nodded.

Beardy was in a private room, with an armed uniformed constable slouched in the visitors' chair. He jumped to attention when Mabaku entered and saluted smartly.

'Yes, yes, Constable,' the director said. 'Go and find another two chairs for us.' The constable marched off, pleased with this challenging assignment. Mabaku walked over to Beardy's bedside. 'How's the leg?' he asked, giving one bandaged thigh a solid thump. Beardy winced. 'Sore, is it?' Mabaku sounded pleased. 'Well, don't get too used to these comforts. You'll be having a much rougher time once we get you out of here. Not recommended, kidnapping the wife of a senior police officer.' Seeing the look on Beardy's face, he continued, 'Oh, they didn't mention that to you, did they? You're in very hot water, Mr Khumalo. Boiling water, I'd say.' Beardy turned away.

The constable returned with the extra chairs, and they settled themselves around Beardy like hyenas circling a wounded impala.

'Then there's the indecent assault on our policewoman,' Mabaku said with satisfaction. This at last elicited a response.

'I didn't touch the bitch! She pretended to be a fucking prostitute!'

Mabaku nodded thoughtfully. 'I suppose that's what prostitutes do,' he commented, 'but she wasn't one, you see.'

'And there's resisting arrest,' Edison chipped in, hoping this was the moment.

'Quite right,' said Mabaku.

Beardy looked disgusted. 'All right, you've made your point. What do you want to know, and what's in it for me?'

Mabaku looked pensive. 'Well, we want to know everything, actually. Who you work for, who was with you, how you got into Botswana, why your friends attacked an assistant superintendent's wife, why you kidnapped his sister-in-law. That would be a good start. As for what's in it for you, if you cooperate, things may go a bit easier on you. That's all I'm offering right now. Let's see how it all goes.'

Beardy shrugged. 'This guy Johannes hired me for the job. I don't know who pointed him to me. Said it was an easy job. Just guarding a house and a woman for a few days in Gaborone. He'd get what he was after, we'd let the woman go – no rough stuff – and get out. I'd get ten thousand pula for a week's work. I had no problems with that.'

Edison was making notes. 'Where did he hire you?'

'Bulawayo.'

'Who were the other men with you here?'

'Johannes and a man called Setu.'

'What were their last names?'

Beardy shrugged again. 'Johannes and Setu, that's all. You think I asked for IDs?'

Mabaku glared at him. 'You said you were cooperating. Now you're lying and getting smart-assed with it.'

'I called him Johannes, the other guy Setu. They called me Khumalo. That's how it was!'

Mabaku walked over to the bed and bent threateningly close. 'Who's Madrid?' he asked loudly in Beardy's face.

Beardy jerked his head away, fear playing in his eyes. 'I don't know any Madrid.'

'Oh, I think your Johannes is very close to my Madrid, who you don't know. Maybe you'd better think again.'

'I don't know a man called Madrid.'

'I didn't say it was a man, but you're right about that. A white man actually. He and your friend Johannes attacked some people at a tourist lodge near Kasane. Ring any bells?'

Beardy turned and looked Mabaku in the eye. 'I know nothing about that.'

Mabaku grunted and returned to his seat.

'How did you get into Botswana?' asked Edison.

'Johannes drove us down from Bulawayo. He had the contacts for the house and car set up already. I don't know who organised that.'

'What about Happiness House?'

Beardy looked surprised. 'That was on Saturday while the others were out tracking down the second woman. I wanted a girl. What of it?' Then it occurred to him how the police knew the location of the Ganzi Street house.

'Oh, shit!'

Mabaku looked bored. 'You have a problem with keeping your pants on, don't you, Khumalo? No wonder they dumped you to face the music when they took off. Want to tell us why they were kidnapping a policeman's family?'

'I didn't know who the women were. Just that we would pick up one and hold her until we got some briefcase that Johannes wanted. He said it was stolen from him.' He paused for a moment and then asked, a little too artfully, 'That true?'

Mabaku looked disgusted. 'I'll ask the questions. What was in the briefcase?'

Beardy hesitated, but evidently decided he had better know something. 'Money,' he said. 'A lot of money. US dollars.'

'How much money?'

Beardy just shrugged. 'A lot.'

'What's this money for?'

'I told you, he hired me to help get it back from someone called Bengu. I don't know how this Bengu got it in the first place.'

'Was it for drugs?'

'Yes. I guess that's right. Drug money.'

Mabaku got up again. 'You're not levelling with us, Khumalo. You know that, and we know that. I guess your Zimbabwe friends might be pretty upset about what you have told us, though. Why don't you think about that while we move you to Central Prison? To more permanent accommodation.'

With that he walked out, followed by Edison.

In the car, Mabaku seemed pensive. 'What do you make of that?' he asked Edison.

'It's half the story. He knows more than he's letting on.'

Mabaku nodded. 'Exactly. He knows Madrid all right. Did you see his face when I asked him? But I think he was telling the truth about the Jackalberry attack. That was news to him.'

'And the briefcase full of drug money?'

'Well, I think the briefcase bit is true – that's what Madrid wanted from Dupie and Kubu, after all. Maybe the money bit, too. But he seemed a bit too keen to settle for the drug money story.'

Mabaku thumped the dashboard. 'Get him out of that damned hospital into a nasty dank cell. Then maybe he'll stop playing games with us.'

CHAPTER 46

Trish and Judith met Kubu at Livingstone's restaurant, and they settled at a comfortably large table. Kubu had a steelworks, and the sisters, who seemed in a celebratory mood, ordered a bottle of white wine. Kubu wondered if he would learn more if he waited until the wine took effect, or if he would then learn nothing at all. But Judith took the initiative.

'Are you married, Mr Bengu? May we call you Kubu? It's such a wonderful nickname.'

'And children?' asked Trish.

Kubu admitted to being married, but that he had no children.

'What about your parents? Where did you grow up?'

Kubu felt he was losing control of the situation. He was the one who should be asking the questions. He finished his steelworks and ordered another.

'When did you decide to become a detective?'

'Well, I've always loved puzzles. My father used to buy them from a street trader, and we'd do them together. Then, as I grew older, I realised that puzzles don't have to be physical things; they can be problems, perhaps difficult problems, but if you apply the same logic to them, you'll find the solution. And my Bushman school friend, Khumanego, taught me something else. That the pieces of the puzzle are often hidden, but still right in front of your eyes. That's how the Bushmen live; they see things we just ignore. Things that are food and drink and danger.'

He looked around, wishing he could enjoy the Chardonnay. 'Where's that waiter gone with my steelworks?' The waiter was nowhere to be seen.

'Well, we must get to business,' Kubu continued. 'I'm trying to understand who Goodluck Tinubu actually was. A freedom fighter who went over the top? A dedicated teacher? A drug smuggler? A victim?' He shook his head. 'He can't be all of these things.'

Judith repeated the story they had told Mabaku, finishing with the sneering indictment of Tinubu by Tito Ndlovu, the ex-terrorist living in England. They paused for the appetisers. Kubu had chicken livers, which were piquant. The Chardonnay would have been excellent to wash them down.

'How did you find out where Goodluck was living? Obviously Ndlovu didn't know.'

Trish answered. 'Well, we found four Tinubus in Botswana, but only one was a schoolteacher. We thought it had to be him. And, of course, we believed he lived near Gaborone.'

'Why did you think he was a schoolteacher living near here?'

'It was in the letter from Shlongwane,' Judith answered.

'What letter?' Kubu was starting to lose the thread being tossed between the two sisters. His veal arrived. It was delicious, and when the last of the lemon sauce had been mopped up with the last fried potato, he was feeling content. But he was intrigued by the mysterious letter.

'What letter?' he asked again. 'Who's Shlongwane?'

Judith picked up the story. 'When we started researching the project, one of the things we did was to scan old copies of the *Rhodesia Herald* from the war period. The newspaper was censored, of course, and you couldn't rely much on what it had to say, but it gave us a feel for the times. One issue reported a schoolteachers' strike. The newspaper said it was unruly and politically motivated, but admitted that the government had misjudged the opposition to closing the school. It mentioned a George Tinubu, who was arrested for leading an illegal demonstration, and we immediately remembered Ndlovu's remark. Tinubu's not a common name. Another teacher called Shlongwane was arrested as well.

'We found in a paper from after independence that the school had reopened and many of the teachers reinstated. We wrote a letter to George Tinubu but received no reply. So on the off chance, we wrote a letter to Mr Shlongwane. He wasn't there, but the school forwarded it to him, and after quite a while he wrote back. He had moved to Harare, and his reply was posted in South Africa.'

Trish leant forward. 'Goodluck wasn't a drug smuggler, Kubu. I don't know what he did in the war, but he wouldn't do that. Not to the children. You'd know if you read the letter.'

'Do you have the letter here?'

Trish nodded. 'I'll fetch it for you after lunch. But to get back to your question, Shlongwane said he didn't know exactly where Goodluck was, but he thought he was near Gaborone. He'd received a call from him once, many years before.'

'What about dessert, Kubu?' suggested Judith. 'Do have something. We have many more questions!'

Kubu wanted to get back to work, but he was intrigued by the letter and feeling mellow after the meal. 'The crème brûlée is good,' Trish encouraged. Kubu protested that he was really too full, but felt obliged to keep them company. How do they keep so slim? he wondered. Must be something to do with the English weather. They've matched me mouthful for mouthful!

By the time they had finished chatting, and Trish had fetched him a copy of Shlongwane's letter, the afternoon was well advanced. The letter was several pages long and written in beautiful script and good English. Mr Shlongwane was clearly an educated and meticulous man. Kubu felt a touch of excitement. Here, at last, was a record from the start of the journey that had ended at a bush camp on the Linyanti. He folded it carefully, to read at his leisure and in private.

At last he took his leave, wishing the sisters well and a good trip home. They shook his hand warmly, saying what a pleasant afternoon it had been, and how much they appreciated his time. As he left, Trish called after him, 'We'll send you a copy of the article when it comes out.'

Kubu missed half a stride. Somewhere during the afternoon, he had forgotten the article they were proposing to write. He wondered if he had said anything he should not have. Especially about Director Mabaku.

CHAPTER 47

Dear Ladies,

Please excuse me for the long delay in replying to your friendly letter of last January. It took several weeks to reach me as it tracked me around this country. Frankly, I pondered as to whether I should respond at all. I am not sure where George Tinubu is, or even if he is still alive. If not, then it is his second passing. I will explain later how that can be.

The things you enquire about took place many years ago. The memory of them is not pleasant and is perhaps dimmed by that, and, perhaps, it is best that these things are forgotten altogether. The world is a different place now, both for better and for worse.

You are writers, so you will remember that Charles Dickens started *A Tale of Two Cities* with the line: 'It was the best of times, it was the worst of times.' I suppose that reveals that I am a teacher of English. But I think you know that already. It was a set book for a final year at a high school where I once taught. I liked the line and remembered it. Nowadays we do not teach or read these books, nor do we study English history. Instead we study African writers and history. Something is gained, but something is lost.

It was the best of times. We were young and keen. We felt an excitement and a mission. There were three of us – George Tinubu, Peter Jabulani and myself – school friends, always together. When we finished high school, we enrolled in the College for Teachers. This was not because our education was paid for, but because we felt a calling. 'The children are our future.' That is what George always said. After independence from Britain, we would run the best school in Zimbabwe. We had ideas, ambitions. I had ideas, ambitions. George laughed at me because he was a teacher and that was what he wanted to do. I thought my ambitions could take the whole country forward! I could be Minister of Education one day, for the 'winds of change' were sweeping through Africa. You must forgive me; I was young, and these things seemed possible then.

But it was also the worst of times. For the door was shut and bolted. In Southern Rhodesia the wind howled outside, but inside there was only a whistling, creeping around the door. And when it became Rhodesia, padding was stuffed in the cracks, and it became stiflingly still.

There came a day Peter told us he was leaving. He could not stand back and wait for others to win our freedom. The next day he was gone. I thought we should follow him, but George said no. 'Our job is to teach,' he said. So George and I carried on at the college, and we talked politics and planned for freedom, but we did nothing. The war growled around us like the sound of traffic on busy streets outside your house.

When we graduated we went to teach at a school outside Bulawayo at a place called Nsiza. We both wanted to go to a country area where we felt the need for good teachers was greatest. The Nsiza secondary school was happy to have us, for we had done well in our training. So it seemed we might wait out the war and bring these children to a new world. But that was not to be.

The school was some way outside Nsiza, and the time came when the government of Mr Ian Smith said it was not safe. That the terrorists – as they called our fighters – would come and attack us and kill the children. I think they were afraid that we were sympathisers and that we would secretly support the fighters. The school was a boarding school where the children lived during the teaching term. An important official came from the Department of Education and explained that the villagers would be moved into Nsiza, that the children could go to school there. He was not clear about what school or whether we were to go too, only that we were all to leave. The headmaster was very upset and said he would write to the Department. But we could all see that he was scared. Of the fighters and of the police. So George stood up and addressed the man from the Department. He spoke very calmly. I cannot remember his exact words after all these years, but he said something like, 'We are grateful for your concern about our safety and that of our pupils here at the school. We are happy to tell you that there is no danger here; these children are the future. No one will touch them. We will stay here with them, and they will be safe. Now you must excuse us, because we have our duties.' With that, he turned and left, and we all followed. Even the headmaster! We left the man in the staff room on his own, so surprised that he left shortly after. Can you imagine such a triumph for a group of schoolteachers?

But triumphs are transitory. A week later a policeman came, this time with an eviction order. We were all to be gone by the end of the month. It was clever, because that was the half-term, and the pupils would go home in any case. Normally we would stay and prepare for the next term. After the policeman left, we assembled again in the staff room. The headmaster addressed us. He told us he had heard from the Department; they understood our concerns, but they said we must obey the police instructions. We would be reassigned to different schools. We would lose no benefits or salary. He sat down, relieved, as though the matter was resolved. I am proud to tell you that this time I raised my hand. What about our education initiatives? I asked. What about our pupils? How could these people destroy our school? The headmaster said we had no option. Then George got up, and we were all quiet, wondering what he would say this time. And I do remember his words, even after all these years. He said, 'The headmaster is right. At least for me there is no option. I will stay here and be ready with my lessons when the pupils return.' Then he sat down.

There was much discussion. Would the pupils come back?

Would they not be kept in the town? Should we not obey the Department? George listened to all this quietly. Then he said, 'Our comrades are fighting and dying. I am not a man of war but a teacher. This is my calling. When the pupils come back, I will be ready with their lessons.' That was all he said. He did not call on us to join him. He just said he would be there. Then he let the talk fly around him like a swarm of desert locusts.

When the new term started, ten of the twelve teachers were there. We had our lessons ready. No pupils came, and a few days later they sent the police under the charge of a black sergeant. The government did not even think we were worth a white officer. The sergeant assured us that the pupils were all being well educated in Nsiza, and that jobs would be found for us. He had trucks to take us and our belongings to Nsiza. He would wait while we packed. We were no longer safe where we were. The army could no longer protect us.

We turned to George; the headmaster was one of those who had not returned after the break. He explained that we were waiting for the children. That they would come back. In the meanwhile we would wait at the school. There was no need for concern about our safety. The sergeant was quiet for a few moments. Then he told us that his orders were that we be taken to Nsiza. We could pack and his men would help us load the vehicles. But we had to leave in two hours' time. George just looked at the sergeant. Then he said, 'I need to finish marking my test papers.' And he turned away.

After two hours, none of us had packed. The sergeant came into the staff room and started reading the emergency regulations that had been promulgated after the Unilateral Declaration of Independence. When he was finished, he told us we must now all get on to the trucks or we would be in conflict with the regulations. George told him that these regulations were illegal, for they had never been signed by the Governor General, who was the only legitimate legal authority in the country. It was the only time I heard him say anything to the sergeant against the regime of Mr Ian Smith and its Unilateral Declaration of Independence.

The sergeant came back after ten minutes with all his men carrying night sticks. Afterwards they said we 'resisted arrest', that we 'punched police officers carrying out their duty', that we 'incited disobedience against the government'. I hope that we did all of these things, but I cannot say. Almost at once I was hit on the head by a policeman, who seemed to enjoy carrying out his duty, and I regained consciousness in a cell at Nsiza police station.

They held us for three months, but we were never charged with anything. We discovered that our colleagues had been released almost immediately, and they had been given postings in other parts of the country. We were the ringleaders, it seems, and had led the others astray. After our release, we looked for jobs for the next teaching year. I wanted to get back to work, George wanted to get back to teaching. But soon we realised there were no teaching jobs available. Not for dissidents and agitators. I found a job at the Wankie coal mine doing clerical work, but for George, they had taken away his life.

After I moved to Wankie, we lost touch, but I heard through the grapevine that he had gone over the border. That could only mean one thing, but I found it impossible to imagine George as a freedom fighter. Perhaps it was Peter Jabulani who recruited him. If so, he should have known no good could come of it. About eighteen months later I heard that George was in a group involved in an attack on a farm and had been killed in a skirmish with the Selous Scouts afterwards. I mourned the man, and I mourned the waste. The world seemed dulled, covered with a layer of the grey coal dust of Wankie. Shortly after, I found a school that would have me as a teacher near what was then called Fort Victoria. I took the job and moved away from the coal and the past.

That, dear ladies, is what I recall of those best and worst of times. Things are different now, and all the things fought for are lost. In those days we thought that the British Government supported us because it felt that freedom was right and that Mr Smith's government was wrong. But now we get no support from Britain against a government even worse. I wonder if all along it was Mr Smith's disobedience that the British Government could not tolerate, rather than his policies.

There is one more thing to add, perhaps the most important for you, and a happy ending. About a year after the end of the war, I received a telephone call at my home near Bulawayo. It was George who phoned. I have no doubt of that, because the things he told me only he could know. He did not say how he found me, only that he wanted me to know that he was alive and teaching in Botswana, somewhere near Gaborone I think he said. He asked me to tell no one. I said I thought he was dead, that he had been killed by the security forces. He did not laugh. 'Yes,' he said, 'that George Tinubu died there. I nearly died, but a good couple nursed me till I was better. When I could travel, I crossed into Botswana.' So that was the death and rebirth of George Tinubu.

I never heard from him again, and he gave me no address or phone number. I think he wanted me to know that he was alive, and as happy as possible for a man cut off from his friends and country, but he did not want me to be in a position to say where he was. But that was many years ago.

I wonder if you will find him, or even if now you will look for him. Does he even wish to be found? But if you do meet him, and the moment is right, remember me to him. I will give this letter to a friend who will post it in South Africa. If God is willing, you will receive it. I wish you good fortune with your efforts.

Yours faithfully,
Endima Shlongwane, BEd

CHAPTER 48

Kubu carefully folded the letter and closed it in his file. So Moremi had been right. Goodluck and Zondo were friends. That was surely important. He came to a decision. The question was whether he could get his boss to go along with it. There was only one way to find out.

'What progress?' asked Mabaku by way of greeting.

Kubu shrugged, looking as depressed as he felt. 'Edison traced the Zimbabweans. They went through Tlokweng, all right. False documents. No car. Someone probably met them on the South African side of the border, and after that they disappeared. They could be anywhere. Joshua Bembo's been very helpful and seems to have the whole South African police force looking for them. But I suspect they may already be back in Zimbabwe. And we only lifted partial fingerprints from the automatic Joy took away from them. We've sent those to Zimbabwe and South Africa, as well as details of the pistol. Nothing back yet. And I'd be surprised if we ever get anything.'

'Well, we made some progress with Beardy. I've no doubt it's this Madrid character who was behind the kidnapping. Beardy said it was drug money, but I'm not a hundred per cent sure.' The director filled Kubu in on the interview. After a short discussion, Mabaku changed the subject.

'Anything on Zondo?'

Kubu shook his head. 'Nothing. I'm sure he didn't come back to Botswana. Joshua's trying to get a higher profile for the search in South Africa, but they're already taking it seriously. One of their men was killed, after all. Director, it's impossible that Zondo vanished. I think the Zimbabwe police may have him. Maybe the secret police.'

Mabaku did not like that idea. 'Well, what about Gomwe? Surely he hasn't also disappeared into thin air?'

'He checked out of his hotel on Monday morning of last week and then vanished. There's no record of him leaving the country. I've asked Notu to look for him in Maun, but Notu wouldn't find someone hiding in his office without help. And Gomwe would be crazy to hang around in Maun if he did kill Boardman. If he went to Maun, he must have driven or flown under an assumed name, because there's no record of a Gomwe flying there that weekend. We've alerted all stations to keep an eye open for him.'

Mabaku looked at Kubu, waiting. The detective hadn't come to his office to tell him this. There must be something else coming.

Kubu looked uncomfortable. 'Jacob, I'm worried sick about Joy.'

Mabaku, whose eyebrows had risen at the use of his first name, started to reassure Kubu, saying that he could have the constable with her as long as necessary. But Kubu brushed him aside.

'She doesn't want that. I don't know what's got into her. One minute's she hoping that the thugs will try again so she can try out her latest karate chop, the next she's in tears that they'll murder Pleasant. And it's affecting her physically too. This morning she was throwing up again. Said it was the strain of the last few days. I'm really concerned. Pleasant seems okay, but she sticks as close to Joy as her shadow.'

Mabaku started to say something, but Kubu rushed on.

'I want them to go to their brother in Francistown until we catch these bastards. They'll be safe with him, and the local police can keep an eye on them. They won't be going to work, following their usual routines, doing all the things that make it easy for kidnappers.'

'Well,' Mabaku commented, 'it's up to you and them. But it's not a bad idea. Will Joy go?'

Kubu nodded. 'Yes, because she's worried about Pleasant, who's as stubborn as she is and wants to go back to work!'

'Fine. I'll arrange the surveillance with Francistown CID.' He pulled the telephone towards him, but Kubu had more to say.

'Director, I'll take them myself.' Mabaku nodded. 'And then I'd like to spend a couple of days in Bulawayo. Private trip.'

Mabaku's eyebrows rose again. 'Oh, a private trip like the *late* Sipho Langa's, perhaps?'

'I want to find out some more about Tinubu. His background's got to be the key. Where did he come from? What made him leave Zimbabwe? How did he get sucked into all this?' He decided it was time to play his trump card. He shoved the letter from Endima Shlongwane across the desk to the director. Mabaku read it carefully. For a few minutes he said nothing. Then he handed it back to Kubu.

'It won't hurt to stir the Zimbabweans up a bit with a visit,' he said unexpectedly. 'But it'll be above board, official permission for everything you do. No cloak-and-dagger stuff.'

'Exactly as you say, Director,' said Kubu demurely.

Mabaku tried to look stern, but his lower lip was giving him away. 'Do what you have to, Kubu, but watch yourself. The Zimbabwe police won't respond well to anyone stamping around on their patch. And they're not quite as strict about habeas corpus as we are.'

Kubu left with a feeling of elation. At last he was going to do something, take the initiative instead of just reacting. But the director's warning stuck in his mind. He would have to be careful. Very careful.

CHAPTER 49

Boy Gomwe had a swim in the pool and then sunned himself on the deck of the Elephant Valley Lodge, enjoying a gin and tonic. A small group of the valley's namesakes were helping themselves to a drink from the waterhole in front of the lodge with equal enthusiasm.

When he had arrived at Elephant Valley Lodge several days earlier and checked in under the name Boy Biko, he knew he had found the right place. It was perfect. It was accessed by a rough dirt track from the border post near Kasane and lay poised a few hundred metres away from the unfenced boundary road. The border patrols between Botswana and Zimbabwe along this border were a joke. With a little care and a few greased palms, anyone could travel across the border and meet a contact staying at the Lodge. The best part was that although less than thirty minutes from Kasane by Land Rover, Elephant Valley was lonely, isolated. No one would notice an exchange of goods for hard currency.

All he had to do was wait for Mandla's contact. He kept expecting someone to join him at the bar, to engage in social chit-chat before revealing himself. But nobody had approached him.

Now it was five days later, and he still hadn't heard anything. He was getting anxious. Had something gone wrong? Had the exchange been cancelled or postponed? None of the other guests looked like drug runners. He snorted. Of course they didn't. They'd be innocuous. His contact would be a regular guy like himself. He toyed with his gold necklace. Relax, he said to himself. Patience. He had to admit that he had enjoyed unwinding at this lodge. Nothing to do but eat, drink and be lazy. Very appealing.

He ordered another drink and sat back to enjoy the elephants at the waterhole. Nice, he thought. Back to nature. Away from people with all their greed and violence. Maybe I'll buy this place when the time is right. But very discreetly, of course.

He looked around. Female company would be nice. As though on cue, Allison Levine, the woman he had met on the morning game drive, strolled over and appraised his strong legs and well-built torso. She was wearing a white one-piece swimsuit, which set off the smooth tan of her skin. She was not pretty, but her figure was fine.

He offered her a drink, and she settled on the beach chair next to him. A joint would be nice, he thought. Perfect for the mood. But Gomwe stayed squeaky clean when he travelled. So while they waited for the drinks he lit a cigarette, and the girl accepted one too.

'What brought you here?' she asked.

'I'm keen on the wildlife. Elephants are great, aren't they?' One had started demolishing a tree not far off. 'Great location too,' he added without thought.

'Certainly is,' she said. 'I've been here a few times. I work in Johannesburg.' She did not volunteer the type of work.

Gomwe signed for the drinks, and they toasted wild Africa. He was starting to like the girl. She really had a great figure.

'Shall we have dinner tonight?' he suggested.

She laughed. 'Yes, dinner is good. Let's have it together!' He laughed too, and she added, 'We can have a nightcap after that. In your tent if you like. You've got one overlooking the waterhole, haven't you? The floodlights are on all night. It'll be wonderful.'

'Sure,' said Gomwe, preening. 'You can lie in bed and watch the game. Great!' Every night, he thought. I'll have a girl like her every night.

The next morning Gomwe would have liked to sleep in, but he'd promised Allison they'd go for a bird walk together. She had spoken about the local bird life with enthusiasm over dinner. He'd joked that he didn't care much for birds of the feathered variety. She'd laughed and said he would when he got to know them. Anyway, she was up before the damned birds and dragged him out of bed.

'You were involved in that Jackalberry business, weren't you?' she asked as they chewed rusks and drank instant coffee on the patio while waiting for the guide.

He nodded. 'How'd you know I was there? Hell of a mess. Cops everywhere.'

'Read about it in the newspaper. Look, the guide must've overslept. Let's go by ourselves. I know the way.'

'Is that safe?'

'Oh yes. I've got you to protect me, haven't I?' She winked at him and set off without waiting for his reply.

It was a brisk walk, and they did not look at many birds. Allison promised a great spot just ahead. Very private and romantic, she said, with a reeded pool. Great for wading birds. But when they got there, it was just a clearing in the bush with a couple of bedrolls on the ground, each with a well-used backpack next to it. A small gas burner supported a sooted kettle. There was a beaten-up Land Cruiser parked at the edge of the clearing, although there were no obvious vehicle tracks leading into the clearing. Two men were sitting in the vehicle. They got out when they saw the couple approach.

'Hello, guys,' said Allison. 'Let me introduce the person Mandla sent us.' But actually she did not make any introductions, and the men did not look friendly. Gomwe decided the walk had been a big mistake.

No one missed Gomwe until after breakfast. Allison said she had joined him for coffee at dawn, and then he had gone for a jog around the camp. He had promised to stay close. She had wandered between the tents behind the lodge itself, looking for bird life in the trees and shrubs. She was excited about seeing a flock of parrots and had asked Douglas, one of the guides, which type they were.

The camp's two guides started a search of the area, one on foot close to the camp, while Douglas took one of the game-viewing vehicles and headed slowly along the track from the Lodge. Gomwe had gone further than expected, and it was a while before Douglas radioed in. He had found him near a small clearing some way into the bush. It seemed he'd had an unfortunate encounter with one of the valley's massive inhabitants.

*

As manager of the Elephant Valley Lodge, Adam Kamwi felt a heavy responsibility for his guests. He wanted them to return in the future, and to tell their friends in foreign countries of their wonderful experiences. And their safety was his highest priority. The radioed message from Douglas could not have been worse news. 'Stay where you are,' Kamwi said after getting careful directions. 'I'll come right away.' He took the other vehicle and headed out.

Crunching his way over the scrub, following Douglas's vehicle tracks, he came to the clearing. Douglas had driven his vehicle right up to Gomwe's body – a sensible precaution with a rogue elephant nearby – and now was standing next to it as he watched Kamwi's approach. The manager stopped, turned off the engine and called, 'Where's the elephant?'

Douglas shook his head. 'I've heard nothing. I think he's moved off.' But there were plenty of signs. Huge elliptical footprints, scuff marks, broken shrubs. Kamwi walked over and looked down at the remains of the man. The elephant had crushed Gomwe's chest cavity, stomping or perhaps even kneeling on him. His khaki bush shirt was crimson-stained, but there was not a lot of blood. His head was at a strange angle, and one cheek seemed to be crushed in also. It was a shocking injury, perhaps a vicious blow with the trunk. Nearby was a signature pile of dung. It was no longer steaming but was still damp, giving off its distinctive sweetly pungent smell, reminiscent of wet compost. It seemed that Gomwe's killer had scant respect for its victim's earthly remains.

Douglas was walking around the body as if he needed multiple perspectives to establish that Gomwe was dead. 'There's a tarpaulin in the vehicle. We can lift him between us.'

'We should call the police.'

'We can't leave him here. There are predators all over the area. I'm not waiting here.' Douglas was adamant. He was already pulling the canvas sheet from the vehicle.

Kamwi shrugged. May as well get it over with. As they dragged the body on to the sheet, it made strange gurgling sounds and an awful smell enveloped them. Kamwi was glad when they had heaved it on to the back of Douglas's vehicle, and he could retreat to the sanctuary of his own.

They took the body to the Kazungula police station, where there was discussion but not much interest in Boy Biko. Then one of the constables opened the wallet found on the body and saw that the man's name was Gomwe. Immediately there was consternation. This was the man the police had been hunting for over a week. The senior officer put through a call to Kasane at once. Soon he was speaking to Detective Sergeant Mooka.

Tatwa arrived with a white man, a Kasane doctor who did occasional work for the police. While the doctor unwrapped the tarpaulin and examined the body, Kamwi spoke to Tatwa in Setswana.

'This is going to kill us! First the murders at that Linyanti place, then the attack there last week, the murder of that tourist in Maun, and now this. Almost worse than another murder!' He glanced at the doctor, and his voice dropped. 'It's not the first time, you know. The elephants around here go rogue. It's the poaching from the Zimbabwe side. I've called the parks people. I want the bastard shot. Sooner the better.' He bit his lip. 'We're already getting tour operators worried about safety issues up here.'

Tatwa was dubious. Maybe the elephant could be tracked, but it seemed unlikely they would find it unless it was still close by.

The doctor joined them. 'Broken neck, smashed rib cage. Knelt on, I'd say. Broken neck is good. Didn't suffer long, poor devil.'

'Who found him?' Tatwa asked Kamwi.

'The staff missed him at breakfast, and we sent the rangers out to look for him. When Douglas radioed in, I went out there myself. It was more than a kilometre from the camp.'

The doctor looked surprised. 'What the hell was he doing out there?'

Kamwi shook his head, disgusted. 'Tourists fall into two categories. The ones who're scared stiff half the time and won't walk to their tents without a guard, and the ones who think they're invincible. Those go around telling everyone that being in the bush is safer than driving a car, and then go jogging there alone.' He shook his head. 'We called the police and brought the body here.'

'Why?'

'Well, it was a violent death! We had to inform the police.'

'No, I mean why did you move the body?'

'We couldn't leave it for the hyenas!' Kamwi grimaced. 'Look, what do you want us to do, Detective? Get the body up to the hospital? Will you notify next of kin and so on?'

Tatwa thought about it. 'Is there any possibility that he wasn't killed by accident? That there could be foul play involved?'

The others looked at him in surprise. The doctor shook his head. 'No man could do that sort of massive damage. You think there's a homicidal maniac out there with a trained elephant?'

'Look,' said Kamwi, switching to Setswana again. 'We don't want this to get worse than it is. Let's get the body to the morgue, try to keep it all low key, and get on with our business. Kasane lives on the tourists. Gomwe – if that's his real name – decided to play Russian roulette and lost.'

Still Tatwa hesitated. 'You'll sign the death certificate?' he asked the doctor, who nodded. Tatwa thought back to Jackalberry Camp. Eight guests gather for dinner on a Sunday night. The next morning two are dead and one has vanished. Before the end of the week the camp owners are assaulted by thugs looking for a briefcase. A few days later another of the guests is murdered in a supposed robbery that actually isn't. Now another of the guests is dead. Five out of eight! Coincidence? He shook his head.

'I'm investigating this as a suspicious death. We'll send the body to Gaborone for a proper autopsy, and I want a forensics team to come with me to the place where the body was found.' Kamwi looked as though he was going to explode, but Tatwa held up his hand. 'No need to make a big scene of it. We'll keep it quiet. No announcements for the moment. Doctor, go ahead with the death certificate. I want to be very careful, but I'm probably wrong. If I am, this'll all be tied up quickly.' He did not say what would happen if he was right.

He called Kasane for the forensics team and asked them to make arrangements for the body to be driven to Gaborone. Unfortunately, autopsies were done nowhere else in the country because of the shortage of trained pathologists.

Tatwa followed Kamwi and Douglas back to the Lodge. His first call was Gomwe's tent. It was a luxurious affair with a queen-size bed, hanging space for clothes, a dresser, and a separate shower and toilet. Judging by the way the bedclothes were tossed back on both sides of the bed and the look of the pillows, Gomwe had enjoyed company the night before. There was a hard-body suitcase on the dresser, and on top of that was a briefcase. Well, Tatwa thought, lots of travellers have briefcases, but just suppose . . .

He took a penknife and checked the catches, careful not to touch the case with his fingers. Both catches snapped back cleanly, and he used the knife to lever the case open to avoid smudging any prints. The lid had a notebook, business cards, a calculator, all neatly held in pockets. The case itself held music magazines and catalogues. But the detective was suspicious. He slid the knife blade down the side of the case until it reached the base. Comparing the knife against the outside of the case, he could tell that the supposed base was much too shallow. There was something hidden below the magazines with their screaming covers. He was sorely tempted to find out what. But he did not want to spoil Forensics' game. He snapped the catches shut using the back of the knife and lifted the briefcase using a handkerchief. It was too risky to leave it in the unsecured tent. Then he went outside to break the latest bad news to Kubu.

CHAPTER 50

Kubu left home at nine a.m. after a good breakfast. He wanted to set off late enough to miss the traffic headed north, and he wanted to leave on a full stomach. 'Your brother knows nothing about food,' he grumbled to Joy. She was busy packing, and ignored him.

Kubu carefully checked his Land Rover, and the family settled in. The plan was for Pleasant and Joy to stay with Sampson for a week, but the vehicle was bursting with luggage. It looked as though they could all survive for at least a month in Francistown. Even Ilia had a huge bag of her favourite dog biscuits.

'You can't always get them,' Joy explained.

'The dog never eats biscuits anyway,' said Kubu. 'She doesn't like them. She always has our scraps. That's why she gets fat and has to have expensive diet biscuits.'

Quick as a flash Joy responded, 'No one would get fat on your leftovers.' Pleasant thought this very amusing. Kubu subsided, and squashed Ilia's rations into the back of the vehicle.

Francistown was a five-hour drive along a road that was good but that offered little interesting scenery. A double-lane highway led them to Mochudi, and after that the road was single-lane, but wide and well maintained. Kubu started to feel they were setting off on holiday rather than fleeing a murderous group of Zimbabwean kidnappers. In celebration, he launched into an aria from *Aida*. Pleasant and Joy also relaxed and hummed along. Ilia was less sanguine and howled when he reached the high notes.

Three hours later they arrived at the small town of Palapye. Ilia, who had slept quietly for much of the trip, started jumping around the car, diving from her back-seat pad into Joy's lap in the front.

'Ilia needs a break,' said Joy.

'Yes, we should stop for lunch,' said Kubu. 'It's after midday.'

'But we've just finished breakfast!'

'We'll have something light,' said Kubu, visualising a double cheeseburger.

Kubu's lunch break was interrupted by the call from Tatwa. He listened with an occasional grunt.

'A vehicle,' he said finally. 'Probably they used a vehicle.'

'The murderers?' Tatwa asked. 'To get to the scene?'

Kubu brushed this aside. 'Suppose you wanted to make it look as though an elephant had crushed someone, you'd need something really heavy. I suppose a sledgehammer might work, but I'd guess that it would produce a different sort of injury. But drive over someone's chest with a heavy vehicle? That would do your crushing for you. Broken neck is easy. You don't need an elephant or a vehicle for that.'

Tatwa hadn't thought of that possibility. He would tell Forensics to check the tyre tracks carefully. Then, changing the subject, he told Kubu about the briefcase with its false bottom. There was silence as Kubu considered the implications.

'Get it to Forensics in Gaborone, Tatwa. I need to close the Tinubu loop in Zimbabwe, but I'll keep in touch. Your instinct was spot on. I don't buy the elephant story. We're treating this as murder.'

CHAPTER 51

After the call, Tatwa went to reception and gave instructions that Gomwe's tent be left untouched until the forensics team arrived. He made notes of what camp manager Adam Kamwi had told him, then considered what his next move should be. Having promised to keep the matter low key, he did not want to start by interviewing all the guests. However, he certainly wanted to talk to the woman who had been the last person to see Gomwe alive, and to the guide who had been the first person to see him dead.

As he came to this decision, he was approached by a woman with an attractive figure and a rather stolid face. Her eyes were moist; she had either been crying or was close to tears.

'Are you the detective? The manager sent me to talk to you. He said he couldn't tell me anything about Boy and that I must speak to you. Something awful's happened, hasn't it? You must tell me.'

Tatwa took her to a more secluded spot on the outside deck, ducking too late to avoid the polished log supporting the thatched roof. He gave the woman a wan smile, shrugged while rubbing his head, and invited her to be seated.

'I'm sorry,' she said. 'My name is Allison Levine. I'm from Johannesburg. I was with Boy last night.'

Tatwa nodded. 'Ms Levine, I'm afraid there has been a terrible tragedy. Your friend is dead. I'm very sorry to bring you this bad news.'

The woman put her head into cupped hands and said nothing for several moments. 'What happened?'

'It's believed that he was attacked by an elephant. Fortunately, it killed him very quickly.'

The woman said nothing, as though acknowledging that her worst fears were realised.

'May I ask you a few questions? Are you up to it?'

She nodded.

'Did you know that his real name was Gomwe? Boy Gomwe?' She looked at him, surprised, and shook her head. Tatwa continued. 'It seems you were the last person to see him. Would you tell me exactly what happened?'

'We got up early, just after dawn. Boy wanted to jog. He said he never missed a day, liked to keep fit. He had a great body.' She broke off and wiped her eyes. 'Anyway, I wanted to watch birds, and he wasn't a birder, so I told him to stick close to the camp while I went for a walk around the grounds. I saw a flock of parrots, which is exciting because they're not often seen here. They were really cooperative, so I called one of the guides to help me identify them. They were Meyer's parrots. I wanted to show them to Boy – seemed romantic, you know? But we couldn't find him. I guessed he'd run along the main track past the camp. Being macho, I suppose. You men are all the same!'

'Where did you see the parrots, exactly?'

Allison gave him a puzzled look. 'They were in the trees behind the pool.'

'And the guide was there too?'

Allison nodded. Tatwa made a note.

'When did you get worried?'

'When he didn't turn up for breakfast. Even with a long run, shower and change, he should've been there by nine. That's when I went to the manager – Mr Kamwi.'

Tatwa asked a few more questions and made notes, but Allison had nothing more to add. She had been due to stay for another two nights, but now wanted to leave as soon as possible. Tatwa sympathised, but asked her to stick to her original schedule in case the police needed her help. She hesitated, but then reluctantly agreed.

At this point Tatwa was informed that the forensics people had arrived. He took his leave of Allison, found the guide, Douglas, and asked him to show them where Gomwe had been killed.

*

Tatwa drove with Douglas – the two men from Forensics followed in their own vehicle – as he wanted the opportunity to quiz the guide on how he had discovered the body.

'I drove up the road a way and then turned south. The paths from the Lodge lead into the bush this way. I drove into the side tracks and open spots on the right and looked around a bit.'

'Why only on the right?'

Douglas glanced at him. 'No footprints crossing the road.'

Tatwa nodded. He hadn't thought of that. Suddenly a flash of blue and purple flew across in front of them. 'What's that?' he asked the guide. 'It's so beautiful.'

'Lilac-breasted roller. Common around here.'

'You obviously know a lot about birds. Did you help Ms Levine with her parrots?'

Douglas nodded.

'Where did you see them exactly?'

Douglas looked at him. 'You interested in birds?'

'Just a beginner. I saw a man with a tame go-away-bird the other day. Fantastic. Sat on his shoulder. Seemed to talk to him. Did tricks.'

Douglas nodded again, concentrating on the driving.

'So where were the parrots?' Tatwa persisted.

'I don't know. Allison just described what she'd seen. Had to be the Meyer's. The others don't occur here.' He slowed, searching for car tracks.

'What made you come this far?'

'I was going to turn back. But there's a clearing up ahead with a waterhole nearby. I thought he might have gone there. It's actually a walking track but I knew how to get the vehicle through the bush from this side.'

They had come to that point of the road. Douglas indicated his tracks and those of Kamwi, before following them carefully through the bush. After a few bumpy minutes they came to an open area. A mixture of shrubs surrounded it, but it was presided over by a massive knobthorn tree. It had survived a dangerous youth and now was serene, too big to be damaged by even the largest elephant. Around it were elephant tracks, some dried dung, and wilting broken branches. There were also multiple vehicle tracks and bootprints. Hardly a pristine crime scene.

'Where did you find Gomwe?'

Douglas gave him a quizzical look.

'That was his real name. Biko was a false name he was using at the Lodge. We don't know why. Yet. Where did you find the body?'

Douglas pointed at a spot surrounded by scuff marks and bootprints. The vehicle tracks converged there. I should have guessed, Tatwa thought.

There was little to show for Gomwe's death. Just some dried blood on the dead grass. The forensics people started to look around, collecting samples and taking casts of the prints. They examined the tyre tracks, checking for any clues to how Gomwe had died.

Douglas stood by with a rifle, but did not look worried. The bush was still now, and quiet but for the bowing of cicadas. While the others worked, Tatwa looked around but did not stray far. He did a full circle of the area looking carefully for tracks. He saw where the elephant had come and gone, noting its direction by the toe-smudge at the front of the elliptical pad mark. He had grown up in the bush and knew how to read its stories. A careless man on a jog or walk, let alone fleeing from an elephant, would leave easy signs of his progress, but he found none. Conveniently, it seemed, Boy Gomwe had materialised in this glade to be mauled and killed by a rogue bull.

CHAPTER 52

The Bengu family arrived at Sampson's house in Francistown shortly after three p.m. A neighbour met them and let them into the house.

'Make yourselves at home,' she said, very graciously Kubu thought, especially as it was not her house. He explored the fridge and, in the absence of the makings of a steelworks, helped himself to a St Louis beer. Joy and Pleasant settled for fruit juice, and Ilia for water.

Unfortunately, Kubu was not fond of his brother-in-law, and the feeling was mutual. Sampson was number two in the Francistown office of the Ministry of Lands and Housing. He was always singing the praises of the government in general and his minister in particular. By contrast, Kubu felt that elected officials were only human, and so it was unfair to expect them to behave in a less selfish way than other people. Thus they needed to be watched carefully and not held in unreasonably high regard. Kubu's viewpoint was much closer to the norm. Sampson was also a jogger, and prided himself on keeping fit. Kubu felt such activities were imports from countries where people did not have enough work to do to keep themselves busy.

However, after an acceptable dinner, particularly in view of the bachelor fare Joy and Pleasant had for ingredients, the men were mellow. Kubu had brought a decent Shiraz, and Sampson had been appreciative.

Sampson had a sketchy knowledge of what had happened to his sisters, but now they filled in the outline and added the colours. He was shocked, but listened with only the occasional exclamation or question. He made no secret of his dissatisfaction with the police. Kubu felt he had a point and did not rise to the comments. After all, he was requesting Sampson's help.

'I'm sorry to impose on you this way, Sampson,' Kubu said once the story was complete. 'We think it's best that your sisters are out of Gaborone until we wrap this case up. We don't expect any more trouble, but there'll be a policeman keeping an eye on them just in case. From a distance,' he added quickly when Joy's brow furrowed. 'I'll be in Zimbabwe for the next two days; after that I'll stay for the weekend, if that's okay with you, and then head back to Gaborone on Monday.'

Sampson said it was fine, although it might be a bit cramped. All of them were welcome to stay for as long as they wished. He asked what Kubu would be doing in Bulawayo, but the detective avoided anything specific.

'No cloak-and-dagger stuff, I hope,' said Sampson with a laugh, making a joke of it. 'The minister wouldn't want anything embarrassing to mar the president of Zimbabwe's visit to the African Union meeting.'

Kubu laughed too, adding, 'I would've thought that receiving the Zimbabwe president in the first place was embarrassing enough.'

Joy spotted an incipient argument and called for dessert. The tense moment passed.

The next morning, Kubu left early and headed for Plumtree. He wanted to be at the border post before it became too crowded. He filled up with gas at the last possible point before Zimbabwe and bought two slabs of chocolate and two packets of cigarettes. He was unlikely to find any fuel available once across the border, certainly not without a long queue. The collapse of the Zimbabwean currency meant that anything requiring hard cash to purchase – such as fuel – was very difficult to obtain. Shortly after that he came to the border post. Even with the early start he had to wait to get through immigration.

He drove through Plumtree, Marula and Figtree. Names of lush fruits for wilting towns, living on custom from visitors from Botswana. When he reached Bulawayo, he checked in to the Holiday Inn and had lunch. He found the food good and cheap provided you were paying in foreign currency at the hotel's special rate. After lunch, he drove through the town, noting lots of activity but unsure what all the people were doing around the poorly stocked shops and garages devoid of fuel. Yet they were neatly dressed and did not look hungry. Zimbabwe's economy was a puzzle. No doubt he would discover worse in the rural areas.

From Bulawayo, he headed north-west for about an hour on a single-lane paved road to reach the small town of Nyamandhlovu. He stopped to consult his map and ask directions, but carefully so that there was no real clue as to whom he wanted to find. He drove past a run-down building that was a hospital, according to a sign faded almost to illegibility. Perhaps people don't get sick here any more, he thought grimly. And so he came to the home of Paulus Mbedi.

CHAPTER 53

When Kubu arrived at the house, Mbedi was hoeing in his garden. His hoe consisted of a straight branch with the bark scraped off, side twigs removed and the knots smoothed out, and a rusty metal head tied on tightly with wire. He was working in a patch of stunted *mielies*, chopping out weeds and breaking the earth. But the ground was hard and dry, and he worked without high expectation. Other vegetables grew in the rest of the small patch of land. Flowers and attractive shrubs were luxuries for people who weren't hungry.

When he saw Kubu battling the gate's rusty hinges, he tensed. The hoe moved to his right hand, and he held it by the middle, off the ground. It had become a defensive weapon. Kubu closed the gate with care, although there seemed nothing to be kept in, and it was useless to keep things out. He took in the vegetable garden with the drunken fence around it, the little house, neat but in need of paint, the chassis of a bicycle with no wheels leaning against a wall.

'I'm Superintendent David Bengu,' he offered in English. 'Are you Paulus Mbedi?' He saw the flash of fear in Mbedi's face and the stiffening of his body, and added quickly, 'I'm with the Botswana police, not from Zimbabwe. Everyone calls me Kubu, which means hippo in my language, because of my shape.' Mbedi relaxed slightly, but did not smile or accept Kubu's offered hand.

'I am Paulus Mbedi. What do you want?'

'I want to talk to you about Goodluck. Goodluck Tinubu.'

Paulus hesitated for just a moment. 'I don't know anyone with that name. Goodluck is a very strange name for a man.'

'I didn't say it was a man.'

Paulus shrugged. 'I don't know anyone called Goodluck,' he repeated.

'Paulus, I'm very sorry to tell you this, but Goodluck is dead. He was murdered three weeks ago in Botswana. I want to find out who killed him and why, and make sure the murderer is brought to justice. I need you to help me. You helped Goodluck before, didn't you? He needs your help again.'

Paulus stood in silence. Death was a regular occurrence in this part of the world, and Paulus expected to bump into it from time to time. But this meeting left a taste of bile, and the fight went out of him. 'You'd better come inside,' he said, putting down the hoe.

They sat at a wooden table in the kitchen, and Paulus gave Kubu tea. It was in a kettle on the wood stove, and he simply added extra water and reboiled it. The taste was bitter from stewing but cut by the sugar Paulus added without asking. He measured two spoons each and stirred it in well. There was not much sugar left.

'How did you find me?'

'The money from Goodluck.'

'There won't be any more?'

'At least not for a while. Perhaps in his will . . .' Kubu wished he had checked. Remembering the cigarettes and chocolates, he reached into his jacket and passed them to Paulus. He should have brought some real food instead. But Paulus accepted the gifts politely with both hands and his thanks. Then they disappeared into a drawer in the small kitchen unit by the stove. Barter was the real currency of Zimbabwe these days, and cigarettes and chocolate would fetch a good exchange.

Kubu was not in a hurry. They talked about the late rains and the bad crops, and drank their tea in peace. When the cups were both empty, Paulus asked Kubu how Goodluck had died, and Kubu told him what had happened. He concluded by saying that Goodluck had been loved and respected in his adopted home and had built up a very successful school. Paulus nodded, knowing this.

'How can I help you? It was very long ago.'

'I need to know who Goodluck was and what happened before he came to Botswana. Then, perhaps, I can understand why he was murdered.'

Paulus thought about where to start. This was a story he had told no one before, and one he had expected never to tell. But now there could be no harm in it, if this policeman was telling the truth. And Paulus believed that he was.

'My wife and I worked at the hospital at Nyamandhlovu,' he began.

'Your wife?' asked Kubu.

'Mary is dead,' replied Paulus, firmly closing that topic. 'She was a nurse-aid, and I cleaned the equipment and the rooms.' He paused. 'I don't work there any more. The money is worth so little, and I don't have transport.' Kubu thought of the remains of the bicycle.

'It was the terrible time,' he continued. 'There was the war, and you didn't trust the whites and couldn't know who to trust among the blacks. We thought we were poor, but that was before . . .' He shrugged, not wanting to mention the president's name aloud. 'Anyway, it was bad. There were terrorists and freedom fighters and police and army. Most people wanted to live in peace. We didn't understand about politics. We still don't.' He wanted to offer more tea but was afraid of running out of sugar. So he continued. 'My friend Msimang had a *bakkie*. He used it for fetching and delivering electrical appliances like fridges when they needed fixing.'

He looked at his own fridge, now a cupboard. He could not afford to get it fixed, and Msimang was long gone. 'He drove here at ten one night and woke us up. We were soundly sleeping because there was work the next day. Perhaps I had drunk a beer or two because it was Sunday. He said he had found a man collapsed by the road. At first he thought the man was drunk, but then he saw all the blood. Msimang thought he'd been shot by the army or the police or vigilantes. He looked around but no one else was there, so he lifted the man and dragged him up on to the metal floor of the *bakkie* like a slaughtered pig. We thought he was dead. He should've been dead. But he was alive. So Msimang and I took him into the house and put him on the spare bed despite all the blood. Mary was a very fussy housewife but she made no complaint.

'I asked Msimang if he wanted some tea, or even brandy, while Mary looked after the man, but he said no. He was keen to go. He didn't want anyone to know he'd been out late at night, and he certainly didn't want anyone to know he'd found this man who might be a freedom fighter. That was why he came to us. He knew the hospital would hand the man over to the army and that he would die. I thought he'd die that night anyway. We wondered what we would do with his body in the morning. Mary said he had three bullets in his back. She bandaged up the wounds, but she said he'd die. We looked through his pockets to see if we could find his name, but there was nothing. So we prayed together for the soul of this young man whose name we didn't know. But God knew his name.'

He seemed to be finished, but his mind was searching through the thirty-year-old scene.

'The next day he was actually conscious but in great pain. I wanted to take him to the hospital, but Mary said we couldn't move him again, and we would get into a lot of trouble. So I stayed with him while Mary went to the hospital. She told them I'd hurt myself and wouldn't come in to the hospital because I'd seen people die there. She was good at making up stories.' For the first time he smiled, and his face was changed. Kubu could see that this man had once been happy.

'She came back with what she could get – pain pills, a scalpel and forceps, which she stole, lots more bandages, penicillin, antiseptic. We had no anaesthetic, though, so I gave the man some brandy and put a stick with a cloth around it in his mouth so he wouldn't bite his tongue.'

'Did you learn that at the hospital?' asked Kubu, incredulous.

Paulus gave a wry twist to his mouth. 'Actually I saw it in an American cowboy film. But it didn't matter. He passed out immediately, and Mary dug out the bullets. I made boiling water and cleaned up. It was as though she was the doctor – a surgeon! – and I was the nurse-aid,' he concluded with pride.

'And he survived?'

Paulus nodded. 'It was touch and go for several days. He was delirious, screaming then passing out. I stayed with him. Mary went to the hospital and got more drugs. She said he was amazingly lucky that not one of the bullets had hit a vital organ or cut a major blood vessel. Amazingly good luck.'

'And that's how he got the name?'

Paulus nodded. 'When he started to improve, and we could talk to him, he would only shake his head if we asked him his name. At first we thought it'd gone with the shock, that he'd lost his memory. But I began to realise that he was scared. That there were people who had wanted him dead, and that it was best for him to stay dead. So we called him Goodluck. And he liked that. He seemed to find it appropriate and funny at the same time.'

Paulus went on, detailing Goodluck's recuperation and how they had pretended he was a family member who'd had an accident and was staying with them to be near the hospital for check-ups. He related how Goodluck started to think of the house as his own home, and Paulus and Mary as the uncle and aunt they pretended to be.

'When did you find out what happened the night he was shot?' Kubu asked, sorry to end Paulus' happier memories.

Paulus shook his head. 'We never spoke of it. It was better that we didn't know some things.'

'Well, when did you learn his real name?'

Again Paulus shook his head. 'He never told us that either. Tinubu isn't his real name. Perhaps you know that?'

At once Kubu was intrigued. He asked Paulus why he thought that. Paulus stared at Kubu, wondering if this was a test of some sort. Then he shrugged and looked down at his empty cup.

'When he became a little stronger, Goodluck said he had a good friend, a comrade, whose name was George Tinubu. He was very concerned about him. He asked me to find out if the police were looking for this man, if they knew where he was. I didn't want to do that. It wasn't safe to attract attention in those days. But he said it was very important, that he owed this man a great deal and had to have news of him. Eventually I agreed.

'So I went to the police station, not the one here in Nyamandhlovu but the main one in Bulawayo. And I spoke to a man there, told him that George Tinubu was missing, and asked if he'd been arrested or if the police knew anything of him. The constable on duty wasn't busy. Perhaps he was bored. He could've told me to go away. Who was I to ask after this person? But he was an Ndebele like me, and instead he decided to help. Many people vanished in those days, and their relatives never found out about them. He asked me when the man had disappeared, and I told him the Sunday when Msimang found Goodluck.

'He went away for a while to check records. When he came back he said that Tinubu was dead. He was sorry for my loss. I asked him what had happened, but then a white sergeant came past and asked the constable what was going on. The sergeant looked angry, and he told me Tinubu was a terrorist, that he'd been killed after a raid on a white farm where the people had been murdered and raped. I was very scared of this man, because I could see he thought that I was also a terrorist, or at least a sympathiser. So I said I was very shocked, that I only knew him slightly, that I was looking for him because he owed me money. But there was hatred in this white man, although I'd done nothing to him. He shouted that Tinubu was in hell, where he belonged, and that his body was rotting in the bush, food for dogs and jackals.

He wanted to see my identity document but I pretended I had left it at home. I knew I was going to be in trouble with this man I didn't know, who hated me. I was shaking. But then someone called him to take a telephone call. He told me to wait. I didn't know what to do, but the constable indicated with his head that I should go, and he pretended to read some papers. So I left quickly, and when I was outside the station, I ran as fast as I could until I was far away. Then I found a bus to Nyamandhlovu and walked home.' He pursed his lips, the memory still degrading after thirty years.

'What did Goodluck say when you told him?'

'He was shocked, of course. He asked for all the details, but I could only tell him the little I had found out. Then he said something very strange that I still remember after all this time. He said, "They must have found the wallet." That's what he said. I didn't understand. Then he started to cry. He was still very weak, and he had lost his friend, so it was not unmanly to do so.'

Kubu waited. After a few minutes of silence, Paulus said, 'I will make some more tea.' He added water and put the kettle back on the hot plate. After a moment's consideration, he added another spoon of tea leaves.

'The next day Goodluck told us that Tinubu had been a good man, a schoolteacher who loved learning and helping people to learn. But the school had been closed and the children sent away, and some of the teachers had left and gone to Zambia to join the ZAPU freedom movement. His friend had been one of those. Then he said that it was better that people didn't look for him, that it would be better to be a dead person. So he would take his friend's name, since he no longer needed it. But in our honour, so that every day he would remember our kindness to him, he would keep the first name Goodluck. That is how he became Goodluck Tinubu.'

Mbedi poured the tea and shared the remaining sugar between the two cups. Then he opened one of the bars of chocolate and shared that also. Kubu accepted both gravely, with thanks.

'Paulus, in fact Goodluck was asking after himself. He wanted to know if the police and the army were hunting for him after that raid. Probably he was scared of what would happen to you and your wife if he was found here with you. He must have been very relieved to know they thought him dead. So he could take back his name. I suppose that he left when he was better? He couldn't risk meeting someone here who knew him, who would bring him back to life.'

Paulus drank his tea in silence. When it was finished, he said, 'Yes, he left a few months later. But why do you think he really was Tinubu?' There was no great surprise in his voice; perhaps he had wondered before about the friend – the schoolteacher – whose identity and profession Goodluck had so comfortably assumed.

Kubu explained about the fingerprints. Mbedi nodded his head in acceptance.

Kubu considered what he had learned. It explained a lot but did not help explain Goodluck's murder. A new thought occurred to him. Goodluck had apparently known Zondo. They had shared drinks together in Goodluck's tent at the camp. Zondo and Goodluck were the same age. Was it possible that some hatred had been intense enough to stretch across thirty years? What actually happened on that night? What had

Goodluck meant when he said, 'They must have found the wallet?' Whose wallet? His own?

'Paulus, you have been a great help to me, and I'm very grateful. I just have one more question. Please think very carefully before you answer. Was there anyone you heard about, or perhaps who came here after Goodluck had gone, who asked about him? Someone who might have been trying to find him? Perhaps to finally settle a score not completed on the night of the shooting?'

Paulus looked at him. 'Why do you ask this?'

'I want to know about anyone – no matter from how long ago – who might have wanted to see Goodluck dead.'

Paulus concentrated. 'Yes, there was such a man. Six months after Goodluck left, he came here with Msimang, in the *bakkie*. Msimang had told him the story, and he said he was looking for the man. I didn't know who he was, but I knew he was one of the fighters, one of the hard men for whom the killing and the terror had become just a job. Perhaps a job he now liked. I told him the injured man had died. That we called the hospital to fetch the body. That they'd handed it over to the police. I knew he couldn't check that. He stared at me for what seemed like a long time. I think he'd heard rumours, and I could tell that he didn't believe me. I think he was deciding what to do about it. But then Mary came out and asked what was going on. She told him the same story I had and asked him to leave. Just like that. And he did, without another word to either of us. We never saw him, or heard of him, again.'

'Do you remember his name?'

Paulus shook his head. 'It was thirty years ago!'

'Could the man have been called Ndlovu?'

Paulus straightened. 'Yes, that's right. I remember thinking that he was named for the elephant. This village is named for the meat of the elephant. Ndlovu. That was his name.' He shook his head. 'The elephant is a noble beast. This man was not noble.'

Kubu thanked Mbedi again for his help and for his hospitality. Knowing that Zimbabwe money was meaningless, and that Mbedi would find a black market for hard currency, he gave him a hundred-pula note. 'It's a loan,' he said. 'I'll recover the money from Goodluck's will.' Both knew this was untrue, but it enabled Paulus to accept the money with gratitude and dignity. But he had a gift for Kubu in return. He went into the bedroom and came back with a small glass jar containing three distorted metal objects. 'The bullets we took from Goodluck,' he said with a hint of his earlier pride in the achievement. 'I kept them. Now you may have them.' Kubu accepted the jar gravely, politely touching his right arm with his left hand.

Kubu shook Paulus' hand and wished him well. On the trip back he looked out at the empty shops and closed businesses around Bulawayo, and thought about Paulus Mbedi and his wife trying to live in peace. What had happened to Mary and what would become of Paulus? It was nearly dinnertime when he reached the hotel, but for once he was not at all hungry.

CHAPTER 54

By Friday morning, Tatwa felt that the pieces were falling into place. He was delighted with the progress they had made in only two days. He wondered if he could reach Kubu in Zimbabwe. Was Kubu's phone on international roaming? Cell phones still worked in Zimbabwe.

Through receipts in his wallet, they had traced Gomwe's movements prior to his arrival at the Elephant Valley Lodge. He had stayed in Nata on the Monday night when Boardman was murdered, which got Tatwa very excited. Nata was where the road from Maun joined the road from Gaborone. Gomwe could have murdered Boardman and then driven to Nata from Maun. But his heart sank when he read the receipt from the Nata Lodge more carefully. It seemed that Gomwe had dined there. He phoned the Lodge to check, and they confirmed that Gomwe had spent the whole evening there, and had left after breakfast early the next morning saying he had an appointment in Kasane. It was not possible for Gomwe to have eaten dinner in Nata, driven the three hours to Maun, committed a murder, and driven back another three hours before breakfast.

In Kasane, he had stayed two nights at the Mowana Safari Lodge. Tatwa checked at the hotel himself. Gomwe had arrived in his car. According to the barman, he drank a lot and also had a short meeting with a black man the evening before he checked out. The two didn't look as though they were friends.

So Gomwe was not a murderer, or at least not the murderer of William Boardman. He had been safely asleep at the Nata hotel on the night of the murder. But he was not an innocent either; his false-bottomed briefcase had turned out to contain traces of heroin. If he was buying, the delivery hadn't been made, or the drugs had been stolen; if selling, where was the money?

Tatwa was sure he was at least half right: Gomwe was involved in a drug operation that spanned Jackalberry Camp and Elephant Valley Lodge. The key lay in Gomwe's murder, and was held by his murderer.

The autopsy had been inconclusive. Gomwe's chest had been crushed and his ribs snapped by heavy pressure. It could be an elephant, or it could be the wheel of a vehicle as Kubu had suggested. His neck was snapped and his cheek crushed by a vicious blow. It could be a raging trunk, or it could be a blunt instrument. But the forensic evidence had been more incisive. The murder scene contained little evidence, but that was to the point. There was too little blood, which on its own was not compelling; when related to the lack of the victim's footprints into the area, it *was* compelling. Tatwa wondered why a bush-wise guide, coming on the death scene undisturbed, had been unable to make these deductions and had carelessly moved the body and trampled the area, destroying evidence. There might be an obvious answer.

Parrots, he thought. Allison's parrots. She said she had shown them to the guide; the guide said she had just described them. One of them was lying, perhaps both.

There was another interesting item in the forensics report. The victim's clothing contained no traces of elephant skin or hair, but there were particles of a canvas material. Were they from the tarpaulin Douglas had used to transport the body, or had the body been wrapped to prevent tyre marks on the clothes?

On a whim he phoned Gomwe's record company in Johannesburg again.

It was before nine a.m., but the manager was already at his desk.

'Detective Mooka? We're still all in shock. Gomwe was one of our best people. Great guy. We're really going to miss him, professionally and personally. Do you have more questions?'

'Just some background information. Who knew Mr Gomwe best at a personal level? Socialised with him and so on.'

'Well, he didn't have really close friends at work. But he and I were quite friendly. Both single, I guess, and interested in football.'

'Did you ever jog together? Anything like that?'

The manager laughed. 'Hardly. Boy said the best exercise took place in bed. Sex was his idea of heavy breathing.'

'You sure he didn't jog or go to the gym or do other exercise?'

'Well, pretty sure. He'd hardly keep it a secret. Most men like to boast about their fitness. He certainly had no reticence about his bed workouts!'

'Thank you. You've been very helpful.'

'I have?'

'Yes, indeed.'

Tatwa said goodbye and hung up. Parrots, he thought. Why did a man who did not like exercise go for a jog instead of watching birds with his girlfriend?

Tatwa decided he needed another interview with Allison Levine. He also wanted to know more about what was in her luggage. But when he phoned the Lodge, he was told she had left at first light. She was driving, on her way home to South Africa. Of course, he thought, she was always scheduled to leave this morning. He tried without success to reach Kubu. He had better speak to the director.

Mabaku had no hesitation. 'Pick her up in Francistown. She can't be further than that yet. Have them go over every nook and cranny of her car. I think we've got a decent chance she's carrying some sort of contraband.'

'What if she objects?'

'Well, she wants to leave Botswana and enter South Africa, right? If she won't let us search her car, I'll get customs to take it apart rivet by rivet. I've got a hunch on this one, Tatwa. We've got them! I want to hear Beardy start singing when we introduce him to Miss Levine!'

Tatwa wondered if it could be that easy. But armed with Mabaku's instructions, he phoned the police in Francistown and asked them to set up a roadblock on the main road from the north. He gave them a description of the girl and, more helpfully, the details of her four-by-four vehicle, which he had obtained from the Lodge. Unlike most guests, she had driven to the Lodge herself.

Well, if she was carrying contraband, she would need her own vehicle, wouldn't she? thought Tatwa.

CHAPTER 55

The Bulawayo central police station brooded over Leopold Takawira Avenue, an attractive colonial building spoiled by heavy security mesh. Kubu parked his car in the parallel parking area in the middle of the wide road and made his way inside. Strange, he thought. Why do I feel uncomfortable in a police station? He checked in with the duty officer and was told that Superintendent Pede was at the CID offices, down the street at the Central African Building Society building. Five minutes later Kubu was ushered into the superintendent's office. Pede was about the same age as Kubu, and about the same height, but much slimmer – in fact quite thin. That, thought Kubu, at least suggests he's honest.

Pede's greeting was polite but cool. 'How can I help you, Assistant Superintendent? Did you just arrive this morning?'

Kubu said he had arrived the previous evening and spent the night at the Holiday Inn. Pede nodded slowly, giving Kubu the impression that he was doubtful. I'd make a dreadful criminal, Kubu thought, embarrassed by his white lie. Good thing I'm a policeman.

'Would you like some tea?'

'That would be very nice.'

They went down the corridor to a tea urn dispensing a well-stewed brew. After that, the ice began to thaw.

'Director Mabaku will have told you that I'm working on the murder case at a camp on the Linyanti. Two men were murdered. A South African policeman by the name of Sipho Langa and an ex-Zimbabwean – now resident in Botswana – called Goodluck Tinubu.'

Pede nodded. 'And the main suspect is Peter Jabulani, going under the false name of Ishmael Zondo. It seems pretty cut and dried. Problem is that you can't find him. Or so you say.'

Kubu bristled. 'And *you* can't find him. Or so you say.'

Pede said nothing.

Kubu sighed. 'Look, I think we're on the same side here. Why don't you trust us?'

Pede gave him a hard look. 'Perhaps if your government would mind its own business and not always side with the British, you'd find us more friendly.'

'Superintendent Pede, what our governments think of each other has little to do with our jobs as policemen. I'm asking for your help as a colleague to apprehend a vicious group of thugs and murderers.'

'What do you want to know?' Pede sounded a little less hostile.

'How come you have Tinubu recorded as deceased?'

'At the time of the war to overthrow the Smith regime, lots of things happened that weren't properly investigated or reported. There was a raid on a farm. The Smith forces responded quickly and managed to catch up with the raiders. They killed three or four. It was the middle of the night. Who the hell knew what was going on? They didn't bother with the bodies. Had other things to do. But they brought back trophies, including a wallet belonging to George Tinubu. Had his fingerprints on it, too. They were on record because he'd been held by the regime's police.

'He was a teacher and had led a protest when they closed several schools to force the villagers into so-called protected townships. He was held under the security laws for three months. I guess he wasn't satisfied with peaceful protest after that.' Pede rubbed his moustache. 'People forget what this country went through. We had to fight for our freedom. Didn't get it on a platter with a new national anthem and a flag-raising ceremony like some countries. We'll go on fighting if we have to. Whatever anyone says.'

'I guess so,' Kubu said blandly. 'So that was it? They declared him dead on the basis of a wallet?'

Pede shrugged. 'They said they took the wallet off a dead body. It's all in here.' He handed Kubu a folder. 'I made you copies of all the documents, prints and so on.'

Kubu thanked him, realising that although the two of them did not see eye to eye, he was getting more help from Pede than he had from Notu.

'Is it possible that the wallet was just on the ground and the soldier lied about taking it off a body? Or that someone else was carrying it for Tinubu or even had stolen it from him?'

Pede shrugged again. 'It's pretty well certain something like that happened, isn't it? It was thirty years ago. Who knows? I suppose you could try to find Smith's soldier boys. But they were guys from the Selous Scouts. They killed a lot of people in hot and cold blood. I don't think they'd remember, or want to talk about it if they did.'

'You're probably right about that.' Kubu hesitated. 'What can you tell me about Zondo? Where does he fit into all this?'

'We've got a detailed file on him too. I can give you some stuff. Background check, where he was born, fingerprints, that sort of thing. We've got information about his other activities as well. But I can't give you that. He's a dissident. Probably working to overthrow the government. As I said, we're willing to fight against people who want to take us backwards.'

Kubu did not want to pursue this line, especially after the earlier tension. 'I understand that. It's an internal matter. But what was he doing in Botswana? We now think that there may have been an exchange of drugs and money at the camp. Was he suspected of involvement in anything like that? Did he have any sort of record of smuggling or drug running?'

Pede had tensed, clearly interested in this theory. 'Did you find money? Or drugs?'

Kubu shook his head. 'It's more complicated than that. There was an issue involving a briefcase. Tinubu obtained one at a pick-up in South Africa. Zondo arrived with a tote. After the murders, Zondo apparently left with his tote, but the briefcase, which was still in Tinubu's tent, was completely empty.'

'These people need money to buy support. It's possible they were just picking up foreign currency. Present from the British, probably, who'll do anything to undermine this country. Maybe it was a lot of money. Maybe Zondo knew we were after him and decided it was enough to set himself up somewhere else.'

'But where? He gets picked up by a plane we can't trace – no flight plan from Zimbabwe, according to your people – and vanishes. To Zambia? Namibia? Angola? They can't find him either.'

'Maybe it was really a *lot* of money,' said Pede sarcastically.

Kubu nodded, defeated by the negativity. And it was true. With enough money, anyone could buy safety and protection in Africa. In most parts of Africa, he corrected himself.

'Less than a week later, the owners of the camp were attacked by two men. They also seemed to be looking for Zondo and for the briefcase. We think they also came in from Zimbabwe.'

'Yes, I read the report. A white man calling himself Madrid and a black man using the name Johannes. We have no record of either of them entering or leaving this country. Why do you think they came from Zimbabwe?'

Kubu ignored the question. 'I see you've followed the reports carefully. Thank you. But there's more that you don't know. We also asked for information on two other men we believe are in the same gang. We have one of them in custody. He has a thick black beard; we called him Beardy. But your people identified him from his fingerprints. His name is John Khumalo.'

This seemed to mean nothing to Pede. 'What did this lot do?'

'They tried to kidnap my wife and did kidnap my sister-in-law. The aim was to blackmail me.' Kubu's voice rang with the anger he still felt. At once he sensed that Pede was on his side.

'Bastards! Attack a policeman's family? That's outrageous! You make this Khumalo talk. Then we might get some answers to this mess. Will you keep me informed? And we'll help any way we can. I swear it.'

Kubu nodded. 'I really appreciate that.' He rose to go, picking up the thin file on Zondo and the even thinner one on Tinubu. 'You've been very helpful, Superintendent. Thank you.'

Pede nodded, and they shook hands formally. As Kubu turned away,

Pede called after him, 'Tell me, Superintendent Bengu, where did you spend yesterday morning?'

Kubu looked back. 'In Francistown, with my brother-in-law,' he said smoothly.

'Of course,' said Pede, as though he had known this all along.

CHAPTER 56

Allison estimated that she would be in Francistown by midday. It was too far to drive to Gaborone in one day, but she wanted to be in South Africa that night. And she had to make the drop-off the following evening.

She was upset about Gomwe's death. She had been told they were only going to persuade him not to muscle in on the drug trade at Elephant Valley, to warn him off. A broken arm, or some other relatively minor but painful injury, perhaps, but nothing about killing him. Now she was worried about the involvement of the police. They were obviously suspicious, not buying the rogue-elephant story. That meant she could become implicated. The tall detective had been polite and had never hinted that she might be involved. Surely he would not have let her leave if he thought otherwise?

She decided to stop in Francistown for fuel and a snack, and then take a short cut into South Africa on a dirt road from Palapye. She wanted to be out of Botswana by nightfall. After this, someone else can play courier to Kasane, she thought. I've had enough.

Just outside Francistown she came to a police roadblock. She wasn't worried, such checkpoints were common in Botswana. But when the policemen insisted that she accompany them to the station in Francistown, she became very concerned. Especially when she saw the roadblock being dismantled behind them.

PART SIX
No Road Through

But there was no road through the woods.

Rudyard Kipling, *The Way Through The Woods*

CHAPTER 57

Kubu's emotions were in turmoil during his drive back to Francistown from Bulawayo. Part of him wanted to believe that Goodluck was the gentle man so many people loved, who was dedicated to preparing the next generation for a better future. On the other hand, it seemed that he had been involved in something illegal. But what? Buying drugs from Zimbabwe? Kubu couldn't imagine a person so dedicated to young children would have anything to do with drugs. Transporting money? That was a possibility. Kubu could imagine Goodluck, who had suffered so much for freedom, taking up the reins to restore it. But who in South Africa had provided the money? Where did it come from? Was it a donation or an exchange? And if an exchange, for what? What did Zimbabwe have to offer in return for money? Gold? Platinum? But surely that was difficult to find and sell without drawing attention. And what was the money for?

Kubu also reflected on the bravery and quiet dignity of Paulus Mbedi, and on the tribulations of Zimbabweans, many of whom had lost family members in the struggle for freedom and were now losing loved ones to the government they had put in power. People are no damned good, he thought, his anger bubbling up again.

He was so wrapped up in his musings that he did not even notice the long lines and delays at the border post; he dealt with them on autopilot. Nor was he concerned by the unusual search of his car by the Zimbabwe customs official, who was polite but surly. It only later dawned on him that it might be that his police colleague in Bulawayo didn't trust him. And how much could he trust them to help him find Zondo?

He was stymied by the Jackalberry murders. Now there were related murders in Maun and near Kasane. Who would be next? Who was responsible? Surely not Zondo acting alone? And where was damned Zondo anyway?

By the time he reached Sampson's home, Kubu was depressed and morose. He opened the front door longing for Joy's consolation.

'Hello! I'm back,' he shouted. 'Come and get me!'

Silence. No bark from Ilia. Nothing.

A chill gripped Kubu. Was it possible that after all the kidnappers had not given up? Could they have been followed from Gaborone? Were Joy and Pleasant all right? He scratched around the kitchen looking for a note or any sign of a struggle. Nothing. Then he noticed a piece of paper on the dining-room table in Joy's handwriting. 'Gone for a walk. Don't worry.' But he did worry. The kidnappers had not been apprehended.

At that moment, his cell phone played its operatic summons.

'Yes?' Kubu's abruptness reflected his anxiety.

'Assistant Superintendent Bengu?'

'Yes. Who's this?' Kubu snapped, not recognising the voice.

'This is Constable Morake of the Francistown police.'

Kubu's stomach contracted. 'Yes?'

'I'm calling because we have someone in custody here connected to the murder in Kasane. Picked her up on her way to South Africa. Tatwa – Detective Mooka – asked me to call you. He said you'd want to speak to her yourself.'

'I'll be there as soon as I can.'

Quickly he phoned Joy's cell phone number. She answered after a few rings. 'Kubu! Are you back?'

'Yes, my darling, where are you? I hope you're not alone out there.'

'Actually we're just walking up to the house.'

He rushed to the front door and saw the two women and Ilia walking down the dusty street. A man, probably a plainclothes officer, followed them a discreet distance behind.

'Joy, Pleasant, I'm so pleased to find you safe. I was very concerned.' He hugged Joy, giving her an emotional kiss, and put his arm around

Pleasant. Feeling ignored, Ilia jumped up and down, pawing Kubu's trousers. 'I missed you too, Ilia!' he said, ruffling her ears.

'They've caught someone who may be involved with the murders at Jackalberry. I'm going to the police station to interview her. I should be home for dinner. If anything comes up, I'll call.'

Joy sensed his eagerness to leave and put off asking about his trip to Zimbabwe. Kubu kissed her again and left.

Pensively, Joy watched him drive off. 'Even though we left him the note, I can tell he was still worried.' Pleasant nodded and said, 'You're lucky to have someone who cares that much.'

Five minutes later, fears for Joy and Pleasant forgotten, Kubu arrived at the police station.

'Her name is Allison Levine,' Constable Morake said with a smile. 'Tatwa was right. We found ten kilos of heroin in a secret compartment next to the fuel tank. It would've been difficult to find if she hadn't been careless. It was all covered in mud, but we noticed some finger marks. Why is someone playing with mud under the car? we asked. Didn't take long to find out. We haven't told her yet that we've found it. And the prints are hers!'

'Good job. Good job,' Kubu said enthusiastically. 'This is the break we needed to tie up the Jackalberry murders with the bastards who've been threatening my family. Miss Levine is going to be in Botswana for a long time. But I need to speak to Tatwa before I see her. Show me a desk I can use, please.'

Kubu kept his conversation with Tatwa as short as possible. He was raring to meet Allison Levine. Tatwa filled him in on what had transpired at Elephant Valley Lodge. He was pretty sure that Gomwe had been murdered. Traces of heroin had been found in a false bottom to his briefcase. They suspected that Allison had lured Gomwe to his death, but had no proof.

Tatwa and his men had found the remains of a camp close to where Gomwe had been killed, but they had no idea who the campers were. They had a vehicle, and there were tyre tracks that headed towards

Zimbabwe. The tracks matched some of those at the clearing where Gomwe had been killed, as did some footprints. Quite likely the vehicle had been driven to the clearing, used to run over Gomwe, and then the tracks were hidden as much as possible. They were checking on this and the footprints. In addition, between the lodge and the corpse they had found two sets of footprints, one of which was definitely Gomwe's. The others were prints from a small shoe – size between six and seven – and those two sets of prints showed that Gomwe and his companion had been walking, not jogging or running.

Tatwa asked Kubu to check Levine's shoe size. He would fax photographs of the prints, and the Francistown police could check against the shoes in her luggage. Tatwa was sure that one of Elephant Valley Lodge's rangers was involved too, but there was no evidence at present.

Kubu could feel the adrenalin beginning to course through his veins. They were closing in on the murderers and kidnappers! It was now only a matter of time and patience.

Kubu turned on the tape recorder. 'It is four fifteen in the afternoon on Friday, the eighteenth of April. I'm Assistant Superintendent David Bengu. With me is Constable Morake. We are interviewing Allison Levine, a South African citizen.' Kubu spoke in English. He checked that she understood her rights. Then he sat and stared at her. He waited all of a minute, assessing and unsettling her. He could see she was scared. Her shoulders were hunched, and her jaw clenched.

'Why am I here?' she snapped. 'I wasn't speeding. And I've got to be in Johannesburg tomorrow by lunchtime.'

Kubu looked at her and shook his head. 'Ms Levine, you and I both know why you are here. And it's not for speeding. All we have to do is agree. And I promise you, we will agree – even if it takes a long time. So, what were ten kilograms of heroin doing in your car?'

Allison did not flinch, but stared into Kubu's eyes. 'I've no idea. I didn't put it there.'

'We found it in a secret compartment next to the fuel tank. It was covered with mud, but you didn't check very well. Your prints were on the mud. Nobody's going to believe you if you say that the drugs were put there by someone else.'

'I don't know about any compartment.' Her voice was taut, her eyes still meeting Kubu's.

'That's nonsense! Tell me who your contacts are – at Elephant Valley Lodge and in South Africa.'

'Contacts for what?'

'Come on, Miss Levine. Don't waste my time. You're a courier for someone in South Africa. You meet a contact from Zimbabwe or Zambia near Elephant Valley Lodge and make the exchange. Your good looks and gender help, I'm sure. You might say they let you get away with murder.'

Allison did not respond, but sat still, staring at Kubu.

'We know your lover-boy Gomwe is involved as well. Did you get your heroin from him?'

Allison sat silent.

'Did you?' Kubu shouted at her, startling her.

'I don't know what you're talking about!'

'Really? Gomwe had traces of heroin in his luggage. You had ten kilos in your car. And you're telling me these things are not connected. Not likely!'

'I'd never seen him before Elephant Valley Lodge. We were attracted. We had a good time. That's it.'

'Ms Levine, you're going to spend the night here. The first of many, I think. Unfortunately, our accommodation isn't as comfortable as Elephant Valley Lodge. But you should start getting used to it.' Kubu paused, staring at her. 'We've got you cold, but what I really want to know is who the others are. Who are your principals in Johannesburg? Who do you buy from? Who are the thugs who've been threatening me and my family? Everyone! I know you are a small fry. But sleep on this. Why should you do life, when the rest are still free? You help me get the others; I'll help you at this end.'

'I want a lawyer. I won't take any more of this crap.'

'A lawyer is your right, Ms Levine. Make sure he's here at eight tomorrow morning, because that's when we meet again.'

*

'Find out who she calls,' Kubu said to Constable Morake when he returned from ensuring Allison was in the cells for the night. 'I doubt if she knows anyone here in Francistown. Maybe she can lead us to her principals.' In reality, Kubu thought this was a long shot. Allison was a bright woman, and he would be very surprised if she made an elementary mistake.

Kubu found an empty office and called Director Mabaku.

'Yes?' Mabaku grunted.

He's got such a welcoming telephone manner, Kubu thought. 'Bengu here, Director. I'm in Francistown.'

'Have you spoken to the woman yet?'

'Yes, but now she wants a lawyer. She denies knowing about the drugs. She's lying, of course. I decided not to mention Gomwe's murder at the moment. I want to keep that for later.'

'Good idea.'

'I think she's a small fry, but I've an idea she could help us find the big fish.'

'Go ahead,' said Mabaku.

'My guess is that she isn't going to give us any useful information tomorrow. Same as today, especially if she has a lawyer present. However, she may have a different view of the world if we add a murder charge, or at least accessory to murder. I think she's in over her head, so if we offer her a reduced sentence or a reduced charge, she may give us her contacts.' Kubu hesitated. 'Do I have your okay to go ahead?'

Mabaku answered slowly. 'Yes. I think it might work. I'll speak to the Director of Public Prosecutions, but I'm sure he'll agree. If you're sure she isn't a big fish, make her an offer.'

'Thank you, Director,' Kubu said. 'Tatwa's doing a great job at Kasane. I think we'll be able to lay both drug and murder charges tomorrow. It shouldn't take long to add the kidnapping charges as well. All in all, very satisfactory.'

After a few more comments, Kubu hung up and set out for his brother-in-law's house, where, he hoped, good food and wine were awaiting.

*

Indeed, Joy and Pleasant had cooked, much to both Sampson's and Kubu's delight. Kubu had bought a couple of bottles of acceptable wine – not too expensive because it would have been wasted on Sampson, but good enough to enjoy. It was a convivial evening, but for Kubu it had been a long day, and he and Joy went to bed early, leaving Sampson and Pleasant to argue politics. Also, Joy was keen to hear more about Kubu's visit to Zimbabwe.

Kubu described to her the strange state of the country, and how he had found Paulus Mbedi. He told her Mbedi's story, and put it in the context of Endima Shlongwane's letter. She listened intently, and then asked Kubu the question he had asked himself. 'Who killed him then? I mean the first time. Who shot him? If it was the Rhodesians, where were the other bodies when he was found by the road? And why would anyone else shoot him in the back?'

Kubu shrugged. 'Maybe he managed to drag himself away from the scene of the attack. Or maybe there were other bodies in the bushes, but Msimang didn't see them in the dark.'

Digging in his overnight bag for sleeping shorts, Kubu found the jar Paulus had given to him. 'These are the bullets they dug out of him.' He passed it to Joy. She looked at the horridly distorted metal lumps. 'Can't you tell what gun they came from? Solve it that way?'

Kubu shook his head. 'If I had a gun that I thought was used to shoot those, we could do a ballistics test. But this all happened thirty years ago.'

'But what about the type of gun?' Joy persisted. Kubu thought about it. 'Well, we could do that. The type of gun used would indicate one group or another. Not evidence, of course, but better than nothing. It's a good idea, my darling.'

Joy preened, then went to the bathroom to shower and get ready for bed. Kubu had finished unpacking, so he scanned the two files Superintendent Pede had given him. As he expected, there was little new information. George Tinubu had been arrested for refusing to follow instructions from a police officer, inciting a disturbance, and resisting arrest. He had never been tried for anything and had been released eventually. Eighteen months later he was supposedly killed in a skirmish with the security forces. There was no doubt about the fingerprints match, and there was a copy of the identity card taken from the wallet. The Rhodesian soldier who reported the matter claimed that the wallet was taken from the dead body of a terrorist shot after the farm raid. There was a description of the raid on the McGlashan farm too. Kubu skimmed it and frowned. Could Goodluck really have been involved in something as brutal as that? Whatever the cause?

He turned to the Zondo file. It was a summary. Zondo had certainly been heavily involved right through the war, but nothing in the file directly linked him to Goodluck. Had they trained together? Been in the same commando unit? Their friendship at the teachers' college suggested it was likely.

At this point Joy returned from the bathroom in her dressing gown. As soon as the door was closed, she let the gown drop to the floor. A burgundy-coloured satin bra just held her full breasts; matching panties set off her silky-smooth chocolate thighs. Burgundy and dark chocolate. Kubu lost interest in the reports immediately.

CHAPTER 58

'Good morning, Ms Levine,' Kubu said as he and Constable Morake entered the interviewing room the next day. 'I trust you had a very uncomfortable night.'

'It's disgusting! Smells like piss!'

'Welcome to prison, my dear. If you think this is bad, wait until you're in a high-security facility.' Kubu looked around. 'Where's your attorney?'

'I've been trying to find one here in Francistown, but haven't got hold of one yet.'

'Well, you have the right to remain silent unless you have a lawyer present. But the longer it takes, the longer you will enjoy the hospitality of our prison system.' Kubu stared at Allison. 'I have to go back to Gaborone tomorrow, so the earliest I'll be able to get back here is next Wednesday,' he improvised.

'But that's four days away!'

'And four nights,' Kubu said quietly. He turned to leave.

'Wait,' Allison said. 'I don't need a lawyer, because there's nothing more to tell.'

Kubu looked at her, noticing her sunken eyes. She might need something to pick her up, he thought. The longer I drag this out, the more desperate she's going to be.

'In which case,' he said, 'I am formally arresting you for possession and trafficking of drugs. In addition, I am going to charge you with being an accessory to the murder of Boy Gomwe. We have evidence now that you lured Gomwe to his death. He didn't jog into the bush and get killed by a rogue elephant. You led him to some of your colleagues, who drove a truck over him to make it look as though he'd been killed by an elephant.' Kubu looked at the shocked woman. 'We may up that charge to murder at a later stage.' He turned to Constable Morake. 'Constable, please take Ms Levine back to the cells.'

'Wait! Wait! Maybe I do know something. Can we make a deal?'

'What sort of deal, Ms Levine? You've got nothing to offer. You just told me so.'

'If I tell you what I know, will you help me?'

'If you admit to the drug charges and give me the names of people involved in this drug ring, I'll do what I can to help you on the murder charges.'

Kubu sat down, reached over to the tape recorder, and switched it on.

'It is eight fifteen on the morning of Saturday, the nineteenth of April. I'm Assistant Superintendent David Bengu. With me is Constable Morake. We are interviewing Allison Levine, a South African citizen.

'Ms Levine, do you agree to be interviewed without the presence of a lawyer representing you?'

'Yes,' she answered quietly.

'Ms Levine, do you admit to knowingly transporting about ten kilograms of heroin from Elephant Valley Lodge near Kasane to an unknown destination, most likely South Africa?'

There was a long pause. She's wondering whether she's doing the right thing, Kubu thought. He waited patiently, letting the silence work on her mind. Eventually she said, 'Yes.'

'We know you've been in and out of Botswana eight times in the last thirteen months, each time to Elephant Valley Lodge. Did you transport drugs each time?' Another pause.

'Yes.'

Kubu could barely hear the response. 'Louder, please, for the recorder.'

'Yes,' she said more firmly.

'Do you bring money from South Africa to pay for the drugs?'

'Yes.' Allison's head drooped as she realised there was no way back now.

'How much money?' Silence. 'How much money, Ms Levine?' Kubu asked sharply.

'I don't know.'

'You don't know?' Kubu was incredulous. 'You don't *know*?'

'I never open the briefcase,' Allison mumbled. 'I can't. It's always locked. I just hand it over and take the packet.'

'Ten kilograms of heroin can be worth millions on the street. That means the briefcase must have had at least several million pula. Actually it probably had dollars – American dollars. Could have been several hundred thousand dollars or more. And you tell me you didn't know how much?'

'I told you, the briefcase is locked. The pick-up has a key. Not me. They don't trust anybody.'

'Who is the pick-up at Elephant Valley Lodge?'

Allison stared at Kubu, gathering her thoughts. 'I give the briefcase to the ranger, Douglas. He comes to my room, takes the money, and gives me the heroin in return. He always has a small backpack with him. No one suspects anything.'

Kubu stood up and paced. 'And then what happens? Where does the money go?'

'The ranger gives it to someone who takes it across the border into Zimbabwe.'

'Who is this someone?'

'I don't know. I've never heard a name or seen anyone. It's easy for the ranger. He's expected to be out in the bush.'

'And on the other side? In South Africa?'

'When I get back to Johannesburg, I call a number. A few minutes later I get a text message with an address. When I get there, I get another text message with another address. I'm sure they're watching me to see I'm not being followed.'

'What's that phone number?'

'They'll kill me if they find out I gave it to you.'

'They won't find out. What's the number?'

'It's on my cell phone under the name "Baby".'

'Then what happens?'

'The last drop-off is always at a busy shopping mall, like Sandton or Fourways. I leave the car and go into the mall. I return to the car after an hour and drive home. I suppose they take the car while I'm in the mall and remove the drugs.'

'And how do you get paid for all these risks?'

'A few days later I find an envelope with cash in it pushed through the slot in the front door of my apartment. It's a lot of money.'

'How much money?'

'About thirty thousand rand.'

'And where do you live?'

'There are some new apartments on Kent Avenue in Randburg, just north of Johannesburg.'

'Please write down the full address, as well as your landline phone number and your cell number. Sign it at the bottom.'

'I don't have a landline, just my cell.'

'So your contacts are expecting you in Johannesburg this afternoon?'

'Yes. If I don't show up, they'll kill me when they find me.'

'You must have a way of alerting them that you've been delayed. You could have had a breakdown or an accident, not so?'

'If I'm going to be late, I leave a message at the same number with an estimate of when I'll be there.'

'Thank you, Ms Levine. That's been very helpful.' He leaned back in his chair and stared at her. She's becoming quite twitchy, he thought. Tapping her foot. Cracking her knuckles. Twisting her fingers. Another hour or so she's going to be desperate.

'Needing a fix, Ms Levine?' he murmured. 'Better get used to it. You're not going to find any in jail. You've been very foolish, my dear.'

He ended the session and turned off the tape recorder. 'Constable Morake here will get you a cup of tea,' he said. 'I'll be back shortly.'

Kubu found the office he had used earlier, shut the door, and went to work.

First he located Mabaku, who was shopping with his wife Marie in the Game City mall. He seemed only too pleased to get a call from Kubu on this Saturday morning. Quickly Kubu recounted the pertinent details of Allison's confession.

'The South African police will want to use Levine to get her principals,' Mabaku said.

'She's expected in Johannesburg later today,' Kubu said. 'I doubt if they can set it up that quickly. Anyway, we can't let her go. We may never get her back if she leaves the country.'

'I'll give Van der Walle all the information,' Mabaku said. 'He may want to try to do something anyway.'

'I can get photos of Levine to Van der Walle,' Kubu said, 'if he wants to use someone who looks like her. I can also arrange for her cell phone to be taken to the border so that the messages will register as coming from South Africa. Someone can pick it up and use it to set up a rendezvous. They can easily get a car that looks like hers. I'll send them the number plates too. I suspect the drug traders won't fall for it, but it may be worth a try.'

'Good, fax all the information to me. I'll send it to Van der Walle.'

'She's suffering from withdrawal,' Kubu said. 'I may be able to get a lot more out of her later. She's beginning to look desperate.'

'Don't let her do anything stupid. Keep an eye on her. Better get a doctor to look at her too. Meanwhile, give Tatwa a call and fill him in.' Mabaku paused. 'I'll have to leave Marie here to finish shopping and go across to the office.' He did not sound unhappy about that at all. Before Kubu could add anything, the phone went dead.

Kubu checked with Morake about the shoes. It looked likely that there was a match between a pair of Allison's shoes and the faxed footprints they had found. Kubu nodded, pleased.

Next he phoned Tatwa, who was delighted to have a reason to bring the ranger in for questioning. He was pretty sure they could now at least charge Allison with being an accessory to murder. He asked Kubu to send the shoes to him as soon as possible.

For the next hour, Kubu filled out the necessary paperwork for charging Allison with the possession and trafficking of drugs. He also drafted a confession relating to the drug charges for her to sign. Finally, he briefed one of the Francistown detectives on all aspects of the arrest, as well as what was happening in Kasane.

Kubu was feeling quite satisfied. A drug charge that would stick; a potential murder charge; and the possibility of finding some high-up dealers in Johannesburg. Now it was time to pressure Allison to get the information he really cared about – the relationship between the drug smugglers and the murders at Jackalberry Camp.

Kubu sat down opposite Allison and completed the necessary preliminaries.

He paged through his notebook, stopped, and then looked at Allison, who was now even more on edge.

'Just a few more questions, Ms Levine.' Kubu stood up and paced. 'How did you know where to take Gomwe on the morning he was murdered? It was quite far from the camp and not easily found.'

He waited, but Allison did not answer. He decided to gamble.

'Come on, Ms Levine, we know you took Gomwe to the clearing where he was murdered. We've identified your footprints with Gomwe's going from the camp to the clearing. You lied, Ms Levine. You said Gomwe went jogging. That's not true, is it? We checked with his friends. They laughed when we suggested that he got killed while jogging. They said if he jogged, he most probably died of a heart attack, not from an attack by a rogue elephant. He wasn't into that sort of exercise at all.' He waited for a response, but Allison did not say a word.

'Anyway, our trackers said that the two sets of footprints – yours and Gomwe's – were walking, not jogging. You're lying, Ms Levine. You knew what you were doing. You deliberately led Boy Gomwe to his death.' Allison was looking down, not meeting his eyes, silent.

'Who told you to take Gomwe to the clearing, Ms Levine? If you don't tell us, then I will charge you with the murder of Boy Gomwe. But you know, I don't think you murdered him. I think you were used. Why would you die for those scum? You know that Botswana has the death penalty for murder, don't you? We aren't soft like South Africa. You kill someone here, you die for it.' Kubu knew this was an exaggeration, but then it was not a lie either.

Allison looked as though she could barely keep herself on the chair. All resistance had drained from her. Kubu was surprised to see that she was crying.

'I just did this for the money,' she whispered. 'I needed the money.' To keep up appearances, Kubu thought. To be able to play the field. To pay for her fixes. He waited.

'I didn't know they'd kill Gomwe,' she said at last. 'Douglas told me that they were just going to teach him a lesson. Show him who ran things around Kasane. That he'd better back off.' A sob racked her body. 'I liked him. I never wanted him killed.' She buried her head in her hands.

Kubu sat watching her cry for a time, deciding she was telling the truth. She thought this was easy money, he thought. An easy game. But the game had harsh rules, which she chose to ignore. He shook his head. Fool, he thought. What a fool.

She asked for a drink, so Kubu fetched her a glass of water. She grasped the glass in both hands and sipped. Several minutes passed before Kubu decided he could continue.

'Ms Levine,' he said quietly. 'I now want to go in a different direction. A few weeks ago, there were two murders at a camp in the Linyanti. We believe that they were drug related, and we think your friend Gomwe was involved; he was a guest there. Then another guest at the camp was murdered a week later in Maun. About the same time, the camp owners were assaulted, my wife was nearly kidnapped, and her sister *was* kidnapped.' He paused, but Allison said nothing. 'We're sure the people you work for are involved in all of this. I need you to tell me everything you know about your contacts, particularly in Zimbabwe. Who are they? Where can they be found? How can they be contacted?'

Allison frowned.

'I think you're wrong,' she said at last. 'As far as I know, Botswana is divided up by different groups. They've sort of carved out the territory between them. Douglas told me that Gomwe was trying to get in on the action. Seems as though he was trying to set something up for himself. Nobody up here had ever done business with him.'

'Have you heard anything about a drug deal in a place called Jackalberry in the Linyanti?'

Allison shook her head. 'But then I wouldn't hear about it. You should ask Douglas. He's closer to things than me.'

For the next ten minutes Kubu questioned and bullied Allison, trying to prise out of her any information that would lead him to the kidnappers. But he got nothing. He eventually decided she had nothing to offer. Frustrated and disappointed, he ground his teeth and thumped his fist on the table, making both Constable Morake and Allison jump. 'Take her back to her cell,' he told Morake, and turned away. Allison shouted that she needed a fix, but Kubu ignored her.

Alone in the office, Kubu closed his eyes to concentrate his thoughts. What were his next steps? He was equidistant from Kasane and Gaborone. Should he go and help Tatwa deal with Douglas, the game ranger, or should he head back to his office and be at the centre of activities? He decided he should head home and leave Tatwa to cope on his own.

What about Joy and Pleasant? Would they want to stay in Francistown for another week, which he hoped would be the case, or would they want to return to Gaborone? He shook his head. He realised he could not predict what they would want to do. He sat quietly for a few contemplative minutes, then picked up the phone and called Sampson's house. Joy answered almost immediately – Sampson had gone to watch a soccer game.

'My dear,' Kubu started tentatively. 'I need to get back to Gaborone. Do you want to stay on with Sampson for another week or so, or—'

'I love Sampson,' Joy interrupted, 'but I couldn't stand another week with him. Pleasant and I were talking a few minutes ago. We're ready to leave.'

'Are you sure you want to go back? We haven't caught the kidnappers yet.'

'You may never get them. We're ready to go home!'

'Okay, okay, we'll leave tomorrow.' Kubu was peeved that he had no say in the matter. 'I'll be back in half an hour. Can you make us some lunch?'

'Lunch will be ready as soon as you get back. I had a notion you might want something to eat.'

Kubu was not sure whether Joy was being sarcastic or funny, so he ignored the comment. 'Thank you, darling. I'll see you in a few minutes. I love you.'

CHAPTER 59

Tatwa was nervous before entering the empty office that served as the interrogation room in the Kasane police station. This was the first interview he had done by himself. Part of him wanted Kubu with him, but another part, struggling to emerge, wanted him to take charge and prove himself. Since Kubu was three hundred kilometres away, there was no option. Taking a deep breath, Tatwa opened the door.

'You don't mind if I call you Douglas, do you?' he said in Setswana to the ranger slumped in the chair on the other side of the table. 'Mr Legwatagwata is a bit of a mouthful.'

Douglas nodded.

'I'm going to tape this conversation as an official record.' Tatwa was nervous and wanted to do everything correctly. It took a couple of minutes to provide the proper introduction on the tape, as well as to read Douglas the customary caution.

'Before I start,' Tatwa said, 'I want to tell you that you're in big trouble. You could spend the rest of your life in jail. But the more you cooperate, the more inclined we'll be to help you. Do you understand?'

Douglas nodded again. Then at Tatwa's prodding he said, 'Yes' for the tape recorder.

'Let's start with the easy stuff. First, we are going to charge you with drug trafficking. Your friend Ms Levine told us that she picks up drugs from you whenever she visits Elephant Valley Lodge. In exchange she gives you a lot of money. Of course, we are always careful to check whether someone is lying. So we did some checking. We found traces of heroin in your backpack.'

'She's talking bullshit,' Douglas spat out. 'Trying to get herself out of trouble. I always thought she was too good to be true.'

'What do you mean?'

'Coming back to Elephant Valley Lodge time after time. Always finding a single guy and then screwing his eyes out.'

'Why would she finger you then?'

'She wanted sex with me, and I turned her down. So she hates me.'

Tatwa pondered this unexpected tack for a few moments.

'How then do you explain the heroin in your backpack?'

'She must have planted it. Insurance if she got caught. Then she could blame it on me. Exactly what she's done. And get me back for rejecting her.'

Allison Levine had not struck Tatwa as someone who would be upset about being rejected by Douglas. She would think he was just an idiot.

'Then how do you explain this?' Tatwa asked, consulting his notebook. 'A few days after she visits Elephant Valley Lodge, every single time, your bank balance jumps by five thousand pula. Same amount every time. Always a week after she leaves. Always a cash deposit. Who are the big tippers, Douglas? You must be an excellent guide and ranger. Five thousand pula. That's nearly my monthly salary. Is it Ms Levine who tips you so generously every time she is here? For what, Douglas? For favours? I don't think so. She may charge for favours, but certainly not pay for them. No, Douglas. I think you get paid in cash every time you deliver the money to your Zimbabwean friends. Only you are too stupid to realise you shouldn't deposit it in your bank account.'

Douglas stared at Tatwa, but did not respond.

'Come on, Douglas. Surely you know who is being so generous to you!'

Douglas continued to stare, but his focus slowly slid from Tatwa's face into the middle distance.

He's feeling trapped, Tatwa thought. Doesn't know what to say. Let's see how he reacts when I put more pressure on him.

'You know how serious this government is about reducing drug usage. Trafficking is not treated lightly. My guess is you'll get twenty years or more for that. At least you won't have to pay your board and lodging, right?'

Still Douglas did not respond. He looked down at his hands.

'However, we know you are a small cog in this business – an important cog, but a small one. If you give us information about the people you work with, I'm sure we can come to a deal.'

Tatwa gazed at Douglas, who wouldn't meet his eyes. He waited until he was sure Douglas was not going to say anything. Then he said, 'Who do you get the drugs from and who do you give the money to?'

Douglas sat, head down. The only movement Tatwa could see was a clenching and unclenching of the jaw muscles. They sat in silence for several minutes, Tatwa hoping Douglas would break, but he did not.

'Okay, Douglas. I've given you your chance to help us. You've blown it. Now we'll deal with the serious stuff. In addition to charging you with trafficking in drugs, I'm also going to charge you with murder – the murder of Boy Gomwe.'

Douglas looked up. 'That's bullshit. And you know it.'

Tatwa continued. 'Ms Levine says that you told her where to take Gomwe on the morning of his murder. You said he needed to be taught a lesson for trying to muscle into the market around Kasane. You knew what was going to happen; in fact you set it up. That makes you one of the murderers.'

'That's a lie,' Douglas shouted. 'She'll say anything to save herself. You've nothing on me except her word. It's all bullshit.'

Tatwa glared at Douglas, knowing he was right. All the evidence was circumstantial. They would never win a case based mainly on Allison's word. Tatwa's self-confidence took a dive. He was sure Douglas was implicated, but how was he to shake him?

Tatwa inhaled sharply. He was his own man now. He had to play the game himself.

'I'm arresting you, Mr Legwatagwata, for the possession of a controlled substance, namely heroin. I expect to add charges of dealing in a controlled substance, as well as of murder. Take him away, Constable.'

'You can't do this,' Douglas yelled. 'You've got no evidence. You've nothing at all. You can't keep me here!'

Tatwa looked at Douglas as he was led struggling from the room.

'You'll have your chance to prove that.' He spoke quietly, with more confidence than he felt. 'You had your chance to cooperate, but now it's too late.'

Tatwa bit his lip, hoping the gamble of keeping Douglas in custody for a few days would make him change his tune.

CHAPTER 60

While Kubu was interrogating Allison, and Tatwa was trying to make progress with Douglas, Moremi was once again walking among the vendors of the Kachikau Saturday market. He was doing three things. His philosophy was that if you could do several things at the same time, perhaps you could fit two or even three lifetimes into one. So he was singing a song of his own composition to an apparently appreciative Kweh. He was thinking of Botswana in the far past, before white people, before Tswana people, before even San people, and how it might have been. Most important of all, he was keeping a lookout for a man wearing a very special hat.

Suddenly he spotted it. He stopped singing and walking, and moved the thoughts of the past out of his conscious mind. Disappointed, he realised that although the man had the right type of build and height, he was not Ishmael Zondo. He stared at the man for a few seconds.

'I'm sure it's Rra Zondo's hat, Kweh. Don't you think so?' While asking the question, he was moving towards the man. One advantage of being thought eccentric was that you could do eccentric things and people were not surprised. So approaching a stranger and discussing his hat was entirely in character.

'*Dumela*,' he began politely. The man looked at him, wondering what this was about. He had heard of the strange cook from Jackalberry Camp. He nodded, but said nothing.

'Your hat is very fine!' Moremi continued. 'Is it perhaps a family heirloom? A man must be very proud to wear such a hat.'

Surprised, the man reached up and touched it. It was an ordinary felt bush hat, quite worn and faded, with a floppy brim all round, good for shielding the face from Botswana's scorching sun. It had three guineafowl feathers carefully sewn on to one side apparently for decoration. When Moremi had asked about them, Zondo had said each feather was for a different type of luck. Moremi had laughed, delighted by the idea and the symmetry. There was no question that this was the same hat. And it seemed that it hadn't brought luck to its owner after all.

'What would such a hat cost?' Moremi continued. 'I suppose it's very expensive. A poor man like me would not be able to afford such a hat.' He could see from the clothes of the hat wearer that he too was poor. He held out his hand in greeting. 'My name is Moremi. I am happy to meet you. This is my bird. His name is Kweh.'

Seeing no harm in this peculiar man with his fixation on hats, the wearer introduced himself. Some small talk followed, in the course of which the possibility of the hat being for sale entered the conversation. Moremi asked if he might hold it, and checked it carefully, particularly admiring the feathers. He asked where it had been obtained, and the man said it was a gift, and then that he had found it, contradicting himself in the same sentence.

Moremi nodded, then, with apparent regret, said, 'My friend, this hat is stolen. I know it's stolen because its owner valued it and wouldn't have given it away or sold it. Now you must tell me how you got it and where.'

Frightened, the man lunged for the hat, but Moremi whisked it behind his back with a flourish. Kweh ruffled his feathers, put up his crest, and stared with beady eyes.

Moremi shook his head. 'Shall we call for help, my friend? Tell them that I am stealing your hat? Tell them how you came to have this hat, and so it is yours?' The man began to edge away, but Moremi added quietly, 'If you tell us the story of the hat, I will buy it from you for a fair price.'

'I found it. It was in the bush, thrown away.'

'Where was that?'

The man gave a complicated description of the location. It was near the airstrip that served Jackalberry Camp. Moremi nodded as if he had known this all along.

'What did you do with the other things you found? The clothes and stuff?'

The man swallowed hard. This madman knew too much. 'There was nothing else!'

Moremi nodded as though in agreement, and jauntily placed Zondo's hat on his own head. Kweh investigated the new addition to what he regarded as his domain.

'What did you do with the other things?'

The man capitulated. 'There was only a coat. It was with the hat. Nothing else. I gave the coat to my brother.' He threw up his hands. 'I kept the hat. You can have it. I don't want it any more.'

Moremi walked away without another word. He knew he could find this man again, knew that Constable Shoopara would now believe him, and call the fat detective or the tall one. But he felt very sad. He had liked Ishmael Zondo and his unlucky hat with the guineafowl feathers. He hummed the snatch of music that had intrigued and puzzled Kubu.

CHAPTER 61

The trip back to Gaborone was uneventful. Unlike Joy and Pleasant, who seemed to have an infinite number of observations about Sampson, his house, his diet, and his apparent lack of girlfriends, Ilia was uncharacteristically quiet. Except for a short visit to the grass ditch at the edge of the road, she slept the whole way.

'What's wrong with the dog?' Kubu asked.

'She's just homesick,' Joy replied.

They had decided to stop for tea at Kubu's parents, since they'd missed their usual Sunday lunch together and Kubu wanted to fill them in on the details of the attacks on Joy and Pleasant. Fortunately he still had the picnic chairs in the back of his Land Rover. He brought one up to the veranda so they could all be seated.

'We must buy some more chairs,' Amantle said to Wilmon, embarrassed by not being able to provide adequate seating. 'When Pleasant comes to visit, we will need at least one more.'

'Why don't you keep this one,' Kubu responded. 'I have several more, and we only use them when we're with you and Father in any case. I can always get it back if I need it.' Kubu knew that buying another chair for the occasional time when Pleasant visited would seem an extravagance to his parents. On the other hand, they would be mortified by not having enough chairs. His offer finessed both issues.

Even before tea appeared, Wilmon and Amantle wanted to hear every detail of what had happened to Joy and Pleasant. Amantle had collected a number of newspapers with reports on the event, and several times contradicted one or other of the younger generation, telling them that the newspaper had a slightly different version. She obviously felt that anything in print must be correct.

When all the details had been laid to rest, Amantle leaned over and touched Pleasant on the shoulder. 'At least you are safe. You must have been very scared. I think I would die if someone kidnapped me. These days you do not know what they might do to you.'

'It was horrible,' Pleasant said, holding Amantle's hand. 'I didn't know whether to cry or scream or keep quiet. Fortunately, they only wanted to use me to get a briefcase from Kubu.'

'Which I didn't have!' Kubu snorted.

'But they didn't know that, did they, darling?' Joy's question rekindled Kubu's guilt at leading the kidnappers on.

Surprisingly, it was the normally quiet Wilmon who spoke. 'I do not understand why it was Joy who found Pleasant. Why did Kubu not do it? You have not rejoined the police, have you, Joy?'

'Father, Joy is a very difficult wife sometimes,' Kubu said, trying to keep a serious tone to his voice. 'I told her to stay at home with two policemen to look after her, in case the kidnappers came again. When she heard about Pleasant, she climbed through the bathroom window and was able to use her friends' help to locate where Pleasant was being held.' Kubu paused. 'I have to say that even though she shows me no respect, I was proud of how she solved the problem. I'll have to ask Director Mabaku whether there is an opening in the CID. At least I'll be able to keep an eye on her.'

Amantle was far from satisfied. 'Have you caught these wicked men?' she asked. 'If you have, you must take the whip to them.'

Kubu smiled to himself. His parents did not understand the difference between the traditional tribal courts, where flogging was an acceptable punishment, and the country's formal legal system, which did not mete out justice in that way.

'No, Mother,' he answered regretfully. 'Unfortunately we haven't.'

Amantle gave a disapproving nod and headed to the kitchen to fetch the tea.

For the next half-hour they talked about Pleasant's kidnapping and the unsolved murders of Goodluck and William Boardman. When Kubu told them that yet another guest who had been at Jackalberry

Camp had been murdered near Kasane, Amantle stood up, fear in her voice.

'Aaaii. Now you make me worried for all of you. These are very bad men. I think a witch doctor must have made an evil spirit live inside them. They are evil! I will not sleep until they are caught and locked up. You were right to go to Sampson's house. But you should have stayed there.'

'I will calm your mother,' Wilmon said, standing up. He touched her gently on the cheek. 'Do not worry, Amantle. Our son is after them. They will never get away. He is more clever than them.'

With his parents standing, Kubu thought it a propitious time to leave. He kissed his mother on the cheek, encouraged her not to worry, and formally took leave of his father, thanking him for taking care of Amantle. Joy and Pleasant cleared the table and took the teacups and plates to the kitchen. They both hugged Amantle and Wilmon. Again Kubu saw the fleeting look of pleasure lighten the reserve of his father's face. He wants to be warm, Kubu thought, but doesn't know how.

Eager to get home, Kubu drove faster than usual from Mochudi and eventually pulled up to the house on Acacia Street only a few minutes after the desert night had enveloped the capital city. He hoped they had done the right thing in returning. The kidnappers were still at large.

CHAPTER 62

Kubu had a restless night worrying about Pleasant and Joy. At six a.m. he made coffee and toast and gave Ilia her biscuits. About half an hour later Joy and Pleasant appeared. He asked them to be careful and to let no one into the house. Before Joy could argue, he kissed her and headed off to the CID.

After pouring himself another cup of coffee, he settled at his desk and found a fax in his in-basket from Kachikau about a hat. He was intrigued. Zondo's hat. Another piece of the puzzle. He closed his eyes, not to snooze, but to let the fringes of his consciousness nibble at the unsolved cases.

Kubu had always loved jigsaw puzzles. The sky was often the hardest part. Too uniform, too blue. Some sneakier puzzles had sky pieces with one almost straight edge. So you would try to fit them into the border of the puzzle without success because they actually belonged in the middle.

Kubu took off his shoes and put his feet on the desk, thinking about pieces of a puzzle made to look as though they fitted in one place, whereas they actually fitted somewhere else altogether.

This was the sight that greeted Mabaku as he entered Kubu's office. Kubu's substantial feet in carefully darned clean socks were nudging his in-basket out of the way. His eyes were closed. Mabaku viewed this for a moment or two with a peculiar mixture of disapproval and envy. 'I can see you're busy,' he said at last. 'I'll come back later.'

Kubu opened his eyes, gave the director an apologetic smile, and waved him to the well-worn guest chair. He maintained his comfortable position.

'Why did Zondo throw away his hat?' Kubu asked. 'He always wore it. What sense did that make?'

'Threw away his hat? What are you talking about?'

Kubu filled the director in on Moremi's discovery at Kachikau.

Mabaku pouted. 'Maybe that was part of his plan? Always wearing the same hat, same jacket. Then abandon them both and put on something else. A disguise by default.'

'Yes, but why didn't he just keep the hat and wear something else?' Kubu asked. 'Why toss it into the bushes? Moremi seemed to think it was important to him. That's why he knew Zondo hadn't given it away.' This is a puzzle piece with a straight side, Kubu thought. But it's not an edge piece.

'I've been thinking about the people at the camp that night,' he continued. 'We divided them into two groups. Those who were divorced from the events – just bystanders – and those directly involved. Who's in the first group, who's in the second? But they were all involved really, you know. Let's go through the guests.'

He started counting on his fingers. 'The Munro sisters. Nice society journalists from a liberal English newspaper? Yes, they are. But they were also tracking Goodluck and Salome through their past. Then suddenly they're all there together. Coincidence, fate or design?' He uncrossed his legs and stretched to get more comfortable.

'The Boardmans. Curio traders and long-time friends of Dupie and Salome. I think William discovered something the night of the murders, or perhaps the next day, and thought he could use it to advantage. Obviously it was valuable enough to make him dangerous. Too dangerous to stay alive.'

Kubu extended a thumb to join the four fingers already raised. 'Gomwe. Definitely involved in drugs, but I'm not quite sure how. Perhaps it was plain greed? I don't know. Perhaps he found what he was looking for at Jackalberry. Perhaps he had to wait until Elephant Valley Lodge. He wasn't an innocent either.' He lifted three fingers on his other hand. 'That leaves the three who were directly involved. Tinubu and Zondo, who were obviously doing some sort of exchange of goods for cash, and Langa, the South African policeman on their trail.' He lowered his hands and rummaged in his desk drawer for a packet of mints. He helped himself and offered the box to Mabaku, who took one without comment. He knew this mood. Kubu was heading somewhere, and it would be worth following.

'Then we have the camp staff. Salome, who connects with Tinubu through the Zimbabwe war. Dupie, and probably Enoch, linked with them the same way. Moremi, who seems to see the relationships between people, even though he's never met them before. Solomon and his wife, who appear to be bystanders, but who knows?' He popped another mint into his mouth.

'So where does that leave us?' Mabaku prompted.

Kubu was concentrating on his mint. 'Madrid and Johannes were expecting Zondo to bring back the money. No question about that. So they're also looking for Zondo. Obviously with no more success than we're having. So where is Zondo? Where is the money? Where is whatever it is they were exchanging for the money? All vanished.' Suddenly he sat up, changing tack.

'What did you get from Beardy?'

'It was Madrid all right. Beardy knew that name, although he wouldn't admit it. And the Johannes who hired him is the same Johannes who terrorised Salome. The fingerprints matched. As I told you, Beardy said it was drug money, but he wasn't really convincing.'

Kubu shook his head, removed his feet from the desk, stood up, and walked over to the window. He suddenly noticed he was not wearing his shoes and looked around vaguely for them. 'And what's Madrid's next move?'

'Beardy doesn't know, or he's not saying. My bet is that he'll give up on this money and get on with making more. We need to keep an eye on Joy and Pleasant, though, in case I'm wrong.'

Kubu was looking at the director, but his mind was moving the pieces of his puzzle around. 'I think we're short of a murder, Director.'

Mabaku looked annoyed. 'I think we've got quite enough murders already! It's getting as bad as the BCMC affair. Why would we want another?'

Kubu did not answer. He collapsed into his chair, replaced his feet on the desk, and wriggled his toes.

'The camp, Director. Madrid *must* go back to the camp.' He nodded firmly and explained why.

PART SEVEN
The Thing Which Was Not

Here he spoke the thing which was not.

Rudyard Kipling, *Three and an Extra*

CHAPTER 63

When Kubu finished the story of the attacks on his family, there was silence on the line for a few moments. When Dupie responded, it was with a single syllable that conveyed shock, surprise, even a touch of guilt, although the last might have been Kubu's imagination.

'Shit!'

'Yes. That pretty much sums it up.'

'What about the one you caught? Has he told you what it's all about?'

'Well, the director has been handling that himself because I'd probably tear the bastard apart. But it seems to be drugs and drug money. The briefcase and the tote are what they're after.'

'So why hit us? Why don't they go after Zondo?'

'I'm sure they have. Either they've found him empty-handed – or only with one hand full – or they're still looking for him, like the rest of us. Something you said to Madrid must've put them on to me.'

'He asked me to describe the policemen who came after the murders,' Dupie said quickly. 'That's all. I had to. They were going to kill Salome!'

'I understand. Can you remember exactly what you said?'

'I think I said you were very large and from the CID in Gaborone. The other detective was tall and slim from Kasane.'

'Nothing about the briefcase?' Kubu probed.

'No, I don't think so,' Dupie lied. 'I can't exactly remember. I was pretty shaken up.'

Kubu grunted. He was not convinced. 'You were asking about Khumalo – the man we caught guarding my sister-in-law. He's cagey, but from what he's said we're pretty clear what their next move will be. Now they know I haven't got the briefcase. So it's back to you.'

'What the hell does that mean?'

'It means we're sure you can expect another visit shortly. And this time they won't leave empty-handed.'

'But there's nothing here!' Dupie's voice was tense.

'You know that, and I know that, but it seems Madrid is convinced that one of us has the money. Perhaps he did find Zondo. I don't know.' Kubu paused, then continued. 'But the good news is that this time he won't have the advantage of surprise. Tatwa and I will be heading out to you with some armed constables in the next couple of days. We'll be ready for him.'

'What about the guests?' Kubu noticed a hint of excitement in Dupie's voice. Perhaps Dupie was relishing getting even, maybe ahead, with a bit of luck and the police on his side.

'How many have you got there?'

'Two couples. Leaving the day after tomorrow. Then a group of six on Friday.'

'Put them off,' Kubu ordered. 'It'll be too dangerous.'

'Hey, wait a minute,' Dupie spluttered. 'They're foreign tourists. You can't just dump them on an airstrip. And anyway, we need the money.'

'Find them another lodge. You want them in the crossfire?'

Dupie didn't answer, but the point was taken. 'When will you get here?'

'I'll fly to Kasane tomorrow and link up with Tatwa. We'll come out in a couple of vehicles the next day. The uniform guys can camp on the mainland, keeping a low profile until Madrid makes his move.'

'Okay. We'll expect you on Wednesday afternoon. Meanwhile I'll hold the fort. This is an island, you know. Easy to defend. Ask—'

'Yes, I know,' Kubu interrupted. 'Ask Winston Churchill.'

Kubu and Tatwa set out from Kasane on Wednesday morning after a good breakfast at the Old House, and even Kubu left satisfied. From there they drove the few blocks to the police station, picked up three constables, their gear, and a powerboat on its trailer, and headed towards Ngoma.

After Ngoma, the road deteriorated to a badly corrugated dirt track, and the going was tough. The policemen stopped at the Kachikau arts and crafts store for soft drinks and rudimentary takeout before heading on towards the Linyanti. After the town the road was wide, but the surface consisted of loose sand with multiple vehicle tracks criss-crossing each other to avoid sink holes, ruts and corrugations. It was necessary to change in and out of low-range gears whenever they hit soft sand, and their forward momentum slowed. By the time they reached the Linyanti, Kubu was hot, irritated, and dissatisfied with packets of artificially flavoured chips.

At the end, they battled to find Jackalberry. Tatwa had done it once by land, but the driver with him had known the area. Eventually they found the track and came to the makeshift jetty. When the vehicles were switched off, it was quiet, even the birds temporarily silent. The dust churned up by the vehicles mixed with the heat haze. Once again Kubu looked at the idyllic waterway, the *mokoros*, and the small motorboat on the far bank. The verdant smell was a pleasant change from the dusty dryness of the south. A lot of water had flowed down the Linyanti since he had seen it last, even though it was only a few weeks ago. Then, he'd had no idea what to expect. Now it was different.

'This is where the answers are, Tatwa. They were always here, not in Gaborone or Maun, or even in Bulawayo.' He nodded in self-agreement. 'Come on, let's attract attention, and Enoch can take us over. The guys can set up camp here out of sight and launch the boat. I want it ready if we need it.'

They got out of the Land Rover and walked to the water's edge. Someone was waving to them from the distant camp. It looked like Moremi.

Kubu was sitting in the tent Dupie called his office. The level of mess was the same, the filing cabinet drawer still jammed open. The Watching Eye still held pride of place in the centre of the work table, and there was still a half-finished mug of cold coffee, the same one as before for all Kubu could tell. This time Dupie claimed his right to the chair behind the desk.

'What's the plan?' he asked.

'Plan?'

'To deal with Madrid and Johannes!'

'Oh, I see what you mean.' Kubu did not have one, so he improvised. 'There are three ways they could come in – by air, over land or by boat. We'll be on the lookout for a boat all the time, and a motorboat will be easy to pick up by the noise. After dark it'll be harder, but we'll have someone on guard at the camp all night. Keep the keys to your outboard motor with you. We have our motorboat if we need to chase them over water. By plane seems unlikely. How will they get here from the airstrip? My bet is that they'll come by vehicle and try to slip across to the camp at night in one of the *mokoros*.'

Dupie nodded. 'Makes sense. Don't worry about the camp; we've had someone on guard at night anyway. The trick will be to catch them on the shore before they get over here.'

'Yes, we'll set up a little way upstream so that the area here looks invitingly unprotected. But we'll be on watch all the time. As soon as they get to the clearing opposite the camp, we'll have them.'

'What if they smell rat-pie and make a run for it in the vehicle?'

'Easy. We just shoot out the tyres. They can't get far. And there's nowhere to go anyway.'

It sounded a bit too simple to Dupie. Would Madrid fall for a trap like that? Or would he have another card up his sleeve? 'What about a chopper? Straight on to the island? It can be done. The Defense Force brought Sergeant Mooka that way after the last attack, although they landed on the mainland.'

'We'll hear it coming, same as a motorboat. We'll be waiting for them. I don't think they could take you and Enoch that way, let alone all of us.'

Dupie smiled. He liked that.

'What do we do in the meantime?'

Kubu shrugged. 'We wait. Lots of police work is like that.' He picked up the Eye, admiring its glassy indigo symmetry.

Dupie reached for it. 'Careful with that. It's valuable.'

'Oh?' said Kubu, giving it to him. 'I thought you said they were all over Turkey.'

'Yes, but this one's special. To me. Like a totem, you know?'

Kubu nodded without evident interest. 'Who else is at the camp at the moment?'

'Just Salome, Enoch, Moremi and Solomon. Solomon's been staying overnight to help keep watch. Beauty sleeps in the village. No guests. We took your advice about that.'

Kubu thought it stronger than advice, but let it go. 'Is it possible any of the staff are working with Madrid? Tipping him off?'

Dupie frowned. 'Why would you think that?'

'Well, it seems odd he just went for you and Salome. Why not Enoch and the others? Did he already know that they had nothing to tell him?'

'Enoch and I go way back. He's as loyal as they come. Solomon and Beauty weren't on the island. That leaves Moremi.' Dupie shook his head. 'You can't seriously suspect him.'

'I think Madrid learned more than you told him. I think we need to watch our step very closely. I'll keep my eyes open. I suggest you do the same.' Dupie opened his mouth to argue, but then closed it and nodded.

'I'll need to ask Salome some more questions too. Some pretty odd things have come out since our last meeting, Dupie. Did you know that the Munro sisters knew of Goodluck before they met him here? And I think Salome had seen him before, although perhaps it's buried in her subconscious now.' Before Dupie had a chance to respond, Kubu continued. 'Then there's William Boardman. He saw something important that night. Important enough to get himself killed.'

'But that was Madrid!'

Kubu shook his head. 'No, we don't think so. Why would Madrid go after him? Unless you – or someone else – told him something about Boardman. Did you?'

'Of course not!'

'I didn't think so.'

Kubu got up and moved to the filing cabinet, where there were two framed photographs. One was of a family with two teenage children – a girl and a boy – standing next to a swimming pool. Behind the family stood a smiling, dark-haired young man of about twenty wearing a bush hat set at a jaunty angle. The second photo was of a single-storey house with face-brick walls and a tiled roof. To one side grew a large, thirsty-looking palm and in the background a range of hills stretched to the horizon. He picked up the family picture, examining it to see if the athletic-looking youth could have become the man across the desk, then glanced at Dupie, who nodded. 'It's Salome's family. That's me in the background.' He indicated the second photo. 'That's my dad's house on the farm in Rhodesia. Nothing left now, no house, no farm. Dad passed away. In hospital in Bulawayo. At least he didn't have his throat cut. They might have saved him, but the doctors were too busy, and the nurses couldn't care less.'

Kubu skipped meaningless condolences. 'And Salome's family?'

'They did get their throats cut. Her mother was raped and killed, and her brother had his genitals chopped off and stuffed into his mouth. Salome was fourteen then. She was lucky, you could say. They'd started gang-raping her when one of the bastards shouted that the Scouts were approaching, and they took off without even bothering to kill her.'

'Were you with those Scouts?'

'Yes. But actually the odd thing is that we were miles away when a terrorist gave the alarm. He jumped the gun. We didn't get there for another half an hour. But we caught up with the bastards.'

'What happened?'

'Took them by surprise.' Dupie pulled his finger across his throat and made a choking noise in the back of his mouth.

Kubu put down the picture. He wasn't looking forward to asking Salome about her experience, but it had to be done. Strangely, Dupie's ambient good spirits seemed restored.

'Time for a drink,' he said. 'It's white wine for you, isn't it?'

CHAPTER 64

While Kubu was talking to Dupie, Tatwa strolled to the dining area. Solomon was setting the tables. The policemen had been invited for dinner. They would all enjoy Moremi's lasagne and well-grilled chops done on the *braai*, with *mielie* meal and tomato gravy. After dinner, two of the three constables would return to their mainland camp in the motorboat and drop off Solomon, who was no longer needed for guard duty.

'You'll be happy to get home tonight,' Tatwa said by way of greeting.

Solomon nodded and went on precisely aligning knives and forks as though royalty were expected. 'Beauty will be pleased,' he commented.

'Are you happy here, Solomon? Aren't you worried about all the things that have happened over the last few weeks?'

'It's my job. And Mma Salome has been good to us. Maybe now we can help her. It'll be all right.' He examined the tables critically and started setting out water and wine glasses.

'That night,' Tatwa began, knowing he did not have to specify which one. 'We think Rra Boardman saw something or learned something. Something so dangerous that it got him killed. Was there anything you can remember that was different that night – maybe something you thought about afterwards?'

'I wasn't here that night. I left after I'd set the table for dinner. I only came across the next morning with Rra Dupie. I don't know what Rra Boardman saw.'

Tatwa sighed. It had been a long shot. 'There was nothing different the next morning?'

'Well, just that Enoch usually fetches us early in the motorboat unless he takes guests out in it. Then we come across by *mokoro*. I heard the boat come over earlier than usual, and then the Land Rover driving away. Enoch didn't come to call us, so I thought we'd take the *mokoro*. But someone had borrowed mine, and the others were out too, so we just waited. About an hour later Rra Dupie came back and took us over in the boat. He told us he'd taken Rra Zondo to the airstrip.'

Tatwa liked to plan his interviews, sketch what he needed to explore and how to go about the discovery. But occasionally a detective finds a question in his mind that has no clear purpose. He had watched Kubu come up with a useful lead that way. So when a lateral question occurred to him, he asked it without hesitation.

'Who had taken your *mokoro*?'

Solomon looked surprised, and shrugged. 'We borrow each other's. It doesn't matter.'

'When did you get it back?'

'It was here. At the camp.'

Tatwa felt a thrill of interest. 'You're sure it was yours?'

'Yes. They're all different. Mine's quite narrow and pointed, faster!'

Tatwa smiled. A turbo *mokoro*! 'You left it at the camp the night before?'

Solomon shook his head. 'No, I went to the village with it that evening. Someone borrowed it in the morning.'

For a moment Tatwa was speechless as the field of potential murderers broadened around him. 'Solomon, this is very important. Do you remember how many *mokoros* were at the camp when you left on Sunday evening? And how many were here when you arrived on Monday morning?'

Solomon looked puzzled. He shook his head. 'Two, maybe three.'

'Were there more or the same number on Monday morning?'

Solomon shrugged. 'I can't remember.'

'Please try!'

Solomon thought, then shook his head. 'It was three weeks ago. Why does it matter?'

'But Solomon, don't you see? Someone could have taken your

mokoro on the Sunday night. To get across to the camp and commit the murders!'

But Solomon pursed his lips and shook his head firmly. 'Can't use a *mokoro* at night. Because of the hippos.'

Tatwa sighed. Something was believed to be impossible just because it was never done. 'Why didn't you tell us this before?'

Solomon just looked at him, and Tatwa knew the answer before he heard it.

'You didn't ask me,' said Solomon.

At this point Kubu and Dupie joined them from the office tent. 'See any weak spots?' Dupie asked.

Tatwa was supposed to have been checking the security of the central area. He shook his head. 'I don't think we'll have a problem. It's like a castle with a moat around it. And the moat is full of crocodiles!'

Dupie laughed. He liked that. He thumped Tatwa's shoulder hard enough to jog his St Louis baseball cap. 'Let's go get a beer to keep your cap company,' he said. 'I think we could all use a drink.'

CHAPTER 65

Dupie made sure they had drinks, then got to work grilling pork chops on the *braai*. The others settled around the dining table, listening to the frogs call and the hippos grunt. Kubu settled himself next to Salome, who had taken the head of the table. Tatwa sat opposite Kubu, with Constable Tau next to him. The other two policemen occupied the foot of the table, leaving two seats for Dupie and Enoch. Solomon hovered.

Kubu noted with approval that Tau was drinking guava juice with ice. He would have the first watch after they went to bed. Tatwa could relieve him. Kubu would take the dawn watch, in time for an early breakfast. That meant that a glass or two now would not be inappropriate, and Tatwa could have one more St Louis beer because the alcohol level was so low. Kubu thought it very unlikely indeed that Madrid would have another go at the camp. It was the residents of the camp he wanted watched to avoid any unpleasant surprises later on.

Dupie arrived with a plate of chops and almost collided with Solomon, who was carrying a tray of lasagne, a big cast-iron *potjie* of *mielie* meal, and a frying pan heaped with a spicy onion and tomato sauce. '*Braaivleis!*' said Dupie with enthusiasm. 'Nothing better! Time for a red, Kubu? I've got some Nederburg Pinotage 2002.'

Pinotage was not Kubu's favourite: Pinot Noir – the noble grape of Burgundy – married way below its station with the peasant Cinsaut. The wine was designed to grow in South Africa's Cape region, but not to grow on the palate, was Kubu's feeling. And 2002 had been an abominable year in South Africa. But he thought it would be snobbish to refuse. And Nederburg wines were good, in general.

Once the main course was presented, Salome said, 'Dupie, won't you bring in another small table there? Pull out the cloth. Then Solomon and Moremi can join us. They're also involved.' It was a thoughtful gesture; Moremi and Solomon were guests for once, as well as staff.

'We don't know what will happen next, Superintendent,' Salome said to Kubu by way of explanation. 'All of us could wake up and find ourselves murdered in our beds!'

Kubu suppressed a smile at this unlikely combination of events. 'We'll keep a strict watch,' he assured her.

'I'll be awake, too. Back-up,' said Dupie. 'The 303 might come in handy yet, with a bit of luck.' He had the rifle leaning against the back of his chair.

'Constable Tau will take the first watch. Ten till two. Will you go next, Tatwa? Two to six. I'll take over from then.'

Salome hadn't touched her food. 'When is this nightmare going to be over?'

The Batswana men were rolling the *pappa* into balls with their fingers and dipping them into the tomato gravy, while gnawing the well-done chops. Each had a large helping of lasagne for variety. Not without regret, Kubu put down his chop bone. 'When we catch the criminals,' he said. 'Not before that.'

'You mean Madrid and Johannes?' asked Salome.

'Well, yes, them also, but I had the murderers in mind. Madrid is after the cash. He didn't send Zondo to bump off Tinubu and Langa. If he had, we wouldn't have heard from him again. He'd have what he wanted. No, Madrid's the injured party looking for his money. We need to catch the murderers and confiscate the money. Once that happens, Madrid will give up.' Kubu looked pensive while he rolled another *pappa* ball. 'You know, Ms McGlashan, it's a funny thing. Every criminal thinks he's smarter than the police. Never considers the possibility of being caught. Worse than that, he thinks he's cleverer than every other criminal. So he'll take on police and criminals all at once.'

Dupie swallowed a heaped forkful of lasagne. 'You're talking about

Zondo?' But Kubu had his mouth full and just shrugged. Dupie spoke across the long table to Salome. 'Don't worry, my dear. Nothing's going to happen. Not while I'm here.'

Kubu noticed the looks that met across the table. Something has changed between them, he thought. Interesting. What had Dupie done to win his lady's favour?

Enoch ate in silence. Suddenly he met Dupie's eyes, and touched his chest as though he were about to cross himself in the Catholic fashion. Dupie glanced away, and Enoch let his hand drop back to his food. From somewhere in the lagoon there came a series of hippo grunts. There was a loud crack, and a tree descended to comfortable elephant-trunk level. The night bush was filled with sounds.

It was left to Moremi to respond to Kubu. 'No, not clever,' he said, shaking his head. 'Not clever! Not clever!' But whether he was agreeing or just commenting was unclear. 'Must go see to dessert. Kweh may eat it!'

There was apple pie bristling with cloves and drenched in custard. It was delicious. Everyone's spirits seemed improved, whether or not they'd had alcohol. Dupie told tales from what he called the 'old' Africa, and everyone had a bad-news story from Zimbabwe.

'How can they let him carry on?' asked Dupie. 'Surely someone can bump him off if that's the only way to get rid of the bastard.'

'It's not that easy. He's got the place tied in knots. Everyone watches everyone else. And everyone is scared of everyone else. Even the police. I was there recently.' Depression and anger sounded in Kubu's voice. Dupie shook his head at the unfathomable ways of Africa.

With Kweh on his shoulder, Moremi brought a large pot of boiled coffee. They heard another tree crashing on the mainland and pachyderms engaging in minor quarrels.

Kubu pushed back his chair, and Tatwa unfolded from his. Constable Tau was deep in conversation with Solomon, but took the cue and jumped up, followed by the other two policemen.

'We'll take Tau up to the lookout,' said Kubu. 'I want him to keep watch across the river. The guys on the mainland will watch the landing. But Tau'll be moving around the island during the night. Don't be concerned.' He turned to Dupie. 'And don't take any potshots!'

The group broke up. Solomon joined the remaining two constables, and they headed for the motorboat and their posts on the mainland. Kubu and Tatwa walked with Tau to the lookout, settled him there, and strolled back to the guest tent near Dupie and Salome. By mutual agreement, the detectives had decided to sleep in one tent.

'Tau'll be asleep in an hour,' said Tatwa.

Kubu shrugged. 'It won't matter. The dangers are here on the island. Not on the mainland or across in Namibia. We'd better keep alert, though.'

Tatwa nodded, but was pensive. He took this first opportunity to tell Kubu Solomon's story about his *mokoro*.

Kubu stopped and turned to Tatwa. 'What does it mean?'

'Well, anyone could've come over from the mainland, committed the murders, stolen the money and the drugs, and been gone by morning.'

'How did they get off the island?'

'By taking one of the other *mokoros*.'

'Did Solomon notice if there was an extra *mokoro* at the landing when he got to the camp?'

Tatwa shook his head. 'He couldn't remember.'

'What about Zondo? He had the money by then. He and Goodluck must have done the swap that night, because he'd arranged to leave early the next morning.'

Tatwa shrugged. 'Maybe not. Maybe he discovered Goodluck's body, realised it was too late, and sat it out till morning.'

Kubu shook his head. 'Why leave the swap to the early hours? No one was watching them. Right after dinner would be fine.'

'Well, maybe they did do the swap. Maybe the murderers hit Tinubu, realised that the money was gone, and settled for the drugs.'

'If they went to the trouble of coming out here, risking a *mokoro* ride through the hippos and crocs, and murdering two people, they knew exactly what was going on. They wouldn't have left Zondo sleeping peacefully with a briefcase full of US dollars.'

'Maybe they stole the money and left Zondo alive?' Tatwa was grasping at straws.

Kubu pouted. 'Then Zondo would have run straight to Madrid, who wouldn't have wasted his time on Dupie and Salome and me. He'd be after the murderers. Anyway, it makes no sense. Why stop at one more murder? Why not just kill Zondo too?'

They resumed walking. Tatwa was silent as he scanned Kubu's argument for leaks, but he couldn't find any damp cracks. It was Kubu who spotted another scenario. Again he stopped in the path, grabbing Tatwa's arm.

'Here's a thought. Suppose they were Zondo's accomplices? He didn't know how things would work out. He didn't know if Tinubu would come alone. Perhaps he mistook Langa for Tinubu's bodyguard. If you were going to pull off a million-dollar heist, wouldn't it make sense to have back-up? They could have set it all up. The others drive from Ngoma, park in the bush. In the middle of the night they steal a *mokoro*, pole over to the island, join Zondo, and hit Tinubu and Langa. They make Tinubu's murder look like a revenge killing. Probably that's Zondo's idea, knowing that at least Dupie would fall for it. Then the accomplices take the money *and* the drugs and head back to their vehicle on the mainland. Zondo has a good night's sleep, wakes early, packs, and Dupie takes him to the airstrip. He insists on being left there, no point in Dupie waiting for the plane. Especially since there isn't one. The accomplices pick him up in their vehicle. He discards his signature hat and coat, selects another passport, and they all head for the nearest appropriate border post – probably at Ngoma. By the time we're in the picture, they're far away. Zondo looks different, his passport is different, and he's driving in a vehicle he isn't supposed to have. Tatwa, that could be it!'

Tatwa stood in the path. The tree frogs were getting excited; the end of summer was offering them their last mating chance. No leaks appeared to Tatwa in Kubu's current thesis either. 'Then we were wrong to come here,' he said. 'The answers aren't here after all.'

Kubu started walking again. 'Perhaps. It's just an idea to explain the missing *mokoro*. I'm not convinced. There must be other possible explanations.'

When they reached the tents close to the central area, they could see Dupie at the water's edge, sinking into the river sand on a camp chair and cuddling his Lee-Enfield .303.

'Did you check with Moremi about the hat?' Kubu asked softly.

Tatwa nodded. 'I spoke to him before dinner. It's what we thought. That hat was Zondo's trademark. Like my cap. He wouldn't have discarded it for a disguise.'

'No, he wouldn't,' said Kubu. Suddenly he stopped again and turned to Tatwa. 'I'm not sure if someone came over from the mainland or not, Tatwa. But the *mokoro* is important. We just have to work out exactly why.'

There was a sudden thrashing in the water and Tatwa jumped back. 'Was that a hippo?'

Kubu shook his head. He knew something about hippos. 'Crocodile,' he said, and walked on to their tent.

CHAPTER 66

Kubu slept lightly and was an early riser. His subconscious continued to process, and he was alert for any sound of a tent opening. At 4.30 a.m. it was still dark, but he was wide awake. He decided to relieve Tatwa; he felt guilty about his unfair allocation of watching duties in any case.

He found Tatwa at the lookout, wrapped in a heavy coat, binoculars round his neck and a police-issue pistol next to him on the bench. He was awake and alert, and scanning with a flashlight. He had heard Kubu lumbering up the path.

'Hello, Kubu. You're early. My watch only ends in an hour.'

Kubu shrugged. 'I'm awake. Go and get a few hours' sleep before the day starts. Could be an interesting one.'

Tatwa hesitated, though he was tired. 'Shall I keep you company?'

'No, get some rest. I want to think, anyway.'

Tatwa handed over the gun and the binoculars and headed towards the tent.

Kubu settled himself and looked around. It was no longer really dark. There was a mauve line of clouds in the east, a false dawn heralding the true one. He could already just make out the river. And the birds were active; the bush was alive with a variety of calls: piping robins, burbling bush-shrikes, raucous go-away-birds. He tried to compete with bars of the Bird Catcher's aria from Mozart's *The Magic Flute*, but gave up, chuckling. By then, the true dawn was turning the clouds into a palette of reds, magentas and oranges. A disc of fire started to rise from the river, spreading colour over the water. God does this every day, Kubu thought. Even if there is no one here to see. He sat for some time watching the sky, river and bush change around him, listening to the bird calls, hearing the harsh and quarrelsome but somehow appropriate barks of the baboons. Hippos grunted on their way back to the water after a night's feeding.

He found himself humming Moremi's melody – the one whose name he couldn't remember. When it was finished, he thought about the *mokoro*. Who had brought it over to the camp? How had he, or they, got back to the mainland? The theory that had brought him and Tatwa to the camp with three armed constables did not allow for a mysterious accomplice from the mainland. Or did it?

Kubu's subconscious demanded attention. The piece of the jigsaw puzzle, Kubu, it seemed to say. It doesn't fit because you're holding it the wrong way up. Try turning it around. Kubu did, and the piece fitted perfectly. Not only was the *mokoro* right to be at the camp, it *had* to be at the camp! Kubu jumped up. That was why William Boardman had been murdered! Now he thought he knew how that had been organised, too. I need a map, he thought. Perhaps Tatwa knows. He almost set off to wake the tall detective, but sighed and settled himself on the bench again. There were loose ends to be thought through and tied off. He needed to work through all the events of the last few weeks. How would he prove his theory? And if he was right, where were the money and the drugs? He was distracted by the grumbling of his stomach. It did not approve of the idea of an early morning without breakfast.

Then he heard someone coming along the path from the camp, and he picked up the gun. But it was Tatwa who emerged from the bush, carrying two mugs of tea. A most welcome sight. Even more so when, having settled the tea, he fished a handful of shortbread biscuits from his pocket and gave them to Kubu.

'Tatwa,' Kubu exclaimed. 'What an excellent thought! Couldn't you sleep?'

Tatwa shook his head. 'I want to get this resolved, Kubu. My first big case. We're no further than we were the last time we were here. We just have two more murders, that's all.'

Kubu shook his head. 'I think you're wrong about that. I think we're much further along. How far is it from here to Maun? Do you know? In hours?'

Tatwa extracted a biscuit from his other pocket and started to gnaw. 'It's a long way. Through the Savuti Game Reserve. Really rough tracks. The best idea would be to take the cut-line road down the firebreak border of the national park. But you'd need a four-wheel drive to get through the sand. Tough going. Why do you want to know?'

'How long do you think it would take?'

Tatwa shrugged. 'Maybe Dupie's done it and could tell us. I'd say six to eight hours, depending on the conditions.'

'And Maun to Kasane? On the main roads?'

'Oh, that's just over six hundred kilometres of paved road. Straight as an arrow. You can do that in six hours, less if you push.'

'He must've been dog tired after all that,' Kubu commented.

'Who?' asked Tatwa, puzzled.

Kubu told him.

CHAPTER 67

After breakfast, Kubu found an opportunity to talk to Salome alone. Dupie was patrolling the island; he clearly thought the police were taking the impending arrival of Madrid too casually. At Kubu's suggestion, Tatwa had accompanied him.

Kubu decided a direct approach was best. 'Ms McGlashan, you recognised Goodluck Tinubu when he arrived, didn't you?'

Salome looked up sharply. 'I've already told you that I did not.'

'But you see, the literary ladies, as my boss calls them – the Munro sisters – linked the two of you. To a farmhouse. Near Bulawayo.'

Salome looked down at her cup of after-breakfast coffee. 'What do you know about that?'

'Only what Dupie mentioned yesterday.'

'It's got nothing to do with what happened here.'

'Please, Ms McGlashan, I have to have all the pieces of the puzzle. I'm sure you're right. It has nothing to do with the murders. But let me decide for myself.'

She looked up from her coffee. 'All right, Superintendent. I was fourteen. Rhodesia was trying to defend itself from the world's ostracism and Britain's anger. It was a nasty, dirty civil war. Dupie talks about the noble Scouts. From what I heard, they butchered terrorists and anyone they thought was a terrorist. The noble president of Zimbabwe talks about the *freedom fighters*. I saw how they butchered anyone they could get their hands on, even civilians. Now he dishes out land to these "veterans" who weren't even born at the time of the war. The war was vicious, bitter. No holds barred. None.'

Kubu nodded agreement, and waited.

'My family had a farm about fifty kilometres outside Bulawayo. My father was a really good man. Good to his workers, good with the land. He loved me and my brother. And he loved my mother. You know, we felt safe! Hard to believe. We heard the stories, but it couldn't happen to us, could it? My father was a sympathiser. He voted against Smith.' She paused, looking at the detective. 'You don't know what I'm talking about, do you? It didn't matter what side you were on, you see. My father was in town when they attacked the farm. They took us by surprise. They murdered and mutilated my brother, maybe the other way around, God help him. In front of me and my mother. He was twelve. Twelve! Then they raped and killed my mother in front of me, and then they started on me. Do you think the *details* are important to your case, Superintendent?'

'Only one. Why didn't they kill you?' Kubu felt the bitterness of his question and of her response.

'Yes, why indeed? They thought the soldiers were coming. One of them sounded the alarm. And they left. I lay alone, naked, bleeding, for what seemed like hours. That's how they found me. That was almost the worst part, but not really.'

'Was one of them Tinubu?'

She looked past him, unwilling to meet his eyes. Unwilling to meet anyone's eyes. There was a long silence between them.

'Was one of them Tinubu?'

'Yes, I think so, perhaps. It was thirty years ago.'

'He was the one who called them off, wasn't he?'

'I don't know what you mean. The leader was raping me. He had first go, you see, since I was a virgin. I understood what they were saying because I spoke the language. There was a line of them, waiting their turn. Like at a bus stop, you know? Laughing and jeering.' She hunched as though protecting herself. 'One guy was telling them to let me be. I was a child. I remember what he said. "The children are our future." Can you beat *that*? While they're *raping* me? The leader told him to get out and keep watch if he didn't want his turn. A few minutes later he rushed in. Said he'd seen lights. The soldiers were coming. The leader didn't believe him, but he couldn't take the risk. He said that if it was a lie, this man would die. They left me there.'

'So this man saved your life?'

'If you like. In the sense that someone who shoots at you and misses saves your life.'

'Was this man Goodluck Tinubu?'

Salome started to cry. Silent tears traced her cheeks. Kubu offered her a napkin, but she pushed it away, got to her feet and walked off. Earlier, Kubu thought, she seemed to be a self-controlled adult. But inside she was still not much older than fourteen.

Dupie and Tatwa found him sitting alone at the table ten minutes later. They pulled up chairs.

'All clear,' said Dupie, satisfied. 'Not a trace of the bastards. You've heard from the guys on the mainland?'

Kubu ignored that. 'Salome told you, didn't she? That Tinubu was one of the terrorists who attacked her family's farmhouse?'

Dupie folded his arms, resting them comfortably on his ample belly. 'Is that what she said?'

'I'm asking you.'

'She thought so. Hell, it was thirty years ago. I told her she was imagining it. Just ghosts from the past. I don't believe in ghosts. And we got the bastards. All of them. No prisoners.' He pulled his hand across his throat.

'Did you check?'

'Check what? The guy was a salesman from Gaborone. Passport was clean. Sure, he was born in Zimbabwe. Does that make him a terrorist?'

'Did you search his tent?'

'Don't be stupid. What for? Souvenirs from a thirty-year-old mass murder? I told her she was confusing Tinubu with someone who might've looked a bit like him. Told her to pull herself together. She accepted that, kept to herself for the rest of the day. But she was okay.'

Kubu stared at Dupie. 'Here's what I think,' he said. 'I think she did recognise Tinubu, and what's more, she was right. I think she got someone here to help her kill him. She couldn't do it alone. Maybe that was you, maybe Enoch, maybe Moremi, maybe someone from the mainland. I don't know, but I'm going to find out.' He got up and headed to his tent without another word.

Dupie looked shocked. 'He's gone bananas! What's he on about? Salome murdering people? It's ridiculous! We all know Zondo did it. You're looking for a scapegoat since you let him get away scot-free! You better talk some sense into him.' His large hand grabbed Tatwa's arm across the table.

Tatwa extricated himself. 'If she's innocent, there's nothing to worry about. The assistant superintendent must have evidence for his suspicions. If you know anything, you should tell us. It may help her.'

For once Dupie was at a loss for words. Then he said, 'You've seen her. She couldn't murder anyone. She's gentle.'

'What about someone who raped her and – it seems – got away with it. Revenge is powerful motivation.'

Dupie shook his head. 'Stupid ghosts. Her and her ghosts. Think it's the first time? She's always seeing ghosts. Always seeing ghosts.' He pushed back his chair and stood up. 'Bloody ghosts.' Then he walked off in search of Salome. Tatwa got up too. He wanted to find Enoch.

Tatwa found him at the makeshift dock. He was working on the boat's outboard motor. He had the casing off and was tinkering with the innards.

'Problem with the motor?'

Enoch nodded. 'Not starting well. Dupie said we must be sure it would be ready in case we have to chase those bastards.'

Tatwa nodded, without comment.

'Think the fuel filter's dirty. I'm just flushing it.' He returned to his work. Tatwa seemed to hold no interest for him.

Tatwa squatted on his haunches next to the boat. 'You seem pretty good at this sort of stuff. What caused the breakdown that time you got stuck on the way to Kasane?'

'Wheel bearing went on the trailer. I didn't have tools, but Dupie brought them.'

'Why didn't you just leave it and head on to Kasane?'

Enoch splashed petrol over the filter. 'Dupie freaked. Said I must wait for him. That the trailer would get stolen.'

'Who would steal it in the middle of the bush? With a jammed wheel?'

Enoch shrugged. 'Didn't matter. I just waited for him. We got it rolling, and he took it back.'

'And you slept in the bush?'

'It was too late to go through to Kasane.'

'Why was that? You can drive that road at night.'

'The Chobe National Park gate closes at eight in the evening. It was too late to get through. And there's bloody elephants everywhere. Not safe to drive at night.'

'Why not come back with Dupie? Head out the next day?'

'Hell, I was halfway there. They didn't need me here. I don't mind being on my own in the bush.'

'Done that a lot, have you? Guess you could tell some stories.'

Enoch nodded, but he did not smile.

'You and Dupie go back a long way?'

'Yes, a long way.'

'Here in Botswana?'

Enoch nodded.

'Before? In Rhodesia?'

'Yes. What of it?'

'You were together there? In the Selous Scouts?'

'Who told you that?'

'Dupie,' said Tatwa, taking a flyer. 'He thinks very highly of you.'

'We were together. You watch each other's back. Nothing ever came at you from the front.' He started reassembling the casing for the motor.

'How did you get to Botswana?'

'Dupie organised it.'

'You'd do anything for him?'

'He owes me a lot. He'd do a lot for me too. Not *anything*. What do you mean?'

Tatwa shrugged. 'Just talking. Were you with him when he got to the farmhouse? Where they were attacking Salome and her family?'

Enoch nodded.

'Must have been bad.'

Enoch shrugged. 'I saw a lot of bad stuff in those days.'

'That night, Enoch, the night of the murders here. Can you tell me anything about it?'

Enoch shrugged. 'Nothing to tell. I was asleep. I saw nothing. I heard nothing. I didn't talk to anyone.'

'You know Mma Salome did it, Enoch. Tinubu was one of the terrorists at the farmhouse. She recognised him. That's how it all started.'

Enoch looked stunned. 'But it was Zondo!' he exclaimed.

Tatwa shook his head. 'Zondo was just caught in the middle, wasn't he, Enoch?'

'You're talking shit! You're crazy! Mma Salome wouldn't kill anyone!'

'Maybe she had someone to help her.'

Enoch turned away, meticulously sorting his tools into the toolbox. When he turned back, he was calm again. 'It's silly,' he said. 'It's nonsense. You should be looking for Zondo.' He picked up the toolbox and started towards the camp. Tatwa watched him go.

Fifty metres into the river was a sandbar. As Tatwa watched, a three-metre crocodile clambered on to it, settled, and opened its jaws, exposing vicious teeth. Tatwa shuddered, thinking of his brother, and followed Enoch back to the camp.

CHAPTER 68

Kubu strolled to a point where he knew he could get a decent signal for his cell phone. He wanted to check on Joy, and he needed to report back to Mabaku. There was a chance that Beardy had finally spilled some beans. He called Joy first.

'Hello, Kubu.' There was noise in the background, and for a moment Kubu was disoriented.

'Where are you, my dear?'

'I'm at work, Kubu. At the daycare centre. Where should I be on a Thursday morning?'

'Oh yes, of course.' The noise was the children playing. He had forgotten that she had insisted on going back to work today. 'How are you feeling?' he asked, covering his slip.

'Fine. How are you?'

'Not bad. We're making progress here. Still confusing, but we'll get there.'

'Good. I'd like you to come home.'

Kubu felt guilty. The conversation was not going well; it felt stilted. 'Karate session this afternoon?' he asked, hoping he had the day right. For once he was glad of her sport. A karate dojo should be safe enough.

'No, I cancelled. Didn't feel like it, really. I said I had a cold. I want to get home. Remember, Pleasant's staying while you're away.'

Kubu hesitated. Joy loved her karate. She always felt like it.

'You're still not well, are you?'

'Kubu, don't fuss. Just a bit uncomfortable. The funny food in Francistown.' She made it sound like a foreign country.

Kubu squared his well-padded shoulders and put down his

substantial foot. 'Darling, this is enough. You must see a doctor. I insist. I'm worried about you.'

'Kubu, don't nag. I'm busy. If I don't feel better—'

Kubu had a flash of inspiration and interrupted. 'What about Dr Diklekeng? You're always saying how good he is. That he doesn't patronise the kids and really listens to them. I'm sure he'd be good. And you know him and like him.' Joy always spoke highly of Dr Diklekeng – the doctor for the daycare centre. Kubu had struck gold.

'Yes, that's not a bad idea. I'll think about it.'

'Do you promise you'll go to see him?'

Joy hesitated. 'Yes,' she said at last. 'It's a good idea.'

Kubu pressed his advantage. 'This afternoon?'

Joy dug in her heels. 'I've got shopping to do, and I don't want Pleasant to be on her own. I'll go tomorrow. Or the next day. I'm a bit busy at the moment.'

Kubu realised he would have to be satisfied with that. There was an outburst of childish noise, and Joy shouted that she had to go. Kubu put down the cell phone and thought about his wife. Suppose she was really sick? What would he do? He felt lost already. He wanted to get home, fetch her, take her to Dr Diklekeng. Do what was necessary. Make everything as before. Instead, he was stuck on a paradise island in the Linyanti, surrounded by people he did not trust. And by crocodiles, he thought sourly.

He pulled himself together and dialled Mabaku's cell phone number, but got a recorded message. Mabaku must be in a meeting. He tried Edison at the CID.

'Kubu! How's it going?'

'Okay, Edison. I can't reach the director. Is he around?'

'Mabaku? Didn't you hear?'

Kubu sighed. How was he supposed to follow the director's movements from the Namibian border? 'Hear what? Break in a case?'

'Break in his stomach, more like. He's in hospital. Perforated ulcer. Couldn't take all the black coffee and stress, I suppose.'

'He's *what*? In hospital? That's impossible. I mean . . .'

'He had awful pain yesterday afternoon, so his wife took him to

Casualty at the Princess Marina. They admitted him right away, and they're operating this morning.'

Kubu had the lost feeling again. 'But we need him!'

'Kubu, he'll be okay.'

'Yes, of course,' said Kubu, embarrassed. 'Who's running the show?'

'I suppose I am at the moment.'

'Good,' said Kubu, not meaning it. Now he really would have to get back. 'Is there anything we need to handle while he's in hospital?'

'He's worried about the African Union meeting. But it's all under control. No problem. We're not really involved. It's Special Service Group stuff.'

Kubu tried to regroup. 'What about Beardy? Get anything out of him?'

'Well, he says he's willing to cooperate. But so far he always has an excuse. Some reason to delay. First he wanted a lawyer, so we got him one. Then he wanted a deal. Now he isn't satisfied with the lawyer and wants one who speaks the Ndebele language. That's not so easy. I think he's stalling, but I've no idea why.'

'Is it possible he expects Madrid to rescue him?'

'From Central Prison? He can't be that stupid. Besides, he doesn't look like a kingpin. If they get to him, it will be to shut him up. There are easier and more permanent ways of doing that than trying a jailbreak. I'm trying to convince him that he'll be safest if he tells us everything he knows. Then they'll have no reason to stop him talking. He agrees, but then has another excuse.'

Kubu ground his teeth. The calls were not going well.

'There is some good news, though,' Edison added. 'The sting the South African police set up for your Ms Levine's contacts. It worked! They put a tracer on her car, and followed it to a house in Bryanston – that's a fancy Johannesburg suburb. Anyway, they found a cosy distribution centre in the middle of the city. They arrested the lot.'

'How high up in the food chain did it go?'

Edison sighed. 'Hard to say. Depends what they can get people to cough up. But there are cut-off points. Hell, it was a big hit. You win one step at a time.'

Yes, thought Kubu. But the real drug moguls always seem one step ahead of that. And don't have to play by the rules. Still, it was a triumph as far as it went. And Van der Walle would owe Mabaku one. That would make the director happy. He would need something to cheer him up in that hospital. Kubu shuddered, remembering his own sojourn there. The food had been awful.

'Okay, Edison, I have to get back to work here. Give the director my best wishes. Tell him . . . never mind. Ask him to phone me when he's up to talking. And let me know how it all goes.'

After the call, Kubu thought about Mabaku. He *is* the CID, he thought. What would we do without him? He shook his head as if to erase these thoughts. He forced himself to think about Beardy. Why was he stalling? Just putting off the inevitable? Or was he waiting for something, and if so, what? Could it be that the convenient fiction Kubu had created of Madrid attacking Jackalberry a second time actually *was* part of the plan?

Kubu felt a wave of urgency. He needed to solve this case before . . . something. And he needed to get back to Gaborone before . . . something. He'd had enough. It was time to stop teasing. It was time to put three aces on the table and to firmly bluff another in his hand. One more day, he thought. Then I'm going back to Gaborone. With everyone at the camp, if that's what it takes. He heaved himself to his feet and went to look for Tatwa. They would need to plan a strategy. And there was something he wanted Tatwa to find in Dupie's office tent. He intended to make the communal lunch an interesting occasion.

CHAPTER 69

Kubu pushed his chair back from the table. 'I can't eat another thing,' he said. 'Nothing more. Perhaps a cup of coffee later. But not now.' He waved Moremi away. His interest shifted to Dupie's rifle leaning against the back of his chair. 'What vintage is that Lee-Enfield of yours, Dupie? Nineteen thirties? Can I take a look?' Dupie passed the rifle to Kubu, who examined it with professional interest. 'Still in good condition. And loaded, I see. I presume you have a licence?'

Dupie nodded, and Kubu seemed to lose interest in the weapon, but did not return it.

'What an excellent afternoon. But the clouds are building up. What do you think, Dupie? A thunderstorm later on?'

Dupie looked at the blackening horizon and shrugged.

'Bit too obvious, isn't it?' Kubu said. 'Lots of noise but no rain. Probably won't be a drop. Funny how we miss the obvious. There's a daddy-long-legs spider that's spun a web by the washbasin in our tent. Quite a character. Catches the mosquitoes. But if you touch his silk, he starts to oscillate in the web. Faster and faster till you can't see him any more. Gone. You see right through him because of persistence of vision. No spider. Nothing to see. Nothing to catch.'

Kubu had their attention. Everyone wondered where this discourse on arachnidean behaviour was heading.

'That was our problem with Zondo. He was there all the time, but we couldn't see him.' Kubu nodded as though this comparison would be obvious to everyone, and said no more.

Oddly, it was the normally reticent Solomon who ventured the question. 'What do you mean, Superintendent? Where was he, and why couldn't we see him?'

'He wasn't moving quickly,' offered Moremi. 'Not quickly. Oh, no.'

'No, he wasn't. Moremi's right,' said Kubu. 'We were always a murder short, you see. We seemed to have enough.' He smiled. 'Too many, even, according to my boss. But we missed out on Zondo.'

'What are you talking about?' asked Salome. 'Is he supposed to be dead?'

'I'm talking about Ishmael Zondo, or Peter Jabulani, if you want to use his real name. I should say the *late* Peter Jabulani. He was the third person murdered that Sunday night. Or maybe the second.' Kubu turned to look at Salome.

'It started with you, didn't it, Salome?' he asked, using her given name for the first time. 'It started when you recognised Goodluck. And you wanted revenge. Understandable enough after what had happened, even though it was a very long time ago.'

Salome blushed. 'I wasn't sure it was him. It could've been my imagination. As you say, it was a very long time ago. Dupie said so too. He convinced me. I just withdrew. Settled down. It was my imagination. They all said so.'

'All?' asked Kubu. 'Were they all involved?' His hand encompassed the group.

'No. I mean Dupie. I was shocked. But then I accepted that it was just my mind playing tricks.'

'But someone agreed to check. Take a look. Moremi, Solomon, Enoch, Dupie?'

'No, no. I just thought it through. No one checked.'

Kubu ignored that. 'The one who stole the keys, right? Didn't need keys to the tent. To the suitcase? Yes. But also to the briefcase. That was a surprise, wasn't it, Dupie? A briefcase full of US dollars. You didn't expect that, but it was just what you needed with things going downhill here.'

Dupie shook his head. 'What the fuck are you talking about, Superintendent? What are you trying to pull here? Whatever it is, it's not going to work.'

'Because you'll all stick to the same story, right? And Salome? She's just a victim. Thought she saw a nightmare from the past. Put it behind her. Nothing there, is there? Just like the spider. And you, Dupie? Everyone's mate. But with a background in the Scouts. Not the *Boy* Scouts, eh? You know about efficient killing, don't you? And how to turn it to advantage. And Enoch. Your sergeant – yes, I know that background, too.' He stared at Enoch, who looked around as if for a weapon.

'Is this what you're looking for?' asked Tatwa. Casually he held up the Watching Eye he'd taken from Dupie's office. Enoch crossed his hands on his chest, as if protecting his heart. Then he got control of himself and forced his hands down. He said nothing.

Kubu pretended to ignore this exchange. 'Maybe Moremi? He owes you, too. No one else would give him a job. He'd help you, wouldn't he? And Solomon? Good, reliable Solomon. He has a family to support.'

Kubu looked round the stricken table. 'You could really pull strings with anyone you liked, couldn't you, Salome? An embarrassment of riches, you might say.' He nodded. 'I think we could have that coffee now, Moremi.' Moremi rose without a word and walked off. But he must have whispered something to Kweh, because raucous clucks and even a 'go-away' came from the kitchen. No one said anything until Salome broke the tension.

'I don't understand any of this. What happened to Zondo?'

'He never left the island,' said Tatwa.

'Of course he did!' Dupie exclaimed. 'I took him across to the mainland on Monday morning. I left him at the airstrip.'

Kubu shook his head. 'You took *someone* across. Someone dressed in a felt hat with guineafowl feathers and a canvas bush jacket. Zondo's hat and jacket were later discarded on the mainland. And that person got back to the island in Solomon's *mokoro*. Solomon himself, maybe?' He glanced at the waiter, who shook his head, but did not contradict the detective aloud.

'That was a neat trick, Dupie, but just a hair's breadth too clever. There was a problem, wasn't there? William Boardman was up before dawn for his birdwatching trip. Had his binoculars as usual. He wondered why someone else was heading across the lagoon wearing Zondo's hat. But he found out soon enough, didn't he?'

Dupie was shaking his head. 'It's all nonsense, Superintendent. I took Zondo across to the mainland, and then we drove to the airport. The reason he was wearing Zondo's hat was because he *was* Zondo, and he was wearing *his own* hat. Not as intriguing as your story. But a lot simpler. Occam's razor!' he concluded triumphantly. Everyone looked at him blankly.

'Is that what you used to cut Goodluck's throat?' asked Tatwa drily.

Dupie snarled, 'This is all bullshit. I took Zondo to the airport. It's not my fault if he dumped his hat and coat there. Maybe he wanted to be incognito? How should I know?'

'I didn't say he dumped his hat and coat at the airstrip. Just that they were left on the mainland.'

Dupie was quiet, but just for a moment. Then he stormed ahead. 'Then Zondo disappeared. You can't try to pin this on us just because you can't find him!'

'Oh, I know where he is,' said Kubu. 'It's like the daddy-long-legs. You can't see him, but he's right in front of you.' He looked out at the lagoon. Everyone followed his eyes. They heard a motorboat starting up on the mainland.

Moremi approached, carrying a tray with coffee, milk and sugar.

Kubu turned to Salome. 'But you had to get rid of William, didn't you? Madrid's visit was quite a bonus in a way, wasn't it? The perfect cover for a hit. Yet another perfect murder your team could put together.'

Salome glared at him. 'Superintendent, you're way out of line. No one here had anything to do with Boardman's murder. He was a good friend. We were all here the night he was killed. With guests. From overseas. They can vouch for us if it comes to that.'

'Not quite,' said Kubu quietly, pointing across the table. 'Enoch wasn't here.'

'He was stuck in the bush!' Salome snapped. 'Dupie had to go out and fetch the trailer. He was halfway to Kasane, for God's sake!'

'So he said,' commented Tatwa mildly. 'Anyone want sugar?' He helped himself to three heaping teaspoons.

Kubu nodded. 'The perfect alibi. Enoch supposedly leaves for Kasane, dumps the trailer, and goes in the opposite direction down the cut-line to Maun. Radios Dupie, pretends he's broken down and needs help. Dupie heads out, also supposedly towards Kasane, but actually towards Maun. Picks up the trailer, takes his time, heads back. Perfect alibi for Enoch, who's halfway to Maun by then. To keep the appointment Dupie set up with William Boardman!'

Dupie got to his feet, and a moment later, so did Enoch. 'This is raving nonsense! Enoch got stuck. He radioed me. Salome heard the conversation, for shit's sake! I went to help him, we fixed the trailer well enough so I could get it back, and Enoch headed on to Kasane in the morning. He was there about nine! Dozens of people saw him. He hadn't driven to Maun! That's hundreds of tough miles through the bush and sand.'

'It can be done,' said Tatwa quietly. 'Check the map. We did. But, of course, you know that already, don't you?' He was also on his feet, facing Enoch. He let the Eye swing from side to side like a pendulum, as though he was trying to hypnotise Enoch. Dupie subsided and sat down. For a few moments no one said anything.

Moremi broke the silence. He turned to Salome. 'Mma Salome, what the policemen say may be true. Or it may not.' He shrugged as though he was discussing the failings of the local football team. 'But this is true. They cannot prove anything. They suspect all of us. But they cannot prove any one single thing.'

Kubu felt a wave of frustration and tried to hide it by swallowing his coffee. He was looking for a crack, a chink. But he had found nothing. They were calm, unsurprised. He knew some were involved, others maybe not. Or maybe they were all involved. He had spelled out how it had been done. But he had no evidence, no proof. Moremi was absolutely right.

'Oh, we'll prove it all right. Don't worry about that. In the meanwhile, everyone stays here,' Kubu said. His eyes moved from the table to the dock, where the other two constables were tying up the police motorboat. There was no doubt about the purpose of their presence now. They would ensure that no one left the island.

Kubu and Tatwa sat on their own, away from the communal area. Kubu had deliberately shown his hand; now he was going to need to play his cards quickly. 'It's the three of them, Tatwa,' he said. 'Dupie, Salome and Enoch. Dupie and Enoch know how to go about this sort of killing, and they had to cooperate to murder Boardman. It would take two people to pull off the camp murders too. Salome was the one who recognised Goodluck, got them to search his tent. She was probably the brains behind it all.'

'What about Solomon and Moremi?'

Kubu shook his head. 'Solomon wasn't even on the island that night – we checked with the villagers, and he was there with Beauty. So what was his role in the whole thing? And why bring up the issue of the borrowed *mokoro*? It was an important piece of the puzzle for us, and he volunteered it. He's not smart enough for a double bluff.' Tatwa nodded, accepting this.

'As for Moremi,' Kubu continued, 'well, he's Moremi. I just can't see it. And he found Zondo's hat. That's what led us back here to the camp. They've both got reason to be loyal to Salome, but murderers? No.' He shook his head again.

Tatwa was thoughtful. 'There were a lot of odd features about the camp murders. Why did they do it that way? Zondo murdered and maybe thrown into the lagoon for the crocs, Goodluck murdered twice – stabbed and throat cut – and mutilated, and Langa casually bashed and dumped in a *donga*?'

'I've thought about that. I think the plan was to murder Goodluck with as little fuss and evidence as possible, dump his body in the lagoon, and pretend he had to get home early and left by plane for Kasane. Easy enough to get rid of his car at Kasane later on.'

'What about Langa? He came with Goodluck?'

'No problem. Enoch would just take him back to Ngoma at the end of his stay. They didn't know he was a policeman. When people came to look for Goodluck, they would shrug. Yes, he was here. Yes, he left early. Said it was an emergency at home in Mochudi. He had arranged a plane to pick him up in the morning. Yes, he was carrying a briefcase when he left. No problem.'

'But?'

'But when they killed him, they discovered he didn't have the money any more. So they came up with the plan of pinning Goodluck's murder on whoever *did* have the money. It would be too coincidental to have both people disappear from the camp on the same day. So they made a virtue of necessity, if you can call cutting Goodluck's throat and hacking off his ears a virtue.'

'How did they know that Zondo had the money?'

Kubu shrugged. 'They probably were watching Goodluck. I don't know for sure. Anyway, they headed for Zondo's tent, took the money, murdered him the same way, probably stripped his body, and then started for the lagoon with its convenient crocodiles. But there was a problem. Langa had seen the money change hands, and his brief was to follow the money, so now he was watching Zondo, and that turned out to be fatal. And there was no time for anything fancy. Not with Zondo's body lying on the path.'

Strangely, but not uncharacteristically, Tatwa was thinking of the people involved rather than the crimes. 'Do you think they were friends after all, as Moremi said? Zondo and Goodluck? Comrades from the Zimbabwe war? There were the two glasses in Goodluck's tent.'

'I'm not sure. That could've been a set-up as Zanele suggested. Just take a glass from Zondo's tent with his fingerprints on it. Exactly the sort of misdirection I would expect from Dupie. Too clever by half.' Kubu shrugged. 'Or maybe they really did have a drink together and chewed over old times.'

'Two fighters for freedom turned drug smugglers. Awful.'

But this time Kubu firmly shook his head. 'I don't buy it. It makes no sense. We don't know much about Zondo, but it's completely against Goodluck's character. Something else was going on. I think we'll know what when we find the money.'

Tatwa nodded. 'That's the one piece of evidence they can't get rid of. The money they had to keep. We've got to find it, because otherwise we've got nothing. With it, the whole pact of silence will collapse. Especially with three people involved. Two's company, but three's a crowd.'

'Someone will break ranks,' Kubu agreed. He rubbed his jowls. But what if we don't find the cursed money? he wondered. Somehow we'll have to get them to break ranks anyway.

His thoughts were interrupted by his cell phone. 'Hello. Bengu here,' he said.

'Kubu! It's Mabaku. These idiots didn't want me to phone you! I feel fine. Come and pick me up and get me back to headquarters. There's lots to do! We've got to get Beardy to tell us what he knows. I've a feeling that it may be important. Very important.'

'Director, I shall do no such thing,' said Kubu firmly. 'You're to stay in hospital until you are completely recovered. We can handle matters here.'

'Bengu, that's insubordination! Get here at once! These doctors will be the death of me!'

And they said I was a bad patient when I was stuck in the Princess Marina Hospital, Kubu thought with a smirk. 'Director, I'm at Jackalberry Camp,' he said gently. 'Why don't you give your wife a call? She can visit you and check with the doctors.'

'Oh yes, I'd forgotten where you were. Marie's here, but she thinks I need to spend a week in bed. Kubu, don't let me down. Phone me as soon as you have anything to report. Hey, give me—'

The line went dead. Kubu suspected Marie had intervened. He turned to Tatwa with a broad smile.

'Director Mabaku's going to be fine,' he said.

CHAPTER 70

Kubu thought about the money. It had to be a lot of money. They'd needed a briefcase. This wasn't a payoff in a fat envelope from someone's inside jacket pocket. And almost certainly it was in an international currency, not rand or pula. If it was in US dollars, it could be half a million dollars in hundred-dollar notes, and the briefcase still would not be full. And if it was in euros, it could be almost ten times that, because euros came in notes up to 500. But apart from issues of size and weight, the briefcase had led to at least four murders. It had to be a lot of money.

'What about the heroin or whatever it was?' asked Tatwa.

Kubu shook his head. 'We don't know what it was. Drugs? Maybe they didn't even keep those. Too dangerous, and impossible to sell quietly unless you have the contacts. Diamonds? We'll never find them. No, we concentrate on the money. We know it existed, and they must've kept it.' He scratched his head. 'Tatwa, what sort of search did your people do when they came out the day of the murders?'

'We were looking for evidence connected with the murders. We weren't looking for money. We didn't know about the money then. But the guys checked all the luggage, all Goodluck and Langa's stuff, of course, and looked over the island. We did a cursory check of thc vehicles, the other tents, the kitchen area. If you're asking if we could've missed a stash of hidden money, the answer must be yes.'

'Okay, that means that they had time to move the money to a better hiding place after we all left and before Madrid turned up. For that matter, Dupie could've hidden it anywhere along the road to the airstrip. We know he went there, because he dumped Zondo's stuff near it. They could even have taken the money to Kasane – you may as well check with the banks. See if they deposited it or accessed a deposit box. Just because something is incredibly stupid, it doesn't mean they wouldn't have done it. But I think the money's nearby. I don't think they would want it out of their control. Especially not with three people in the know. I'll bet it's within walking distance of right here.' He heaved himself to his feet. 'Let's go and find it.'

A different type of search took place around Jackalberry Camp. Two of the constables walked the island, looking up into the trees for anything unusual that might indicate a package. Kubu scanned the messy bird's nests in the dead trees near the water's edge with binoculars. Tatwa took on the kitchen area, opening boxes of provisions in front of a scandalised Moremi and an irritated Kweh. The third constable, accompanied by Salome, went through each tent, quickly checking the vacant ones and going carefully through the staff accommodation.

Kubu finished first and returned to the reception area. He found Dupie there, drinking tea and looking smug. 'You're howling up the wrong tree, Superintendent. You're not going to find anything because there's nothing to find. What's next? Dig up the island for buried treasure? Dredge the lagoon?' He laughed.

In fact, Kubu had thought about the money being buried or hidden in the lagoon and had rejected it. The crime was opportunistic, in the sense that they'd planned it when they found the money. He did not think that a suitably strong or waterproof container would have been available. But it was a concern. If he was wrong, there were hundreds of places the money might be. They might never find it.

'I want to look at the stuff on the mainland. The vehicles and that shed you have there. Any objection?'

Dupie shrugged. 'Help yourself. But everything is locked. Has to be, with the village just down the river. I'd better come with you. I'll get the keys.' He swallowed the rest of his tea, climbed to his feet, and headed to his office tent. At the same time, Tatwa appeared from the kitchen, wiping his head with a tea towel. He had been through everything, concluding with Kweh's perch-cupboard. Kweh had been so outraged that he had broken his strict house training. Kubu could not help smiling, as he detected a note of triumph in the raucous 'go-away, go-away' that followed Tatwa's departure.

'Nothing,' Tatwa announced, dumping the wet towel. 'They're low on provisions too. Either they're not expecting to be in business much longer, or they've delayed stocking up because of the Madrid story. And Moremi's in as bad a mood as Kweh now. Don't expect a gourmet dinner.'

Kubu pouted because Tatwa expected that. But actually he was keen to get home, touch base with Mabaku, and most of all see Joy. Perhaps he would have to take her to Dr Diklekeng himself. And he felt the urgency again. Something was going to happen. Perhaps they would break the case given enough time, but instinctively he felt that time was exactly what they didn't have.

'I want to check the boat and the vehicles and look around at the landing on the mainland. Dupie will come with us. He's gone to fetch the keys.'

The boat had a sealed fibreglass hull and a few storage compartments that were damp and stuffed with life jackets and fishing gear. Nevertheless, the equipment was unpacked and the compartments checked with a flashlight. It was soon obvious to Kubu that there was nowhere on the boat where you could hide anything, let alone the amount of money he thought was involved.

They took the police launch to the mainland. There they carefully checked the camp's vehicles, looking for extra tanks or compartments. Both vehicles had second tanks for long-distance driving; both contained fuel. They checked under the seats, inside the seats themselves, and in the small camping fridges whose contents kept guests cheerful on game drives. The open Land Rover had long since lost the sealed dashboard area, but there was closed space behind the Toyota Double Cab's façade. It was large enough. Kubu asked Dupie to disassemble it.

'Hell, that's a big job. I don't want my vehicle messed up because you're on a wild goose chase.'

'Then we'll have to impound the vehicle and take it apart in Kasane.'

'Like hell you will! Shit! Okay, I'll get some tools from the shed.'

'I'll come with you. I want to look at the shed anyway.'

Dupie battled briefly with the rusted padlock on the door of the small storeroom and then creaked open the door. There was no window, but enough light came in through the door to be able to see. The place was as messy as Dupie's office. You can judge a workman by his tools, thought Kubu. Someone had told him that; he was not much of a workman himself. There was a scatter of wrenches, screwdrivers and other tools on a rickety wooden workbench. They had to step over a drip pan for oil changes – still containing oil – to reach it. A couple of spare tyres leaned against one wall next to a hopelessly distorted wheel rim and some tyre irons and clamps. Clearly Dupie did – or tried to do – much of his own maintenance for the boat and the two vehicles.

Dupie cursed.

'Your bloody people took half my tools! When am I going to get them back, hey? How long does it take to check if they were involved in whacking Langa?'

Kubu treated the question as rhetorical. There were some greasy boxes under the workbench. He pointed to them. 'Spare parts?'

Dupie glowered. 'Yes. You want to check? Help yourself while I waste my time pulling the vehicle apart.' Carrying a selection of screwdrivers and wrenches, and a pair of pliers, he headed off. Kubu was tempted to let it go. But it could be a bluff. So he started on the boxes.

Ten minutes later he emerged into the sunshine, blinking, and with nothing to show for his efforts but greasy hands. He tried to clean them with a rag from the boat. By the time he felt he could survive until soap was accessible, Dupie had the dashboard off, and Tatwa was shining the flashlight and poking around inside. He shook his head when Kubu approached.

'You satisfied?' asked Dupie. 'Can I put it back together now?' Tatwa was checking depths from the engine side to be sure there was no hidden compartment. He nodded. It was another blank.

'Thanks. Much appreciated,' said Dupie sarcastically. Kubu was looking at the inside of the vehicle doors. 'Do the windows open?' he asked.

'Of course the windows open,' said Dupie with irritation. Then he guessed where Kubu was heading. 'Oh shit. You want me to take the door panels off too? Well, why the hell not?' He started viciously levering them off with a screwdriver. A lot of dust and rusty mechanism was exposed, but not a single dollar bill.

Kubu took another look under the vehicle. Like many *bakkies*, the spare wheel was held under the vehicle with a protective plate. It kept the tyre out of harm's way. It also meant that the wheel's centre cavity was hidden. That could hold a lot of money.

A stream of invective was coming from the front of the vehicle, where Tatwa was trying to help Dupie replace the dashboard. The screwdriver had slipped and gouged Dupie's hand. Kubu decided to wait a while before raising the issue of lowering the spare wheel. He noticed that the front driver's tyre was a bit flat. Maybe Dupie would want to change it. He left Dupie and Tatwa to their struggles and wandered over to the Land Rover. It had two spare wheels, one on the hood and one fixed to the tailgate. Neither rim had any significant space for hiding money. He scanned the river bird's nests again with his binoculars, checked around the shed, and got back to the Toyota Double Cab in time for Dupie's satisfied grunt as he tightened the last screw.

'Your front tyre's a bit flat,' Kubu offered.

Dupie took a look at it and tried a kick. 'Well, I'm not going anywhere, am I? I'll pump it up when I am.'

'I'd like you to take down the spare.'

Dupie did not even argue. Without a word he rummaged in the vehicle and appeared with a tyre spanner and jack handle. Then he said to Tatwa, 'You'd better do it. Neither of us will fit under there.' Suddenly in a better mood, he offered Kubu a wink. So it was Tatwa who emerged five minutes later, covered in dust. He had lowered the wheel far enough to check there was nothing hidden, and then cranked it back into place. By that time Dupie had locked the shed. He accepted the vehicle's tools from Tatwa and packed them away, locked the Toyota's doors, and rubbed his hands on his shorts.

'Tell you what, you owe me a beer. On you this time, Superintendent.'

In spite of himself, Kubu smiled. But why was Dupie suddenly in a good mood? Was the beer something of a celebration? Had they, after all, missed something? If they had, Kubu could not think where. He sighed and relaxed.

'Okay. I'll buy you a beer.'

CHAPTER 71

Despite Dupie's sudden bonhomie, it was a sombre evening. Dupie drank his beer and took himself off, leaving Kubu and Tatwa to ponder the disappointments of the day. Kubu tried to phone Mabaku, but the call went straight to voice mail. Kubu smiled. Marie must be in full control.

Next he tried Joy. She answered, but sounded tired and distracted, and again asked when he would be back. The stress is starting to tell, he thought. He told her they would be leaving tomorrow. The thought had become a decision. He had to get back, and anyway, his investigation was stalled. Tatwa, pretending not to listen, was relieved. He too could see no point in hanging around the camp.

They walked up to the lookout to watch the sunset. It was as spectacular as the sunrise, but this time brought no inspiration. Then they wandered back to the bar, and in Dupie's absence, Kubu opened a bottle of cold Sauvignon Blanc. Dupie arrived back shortly afterwards, changed and showered. He was friendly, but thoughtful and restrained. There was no sign of Salome or Enoch until dinnertime.

As Tatwa had predicted, dinner was not gourmet fare. Moremi produced cold meats, bread and cheeses, salad and fruit. He had little to say to anyone, and retired early with Kweh. Solomon and Enoch followed soon after. Dupie brewed a pot of coffee while Salome sat in hostile silence with the detectives. The three constables had set up camp near the landing. The pretence of an attack from Madrid had been abandoned. It was clear to everyone now that the policemen were there as guards, not protectors.

When Dupie arrived with coffee and a bottle of port he and Kubu had opened the previous night, Salome broke her silence.

'What's going to happen now, Superintendent? Are you still trying to prove that we're all bloodthirsty murderers?'

Kubu took his time before replying. 'I think some people here are responsible for the deaths of four men. They did it for money, and they did it for revenge. I'm not sure who they are, but I have five suspects. I intend to make a decision soon as to how to proceed. I'm afraid it's going to be very unpleasant for everyone. It would be very helpful if at least the innocent parties started telling me the truth.'

'Would you recognise the truth if you heard it? Can you distinguish innocence from guilt, Superintendent? I don't think so. You've already made up your mind, haven't you?' Salome left her coffee and got to her feet. 'I'm going to my tent. Good night, Dupie.'

Kubu sat impassively, but smarting from her words. Was he victimising this woman? Was he biased by her past and by the soft spot he had developed for a man he would never meet but felt he now knew? He decided he was tired, and was about to call it a day, but suddenly Dupie became sociable. He poured the three of them a port, and when Tatwa politely refused, pushed the second glass towards Kubu.

'Salome's under a lot of strain, Superintendent. Has been since all this started. No, from long before that. Maybe thirty years before. She's had a hard life. But we're all grateful to her. All of us would do anything for her.'

'Are you trying to tell us something, Dupie?' Kubu was instantly alert.

'I'm asking you to understand her and to understand us.'

Kubu nodded, waiting. There would be more. Tatwa knew this exchange was between Kubu and Dupie; he sat quietly, withdrawn, unobtrusive despite his height.

'I'm going to do what you asked. I'm going to tell you some things I omitted before. But it's going to hurt me, Superintendent. I'm not doing it for you. I don't care about your damn case. I'm doing this for her. I want you off her back.' He swallowed the port in one gulp and helped himself to another.

'There's something else I want you to know. Enoch and I go back a long way.' He hesitated, and Kubu interjected. 'To the Rhodesian war? Yes, I know.'

'Much further back. To when men walked outside their caves at night in fear of predators. Tigers. Sabre-tooth tigers. And you had to rely on another man to back you up, whatever happened. Whatever happened. It was like that in the Scouts. Our strength was in backing each other up. No matter what happened. No matter what was done to us. No matter what we did. You know what I'm talking about?'

He shook his head. 'You've no idea, have you? It's like the Watching Eye.' He turned to Tatwa. 'You'd better give that back. It's mine, and it's important. You understand?' Neither policeman reacted, so Dupie shrugged in disgust. He worked on the port for a while.

'Enoch and I were like that. Did we save each other's lives? Sure we did. That wasn't a big deal. That was a *by-product* of what I'm talking about. The Eyes . . .' He struggled, trying to explain. 'They're *symbols*. You know?'

Kubu did not know at all. But he did not want to hear about Dupie and Enoch, nor about the Rhodesian war. He wanted to hear about a Sunday night three weeks before. Dupie finished another port. Suddenly he was matter-of-fact. The sober, practical man, not the slightly tipsy philosopher.

'Okay, I'd better tell you some things that happened. That I didn't tell you before. Some of the things you said are true, after all. It's just your deductions that don't work. Not quite Sherlock Holmes after all, perhaps.'

Kubu did not react. He took a contemplative sip of port. He didn't need to push. He knew Dupie would say what he had to say. Tatwa was so quiet and still that Kubu had to check his eyes to see that he was still awake.

'Well, you were right about that day with the trailer. Enoch asked me to help him set up an alibi. He was going to head out a way – not far – push the trailer into the bushes at a place we know and leave it there. When he called, all I had to do was go out there, hang around for an hour or so, and then head back with the trailer. And tell the story about the wheel bearing.'

'And what was Enoch doing while this was happening?'

'I don't know. He didn't say. He just said he had something he needed to sort out. That he'd be back the next day after he'd done the shopping in Kasane. I don't know where he went.'

'You didn't ask?' It was Tatwa's incredulous interjection.

Dupie looked at him and shook his head. 'No, I didn't ask. He said it was important, and he needed my help. It was like in the war. We didn't ask. We just did what was necessary. Like the Eyes. Like that. I didn't even think about asking.'

Kubu nodded. 'What else?'

'What do you mean, what else?'

'When Enoch left you, he drove to Maun and killed William Boardman. Why?'

'I don't know that he did that! I know he did something, that's all.' Dupie looked at Tatwa, as though he might understand.

'Was it a return favour?' asked Kubu. 'For your asking Enoch to pretend to be Zondo on the boat?'

'That *was* Zondo! I swear it. Everything I've told you about Zondo is true. And we don't tally favours.'

'So you still stick to the story that Zondo was behind all the murders?'

'That's what I thought.'

'Ah. No longer *think*?'

Dupie seemed very uncomfortable, and refilled his glass before he replied. 'Shit! I might as well tell you now. Salome did ask me about Goodluck. I thought it was her ghosts, but I promised I'd check. But I needed to keep Goodluck chatting after I lifted his keys. So it was Enoch who searched his luggage. The briefcase too, I guess.'

'And what did he find?'

'He said he found nothing. Nothing. I told Salome. I don't think she believed we'd even looked. She was sure about Goodluck. God knows how she could be after all these years. But she was right about him, wasn't she? I guess there are some faces you never forget.'

'So Enoch knew about the money, but he didn't tell you. And the next morning Goodluck and Langa were dead. But you took Zondo to the airstrip.'

'Look, it could still've been Zondo. He knew about the money and the drugs. Maybe Enoch knew too, but it doesn't mean it wasn't Zondo who was the murderer.'

Tatwa came to life. 'Anyway, why would Enoch kill Boardman? What would be the point?'

Dupie stared into his empty glass. 'Well . . . if Enoch had the money, he needed to hide it. He and Boardman went out together that morning by *mokoro*. Maybe William was in on it. Maybe he just spotted Enoch hiding something. Maybe he wanted a cut, for God's sake! The man was a greedy son of a bitch. He ripped me off a dozen times for artworks. I know he did. Greedy son of a bitch.' He poured another port.

Kubu had just finished his first. Tatwa's full glass was still in front of him, and he took a small sip.

'So this is what you're deducing,' Kubu said. 'Enoch took Goodluck's keys – at your request – checked his luggage and found the money. Salome was convinced Goodluck was one of the gang who attacked her in the war. That made Goodluck a bad guy with a lot of money. Enoch bumps him off and hides the money on the *mokoro* trip with William Boardman, who – when the bodies are discovered – deduces what he was hiding. Then he wants a cut, and Enoch obliges in Maun, with your help for an alibi.'

'I'm not saying all that. I'm just telling you what happened.'

'Is there anything *else* you've left out? Now would be a really good time to tell us the full story.'

Dupie shook his head. 'I would've trusted Enoch with my life. Hell, I've trusted him with my life lots of times.' He paused. 'You know what hurts? Not that he killed this man. I understand that. Probably deserved what he got. And what he's getting.' He pointed downwards. 'What hurts is that he cut me out. That's what hurts.'

He lumbered to his feet. 'So now you've got what you wanted, right? The *truth*. Let's see if you can recognise it, after all.' He walked to his tent, his step slightly unsteady.

*

Kubu and Tatwa looked at each other in silence until they heard the toilet flush and then Dupie's tent zip up.

'What do you think?' asked Kubu.

Tatwa shook his head. 'I don't believe it. All that business about how close they are? But Enoch goes behind Dupie's back to murder someone for money. And Dupie lies for him, but then shops him to the police. More in sorrow than in anger.'

'It's a lot of money. That much money does things to people.'

'It was enough money to share. Plenty of money to share.'

'It's a good story. But like so many of the other stories, it comes unstuck with Zondo. Just by coincidence he decides to leave the next morning, ahead of schedule. Fortunately he doesn't trip over any of the dead bodies on the way to the boat. Then Dupie drops him at the airstrip, where he abandons his favourite hat and jacket and disappears. *Without the money*. Why on earth would he do that?'

'What if he found Goodluck's body and took fright? With the warning mutilations, I'd be terrified if I were him. I'd leave in a big hurry.'

Kubu nodded. 'It's not impossible. But remember he arranged to leave early the next day before the murders took place, according to Dupie.' Kubu was thoughtful, wondering whether Dupie might tip off Enoch either casually or on purpose. Enoch knew the area like the back of his hand.

Constable Tau joined them for a moment to get a soft drink on his way to take over the watch at the dock. Kubu passed him an orange juice.

'Keep a careful watch on the *mokoros*, Tau.' He held up his hand when Tau started to protest. 'Yes, I know it's too dangerous to use them at night. Tell that to Director Mabaku if someone slips away in one of them.' Then he had another thought. 'There's something else I want you to do.' He gave Tau some further detailed instructions.

'Just to be on the safe side,' he said in response to Tatwa's quizzical look. Then he smiled, thinking back to Dupie's tale. 'It doesn't really matter how much of this story is true, does it, Tatwa? They've started breaking ranks. Tomorrow we can tell Enoch that Dupie's trying to shove the whole thing on to him. Then Enoch will have another story that we can take to Salome, and soon they'll be tripping over each other's lies.' Kubu poured himself a celebratory final glass of port, and toasted in the air with it.

'We've got them, Tatwa,' he said. 'We've got them!'

CHAPTER 72

The next morning again there was a strained atmosphere. The team spirit generated by the fiction of Madrid as the common enemy had been replaced by reality. The policemen constituted an occupation to be tolerated, not reinforcements to be welcomed.

Moremi set out a buffet of cereals, yogurts and fruit salad, and then took orders for eggs. Clearly he disliked the new scenario, but he didn't let his distaste run to a desire to see Kubu starve. He delivered a heaped plate of scrambled eggs, bacon and lashings of toast. Tatwa stuck to the buffet. He was restless.

'We haven't seen Enoch this morning, Kubu. I hope Dupie didn't have a change of heart and tip him off.'

Kubu finished a mouthful. 'Where would he go? The constables guarded the boats all night.'

'But he could get out overland. If you're willing to wade through the marshes. I'm worried.'

Kubu was not going to upset his breakfast. A proper breakfast was a prerequisite for a successful day. He just grunted. 'Nowhere to go once he gets to the mainland either. Check if the two vehicles are still there.'

Tatwa walked to the river's edge and looked through his binoculars. The vehicles were still exactly where they'd been the day before. He told Kubu, who nodded and finished the last piece of toast. Moremi poured them coffee.

Dupie joined them, carrying his own plate from the kitchen. 'Morning.'

'Where's Enoch?' asked Tatwa.

'He was around earlier,' said Dupie vaguely. 'He's not a big eater.'

That was the end of the conversation, until Kubu had finished a second cup of coffee and Dupie had finished his fried eggs.

'Could you find him for us?' asked Kubu. 'After what you told us yesterday, we need to talk to him.' Dupie nodded and headed back to the kitchen.

'Let's go to the office tent,' said Kubu. 'I don't fancy interviewing Enoch here.'

They settled themselves and waited. Tatwa had brought the Eye with him; he placed it gazing upwards in the middle of the mess of papers on Dupie's desk. It'd had an unsettling effect on Enoch once before.

When Enoch arrived he was carrying a backpack, wearing khaki shorts and sporting a multi-pocketed fishing jacket over his shirt. Tatwa breathed a sigh of relief, but Kubu was puzzled by the backpack.

'*Dumela*, Enoch,' he said. 'What's the backpack for?'

Enoch dumped it beside the tent flap. 'Dupie told me you'd take me to Kasane. So I packed my stuff.' Kubu's eyebrows rose. So Dupie *had* been talking to Enoch.

'Sit down, Enoch,' he said, indicating the chair opposite, with the Eye between them and Tatwa to its left. Enoch looked down at the Eye, shook his head, and remained standing.

Kubu shrugged. 'Enoch, we think you've been lying to us. About the Monday before last, for a start. The day that you supposedly broke down in the bush.' He made a show of consulting his notes. 'You said that the trailer broke a bearing on the way to Kasane, that Dupie came out to help you and towed it back, and that you slept in the bush before heading on the next morning. Is that right?'

Enoch nodded. He stood as if before a court martial. Kubu stared at his face, then deliberately glanced down to the Eye, taking Enoch's gaze with him.

'But, you see, Rra Du Pisanie says it's not true. Actually, you arranged with him to abandon the trailer, undamaged. He picked it up and brought it back. You had long gone. To Maun.' Dupie hadn't said this, but Kubu banked on Enoch not knowing that.

'I have a girlfriend in Kachikau. I spent the night with her. Dupie covered for me. That's all.'

'Why would he need to cover? You're not married, are you?'

'Yes. I have a wife in Francistown.'

Tatwa looked at him. 'Don't be stupid, Enoch. Every Motswana man has a mistress! Except Kubu and me, of course. No one needs to cover for that. Not with the wife as far away as Francistown. And Dupie wouldn't have put himself out for that. We know what you did. You drove to Maun and tortured William Boardman to death, didn't you? But that was easy, wasn't it? After you'd killed Goodluck, Zondo and Langa right here.' Tatwa leaned forward and lifted the Watching Eye as though to examine it. It oscillated and flashed the sunlight from the tent opening into Enoch's face.

Enoch's reaction was so sudden that it caught both of them off guard. He grabbed the Eye, slammed it on the desk, and smashed it with something in his fist. Shards of indigo glass flew everywhere. Both detectives recoiled, instinctively closing their eyes. When they opened them a split second later, they found themselves looking at Dupie's service revolver. Kubu cursed himself under his breath. This man was a fighter, a real veteran of a real war. How could he have been so stupid? No constable was present; no one had searched Enoch. It was all too casual. Kubu had ignored the fact that this man was a multiple murderer. He forced himself to relax in his chair.

'Don't be silly, Enoch. That's not going to get you anywhere. There's nowhere to go, nowhere to run. We know you weren't the mastermind behind the murders. Let's put the blame where it really belongs. You were helping Dupie, weren't you?'

Enoch pointed to the smashed talisman with his left hand. 'That's finished!' he shouted. 'I did it for her! You understand? Not for him, for her.'

Kubu nodded, at sea. 'I understand, Enoch. Let's talk about it. There's no way out of here. Just put down the gun, and we can work it out together.'

Enoch did not answer. He pointed at Tatwa with the revolver. 'I'm leaving now,' he said. 'He's coming with me. You tell your people that if they try to stop me, I'll kill him first. You tell them.' Returning his aim to Kubu, he yanked Tatwa up with his left hand. 'Turn around,' he said.

Having no choice, Tatwa turned with his back to Enoch. Enoch patted him down, keeping his eyes on Kubu. 'Okay. Pick up the backpack. Slowly.'

Tatwa bent over and lifted the pack. It was heavy. Stuffed. 'What's in here,' he asked, but Enoch ignored him.

'Get out there,' he ordered Kubu, indicating the tent entrance. Then he followed, Tatwa first.

Tau and one of the other constables were drinking coffee in the breakfast area. The third was probably in the kitchen.

'Tell them!' said Enoch.

'Hold your fire!' shouted Kubu, hoping the constables were armed. 'He's got a gun on Detective Mooka!' Both policemen jumped up, alert. Enoch had made a mistake. He could probably have walked right past them with Kubu and Tatwa, almost unnoticed. Now he had four potential adversaries instead of two. That was little comfort to Tatwa. He could feel the gun in the small of his back, pressing against his spine.

'You stay here,' Enoch told Kubu.

'Enoch, you're just making it worse. You can't escape. Where would you go? Give me the gun and we can make a deal. Arrange something.'

'Stay here!' Enoch repeated loudly.

Dupie ran from the kitchen, followed by the third constable. 'What the hell's going on?' he demanded. Then he saw the revolver. 'Oh shit! Enoch, you gone mad?' Enoch ignored him and backed away, holding Tatwa as a shield between himself and the others.

He carefully made the hundred metres to the jetty. The others moved forward in a circle but did not crowd him. They had no doubt that he would kill Tatwa as a last resort. Enoch worked his way to the camp's motorboat.

'Put the backpack in the boat.' While Tatwa did so, Enoch untied the boat and pushed it out. The gun never wavered from Tatwa. 'Now wade out and get in, slowly.' Tatwa knelt to undo his sneakers, but

Enoch shoved him so hard he nearly fell. 'Forget your shoes! Get in the boat!' Tatwa waded out, and Enoch followed. His attention was now on Kubu and the others, and he pointed the gun at them. But Tatwa was climbing gingerly into the launch and did not notice that. A moment later, Enoch was in the boat with him, the gun at Tatwa's head again. In those few seconds, Constable Tau had got his gun unholstered and had it behind his back, waiting for a chance. Enoch would need both hands to start the outboard motor. But when he had inserted the ignition key, he spoke to Tatwa. 'You do it,' he told him.

Tatwa looked at him, and at the revolver. He knew this was going to end badly. He might as well make his play now. 'No,' he said.

Enoch looked at him, sensing the resolution. 'Okay,' he said. 'Then we're stuck here. That's the idea, isn't it? Sooner or later one of them shoots me, and it's over?' Tatwa said nothing. 'I told them to stay at the dining area,' Enoch continued, indicating the policemen on the shore. 'But they don't listen either. So start the motor. The fat detective is in range. I'm a dead shot with a revolver. You want to try me?' Tatwa said nothing, holding his ground. Kubu was well back.

'Superintendent,' shouted Enoch. 'Come here. I want to make a deal. The others stay back. Not a step closer.'

Kubu moved gingerly forward until he was near the boat. 'What's the deal?'

'Tell him to start the motor. Otherwise I shoot you both. I can kill you before they get me. Easy.'

Kubu considered the situation. 'Start the motor, Tatwa,' he said.

Tatwa considered too. Then he leaned forward, and with three sharp jerks started the outboard. It roared. Two large crocodiles, disturbed, exited the sandbank into the water. Enoch guided the boat slowly into the lagoon. 'Sit on the edge,' he told Tatwa, indicating the side of the boat with the gun.

'So when you shoot me I'll fall over? No. I'll stay here. You can have a dead body weighing down your boat, if that's what you want.'

'If you do what I say, I promise I won't shoot you. I swear it on my ancestors,' said Enoch.

Tatwa looked into Enoch's eyes, strangely believing him. Then he shrugged and perched on the side of the boat. The next moment Enoch jumped forward and shoved him off into the water. Then he opened the throttle, and the boat jerked forward.

Tatwa had not expected this. He should have, but he had focused on the gun. The water closed over his head, and he held his breath, panicked. He could not swim. And there were crocodiles! His head broke the surface, and he heard shots. Constable Tau had run to the bank and had fired at Enoch, who had retaliated by firing back not at Tau but at Tatwa. Tatwa heard the whine of the bullet. He churned with his feet and yelled, 'Help! Help! I can't swim! The crocodiles, oh God, the crocodiles!' His head went below the water again, and he choked.

Kubu was at the water's edge too. He shoved Tau towards the police launch. 'He'll drown! Forget Enoch. Get Tatwa!' He fumbled in his pocket, coming up with the launch's keys. 'Thank God!' he said, tossing them to Tau.

Tau grabbed them, ran to the dock, and jumped into the boat. He started it with one pull, threw off the tie rope, and headed out into the lagoon at full throttle. Tatwa was thrashing in the water, trying not to sink.

'Tatwa!' Kubu shouted. 'Kick off your shoes. They're pulling you down. Lie on your back. You'll float!'

Tatwa tried to obey the conflicting instructions, but the shoes were laced on and wouldn't kick off, and when he tried to float on his back, they dragged him under. He flailed his arms, tried to pull himself up, and took a lungful of water. He was coughing again and starting to panic. Oh God, where were the crocodiles?

But Tau was nearly there. In fact, he cut the motor too late and realised he would drift past. He leaned out, holding an oar. 'Grab it, Tatwa, grab it!' But it was just out of reach.

Suddenly Tatwa felt something large and solid rub his leg. Perhaps it was a submerged log. But maybe not . . .

With a high-pitched scream, he flung himself forward, away, kicking the thing behind him. Miraculously, that propelled him towards the boat, allowing him to grasp the oar and climb up it towards the boat. He nearly pulled Tau into the water, and between them they almost capsized the boat. They landed in a heap in the middle, as it swayed wildly from side to side, taking water. Tatwa was still screaming, but Tau put a hand over his mouth. Slowly the boat settled.

Tatwa huddled in the middle of the boat, shivering. Tau asked him if he was okay, but Tatwa just looked at him. 'It was a crocodile,' he said. His teeth started to chatter.

Against all the odds, Tatwa's St Louis hat floated next to the boat. 'Your lucky hat!' Tau exclaimed. Tatwa ignored it, so Tau leaned over, scooped it up, and tossed it into the boat. It floated. He realised the water in the boat was above his ankles. Chasing Enoch was out of the question. With a couple of solid pulls, he got the motor going and headed for the group on the shore.

Tau ran the boat aground, cut the motor, and Kubu helped Tatwa out. 'My friend, you gave us a bad scare. You need a change of clothes and a stiff whisky. In that order. Come on.'

Tatwa shook his head, dripping. 'It was definitely a crocodile,' he said. 'A huge one.' He was starting to feel ashamed of the panic that had probably saved his life. 'My brother was just ten years old,' he added. Kubu was puzzled, but didn't pursue it.

They could still hear the distant sound of Enoch's motorboat, which had disappeared around a bend upstream. Enoch and his backpack – presumably stuffed with Goodluck's money – were gone. He had kilometres of the Caprivi on the Namibian side and kilometres of wild Linyanti on the Botswanan side in which to disappear.

CHAPTER 73

While Tatwa showered and changed and regained his composure, Kubu was in contact with the CID in Kasane. They promised to contact the Defense Force and get a spotter plane into the area as soon as possible. With low passes over the river, they would certainly pick up Enoch if the boat was still on the water. But it would take at least an hour. They would see what could be done about a helicopter. Once Enoch was found, they needed to be able to get on the ground to arrest him.

Tau and another constable had baled out the police launch and were ready to head off after Enoch. Kubu was pleased about the ace he had hidden up his sleeve the night before.

'He can't get far. Keep in touch using the radio, and don't engage him in a shootout. If you spot him, keep out of range, stay on his tail, and wait for reinforcements from the Defense Force. I don't want one of you floating around in the river. We've had enough close calls today.' Tau promised to be careful, but went off excited. Minutes later Kubu heard the launch start up. The chase was on!

When Kubu closed his phone, Dupie came up shaking his head. 'Damn!' he said. 'I would never have believed it unless I saw it. Enoch, after all these years.'

'I want to show you something,' said Kubu. He led the way to the office tent and entered first so he could watch Dupie's face as he came in. The desk was still showered with chips and pieces of the broken Eye. Dupie's jaw dropped. 'Shit!' he said. 'How did this happen? I told you it was important.' Now he sounded genuinely shocked and angry.

'Enoch. And what he said was: "That's finished. I did it for her. Not for him, for her." What do you think that means?'

Dupie just shook his head. 'I don't know what to think. Why did he smash the Eye?'

'Perhaps he was announcing the end of a connection, Dupie. The end of a relationship. After this, you're on your own. Could that be it?' But Dupie did not answer. He backed out of the tent, visibly shaken. Salome was calling him.

Kubu could hear Dupie telling Salome and the camp staff what had happened. Already the story was becoming distorted. Salome started to sob, and Dupie broke off to comfort her. Kubu scowled. Things were complicated enough. It was time to contact Mabaku and to decide on the next step.

Mabaku had escaped from home and was at the office. He was tired and sore and did not need any bad news. But that was what he got. Serves me right for not listening to Marie, he thought.

'So let me get this straight, Kubu,' he said, when Kubu had filled him in on the events of the last two days. 'You suspected Enoch because Du Pisanie tipped you off about him. You practically arrested him, but it didn't occur to you he might be armed? So he's now escaped – with the money, you say – and we have the Defense Force scouring the country. Two countries, actually. Did anyone think of informing the Namibian police?'

'I'm sure Kasane will do that. The Defense Force will have to tell them about the plane, and the chopper, too.'

'I'm sick to death of people being sure about things. Maybe they'll forget, too. Get on to them and discuss it with the police there yourself,' Mabaku growled.

Kubu hadn't forgotten. He had just thought it politic to phone Mabaku first. But he didn't want to waste time arguing. 'Yes, of course, Director,' he said. 'But it's not as bad as it sounds.'

'Why not?'

'Because as a precaution, I told Tau to empty the camp motorboat's fuel tank last night. Enoch won't be able to get far.'

'Well that's something, I suppose,' said Mabaku, impressed in spite of himself. 'But let's leave Enoch to the local police. I want you back here; I can't rely on Banda. Enough of playing cat and mouse on the Linyanti. It looks like it was actually cat and lion, with you as the cat. At least you weren't the mouse!'

Mabaku's instruction was good news for Kubu. It coincided with what he wanted to do anyway. I must call Joy, he thought, worried again. 'Yes, Director, that was my intention. What shall I do with Du Pisanie and McGlashan? Bring them in to Kasane, or leave them here?'

'What have you got on them?'

'Well, not much directly. Dupie told me a nonsense story about covering for Enoch the night he murdered Boardman, and I suppose the implication of what took place this morning is that Enoch is the culprit. But I don't believe he did it on his own. I think all three are in on it. Dupie's latest piece of play-acting was a set-up.'

Mabaku grunted. 'Hold them as material witnesses. I don't want legal hassles to add to everything else now.'

'They'll argue that they're citizens of good standing and not going anywhere. My suggestion is that I impound their passports and leave them here with two of the constables to watch them. For their own protection, that is. We still haven't resolved the Madrid issue.'

'Don't remind me. And Edison's come up with nothing more from Beardy. Well, this will be a lesson to me. I can't afford to get sick and be away for two days.' He mulled over Kubu's proposal. 'Yes, do what you suggested. Once we catch Enoch, we'll have him singing a different tune. Then we can get Dupie and Salome to come and supply the words.' There was an interruption, and Kubu could hear Mabaku's secretary telling him the commissioner was on the other line.

'Kubu, I've got to go. See if you can arrange things for the rest of the day so that you don't drown any of my detectives, don't start a war with Namibia, and don't release a horde of murderers into the community. Do you think you can handle that?'

Kubu said he thought he could, and the director hung up. Kubu wondered why his careful moves – with real results in this case – always seemed to come across as bumbling incompetence when summarised by the director. But Mabaku was right about the Namibians. He needed to call them.

*

When Tau radioed in from the police launch, the news was mixed. They had found the motorboat stuck on a sandbank in the river, and, indeed, it had run out of fuel. But there was no sign of Enoch. Obviously he had rowed it to the shore and then pushed it out into the current. So there was no indication of where he had landed, or even on which side of the river. They were only about fifteen minutes away, so Kubu told them to come in. There was no point in them sitting on the river on the off chance that the spotter plane would find Enoch nearby. He would have gone to ground by now in any case. However, Kubu's plan had worked to the extent that there was a relatively small area in which he could be hiding, and he must be relatively close.

Tau was back at the camp by the time the spotter plane arrived. There was a side benefit: it was a six-seater with only four people in it. When it went back to Kasane, Kubu and Tatwa could get a ride, saving the four-hour drive in the Land Rover, on their way back to Gaborone. Kubu relayed the information on where the boat had been found, so the plane had a reasonably well-defined area to search.

Tatwa joined Kubu to wave as the plane flew low over the camp. He was looking better, dry, in clean clothes, and thankful for the large neat whisky that had started a bout of coughing, expelling most of the river still in his lungs.

'I spoke to the director, Tatwa, and he said we should leave the manhunt to the local police. You've got stuff to tidy up on the Gomwe case, and I need to move the Madrid business forward. Let's get packed up. We're going home.' As Kubu expected, Tatwa made no objection.

Kubu made the situation clear to Dupie and Salome and the staff. They were all material witnesses, and there would be more questions once Enoch had been caught and had told his side of the story. They were to stay in touch by phone, and make no trips off the island without letting Tatwa know, and in any case no trips out of Botswana. To emphasise the last point, Kubu took their passports, and told them that two of the constables would remain on the island.

Dupie laughed at that. 'How long does this charade go on? We have a business here, you know. Lives to lead. Enoch's a bush man. You may never find him out there.' He gave a broad wave, encompassing Africa.

Kubu was not in the mood for banter. 'It goes on until I say it stops.' He looked at Tatwa. 'We better get going. I expect the plane will have finished its search in an hour or so.' Then he hesitated, not sure how to address the others.

'Thank you for your cooperation,' he said at last, brusquely, and turned away.

Reaching the mainland felt like a release. Jackalberry Camp had become a prison, haunted by death. While Tau organised the luggage, Kubu and Tatwa took a last look around. 'What did you find in that shed?' asked Tatwa, pointing to it.

'Just tools for the vehicles and the boat. Looks like Dupie does a lot of his own maintenance. Oil changes and the like. Stuff to fix tyres also. I guess they get a lot of punctures from the acacia thorns in the bush . . .' His voice faded away, his mind following a lateral thought. Suddenly he grabbed Tatwa's arm. 'The tyres, Tatwa, they change the tyres!'

Tatwa frowned. 'Well, every car has a jack and stuff to change a wheel.'

'Not the wheel, the tyre. They've got tyre irons to get it off the rim and inner tubes to reinflate it once they've fixed the hole. But once the tyre's off . . .'

'You could put stuff in it!' Tatwa joined in. 'Stuff like money. Were there any wheels in the shed?'

Kubu hesitated, then shook his head. 'I remember a dented rim and a tyre, but not a tyre on a rim. But it could be one of the spares on the vehicles.'

'The one you have to crank down under the Double Cab? That's the best hidden.' Tatwa's heart sank. Getting at that wheel was a lot of work. But Kubu shook his head.

'That vehicle has only the one spare. They wouldn't risk driving on a million dollars. It'll be one of the Land Rover spares. My guess would be the one on the back door. I wouldn't put it on the hood over the hot engine, would you?' Tatwa shook his head, but Kubu was already walking towards the Land Rover.

Now they were faced with another problem. How could they tell if the tyre was a disguised bank box? Tatwa had an idea. He found a twig, jammed it in the tyre valve, and was rewarded by a satisfying hiss of escaping air. Having tied up the boat and loaded the luggage, Tau joined them, puzzled by why his superiors were sabotaging Dupie's vehicle. If the idea was to stop him escaping, it seemed to Tau that letting down one of the tyres on the ground might be smarter.

Sooner than expected, the air in the tyre stopped hissing out.

'It was pumped up just enough to keep everything in place,' Kubu said, tensely. He felt the tyre, but it remained hard and still firmly on the rim. 'Damn! Get it off the door, Tau. There must be tools in the police Landy.'

Dutifully Tau found the wheel spanner and spun off the nuts. He and Tatwa lifted the tyre on to the ground.

'Now what?' Tatwa asked. But Kubu already had the wheel on its edge and slowly rolled it over the ground. They heard something shifting around inside.

Kubu turned to Tatwa, triumphant. 'Get on the radio and tell the plane to wait. We're going to have something pretty spectacular to take back to Kasane. Much more interesting than Enoch's backpack stuffed with old newspapers or whatever.

'Tau, take the boat back to the camp and fetch Dupie and one of the other constables. Tell Dupie to bring the keys to the shed. Tell him we need to look inside there again.'

But Dupie had been watching them from the lookout through binoculars. He sighed. He had come so close. But it seemed that his last roll of the dice had come up snake eyes.

Dupie watched in disgust as the constables battled with the tyre irons. 'You'll wreck the wheel if you're not careful,' he complained. 'What the hell is this all about anyway?' But it was obvious what the hell it was all about when they finally got the rim free. Kubu pulled out the flat inner tube, shook out the tyre, and flooded the sand with money. The notes were wrapped into packets in thin plastic. Kubu picked one up, pulled off the wrapping, and flipped through the stack of hundred-dollar bills with his thumb. Then he counted the packets. Their earlier speculation of half a million dollars looked close.

'Shit!' said Dupie. 'That's where he hid the money, hey?' Kubu looked at him enquiringly. 'Enoch!' said Dupie in an unconvincing reply to the unasked question. Kubu ignored that.

'Morné Du Pisanie, I am arresting you in connection with the murders of Goodluck Tinubu, Peter Jabulani – also known as Ishmael Zondo – Sipho Langa, and William Boardman. You are not required to say anything at the moment, but take note that anything you do say will be recorded and may be used in a court of law. Do you understand what I have told you?'

Dupie said he did, while Tau handcuffed him and searched him for weapons. A good idea, Kubu thought.

'I'll need some things,' said Dupie. 'Till you catch Enoch, and this is all cleared up.'

Kubu nodded. 'Tatwa, take Dupie back to Jackalberry. Arrest Salome too, and then get them to Kasane. Leave one of the constables at the camp to keep an eye on Moremi and Solomon in case we were wrong about them. I'm going to take the money and catch that plane. If I hurry, I can still get back to Gaborone today. Tau can drive us to the airstrip. Okay?' Tatwa nodded. He too was high on the mixture of triumph and excitement. He headed back to the police launch.

Kubu searched for something to hold the money. There was the boat tarpaulin, but it was much too big. He needed to catch the plane! At last he grabbed Tatwa's backpack and emptied its contents on to the back seat, rescuing a couple of T-shirts that ended on the dusty floor. Then he and Tau stuffed the money into the backpack, dumped Tatwa's clothes on the tarpaulin, scrambled into the vehicle, and took off. They made a fine pace over the bumpy road, as a few items of Tatwa's underwear they had missed escaped into the African bush.

PART EIGHT
One May Fall

One may fall, but he falls by himself,
Falls by himself with himself to blame.

Rudyard Kipling, *The Story of the Gadsbys*

CHAPTER 74

By the time Kubu landed at Gaborone, he was tired but content. The money was safely locked away at the police station in Kasane, Dupie and Salome were being held there, and Tatwa was keeping a close watch on them. Enoch had survived the day, but could not remain at large for long, now that they knew pretty well where he was. Best of all, Joy would be waiting to meet him at the airport. So he grabbed his luggage and looked around for her, his mind on a delicious dinner with good wine, and a beautiful woman before, during and after. When he saw her, he dropped his case, folded her in his comfortable bulk, lifted her off the ground, and kissed her with the passion of absence.

'Oh Kubu, put me down! Everyone's watching! You're embarrassing me!' she said through her laughter. Indeed, many passengers glanced at them, the bored expressions of business travel replaced with smiles.

'My darling, I've missed you and been worried sick about you, but now we are back together and everything is fine.' Kubu confirmed this remark with another kiss, this time with all feet on the ground.

'Oh Kubu, you got them? Solved the case?' Joy was breathless.

'Well, I know who did what and how. One suspect is still at large, but the others are in custody. We'll have it all wrapped up in no time. And after this, I'm not budging from Gaborone.' He picked up his bag and headed for the exit with his arm around her shoulders.

'Will Pleasant and I have to testify? Identify the suspects?'

Suddenly Kubu realised that they were talking about two different cases. 'Well, we haven't got that lot yet. This was the Jackalberry Camp murder case.' Seeing her disappointment, he rushed on. 'But it's all linked. We've got the money that the kidnappers were after, and it will be all over the newspapers tomorrow. They won't dare set foot in Botswana again. And Beardy is going to tell us everything we want to know. He's just looking for a deal.'

But Joy was not consoled. 'Kubu, I'm so tired of worrying about myself and Pleasant. I wish you could catch these people. I think they might try again. We're scared.'

'My darling, I had to go to Jackalberry to solve this case, but now it's done and I'm staying right here. The whole thing is just about wrapped up! There's absolutely nothing to worry about.' He sounded much more cheerful and confident than he actually felt. He leaned over for another peck, and Joy responded before quickly turning away, but not before he had seen the wetness in her eyes.

When they reached the car, it was shaking from Ilia's jumping and barking. She was trying to squeeze herself through the small gap at the top of the window that Joy had left open for fresh air. There was nothing for it but to open the door and let her dive into Kubu's arms and do a complete lick and polish of his face.

'You're impossible, Ilia. You're so badly behaved. But I love you. Now get back into the car so we can go home. I very much hope that your mother has a fine dinner waiting for both of us.' Eventually they managed to get Ilia sufficiently under control to get the doors closed and the trip home under way.

'How have you been feeling, my love?' asked Kubu, realising he was on shaky ground.

'Oh, much better. I'll be fine now that you're back. It was all just the stress and worry.'

'Is that what Dr Diklekeng said?'

Joy shook her head. 'I'm so much better, I didn't want to waste his time. Anyway, let's talk about something else. I've made a delicious curry, and I've put a bottle of Gewürztraminer in the fridge. See? I'm learning which wines go with what. And Ilia can have the sauce over her dog biscuits. She'll love that. And then we can have a nice quiet evening together. Quiet until a bit later on, that is.' She gave him a naughty smile, her good humour apparently restored. Kubu marvelled at how neatly she had changed the subject. He could already smell the spices, taste the fruity richness of the wine, and feel the touch of her soft hands on his body. He must stop nagging her. All would be well.

'How is the karate going?' he asked, once more on bedrock.

'Oh, I'm not sure I want to go on with it. I've got so much on my mind, so much to do. I'll think about it. You're here to look after me now.'

Kubu felt the rock turning to sand. She loved her karate. 'As a matter of fact, I need a check-up too,' he said. 'That strain in my shoulder has been worrying me a bit again. I'll make an appointment with Dr Diklekeng, and we can go together.' Catching Joy's developing scowl, he used her technique of changing subjects and scrambled back to solid ground.

'Tell me about the curry you made. Is it a new recipe or an old favourite? I want to hear the details.'

Joy laughed in spite of herself, and started talking about meats and spices. Ilia barked as though this discussion was much more interesting.

Early the next morning Kubu headed to the office. He expected to have an exciting day, but he was disappointed. Up to now he had been active, exploring aspects of the case in Gaborone, Bulawayo and Jackalberry. Here he found himself at the eye of the storm, in the centre, with everything happening around him but just out of reach. It was Tatwa who was trying to get Dupie and Salome to break and tell the true story of that fateful Sunday night. So far without success. It was the Namibian police and the Botswana Defense Force that were scouring the border area for Enoch, who had so far eluded them. Now that Mabaku was trying to keep one step ahead of his wife and doctors, it was Edison who paid daily, unprofitable visits to Beardy. Even Joy wished to go her own way, finally agreeing to visit Dr Diklekeng, but on her own.

What was Kubu supposed to do? He picked up the jar containing the bullets Paulus Mbedi had given him and headed to Ballistics. By making a nuisance of himself, he persuaded them to take a look immediately, and they became intrigued by the story. After analysis, they confirmed what Kubu had already guessed. He thanked them and went back to his office.

AK-47 bullets. Used by the Russian-armed fighters in Africa. Goodluck had been shot in the back by one of his comrades. Perhaps one who had a score to settle after the raid on the farm.

But Kubu was no further with the case. Those comrades had died in a firefight with the Selous Scouts, including Dupie and Enoch. They couldn't be involved in a chain of murders in Botswana, thirty years on. Something else had driven Goodluck to Jackalberry. But what? Kubu thumped his fist on the desk and watched the effect on his pencils with satisfaction.

At last he could stand his own company no longer and phoned Ian MacGregor.

'Ian, it's Kubu. I'm back.'

'Kubu! And successful, I hear. Money found, villains arrested. Time for a celebration.'

'At eleven in the morning?'

'I meant after work.'

Kubu was tempted. 'Ian, I can't. Joy's seeing Dr Diklekeng. She's still not right. And I don't want to leave her alone. We haven't caught the kidnappers, and they're the ones I'm really worried about. In the meanwhile I'm sitting here counting my buttonholes.' He tried to keep any hint of self-pity out of his voice, but was not entirely successful.

'Ah, Kubu, always the man of action,' said Ian with a hint of uncharitable irony. 'Did you find the drugs they were smuggling?'

Kubu shook his head, forgetting Ian couldn't see it. 'No. Actually I don't believe there are any drugs. It doesn't fit Goodluck's personality.' He described his visit to Zimbabwe and what he'd learned there, and at Ballistics a short while before.

'It's a sad story,' said Ian. 'Hang on, let me get my pipe.' Obviously he was not in a hurry and intended to concentrate on the issue. Kubu was glad of that. A minute later Ian was back.

'Right. I'm settled. Now where were we? Ah, the drugs. You say he was a good guy. Is it possible he was selling drugs to help Zimbabweans?'

'It doesn't add up. He was involved with a small support operation for Zimbabwean refugees in Gaborone, but he gave his time, not money. At least not a significant amount. They confirmed that to Edison early on.'

Ian digested this, but did not want to abandon his theory so easily. 'Maybe it was money collected for people in Zimbabwe, and he was just a courier. Could that be it?'

'Too much money. It was more than half a million US dollars.'

Ian took his pipe out of his mouth and whistled. 'That's a lot of money! Enough to start a small war. Pity you don't get a percentage.'

'I wouldn't want any of that money. The notes should be printed in blood red, not green.'

'And you found nothing else? Just the money?'

Kubu confirmed that.

'Could it have been a payment, then? For services rendered, or to be rendered in the future?'

This was a new twist. Kubu had always visualised an exchange. Zondo and Goodluck swap money and . . . something. But suppose there was no swap? Suppose the money was simply to be delivered to Zondo. Perhaps, then, Goodluck's involvement made sense. He was just the courier. Of enough money to start a small war. Kubu bunched his fists as his subconscious kaleidoscoped ideas.

'Ian, you've been very helpful, as always. I have an idea. Let me check up on it and see if it makes any sense before I waste any more of your time.'

Ian sighed. He was used to this. Occasionally Kubu needed someonc to help with his lateral thinking, but once a sideways thought came along, he would be off on his own again. Telling Kubu he was welcome, and that they must get together soon, he hung up.

Kubu scrabbled through his file until he found the report from Forensics in Kasane. He scanned it until he came to the list of Goodluck's personal effects found in his tent and in his tote. He was looking for some hint of what Goodluck had been doing, something that Dupie and Enoch would have ignored when they went after the money. Something that would lead him to Madrid and the thugs who had dared to threaten his family. He wanted them very badly indeed.

There was nothing. Inexpensive clothes of the type found in any clothing chain. Two pairs of sneakers. A hand-knitted jersey – something made by his mother, a girlfriend, grandmother? He had been wearing it the night he was killed; threads from it had been caught on thorns at the lookout. Sun hat, glasses (reading and sun), but no binoculars, camera, or anything for the wildlife enthusiast, such as an animal or bird book. A copy of the *Botswana Gazette*. Some notepaper but no notes. A copy of Mandela's autobiography, *Long Walk to Freedom*, with a bookmark on page 120. A digital watch (with no alarms set). Forensics had been meticulous, Kubu thought with approval. A Maglite flashlight. A road map of Botswana. A packet of liquorice allsorts, which ants had discovered. Goodluck liked sweets, so what? The holdall was a cheap plastic carrier, no special marks or compartments. Goodluck's briefcase, which had caused all the grief for Joy and Pleasant, was with Forensics in Gaborone.

It looked like a meaningless collection of items that anyone might take on holiday. But he wasn't on holiday, thought Kubu. Hence no nature stuff. What about the map? Why didn't he leave that in the car? Perhaps he thought he might need his bearings if something went wrong. What about the newspaper? He probably bought it in Mochudi before he left for Kasane.

But Kubu couldn't let it drop. He phoned Tatwa.

'Oh, hello, Kubu. Still no joy from Dupie or Salome. They just stick to their stories. Dupie insists it must've been Enoch who hid the money in the tyre of the spare wheel. Salome is adamant that she knows nothing about the money or the murders. I haven't been able to trip either of them up. You know, even with the money, we need Enoch to get them convicted.' He sounded discouraged.

'Cheer up. They'll get Enoch,' Kubu told him confidently. 'I phoned about something else, actually. Goodluck's stuff. Was it all fingerprinted, checked for notes, that sort of thing?'

Tatwa dug out his file. 'Yes. Nothing unexpected about any of it.'

'Even the map and the newspaper?'

Tatwa scanned the report. 'So it says. The map was the standard Veronica Roodt one and had fingerprints from Goodluck and Langa – what you'd expect since they drove together. The newspaper was the *Gazette*. Anyway, it was an old paper; they thought Goodluck probably used it for padding.'

Suddenly Kubu was interested. 'What do you mean, *old*?'

'Well, it just says it was old.'

'What did he have that was breakable?' There was something here. There had to be.

Tatwa looked through the list of effects again and admitted that nothing seemed to need padding.

'Tatwa, can you lay your hands on that newspaper? While I hang on? I've got a feeling it might be important.'

Tatwa pointed out that it was nearly lunchtime, which he thought would close the discussion, but Kubu said he would wait. Tatwa promised to phone back as soon as he located Goodluck's newspaper.

It took fifteen minutes. 'It's a copy of the *Gazette*, Kubu. Dated the week before Goodluck's Jackalberry visit. It's not scrunched up or anything, but it's a bit creased. Maybe he had it in the holdall.'

'So he packed it. What's in it?' asked Kubu. He wished he had the newspaper in his hands to tell him its story directly.

'In it? Speech from the president, announcement of the plan for the African Union meeting, schedule of all the leaders' visits and so on, something about the police getting an air wing. That's the front page.'

For a full minute there was no response, and Tatwa checked that Kubu was still on the line. When a reply finally came, Kubu's voice was tense, although the words were bland enough. 'Read what it says about the Zimbabwe visit,' he said. Puzzled, Tatwa did so.

' "The Zimbabwe delegation will include the president himself and several senior members of his government. Clearly the high-level delegation is intended to emphasise the legitimacy of the government after the recent contested elections and broad criticism by the government of Botswana. The delegation will stay a week in Gaborone. Meetings with the Botswana government are also planned." Then there's a list of the delegates attending and some comments by the president. Do you want me to read that too?'

'No, that's okay,' said Kubu. 'It's like the road map. He had it with him just in case they needed those details. Thanks, Tatwa.'

'Needed them for what? What do you mean, Kubu?' But to Tatwa's annoyance, the only response was the dial tone.

Kubu looked for Edison and found him at the tea urn. 'We're going to interview your Mr Beardy,' he said, by way of greeting.

'Now wait a minute,' said Edison. 'Firstly, he's not *my* Mr Beardy. But more importantly, you know the director's rule. You don't go near Beardy. Too much personal involvement. You can't come.'

'Edison, this could be really very important. I promise I'll just ask a couple of questions, make a few suggestions. Never raise my voice. Not once.'

This did not encourage Edison much. He was still getting black looks from Mabaku over the blown trap for the kidnappers. 'We have to get Mabaku's approval first,' he said firmly.

'Edison, the director's otherwise occupied. He'll agree once he has the facts. But we do have to get something to eat first. I'll buy you lunch at the Delta Café on the way.' He was already striding off to his meal, and Edison knew it was hopeless to argue. He sighed, and then hurried to catch up. He liked the Delta Café.

'Who's the fat guy,' Beardy asked Edison, pointing rudely at Kubu.

'I'm the man whose sister-in-law you kidnapped and whose wife you tried to abduct and, no doubt, rape.' Kubu said it calmly, as he had promised, but it clearly affected Beardy. He shrank back into his seat.

To Edison's relief, Kubu continued, 'Don't worry. I know you were just doing a job. I'm here to tell you it's all over. The Zimbabwe secret police have got Madrid and all the other ringleaders. They'll be having a very uncomfortable time from now on, I expect. But not for all that long, I imagine. You're very lucky to be in custody here. There, you'd probably be sleeping on a concrete floor. No toenails left, either. And I doubt you'd have much interest in prostitutes again.'

Beardy and Edison both had faces awash with surprise. Edison had no idea what Kubu was talking about and was scared the situation might get out of hand. But Beardy was shocked. He opened his mouth, started to say something, and then shook his head. 'I've nothing to say. I want to be treated as a prisoner of war, not as a common criminal.'

'Oh, nothing common about you. Kidnapping, attacking a policewoman, accessory to the assassination of the leader of a neighbouring state. Not common at all. I think we're going to find lots of other charges for you too.'

Suddenly Beardy's demeanour changed. Kubu had overplayed his hand. Beardy clammed up. After that, he said nothing except that he wanted his lawyer. Even a threat to extradite him to Zimbabwe produced no reaction.

But Kubu felt he had enough. 'Come on, Edison. We know what's going on now. Let's get it to the director.' Edison, who had absolutely no idea what was going on, agreed readily, and they left.

Mabaku listened carefully, interrupting only when he needed clarification or an extra detail. When Kubu had finished, he turned to Edison. 'I thought I had made myself quite clear about the professional conflict of Kubu being involved with interviewing Beardy?'

Edison looked from side to side, wondering how a promising lunch had led him into so much trouble. Kubu came to his rescue. 'I insisted, Director. You were involved with the meeting about security for the African Union meeting, and I felt there wasn't a moment to lose. I gave Edison no choice.' Edison nodded, relieved.

Mabaku decided to let the matter drop. 'Let me see if I have this fantastic story straight. Tinubu was a courier taking money to overthrow the government of Zimbabwe. And it's certainly a government most people would like to see changed. This Madrid character is the fix-it man, and the money's destined for him and his men. Dupie steals it, Kubu sticks his neck out, and both of them are on the receiving end of Madrid's anger. Beardy – one of the mercenaries – gets caught, but the others get away.

'Let's summarise the evidence for this hypothetical plot to assassinate the president of Zimbabwe.' He counted on his fingers. 'One, Kubu doesn't see Tinubu as a smuggler – or at least not a drug smuggler – because he's a nice person, likes kids. Two, Tinubu took a newspaper outlining the itinerary for the various visiting presidents' trips with him to Jackalberry. Three, he had deep ties to the country from the war days, and he was involved with a support group for Zimbabwean refugees in Gaborone. That could've been the hippo's ears of his political involvement, with a lot of undercover stuff below the surface of the water. Four, Beardy was shocked by the lie that all his comrades are being held by the Zimbabwe police – and particularly Madrid, who he's never admitted knowing. Five, he asked for treatment as *a prisoner of war*.' He had to start on the fingers of his other hand. 'And six, Madrid has the resources and the balls to pull off the kidnapping of a policeman's family. Not the sort of thing you'd expect from a drug ring. Is that about it?'

Kubu nodded. Mabaku had summed it up very well. Mabaku turned back to Edison. 'What's your take on this?'

Edison squirmed in his chair. He had nothing to go on but his gut feeling. But Kubu was right, usually.

'I think Kubu may be right,' he said at last.

Mabaku walked to the window and gazed out at Kgale Hill. 'We're talking about two days from now. We can't afford to be wrong about this. Frankly, I think the evidence is very tenuous. The only thing that jolts me is Beardy claiming status as a prisoner of war.' He waited, but no one commented. He ground his teeth, ignored a twinge from his stomach, and headed for the telephone.

'I can't afford to ignore this, no matter how remote the chance of its being true. I need to talk to the commissioner right now. In private.' Kubu and Edison got up and left Mabaku holding the time bomb they had passed to him.

Mabaku knew how to get the commissioner's attention quickly, and fifteen minutes later he had outlined the whole story.

The commissioner was silent for what seemed like an age. 'This man who calls himself Madrid. Is that his real name?'

'I have no idea, Commissioner. It's the only name we have heard used.'

'Ah. And it was used in the context of the attack on the tourist camp you mentioned? Nowhere else?' Mabaku admitted this was so. 'Ah. And apart from what we might charitably call an *informed hunch* from your assistant superintendent, the only evidence we have to connect the man you have in custody with this hypothetical plot is the remark that he wants to be treated as a prisoner of war? Completely ridiculous! The Republic of Botswana is not at war, and in its entire history has not been at war, with any country.'

'He misused the term, but it was clear what he meant, I should think.'

'Ah. And what is that?'

'That he is fighting in an army. Against a country.'

'But not this country. Don't you think he might rather ask for political asylum? No, I think we are setting too much store by the ravings of a dangerous criminal who's in custody for kidnapping a policeman's sister-in-law. The same policeman who has now come up with the idea of this extraordinary plot.'

'Nevertheless, Commissioner, we have a situation here.'

'Ah, yes. A situation. Mabaku, I recognise your commitment. I have repeatedly emphasised the importance of the African Union meeting going smoothly, without embarrassment or hitches. You have taken that to heart most commendably. What I'm going to tell you now is *absolutely confidential*. Keep it strictly to yourself. We have been assured by all parties that the president of Zimbabwe will not be in danger while he is in Botswana. Do you understand me? *By all parties*.'

Mabaku thought he understood.

'However, I will deploy additional men and demand additional vigilance. We can't afford to be complacent.'

This sounded more promising. 'Should we see what we can shake out of the bearded Khumalo, then?'

'Why not? He's the only connection with the kidnappers. We need to tie that up as quickly as possible. But you do it yourself, Mabaku. Keep Bengu out of it. He's too personally involved. I would've thought that was obvious to you anyway.'

Mabaku agreed, accepting the implied rebuke, and promised to handle the matter himself.

The commissioner continued. 'Report anything you learn directly to me. And for God's sake, keep any hint of this out of the newspapers. Is that absolutely clear, Director Mabaku?'

'Yes, Commissioner.'

'Well then, have a good evening, Mabaku. It's very encouraging to know I have your full support. Good night.'

Mabaku put down the phone and wiped his forehead with a handkerchief. He was sweating, although it wasn't really hot. Must be the operation, he thought. Marie was right as usual; I should've stayed at home for a few more days.

Kubu fidgeted while waiting for the director. Joy would be home by now and probably had news she wanted to share with him. Hopefully not bad news. When Mabaku called them back in, he hoped the matter would be resolved quickly, and he was not disappointed.

Mabaku leaned back and folded his arms. 'I fully appraised the commissioner. He says we don't have enough evidence to take the matter further.'

Kubu was not surprised. 'Yes, I thought he might say that. Don't rock the boat.' The phrase made him think of poor Tatwa in the river. 'Just give us a few more hours with Beardy and authorise a deal for him. We'll get a full confession in exchange for a light sentence.' He looked at the director's resolute expression. 'A few hours tomorrow, that is,' he added, remembering Joy.

Mabaku shook his head. 'The commissioner's instructions in this matter are absolutely clear. I'm to follow up with Beardy personally.' He held up his hand as Kubu started to protest. 'I'll pursue your idea. Don't worry, I'll get to the bottom of it. Tomorrow if I can. You're to keep out of it, though. Is that clear?'

Kubu nodded, having no option but to accept.

'Now,' said Mabaku more kindly. 'You need to get home to Joy. Good evening, Kubu, Edison.'

Edison, who had been fairly confused all along, smiled, nodded and left. Kubu wanted to suggest how to approach Beardy, how to follow up. But he realised the issue was completely out of his hands now. So be it.

'Good evening, Director Mabaku,' he said. 'I'll see you in the morning.'

CHAPTER 75

Enoch bashed through the buffalo grass, his boots sinking into the mud of the Linyanti marsh. His backpack was comfortable now with the newspaper and rocks jettisoned. It contained only minimal clothes, an old sleeping bag, food, a water bottle, a waterproof wallet stuffed with various currencies, and some equipment. Midges buzzed around him as he walked, biting when they could. He ignored them. He was used to these conditions, and despite the discomfort, he was happy. He felt free. Perhaps for the first time in thirty years.

His intention had been to head much further into the flood plain and land on the Botswana side. There were people there who knew him, people he could trust, but there were far more who did not know him and who were thus even more trustworthy. But when the boat ran out of fuel, he was too close to the areas that the Defense Force patrolled. So he had chosen the other shore. In any case, Namibia would lose interest in finding him long before Botswana did. He smiled, recalling the tall, thin detective churning up the water and screaming his head off, while the big one freaked on land, too fat to do anything useful.

But they'd had the last laugh. He was positive the boat had been fuelled up; someone had deliberately emptied the tank. The spotter plane had come much sooner than he had expected, too; he had been forced to spend the day huddled in a thicket like a lion cub secreted from hyenas. And the night had been spent uncomfortably in a tree, out of reach of predators. A helicopter had been active during this morning, but had taken itself off after a few hours, probably to scan the Botswana side. Now he needed the perfect camouflage, a small village out of contact with the world. Somewhere safe to rest and plan his next move.

He checked his cell phone; he wanted to be out of range. A village with reception would have a communal phone and thus contact with the outside world. At first there was no signal, but suddenly it strengthened and a Namibian network offered its services. He cursed, and headed on.

An hour later he saw smoke spiralling above the tall grass. It was some way off and back towards the watercourse. It might indicate a fishing village. He had little option now, the day was getting old, and soon he would have to find a place to spend the night. Building a fire was out of the question, so his best bet was to head for the smoke. Even if it turned out to be poachers, he could join them for the night. He had money to pay his way. And he had Dupie's revolver, only one shot fired, as a last resort.

He had to detour as he came to waterlogged areas where the flood had spread into the marsh. He was beginning to fear he would not make it before dark when he came to a ridge running parallel to the game track he had been following. It was worth the short climb to get a view of where he was.

From the top he could see that the land fell away steeply to the flood plain, which was now reclaimed by the Linyanti. A group of temporary huts formed a horseshoe around a small bay. There were *mokoros* and drying nets. And in the valley there would be no cell phone reception. It was perfect. But there was a problem. A large group of elephants had taken the middle ground between him and the village. They were decimating the foliage of the trees scattered on the lower hillside above the waterlogged plains. It was a breeding herd with females and calves. The villagers were making a big fuss and the damp grass fire causing all the smoke was probably to keep the elephants at bay. Enoch sighed. He was tired and hungry, and he wanted a place to sleep where he did not have to worry about hyenas and lions. If he tried to outflank the herd, it would be a long way around, and it might even leave him stranded in the dark. He put his hand to his breast, feeling for the Watching Eye that had hung around his neck, the Eye that matched Dupie's. But Dupie's Eye was in a thousand pieces, and he had thrown his own into the Linyanti. That time was past. He slung his pack over his shoulders and headed down the hill towards the village.

At first it seemed that the elephants would ignore him. He had to pass through the herd, but he kept as far as possible from any individual, and particularly from the females with young. He made no effort to be quiet, feeling it was better not to behave as a stalker. One or two lifted their trunks to smell the air, flapped their ears threateningly, and pawed the ground, but he passed by, and they let him go. He thought he was through the herd, home free.

Suddenly he came upon a young female with a younger calf, who had lagged behind the herd to enjoy the green papyrus and the sweet river water. They saw each other at almost the same moment, and the cow panicked. She gave a shrill, high-pitched trumpet and charged, determined to eliminate this threat to her youngster. The baby trumpeted too, impressed by the noise he had created but unsure what the fuss was about. Luckily, Enoch was on a fairly steep part of the ridge, and there was a huge baobab to his left. He had time to duck behind it before the female thundered over the spot he had been occupying seconds before. She turned to find him, knowing exactly where he was, but her calf, still producing shrill imitations of his mother, was right behind her. The threat was no longer between them and the herd. She trumpeted again, turned surprisingly quickly, and started up the hill at a pace so fast that her baby could barely keep up. In seconds they were gone.

Enoch waited a few minutes while his heart rate returned to normal and his muscles relaxed. He had been set to leap into the baobab, one tree in which he would be safe from the most determined elephant, but only if he had made the first branch three metres above his head. It seemed that Eye or no Eye, his luck had held.

Calm now, he made his way down the hill to the village. They were not Batswana, but understood Setswana. He told them he was surveying for a mining company and showed them his GPS. He asked if he could use his cell phone. At first they did not understand, but when he showed it to them, they laughed loudly and shook their heads. They wanted to know how he had managed to get around the elephants. He told them he had walked through the herd. It was all in a day's work. He became an instant celebrity.

Two women were cooking fresh fish, wrapped in aromatic leaves, over open coals from the fire, while another stirred a pot of the ubiquitous *mielie* meal for *pappa*. The men invited him to join them, and he accepted graciously, but insisted that he pay his way. He had pula, not Namibian dollars, but that was fine.

'The white men have lots of cash,' he explained, and they nodded in sage acceptance. They had calabashes of beer and enjoyed his company the better for the money. The evening was fine, and Enoch relaxed for the first time in days, maybe in years. When the meal was over and all the beer was gone, he shared a hut with a single man in the group and slept the sleep of the exhausted.

But one of the older men, toothless and early to bed, religiously listened to the news on a portable shortwave radio every night at nine p.m. Usually, there was little he understood and less of interest. But this was a special night. This night was different. Enoch's luck had just run out.

CHAPTER 76

It was nearly six p.m. when Kubu got home, and he approached the gate in an ambivalent mood. Should he have called? But he did not want to be physically separated from Joy if the news was bad. He had meant to be home early, but the issue with Beardy had made him late. Wasted time, he thought bitterly. They weren't taking the Zimbabwe plot idea seriously. Anyway, he had done his best.

As usual, Ilia was at the gate making a huge fuss of her returning master. There was nothing for it but to put her in the car so that Kubu could drive in without worrying about where she was. It calmed her down, too. He parked the car and went up to the house. It was still light, but Joy was not on the veranda. Kubu swallowed hard and opened the front door.

'My darling! I'm here!'

'I'm in the lounge, Kubu.'

Joy was relaxing in an armchair, reading a magazine. She was wearing one of his favourite dresses, one she had bought for a fancy reception to which they had been invited the previous year. It traced and hugged every curve, and with subtle make-up, Joy had been the most beautiful woman there. For a moment Kubu wondered if he had forgotten that they were going out, but then he saw the dining table set for two. The special dinner service was in use, and two tall candles waited to be lit. A delicious aroma of oxtail stew wafted from the kitchen. I've forgotten some special anniversary again, Kubu thought, worried. He stood gaping at Joy, still holding his briefcase.

'Do you want a steelworks, or will you open some wine?' Joy asked, putting down the magazine.

Kubu played for time. 'A steelworks will be wonderful to start. You look ravishing. My favourite dress! I'm very spoiled.' He dropped the briefcase, lifted her in his arms, and gave her a long kiss, which left them both a little breathless.

'I love this dress. I thought I'd wear it for you tonight. I may not be able to wear it for a while.'

Kubu just nodded. 'What did Dr Diklekeng say?' he asked.

'I'll tell you in a minute. Let me get the steelworks first.' She was already busy with it. 'Why don't you choose a wine? We're having the oxtail stew you like so much.'

'We need something heavy with that. What do you feel like? A Shiraz or a Bordeaux blend?'

'Whatever you prefer. I'll just have a sip to taste.'

Ah ha, Kubu thought. He busied himself opening a rich Shiraz from Stellenbosch, which could breathe while they had the soft drinks.

'So,' he said complacently when they were settled. 'We are going to have a baby!'

Joy's jaw dropped. 'Yes, that's what Dr Diklekeng told me. I was shocked! But how on earth did you know? You didn't phone him, did you?' There was an edgc to the last question.

Kubu laughed. He swallowed the steelworks, jumped to his feet, and lifted Joy into the air, against token protest. 'My darling, you are the most wonderful woman in the whole world – and that's counting all the ones in China, too – and I love you desperately. You've made me happy since the day we met. Now you give me this wonderful gift we no longer dared hope for. I love you for ever!'

'Kubu, put me down! You're making me dizzy. Now, how did you know?'

Kubu put her down, but squeezed into the armchair with her. This forced her on to his lap, which was fine with both of them. He put his arm around her shoulder.

'My darling, you must remember that I'm one of Botswana's ace detectives. It's my business to sift clues, always be alert, integrate data. Even today I discovered a dastardly plot against a head of state. Now let me explain to you how a great detective deduces the truth from a few scattered clues.'

Joy rolled her eyes in mock despair.

'First, I know you went to the doctor today. Clearly the news was good, but not being seriously ill isn't cause for major celebration. The best dining service, your husband's favourite meal, candles, a dress that even now, despite the wonderful aromas wafting from the stove, may force dinner to be delayed.' He kissed her deeply again. 'So clearly something's up. But what? A forgotten anniversary? A hippo never forgets! It must be the news from the doctor. And the ace detective picks up little clues. Why only a *sip* of wine? You usually have a glass or two. Why would you not wear this dress for a while? Could it be that your figure will change? Even though we were told that it was very unlikely indeed that we'd have children, the ace detective deduces the correct conclusion!'

Joy, who had gazed appreciatively into his eyes during the first part of this recitation, was no longer looking at him. She had spotted the magazine that she had been reading lying on the floor.

'Kubu! You saw my magazine, didn't you?'

Kubu nodded gravely. 'That too. Another clue!' The magazine had a smiling cherub on the cover and *My Baby* in block letters across the top. Joy picked it up and gave Kubu a playful clout with it.

'You pig!' she said. 'How could you pretend? Ace detective indeed.' But she was laughing so much she could hardly get the words out. Kubu used the moment to start caressing her. The stove had to be switched off, lest the stew burn.

Half an hour later, the stew was even better. Kubu wolfed it with lashings of vegetables and copious glasses of Shiraz. Joy ate little and drank less. There was a dreaminess about her.

'Kubu, you are really happy about this, aren't you? Our lives will change, you know.'

'My darling, I'm happy beyond my wildest dreams. How can you doubt it? But how come you didn't know? I thought women always knew these things.' He sounded a touch embarrassed.

'But Kubu, you know I'm very irregular anyway, and I'd given up hope after those visits to the specialist and everything. But

Dr Diklekeng said it was all your doing. Trust a man to say that!' She laughed.

Kubu was so happy that he almost turned down a third helping. But it was a special occasion, so he indulged himself. 'I wonder if he'll be interested in cricket?' he mused, as he helped himself.

'Kubu, it may not be a boy, you know. You won't mind if it's a girl, will you?'

Kubu laughed. 'A girl will be excellent. Think of all the wine we can buy when we get the *lobola*!'

'Oh Kubu, you're quite impossible! You'll be a terrible father, getting your children involved with ridiculous sports that no one else understands, and pretending that they are ace detectives, and encouraging underage drinking, and I've no idea what else but I'm sure I'll find out. But I am so glad that you are you.'

Kubu winked. 'Is there any dessert?' he asked.

CHAPTER 77

Kubu and Joy couldn't wait to tell his parents. It took restraint not to phone them first thing on Sunday morning, but they decided to wait until they got to Mochudi. Kubu wanted to celebrate at the best restaurant in Gaborone, but Joy cautioned him that his parents would be uncomfortable with both the surroundings and the extravagance. If anything, Wilmon would say, they should cut back on their spending to prepare for the arrival of his first grandchild.

After much discussion, Kubu and Joy decided to do what they often did – take lunch and eat it on the veranda of his parents' house. That would be more in keeping with the way his parents thought. The only deviation from the norm was that Kubu stopped at a supermarket on the way out of Gaborone to buy a bottle of sparkling grape juice; non-alcoholic, of course. Kubu loved celebrations and couldn't resist something different, albeit not what he would have offered wine-loving friends. For them it would have been real Champagne, and had Wilmon known the cost, he would have been scandalised.

The trip north seemed interminable. Even Ilia sensed something was different. She kept trying to climb over the back of Joy's seat into her lap. Even when pushed back, she would put her paws on the back of the seat and lick Joy's ears. Neither Kubu nor Joy had the heart to stop her.

When they opened the car doors in front of Kubu's parents' house, Ilia streaked up the steps into Wilmon's waiting arms. It's sad, Kubu thought, that the old man is able to display more emotion to the dog than to his wife. It's a generational thing, he thought. People didn't express feelings openly in the old days.

After ritual greetings, Amantle brought out a tray of tea, adorned with a gift of mixed biscuits from Joy, rather than the usual Marie biscuits. The time had finally arrived to break the news. Joy glanced at Kubu and nodded.

'Mother, Father,' Kubu said with a straight face. 'I've told you that Joy hasn't been feeling well since they tried to kidnap her. She's a stubborn woman, so it was only yesterday that she went to the doctor . . .'

Amantle put one hand anxiously to her mouth. Wilmon's impassive face showed the trace of a frown.

'Well,' Kubu continued, 'the doctor told Joy that she wouldn't be well for several months and ordered her to change her diet. He also ordered her to stop drinking alcohol.'

Wilmon nodded in agreement. He would certainly give similar advice.

'What is wrong with her?' Amantle asked. 'It is nothing serious, is it, Joy?'

Playing along with Kubu's game, Joy hung her head. 'Kubu must tell you,' she said demurely.

'Kubu, tell us. You know we will do what we can to help.' Amantle was becoming impatient.

'We'll need both of you to help,' Kubu said. 'It's something we're not prepared for.' He paused for effect. 'Mother, Father, before Christmas you will become grandparents. We are having a baby!'

Amantle jumped up and hugged Joy. 'The Lord has blessed us!' she said with a huge smile. 'That is the best news in the world, is it not, Wilmon?'

Wilmon, who was struggling to his feet, had a rare full smile. 'I knew my son was a man,' he said, 'and my daughter-in-law has brought us great happiness. We have prayed for this day ever since you were married. Even this morning I asked God to bless you with children.' He shook Kubu's hand and uncharacteristically patted him on the shoulder. He would have shaken Joy's hand too, but she was having none of it. She hugged him tightly and gave him a big kiss. A little flustered, he extricated himself, took a step back, and stood grinning.

'We must celebrate!' Kubu said. 'I have brought something to drink.

Joy, get some glasses while I open the bottle.' He unzipped a cooler bag and took out the sparkling grape juice. 'It's non-alcoholic, Father. I know that you'd disapprove of drinking alcohol on the Sabbath, even on such an occasion.'

'Thank you, my son,' Wilmon said. 'I know you would prefer something different.'

A few minutes later the four drank a toast to the couple and the unborn baby. Joy and Amantle could not stop talking, so when they had emptied their glasses, Wilmon suggested a walk. Kubu knew he wanted to share the good news with the neighbourhood as quickly as possible.

To some he would say, 'You know my son, the senior detective in the police? His wife is pregnant, and he is going to be a father!' To others, 'My son has just told Amantle and me that we will be grandparents by the end of the year. Is that not wonderful?'

It took an hour for Wilmon and Kubu to do the rounds. Kubu was touched by how respectfully his father was treated, how happy people were for him. There's more to this man than I know, he thought. Why can't children know their fathers and mothers as friends as well as parents?

When they were all again seated on the veranda, some of the women's excitement had dissipated. Now there was a comfortable warmth among the four. Kubu was absent-mindedly humming Moremi's melody.

'Oh, Kubu,' Amantle exclaimed. 'You remember that song! I used to sing it to you when you were a child.'

'What is it? I've been trying to remember.'

'It's called "Sala Sentle". It is very beautiful.'

Memories flooded Kubu's mind. Memories of a happy childhood. Now he remembered the Tswana farewell song. He wondered if it had some special meaning to Moremi.

'Are you going to give up work?' Amantle asked Joy.

Joy had anticipated this question from her mother-in-law, but had not yet discussed the matter with Kubu.

'I will keep working for now. But I'll stop later in the year to get ready. After the baby's born, I'll stay at home for a while.'

'I was always at home,' Amantle said. 'It is important for a child to have a parent who is at home.'

'I agree,' Joy said, 'but I enjoy my work a lot also. I'll wait and see. I can't predict how I'll feel.'

'Mother,' Kubu interjected. 'Joy and I haven't discussed this yet. I'm sure you know that we'll do what is best. You and Father gave me the greatest gift of all, and Joy's parents did the same for her – a loving home with lots of good common sense. We'll do the same for our child.'

'Oh, Kubu!' Amantle started to cry. 'I am so proud of you both. We are so lucky, are we not, Wilmon?'

Wilmon nodded agreement.

A loud bark interrupted the proceedings. In all the excitement, they had forgotten about Ilia, who was feeling neglected. What about me? she seemed to say. I'm still here. Wilmon patted his lap, and Ilia jumped up immediately. Kubu leaned over to give her half a wafer biscuit that he had been saving. He was sorry to part with it, but Ilia deserved a treat.

If Kubu thought that this Sunday could not get better, he was wrong. On the way home, his cell phone rang. He pulled on to the dirt verge and stopped.

'Yes, Tatwa,' he said, recognising the number. 'I'm having a wonderful day. Please don't spoil it.'

'Good news, not bad,' Tatwa said. 'They've caught him!'

'Enoch?'

'Yes! The Namibian police are holding him in Katima Mulilo. They got a tip from the headman of a fishing village on the Linyanti. Enoch was staying with them, as bold as you please.'

'That's wonderful, Tatwa! Now we can . . .' He stopped and corrected himself. 'Now *you* can wrap up the whole Jackalberry affair. Call the director and have him arrange with the Namibians for you to go and interview Enoch.'

'I've already done that, and I can go tomorrow!' Kubu could hear the excitement in Tatwa's voice.

'Excellent. I'm sure you have all the angles covered, so go to it. See if you can get a confession from him. Unlikely, but worth a shot. I assume the director has started extradition proceedings?'

'He said he would, but it could take some time.' Tatwa paused. 'Kubu, have you any advice? I didn't make much headway with the ranger from Elephant Valley Lodge. I'm worried I won't do a good job tomorrow. I don't want to ruin the case.'

'You'll be fine, Tatwa. I think you'll find the Rhodesian civil war is at the root of all this. Get into Enoch's past. And don't forget *you* are asking the questions. No need to answer his or offer any information.'

Then it was Kubu's turn to share good news. Tatwa was delighted and congratulated them both. Kubu realised that the whole of Kasane's police force would know by morning. He smiled, looking forward to the avalanche of good wishes.

CHAPTER 78

Tatwa was so eager to get to Katima Mulilo that he left Kasane at six a.m., which was the earliest he could drive through the Chobe National Park on the way to Ngoma Bridge. The border post was clogged with trucks, and he sat patiently for about fifteen minutes before he remembered that his boss had arranged expedited transit for him with the Namibian authorities. He had been rehearsing his questions with such concentration that he had forgotten this. With a big smile, the tall man drove to the front of the line, where the Botswana border guard waved him through. Much the same thing happened at the Namibian control point, except that his passport was stamped. Even with the needless delay, he was in Katima before nine a.m.

He had coffee with a senior detective, who told him how they found Enoch. Apparently Enoch had stumbled upon a small village, with a story that he worked for an exploration company. After dinner, one of the elders listened to the evening news on the radio, learning of a massive manhunt for a murderer from Botswana. Enoch fitted the description. The next day the old man borrowed the communal cell phone and climbed to the top of a ridge, where he could get reception. Luckily there was already a police patrol not too far away looking for Enoch, and they caught him a few hours later heading into the bush. He did not resist arrest, but admitted to nothing except his name. He refused to answer any questions.

'Well,' Tatwa said, 'time to try my luck!' He wondered how he would react to seeing the man who had almost killed him.

His colleague escorted him to an interrogation room, where Enoch was seated at a table, cuffs on his legs. He looked up as the two men entered, but said nothing. 'Good morning, Rra Kokorwe,' Tatwa said politely in Setswana. He was pleased he felt no anger; he did not want revenge, just that Enoch pay for his crimes.

'The Namibian police said I could talk to you before you're extradited. My colleague here has offered to tape this session. He has told me that you know your rights both here and in Botswana.'

Enoch stared at him, his face expressionless.

'When you return to Botswana,' Tatwa began, 'this is what you will face. Resisting arrest, kidnapping, and the attempted murder of a policeman. That's when you pushed me off the boat into the river. Also, the murder of Sipho Langa and Goodluck Tinubu and the theft of about half a million US dollars. We have the money now, by the way.' He looked across the table at Enoch, but his face still revealed nothing. 'The murder of Peter Jabulani, known to you as Ishmael Zondo. And the murder of William Boardman in Maun.'

Enoch's continued silence began to erode Tatwa's confidence.

Tatwa stood up, but Enoch looked down at the table rather than strain his neck. 'Why did you kill Goodluck Tinubu?'

Enoch did not reply.

'Rra Kokorwe, keeping silent won't help you. We've enough to put you away for life without Goodluck's murder. The longer it takes you to help us, the less we will help you.' Tatwa sat down again. Minutes passed.

'Okay,' Tatwa said at last. 'Let's start at the beginning. Tell me how you know Rra Du Pisanie.' As he said this, he noticed a shadow cross Enoch's face, sadness rather than anger, resignation rather than resistance. Perhaps I can get something from him after all, he thought.

He stared into Enoch's eyes. After a lengthy silence, Enoch shifted slightly in his chair. Tatwa waited patiently. Then Enoch spoke. 'I met Dupie because I was in the wrong place.'

Tatwa looked hard at Enoch, trying to understand. He decided not to say anything.

'I had dreams that this is how my journey would end. My ancestors were always angry with me.' Enoch spoke so quietly the two policemen had to lean forward to hear. 'I must've done something bad when I was young, but I don't remember. Maybe stealing milk from a neighbour or missing school to play in the river? Surely these things are too small for ancestors to be angry.' He paused, and the policemen said nothing. Tatwa knew what Enoch was talking about. Although he was a Christian, he too believed that everyone's life was influenced to some degree by their ancestors.

'From when I was a boy, I was in the wrong place.' Enoch swallowed, trying to wet his throat. Tatwa's colleague gave him a glass of water. He drank half, and then continued. 'When I was about eight or nine, I walked home after school. It was late. I was playing soccer with friends, so I walked across a farmer's field to save time. The next day I was in school, and the headmaster called me to his office. The farmer was there. He said he'd seen me in the field, and I'd let his cows out, and a calf was dead now, eaten by a leopard. I told him all I did was climb the fence and walk across. The cattle were there, grazing. I didn't even go near the gate. The man shouted that he'd seen me open the gate. I started to cry. I promised that I hadn't done anything. The man turned to the headmaster and told him that if he didn't punish me, he would do it himself. The man was white and had a bad temper, so the headmaster listened. I got a terrible lashing. I had done nothing.'

The two policemen were drawn to Enoch's story.

'That's how my life is,' Enoch continued. 'I'm always in the wrong place. My ancestors are always frowning.' He took a sip from the glass. 'And now I'm here. What are they thinking now?' He shook his head.

'When I was sixteen, my father took me out of school and made me join the army. "Do you good," he said. "You can make some money; help the family." It was okay. We were treated okay by the whites. Even after the war started. They trusted us.' Enoch took another sip of water. 'One Sunday I stayed in the barracks. Most of the others had gone to Bulawayo for the weekend. I was lying on my bed. The district commander came in and shouted that we should go to his office. I think there were five of us. We got dressed and ran to the office. There was a big white man there with the commander.

' "This is Major Du Pisanie," the commander said, "from the Selous Scouts. He needs some men. You've volunteered. You leave in thirty minutes. Go!" I didn't want to go. There were bad stories about the Scouts. If I was in town that day, I wouldn't have gone. I wouldn't have met Dupie. I wouldn't be sitting here. I was in the wrong place again.'

There was a long silence, and Tatwa was afraid that Enoch would say no more. But he was only collecting his thoughts. 'People say that the Scouts were the best. We were. But we were also the worst. We did what we wanted, when we wanted, sometimes to innocent people.' Enoch struggled to maintain his composure. Several times he sucked in breath as though he was about to sob. 'And I was one of them. I became like Dupie. And my ancestors shook their heads.'

He stopped talking. Tatwa noticed that one of Enoch's eyelids was twitching.

'How did you become so friendly with Dupie?' he asked.

'We never became friends, but something happened near the end of the war. We learned that some workers at a farm near Bulawayo were supporting the freedom fighters. Giving them shelter and food. We went to find out what they knew. We got there at midnight and dragged the men from their beds. We stripped them and tied them to trees. Some of us started to torture them.' Enoch shook his head at the memory. 'We were laughing as they screamed. I still hear the screams.' He paused. 'Turned out later we were on the wrong farm.' He shrugged his shoulders.

'Go on,' the Namibian policeman said, transfixed by Enoch's story.

'As we left, a man jumped from the bushes and rushed at Dupie. He had a big cane knife. He must have been peeing or something when we arrived. I didn't have time to pull my revolver, so I jumped in front of him and took the blow on my shoulder. Dupie was able to shoot him before he could strike again.'

Enoch continued to sit erect in his chair, but he looked as though his words were stuffing slowly being pulled from inside him. He seemed to shrink right in front of Tatwa, defiant and defeated at the same time.

'I had a deep wound through my shoulder. It was bleeding badly. I thought I was going to die, and I was glad,' Enoch whispered, drawing the two policemen closer. 'Dupie wasn't sure what to do. He didn't like me, didn't like any blacks, but I'd saved his life. In the end, he carried me almost a kilometre to where we'd left the vehicles. Without him, I would've died. After that we were partners. Looked out for each other. But never friends. Never friends.' He drained the glass.

'After the war, I went back to my village. Dupie left Rhodesia. He couldn't accept being ruled by the terrorist leaders. About two years later, he came to the village. Said he needed someone to help him run hunting trips in Botswana. Someone to look after his back. Someone he knew he could trust. Would I go? So I did. There was no work for me in Zimbabwe. When he went to Jackalberry twelve years ago, I went too.'

'What about the Eye?' Tatwa asked, remembering Dupie's office. He could see Enoch fighting to maintain a semblance of composure.

'The Eyes came later. We took a group of businessmen hunting in the Central Kalahari. They were from Turkey. One of them walked right into a pride of lions lying in the grass. A lioness attacked him. Luckily we were close by and shot it before she killed the man. He wasn't even badly hurt. Rips on his chest, but nothing terrible. He was grateful and gave us money and two Eyes. He made us promise that we would never get rid of them. He said they were for good luck and would protect us. I hung mine around my neck. Dupie carried his in his trousers. But we didn't really believe him.'

Enoch shook his head. 'A few months later I went to see my family. I was waiting to catch a bus in Bulawayo. Someone tried to stab me and steal my money. The knife hit the Eye under my shirt. It saved me. When I got back and told Dupie, he said the same had happened to him. It was a cool night and he was camping, sleeping in the open. A mamba lay next to him for warmth. When Dupie woke up he scared the snake. It struck at him, but hit the Eye. After that we believed. What happened with the one happened with the other.'

'And the night of the murders at Jackalberry?'

Enoch shrugged. 'When Goodluck arrived, Salome thought he was one of the men who had raped her thirty years before in the war. Dupie didn't believe it. She often had nightmares about it. Sometimes she thought some guest at the camp had been there. It was difficult for

Dupie because he loves her. But he didn't believe her. Anyway, he asked me to check Goodluck's tent. I managed to get his keys and found a briefcase full of dollars. I told Dupie, and he saw a way to save the camp. You know Salome was running out of money?'

Tatwa nodded.

'I think he always loved Salome. Maybe he thought this was a way to show his love. To get her to love him. So he made this plan to kill Goodluck and steal the money. He thought Goodluck deserved this.' Enoch stopped talking.

'Tell us what happened, Enoch. What happened that night?'

Enoch remained quiet, head down, shoulders now slumped.

'Tell us. What happened?'

Suddenly Enoch sat upright and stared into Tatwa's eyes. 'Dupie killed Goodluck. He knocked him out with a wrench and stuck him through the chest with a sharp wire stuck into a piece of wood. Something from the war. Then he grabbed the briefcase and I lifted the body. We meant to throw it in the river. But suddenly Dupie realised the briefcase was too light. It was empty. He's quick, Dupie. He always was. He told me to drop the body, and he cut the throat and ears. I didn't know what he was doing, but he'd made a new plan. Goodluck must've given the money to someone else at the camp, and he guessed it was Zondo. So we went to his tent, made him give us the money, and then we killed him. We carried him to the river, and pushed him into the current.'

A chill ran through Tatwa, thinking of the body sinking in the water with monster scavengers.

'Unfortunately Langa was snooping around and saw us. I had to kill him too.'

'What happened to the murder weapons?'

'Dupie put them into a bag and threw it in the river.'

'What happened next?'

'In the morning, I wore Zondo's hat on the boat in case someone saw us on the river. Dupie wanted people to believe that Zondo had left, that he was the murderer. It would've worked, but Rra Boardman was up early looking at birds.' He shook his head. 'The ancestors again, you see? Well, he saw through his binoculars that it was me, not Zondo, in the boat. He tried to blackmail Dupie.'

'So you had to get rid of him too?' Tatwa said.

'Yes,' said Enoch, finally. 'We had to get rid of him too.'

Tatwa had the confession he wanted. The case was solved. Why was he not elated?

'My ancestors knew I would end up here,' Enoch said. 'It is how my life was to be.'

He put his arms on the table, his head on his arms, and said no more. Tatwa and the Namibian policeman tried to get more details, but to no avail. Enoch had told his story. He had nothing more to say.

CHAPTER 79

On Monday, at eight a.m., Mabaku arrived unannounced at the Central Prison and had Beardy brought to an interview room. He waved away the guards, who withdrew doubtfully. This was against procedure. Beardy wanted his lawyer, but Mabaku dismissed that with contempt.

'It's time for us to have a private talk, Mr Khumalo. You've not been very helpful. Lots of promises, lots of delaying tactics, no delivery.' Beardy started to protest, but Mabaku frowned him to silence. 'Yes, you've told us all about the kidnappings. Everything we already knew. But not what it was all for.' Again Beardy tried to interrupt and again Mabaku ignored him. 'Well, we know now. Assistant Superintendent Bengu has unorthodox methods, but they sometimes pay off. You were part of a plot to depose – perhaps assassinate – the president of Zimbabwe. We don't yet know all the details, but we will. This will be very embarrassing for the Republic of Botswana. It seems that we were also used as a conduit to finance this attempted coup. We will, of course, cooperate fully with the Zimbabwean authorities. But we don't want to look incompetent. We want to be able to show them that we took every step to avoid an illegal action against their government.' He glared at Beardy. 'You can help us. If you do, we will recommend leniency on the kidnapping charges. You'll want to be in a Botswana prison for the time being, safe from extradition to Zimbabwe, won't you, Mr Khumalo?'

Mabaku sat back, folded his arms, and waited. If Beardy called his bluff, he would have no options left. It all depended on whether Beardy believed the plot had failed and moved to save himself, or whether he decided that if he kept silent, all might still be well. Mabaku stared at him without blinking. At last Beardy dropped his eyes. That was when Mabaku knew he had won.

Mabaku went straight to the commissioner. He was involved in an important meeting, but Mabaku persuaded his assistant that he had to see him immediately. A few minutes later he was ushered into a small meeting room. The commissioner had been talking to the Minister of Foreign Affairs and International Cooperation. He introduced Mabaku and invited him to sit. 'I think I know what you are going to tell us, Mabaku. The minister should hear it directly from you.'

'Thank you, Commissioner,' Mabaku said. Turning to the minister, he continued. 'I have a confession from a certain Mr John Khumalo, who is being held in connection with the kidnapping of Assistant Superintendent Bengu's sister-in-law. It probably won't stand up in court, because I embellished the truth a bit, but the purpose was to discover what was going on. Before it was too late.'

'And that is?' The minister seemed only mildly interested.

'A plot to overthrow the president of Zimbabwe. A coup is planned for the period that he is out of Zimbabwe, when he is here in Botswana for the African Union meeting. What's more, it is being financed by monies smuggled from South Africa into Zimbabwe. Through Botswana.'

The commissioner cut in. 'After you spoke to me last night, Mabaku, I decided that I should apprise the minister of the possibilities you suggested. He wasn't as surprised as I expected. It seems there have been rumours developing over the past few weeks. We knew nothing. So we said nothing. Now we know something.' He stopped and looked at the minister expectantly.

The minister rubbed his beard, making a sandpaper noise. 'Director Mabaku, you are aware, I'm sure, that the relations between ourselves and the current leadership of Zimbabwe are very strained. Since we rejected the 2008 election results, we have been almost alone in southern Africa in opposing the regime there. We had great difficulty accepting that Zimbabwe's president will be here for the African Union meeting, but it was made clear that if we interfered, the meeting would move elsewhere.' He looked at Mabaku with more intensity. 'What do you think we should do with this information now, Director Mabaku?'

Mabaku looked back without blinking. 'Minister, I'm a policeman, not a politician. I enforce the laws of the country. I have no doubt that many laws have been broken. Laws of this country and of another. We are obliged by protocol to inform that other country. Without delay.'

'Even if that removes the possibility of a different sort of government taking the reins in an important neighbouring country?'

'Minister, as I said, I'm not a politician. But I haven't noticed great democratic progress in countries where governments came to power in coups or military takeovers. I believe in the rule of law. The end is desirable, but it can never justify inappropriate means.'

The minister rose and held out his hand. 'Thank you, Director. I'm glad we have people like you running our police force. We'll think about what you've told us. In the interim, I trust you will keep this meeting and everything you have learned today in the strictest confidence?'

Mabaku gave a stiff nod, shook hands, and left for his office at Millennium Park.

That afternoon, General Joseph Chikosi received a message from a contact he trusted. The message was short. The general and his key men had very little time to flee the country. The government would soon be looking for them. And once it started looking, they would not be hard to find. The general felt obliged to tell Madrid. He, too, would soon be in serious danger. Chikosi didn't really care about that, but he had his honour. However, Madrid was nowhere to be found. It seemed Madrid's spies were even better than those of the leader of the coup,

That evening, the government of Zimbabwe announced that due to pressing business, the president would not, after all, attend the African Union meeting. A deputy with full rights to speak on behalf of the government would stand in for him. This came with a very gracious apology to the government of Botswana. It seemed relations were on the mend.

*

The evening before, a charter flight left Zimbabwe headed for Argentina. None of the passengers went through customs or immigration formalities. The plane's cargo was in sealed boxes that also were not inspected. One of the men was a short and swarthy European. He spoke in Spanish to the pilot, who nodded without surprise. The flight plan had just changed, but Zimbabwe air traffic control would not be informed.

Madrid settled himself into an aisle seat. He started to relax. He had played double or quits with Joseph Chikosi and had lost. Shoving some US dollar bills into his wallet, he came across a 1,000,000 Zimbabwe dollar note, a souvenir. Madrid laughed, partly at the size of the note – worth less than ten US cents on the black market – and partly because he had offered it in answer to Johannes' question about how much he would spend to spring the bearded idiot from a Botswanan jail.

He signalled for a beer. He was philosophical about the Zimbabwe project. He was leaving empty-handed, but there would be another country, another opportunity. There always was.

The plane started to taxi to the runway, and he checked his watch. It was 6.30 p.m. Good. He had told his Zimbabwean contacts he would leave early the next morning. He fully expected the airport to be full of soldiers by then. They had skins to save too.

The plane took off and headed west over Zambia and Angola, then out over the ocean. As Madrid sipped an ice-cold beer, the huge ball of the setting sun spread blood over the African Atlantic.

CHAPTER 80

As soon as he came in the next morning, Kubu tossed his briefcase on to his desk and barged passed Miriam into Director Mabaku's office. Warily, Mabaku looked up from his desk. 'You made Beardy talk, didn't you?' Kubu threw himself into a chair, which creaked ominously.

'Yes, Kubu, you were right.'

'But they knew already, didn't they?' said Kubu shrewdly. 'That's why I heard nothing from you. They were just keeping a low profile, hoping it would all work out.'

Mabaku was puzzled. 'Who knew?'

'The commissioner! The minister! The great Republic of Botswana! We were in on it, weren't we? More what the world expects from the CIA than from the Republic of Botswana.'

'Kubu, this is nonsense. I'm sure the commissioner knew nothing about the planned coup. I'm not saying no one knew what was going on in Zimbabwe. It all seemed rather neat, didn't it?'

'And my family was attacked because the politicians decided to dabble in the affairs of another country!'

Mabaku was getting irritated. This was an issue that should be left well alone. 'You may recall that *you* were the one who got Madrid on to your family. That had nothing to do with any high-ups. I was furious with you at the time, and I was right.'

Kubu had to accept the justice of this.

Mabaku spread his hands on the desk in a conciliatory gesture. 'We didn't engineer this. That's for certain. You think they'd pick someone like Goodluck Tinubu to courier more than half a million dollars from South Africa? Hardly. I'm sure no one in the government even knew about him, otherwise I'd have had a lot more heat when they discovered he was dead.'

Kubu had another thought. 'Maybe it was the South Africans? That would explain their shadowing of Tinubu without letting you know. Maybe the money was raised by powerful people ready to support the coup. Maybe it started life as South African rands before it morphed into US dollars.'

Mabaku shrugged. 'The South African government has always seemed pretty hands-off about Zimbabwe. Rich, well-connected individuals putting up the money to further their own agendas? Well, that's certainly possible.'

Kubu wriggled in the chair, causing more creaking protests. 'A good man, a citizen of Botswana, was murdered for that money. Money for an illegal plot. And we turned blind eyes to it.'

Mabaku shook his head. 'It won't stand up, Kubu. Goodluck knew what he was doing, and he must've realised the risks. What happened was the result of a confluence of circumstances.'

'So Goodluck's life was wasted twice.'

'Well, I had a call from the commissioner this morning. It seems a pretty clear message got through to the president of Zimbabwe. We may see some changes there in the future.'

Kubu thought for a moment. 'Perhaps,' he said.

Mabaku spotted the hesitation, the waning of steam, and slyly moved the subject to the Jackalberry case. 'Tatwa's very pleased with himself. Getting that confession from Kokorwe really tied up the case. He's done a good job. Impressive. Of course, you were the brains behind it. When you decided to use them.'

'It was a joint effort. Tatwa's a good detective. He's got brains too. He's learned a lot from this case.'

'What was the final story of the murders? I've got Tatwa's report, but I haven't had a chance to read the details yet.'

Kubu thought for a moment to get the pieces of the story in the right order.

'Well, it was pretty much the way we'd worked it out already. Salome thought Goodluck was one of the group who'd attacked her and murdered her family, so Dupie snooped around in his tent. He was intrigued by the briefcase, which looked out of place with the old suitcase and cheap clothing Goodluck had with him, but it was locked. So he got Enoch to filch Goodluck's keys and investigate at dinnertime. That nearly went wrong, because Goodluck realised almost at once that the keys were missing and made a hell of a fuss. But they pretended he'd dropped them at the buffet.

'Enoch had an amazing story to tell Dupie: the briefcase was full of hundred-dollar US bills. From there, greed and revenge egged each other on. The plan was to murder Goodluck late that night and dump his body in the river. The crocodiles would take care of the rest. Dupie would pretend to take Goodluck to the airstrip early the next morning, giving a family emergency as the reason. So there'd be no murder in evidence at all. Obviously people would look for Goodluck, but the people who were expecting the dollars would put two and two together and get five: that Goodluck had taken off with their money. Dupie and Enoch might've got away with that.

'But the plan went wrong, because when they'd killed Goodluck, they found he no longer had the money. He'd passed it on to someone else. I think this is why Goodluck was found on the floor. They were about to drag him to the river and throw him to the crocs when they realised the money was missing.

'So Enoch and Dupie had two problems. First, who had the money, and second, how to deal with killing two people. No one would buy a double family emergency that forced two completely independent people to leave the camp early and then disappear.

'They solved the second problem by actually making Goodluck *look* murdered. Dupie got clever and mutilated the body to make it look like a revenge killing of some kind. He knew we'd see through that, but his idea was that his hypothetical murderer would want to apply some misdirection to point away from the money.

'As to who had the money, they assumed it would be one of the black guests. The choice was between Zondo, Gomwe and Langa. Langa seemed unlikely. He had come with Goodluck. Why give him the money at the camp when they could do it in comfort in the car?

Gomwe was a possibility, but he came from South Africa. Why travel across the whole of Botswana to do the exchange? What was wrong with Mochudi itself? That left Zondo. Flown in from Zimbabwe by charter. It made the most sense. So they went after him, and they were right.'

'So it was Zondo who ended in the river?'

'That's right. And the story of the family emergency was transferred to him. They even dressed Enoch in Zondo's hat and jacket in case anyone was up and watching when the two of them left, supposedly Dupie and Zondo going to the airstrip. On the mainland, Enoch borrowed a *mokoro* – it turned out to be Solomon's – to get back to the camp and take William Boardman birdwatching, while Dupie drove towards the airstrip and got rid of Zondo's hat and coat. Our lucky break was when those were found.'

'What about Langa and Boardman?'

'Langa was following Goodluck. He must have realised the money had been passed on to Zondo, so he transferred his attention to him. Maybe he heard something and went to check. Anyway, he came upon Dupie and Enoch coming back from the river with bloody hands. He challenged them. That was a fatal mistake.

'As for Boardman, he was up even earlier than usual, going about his birdwatching, and saw the two men crossing the river in a *mokoro*. Of course he had his binoculars with him and took a look. He spotted that it was Enoch and Dupie, and probably wouldn't have thought any more about it, but he was surprised by Enoch's hat. Exactly like Zondo's. Dupie had been too clever again. But it wasn't spotting the hole in Dupie's story that was Boardman's fatal mistake, it was trying to use it for blackmail.'

Mabaku shook his head at the wiles of people. 'And they pulled that murder off by setting up a meeting between Dupie and Boardman in Maun, and pretending that Enoch had broken down along the road to Kasane when in fact he made his way along the firebreak road to Maun, killed Boardman, and headed back to Kasane on the main road, even making a cell phone call to try to confuse the time of death.'

Kubu nodded. 'Yes, that's exactly what they did. I wonder if Notu is still trying to find his robbers!'

'Has Du Pisanie admitted all this yet?'

Kubu shook his head. 'No, he's sticking to his story: it was all Enoch acting on his own. He only admits providing Enoch with an alibi for the trip to Maun. But no judge will buy that in the face of Enoch's coherent confession and the disappearance of Ishmael Zondo. Dupie claims Zondo vanished because he still had the goods he was going to swap for the money. But that's nonsense. In fact, I no longer think it was a swap. It was payment for services about to be rendered. To the new interim military government of Zimbabwe.' Kubu snorted.

'What about the McGlashan woman? What was her role?'

Kubu looked pensive. 'First I thought she was the brains behind the whole thing, but now I'm not sure. She claims she knew nothing about what was going on, and she's been pretty convincing. She may have known about them, but she certainly wasn't actively involved in any of the murders. Enoch is adamant that she knew nothing at all, and he has nothing to gain by saying that. Frankly, whether she knew about the crimes or not, I don't think we have a case against her unless Enoch and Dupie change their stories. We'll sweat them a bit longer, but then we'll have to let her go.'

Mabaku nodded slowly. 'Good work. How did you eventually get four when you put two and two together?'

Kubu shrugged, a little amazed that the director was so complimentary this morning. 'It was a lot of small things. Goodluck had his throat cut after he was dead, and Boardman was tortured after he was dead. It seemed an odd coincidence. The two glasses in Goodluck's tent, with Zondo's prints on one. Why would Zondo leave a glass there after murdering Goodluck? In fact, Dupie brought the glass there from Zondo's tent after the murders. Then there was Zondo's disappearance. Even if he'd planned the whole thing carefully, it was hard to imagine he could vanish so perfectly. We thought maybe the Zimbabwe police had him, but my visit there convinced me otherwise. And if he had gone to – say – South America, then Boardman's murder was unconnected. That seemed unlikely.'

Kubu had more to tell. 'Finally there was the issue of Zondo's hat. Why would he discard it? He always wore it at the camp. First I thought that he'd deliberately used it as an inverse disguise – attracting attention to the hat rather than to himself – but Moremi said he had an attachment to it, and I believed him. That meant the hat was discarded because Zondo wasn't around any more. Once I had that insight, the rest came easily.'

Mabaku came round from behind his desk and gave Kubu a thump on the shoulder. 'Well done! It seems the hippo outfoxed the crocodiles!'

Kubu thought of Zondo's consumed body, and Tatwa struggling in the river. 'Maybe,' he said sombrely. 'But it was a close thing.' He rose to leave, but another thought occurred to him.

'You know, Director, you and I don't believe in coincidences. Yet in this case there was a huge one. It nearly derailed everything by sending me off in the wrong direction.'

'The Gomwe murder?' Mabaku suggested.

'Yes.' Kubu shook his head. 'The timing seemed perfect – Gomwe coming back to Botswana just as Boardman was killed and then being murdered himself. But actually he was trying to muscle in on the trans-frontier drug trade. Perhaps the money people in South Africa tipped him off about Jackalberry, and that's why he was snooping around when Goodluck was there. But actually his death wasn't directly connected to the money destined for Zimbabwe. I was so desperate to catch the people who were threatening Joy and Pleasant that I convinced myself that Gomwe's murder was the key. That was almost a huge mistake.'

Mabaku nodded slowly, digesting this. 'How's Tatwa doing on that case?'

'It's going to test his skills even more than the Jackalberry one. We've got the woman and the ranger on various drug charges – that's open and closed. But as for the murder charges, I don't know. They both claim that the other's accusations are lies. I'm not sure we have enough hard evidence to convict them. Anyway, we'll see. Tatwa's developing into a very good interrogator. Maybe he'll get a breakthrough.'

'And Van der Walle owes me one for his bust in Johannesburg. That's always useful.' Suddenly Mabaku was serious again. 'Things are still pretty confused in Zimbabwe, Kubu, but we've asked the government for help to track down Madrid and his thugs. The commissioner has made it clear that if they want cooperation from the Botswana Police Force in the future, they need to deliver on this one.'

'But they'll never give us Madrid if they catch him!'

'Yes, we know that. We just want to be sure he doesn't get away. Once they've got him, he's no longer a threat. To anyone.'

Kubu realised that this was the best resolution he could hope for. He was grateful the commissioner had moved so quickly, and was beginning to feel a little ashamed of his earlier outburst.

'Thank you, Jacob. And thank you for your support when things were going badly for me. You won't regret it.'

Mabaku smiled. Suddenly he stuck out his hand and warmly shook Kubu's surprised one. 'Oh, and congratulations!' Realising that Kubu was lost, he added, 'On becoming a father, of course.' Kubu's mouth worked. How on earth did Mabaku know these things? It seemed Mabaku could read this thought too. He laughed. 'Oh, I phoned for you yesterday when you were out, and Joy told me. She didn't mention it to you?'

Kubu shook his head, but he had a broad smile. Just the reminder was enough to restore his good humour.

Mabaku gave him another playful thump. 'Your life's going to change, Kubu. But you'll never be sorry, not for a moment. My kids are grown up now, but they still give us a lot of pleasure. The first twenty-five years are the hardest, though!'

Kubu grinned. 'We'd better get back to work,' he said.

EPILOGUE
All Alike

He walked by himself, and all places were alike to him.

Rudyard Kipling, *Just So Stories*

Salome walked around the camp thinking of what had been lost and what had been gained. It was not for the last time. She would need at least two trips to Kasane to move the items that were not part of the sale of Jackalberry Camp. She had been lucky to find a buyer who was willing to negotiate the extension of the concession and pay her a fair price. For the first time in many months she looked around at the river and the view of the hills, hurting from the beauty. Scattered clouds were gathering on the horizon. She would go to the lookout for the sunset. It should be spectacular.

One more commitment remained. She was tempted to shrug it off, just as she was trying to shrug off the life and the events that had led her to this point. Why, when things were changing for them, had Dupie thrown it all away on a quest for revenge and riches? She shrugged. She needed to move on while there was still time for her to build a life. If there is still time, she thought wryly. Wherever I go, I take myself with me. But she had made a promise, and she did not want any open doors left behind her.

She needed a spade. Take a spade, Dupie had said from behind the heavy prison glass. She had seen him just that once after her release. Will you come to see me again? he had asked. With sadness in her heart, she had said she would not. He had nodded, almost relieved. That was when he had told her where to go, and to take a spade. He had asked her to promise that she would, and after hesitating, she had given her word. They owe it to you, he had said. So now she needed to close this one remaining door.

The spade, used to trim the camp paths, lived behind the kitchen, so she went to fetch it. There she found Moremi. As always,

Kweh was on his shoulder, clucking and eating a marula.

'Will you stay, Moremi?' she asked. 'You're a wonderful cook; the new owner will be lucky to have you. He'll probably pay you much more than I could afford to. I'll write a reference, if you like.'

Moremi smiled, but shook his head. 'We're going to see the world, Kweh and me. Kasane, Francistown, maybe even Gaborone!' He did a little pirouette, disturbing the bird. 'Don't worry. We'll be fine. You too. We'll all be fine. It is time.' He started to hum the farewell song.

Salome picked up the spade. Moremi watched her as she walked off.

Where the camp path ended, she had to push through bushes to get down to the river. There was a small inlet with a quiet bay surfaced with fine mud. Salome had no idea what she was looking for, or what was there to find, but she took off her sandals, checked for crocodiles, and waded into the water in her shorts. There was a large log jammed between rocks, red and shiny from water wear. Where Dupie had told her, she started to dig in the silt behind the log. More accurately, she scooped the mud away. Very soon the spade hit metal, and she stepped back, waiting for the now cloudy water to clear. Then she could see a mud-stained muslin bag. Leaning on the spade, she reached down with her right hand and tried to lift it out, but it seemed stuck in the river. After a few tugs, she tossed the spade on to the shore and used both hands to dislodge the bag. It didn't seem large, but it was very heavy. She supposed it was waterlogged and weighed down with mud. There was another bag below the one she had moved.

Salome dragged the bag to the shore and unwound the wire tie. Then she saw the golden gleam. She lifted out the top bar, shiny, unsullied by the mud or water. On the top was stamped '1 kg', with a mark indicating the source and the purity. A kilogram of Zimbabwean twenty-carat gold, with a value of over thirty thousand US dollars. And the bag was full. And there was at least one more bag in the river. There could be a million dollars' worth of gold here, she thought, amazed.

They owe it to you, Dupie had said. Who? The terrorists who had killed her family and distorted her life? The people of Zimbabwe? The politicians who had maimed the country as badly as she had been maimed? She stood and thought about this gold and the money for which, she supposed, it was to have been exchanged. Money and gold that had taken four lives, as well as the freedom of Dupie and Enoch. Should she turn in the gold to the police? Be free of it once and for all? But they would give it back to the greedy politicians. Should she keep it as repayment of a debt everyone else had forgotten? Or would someone come looking for it, bringing more pain?

Eventually she retied the wire, dragged the bag back into the river, and covered it again with the sandy mud. Perhaps there would be a time for it, but that was not now. She washed her hands and feet in the river and put on the sandals, slippery on her wet feet. She pushed through the brush back towards the camp. Perhaps Moremi had made coffee.

Authors' Note

On 11 November 1965, the white minority government of Rhodesia under Ian Smith unilaterally declared independence from its colonial parent, the United Kingdom. This triggered a bitter struggle between the forces of the government and the black freedom movements operating from the surrounding black-controlled countries. At first the government soldiers (who were black as well as white) had the upper hand, but as international sanctions started to bite in the land-locked country, it became clear that they would not be able to hold on to power. As in all guerrilla wars, the liberation movements resorted to terrorist tactics that were soon matched by those of the government forces.

Eventually an internationally supervised election was held, leading to the government of Robert Mugabe's Zimbabwe African National Union. The newly named Zimbabwe seemed to have a promising future fuelled by mineral and agricultural wealth, infrastructure, and wonderful tourist attractions. However, in recent years the world's press has reported that the economy has collapsed, agriculture is in ruins, and most of the people live in poverty. With their currency valueless, many Zimbabwean families survive on small amounts of money sent home by relatives working in the surrounding countries, particularly the economic powerhouse of South Africa.

To the west, Botswana too faced pressure from illegal immigrants. Situated on the Chobe river, Botswana's northernmost town, Kasane, has grown to be a tourist Mecca. Dramatically different from the desert regions in the south of the country, it has lush vegetation, perennial water rich in hippos and crocodiles, and elephant herds that occasionally wander into the town from the neighbouring Chobe

National Park. But it is an outpost: from a point near the town one can see Namibia, Zambia and Zimbabwe.

Like all wars, the Rhodesian bush war forged strange relationships, both good and evil.

Acknowledgements

In our first book, *A Carrion Death*, we introduced Detective Kubu, and he struck a chord with readers. We've been delighted by all the support he's received both in reviews and in personal communications. We'd like to thank everyone for their interest, comments and enthusiasm.

Among the first Kubu supporters were our wonderful agent Marly Rusoff and her partner Michael Radulescu. We thank them for that and much more. Marly introduced Kubu to Claire Wachtel, Senior Vice President and Executive Editor at HarperCollins, who bought this book as well as *A Carrion Death*. We are very grateful for her strong guidance, which has greatly improved our books. Sherise Hobbs, Senior Commissioning Editor at Headline Publishing Group in London, became another Kubu fan and bought subsidiary rights from HarperCollins. Her input on both books has been invaluable. Our thanks also go to Jane Selley for her meticulous copyediting. Indeed, we are grateful for all the support and encouragement from the team at Headline.

As with our first book, many people have provided input and suggestions. While the curiosity of a new writing partnership might have motivated the help they gave on the first book, we are delighted that they have been willing to extend their support as enthusiastically and unselfishly to a second.

The job of focusing the setting for Jackalberry Camp fell to Peter Comley and Salome Meyer. They hosted us at their wonderful property near Kasane, and then spent a week driving us around northern Botswana making sure that we understood the environment of the Chobe and Linyanti rivers. We thank them for the benefit of their encyclopedic knowledge of Botswana, formed in a lifetime of living and working there, and for their wonderful company.

We particularly want to thank Thebeyame Tsimako, Commissioner of Police in Botswana, for taking time from his demanding schedule to give us comments and advice, and for helping with our requests. We also want to thank Superintendent Ntaya Tshepho and others at the Kasane police station for showing us around and answering questions about policing the area. They have important work to do, but managed to find time to satisfy a couple of inquisitive writers.

Despite the efforts of all these talented and generous people, and the breadth of their knowledge and experience, the book may still contain errors. A writing partnership is wonderful for many reasons. Among them is that we each have the other to blame!

Michael Sears
Stanley Trollip

Glossary

Amarula	South African liqueur flavoured with marula fruit.
Bafana Bafana	South Africa's national soccer team. Literally 'The Boys, the Boys'.
bakkie	South African slang for a pickup truck.
Batswana	Plural adjective or noun: 'The people of Botswana are known as Batswana.' See Motswana.
biltong	Meat dried with salt, pepper, coriander and other spices. Similar to beef jerky (but much tastier!).
bobotie	South African Malay dish based on lightly curried ground lamb.
braai/braaivleis	South African term for a barbecue.
Bushmen	A race small in size and number, many of whom live in the Kalahari area. They refer to themselves as the San people (see Khoisan). In Botswana they are sometimes referred to as the Basarwa.
Debswana	Diamond mining joint venture between De Beers and the Botswana government.
donga	A dry river course, usually with steep sides.
dumela	Setswana for 'hello' or 'good day'.
Khoisan	Name by which the lighter-skinned indigenous peoples of southern Africa, the Khoi (Hottentots) and San (Bushmen) are known. These people dominated the subcontinent for millennia before the appearance of the Nguni and other black peoples.
koppie	Afrikaans for 'small hill'.
kubu	Setswana for 'hippopotamus'.

Landy	Term of affection for a Land Rover.
lechwe	Type of water-loving antelope (*Kobus leche*), common in the wetter areas of Botswana.
lobola	Bride price (originally in cattle) paid to the bride's parents in African tradition. Sometimes used to set up the newly married couple.
marula	*Sclerocarya birrea*. Large African tree, member of the mango family, with tasty greenish-yellow fruit.
mokoro	Water craft commonly made by hollowing out the trunk of a sausage tree (*Kigelia pinnata*). Also made from other trees. It is propelled by a long pole held by someone standing on the back.
mielie	Maize or corn.
Mma	Respectful term in Setswana used when addressing a woman. For example, '*Dumela*, Mma Bengu' means 'Hello, Mrs Bengu'.
Motswana	Singular adjective or noun: 'That man from Botswana is a Motswana.' See Batswana.
muti	Any sort of medicine or potion. The term usually refers to medicines prepared by traditional healers or witch doctors.
pap	Smooth maize-meal porridge, often eaten with the fingers and dipped into a meat or vegetable stew.
pappa le nama	Pap and meat.
potjie	A three-legged metal pot used to make stews over an open fire.
pula	Currency of Botswana. Pula means 'rain' in Setswana. 100 thebes = 1 pula.
quelea	Small seed-eating bird (*Quelea quelea*). Huge flocks in flight can resemble clouds of smoke.
rand	Currency of South Africa. 100 cents = 1 rand.
riempie	Leather strands that are interlaced to make chair seats.
rooibos	Red herbal tea made from a plant native to southern Africa (*Aspalathus linearis*).

Rra	Respectful term in Setswana used when addressing a man. For example, '*Dumela*, Rra Bengu' means 'Hello, Mr Bengu'.
rusk	A kind of hard cake-like sweetened biscuit.
San	Bushmen people. See Bushmen and Khoisan.
Setswana	Language of the Tswana peoples.
steelworks	Drink made from cola tonic, ginger beer, soda water and bitters.
thebe	Smallest denomination of Botswanan currency (see pula). 100 thebes = 1 pula.